The Shadow Catcher

Michelle Paver

CORGI BOOKS

THE SHADOW CATCHER
A CORGI BOOK : 0 552 14872 5

First publication in Great Britain

PRINTING HISTORY
Corgi edition published 2002

1 3 5 7 9 10 8 6 4 2

Set in 11/12pt Sabon by
Phoenix Typesetting, Burley-in-Wharfedale, West Yorkshire.

Corgi Books are published by Transworld Publishers,
61–63 Uxbridge Road, London W5 5SA,
a division of The Random House Group Ltd,
in Australia by Random House Australia (Pty) Ltd,
20 Alfred Street, Milsons Point, Sydney, NSW 2061, Australia,
in New Zealand by Random House New Zealand Ltd,
18 Poland Road, Glenfield, Auckland 10, New Zealand
and in South Africa by Random House (Pty) Ltd,
Endulini, 5a Jubilee Road, Parktown 2193, South Africa.

Printed and bound in Great Britain by
Clays Ltd, St Ives plc.

THE SHADOW CATCHER

THE MONROES OF FEVER HILL

(Names in bold capitals are those of principal characters in *The Shadow Catcher*)

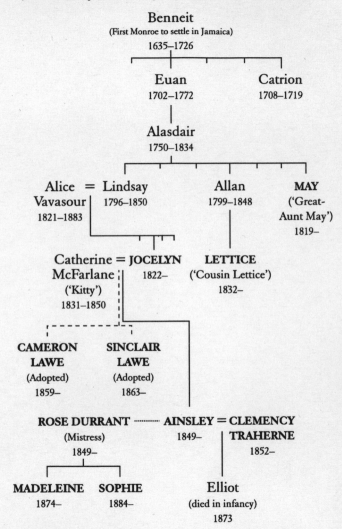

Benneit
(First Monroe to settle in Jamaica)
1635–1726

Euan
1702–1772

Catrion
1708–1719

Alasdair
1750–1834

Alice Vavasour
1821–1883
= Lindsay
1796–1850

Allan
1799–1848

MAY
('Great-Aunt May')
1819–

Catherine McFarlane
('Kitty')
1831–1850
= JOCELYN
1822–

LETTICE
('Cousin Lettice')
1832–

CAMERON LAWE
(Adopted)
1859–

SINCLAIR LAWE
(Adopted)
1863–

ROSE DURRANT
(Mistress)
1849–

AINSLEY
1849–
= CLEMENCY TRAHERNE
1852–

MADELEINE
1874–

SOPHIE
1884–

Elliot
(died in infancy)
1873

PROLOGUE

Jamaica, 1895

She is dizzy with hunger, and the laudanum is making her sick. It's becoming harder to think in straight lines.

What is she doing out here, and why did she forget to put on her riding habit? What made her think she could tackle a jungle in her underclothes?

Mosquitoes whine in her ears as she wades through the hot green shade. The rasp of crickets is deafening. She steps on a dumb-cane leaf, and poison oozes like milk.

The forest is watching her, waiting to see if she will survive. Bird calls echo through the canopy. A cinnamon streak brushes her shins, and through the leaves she catches the red eye of a mongoose.

She doesn't belong in these demon-haunted hills. They're not for white people. They're for outlaws and witches and the ghosts of runaway slaves. Even the names are haunted. Turnaround. Disappointment. Look Behind. If she weren't so dizzy, she would be frightened.

Beneath her feet the ground is soft with rottenness, but through the vegetable stink she can smell the blood on her hands. Her husband would be appalled. He has always had such a horror of blood.

Why is everyone obsessed with blood? Bad blood. In cold blood. Dr Hay's Tablets to Purify the Blood. Vice, insanity and disease. It's all in the blood. At least, that's what they say.

On a tree trunk an emerald lizard watches her pass. She wonders what it sees. Everyone seems to see someone different when they look at her. But whatever they see, it's mostly bad. Actually, it's all bad.

Her husband says she's insane, for she never does what he says. 'Woman's purpose', he tells her, 'is to praise and to obey. If you cannot accept that, it is because you are not a proper woman.'

Dr Valentine says that she has nerve fever, and must become a child again, so that he can re-create a more appropriate personality.

The washerwoman who talks to ghosts tells her that she's dangerous. 'You bring trouble to this house, Miss Maddy. You not who you say.'

And her lover says he doesn't know her any more, and walks away. After what she did, she can hardly blame him for that. But she does, just the same.

She reaches a clearing where hummingbirds dart and hover in the dusty sunlight. Beyond it the forest is thinning, and on a distant slope she sees an enormous silk-cotton tree. Its outstretched limbs are draped with strangler fig and Spanish moss, and orchids like little darts of flame.

Is that the Tree of Life of her mother's stories? Has she found Eden? Has she? In Eden everything is wilder and more alive. The sun shines more fiercely, the rain strikes harder, and the leaves are so green that it hurts your eyes. And deep in the forest stands the Tree of Life, and from its branches the creepers hang down to the ground, and at night after the rains they're speckled with fireflies, and you can smell the vanilla flowers and the sweet decay.

Behind her a branch snaps. She whips round. But the clearing is empty.

Her mind floods with clarity. She understands why she is here, and why she is frightened. Only one man knows where she is, and if he finds her, it's finished.

Another twig snaps. She hears the chink of a bridle, and forgets to breathe.

One way or another, it won't be long now.

PART ONE

CHAPTER ONE

Galloway, south-west Scotland, March 1884 – eleven years earlier

The important thing, her mother always said, is to think for yourself.

Then she would bundle Madeleine into hat and coat and galoshes and muff and send her out onto the beach – with orders to find ten different kinds of seaweed, or learn how the Corsewall lighthouse got its name. Come back when you're hungry, she would say. And watch the tides or you'll drown.

What will I look like drowned, Madeleine would ask. Will you take a photograph of me?

Several, her mother would reply. And if I'm lucky I might get one published in *Amateur Photographer*.

Watch the tides, and think for yourself. As Madeleine stood at the edge of the Forbidden Kingdom, she thought, well at least I am thinking for myself. Although this probably wasn't what Mama had in mind.

Her breath steamed in the frozen stillness, and cold seeped through her cork-soled boots. But she couldn't stamp her feet in case she alerted some guardian of the forest.

Before her the carriageway swept through the great iron gates and disappeared into the shadows beneath the trees. To her right the gatehouse loomed. Frost filmed its blind marble windows. Icicles waited to fall from the roof. In the pediment a marble crow hitched its wings to fly away, while a marble snake writhed in its claws.

Madeleine was vaguely aware of some story in the Bible about a snake, and that the snake was not the hero. She wasn't sure if there was a crow in it as well. Her mother often said they must make a start on the Bible, but they never did. 'I'm sorry, Maddy,' she had said only the week before, 'I'm too ignorant and undisciplined to make a good teacher.' Madeleine strongly disagreed. Her mother knew singing, photography and tropical plants and animals; and she could tell stories about magic trees and dapper little talking spiders, in the sing-song language of Jamaica that she called *patois*.

There was a thud behind her. She spun round. A big black crow was watching her from a swaying branch. It fixed her with bright, unfriendly eyes.

'Go away,' she told it.

The crow gave a croak and flew off into the trees. Snow drifted down from the branch. The stillness returned.

It was just a crow, she told herself. But she didn't like the fact that it had understood what she said.

Through the gates, the woods were dark and haunted: warning her not to enter the Forbidden Kingdom. She groped for Mister Parrot in her pocket, and slipped off her mitten and gave his fuzzy felt wing a reassuring squeeze.

The Forbidden Kingdom was not, of course, its real name; that was Strathnaw. The Forbidden Kingdom was merely what her mother called it when she was angry – because Papa had said that they must never visit it on any account. 'Then why on earth *take* a house two hours away from the wretched place?' Mama would blaze at him during one of their rows.

'Because it's secluded and within our means—'

'Nonsense. It's because you miss them, and you want to retain some sort of link, however tentative—'

'Rose, no.'

'Tell the truth! You miss them. Heaven knows, I understand. What I don't understand is why you won't allow us to make an approach, not even for Maddy's sake. She's ten years old, and she's never seen the place where you—'

'There would be no point.'

'Of course there's a point!'

And so it would go on, while Madeleine listened on the landing until Hannah poked her head round the kitchen door and shooed her back to bed.

The last row had been a fortnight ago, just before Papa went back to his regiment. He had lost his temper and stormed from the house – but returned much later with an armful of hothouse lilies. Her mother had thrown them back at him ('Damn you, I'm not an invalid!'), then burst into tears. Madeleine had crouched against the banister, picking at the varnish and wondering what to do. Her mother never cried.

Dr Baines said it was just the usual 'morbid despondency of a lady near her time', and prescribed warm milk (which her mother detested), and a little phial of cocaine drops for her sore gums.

It didn't help. Recently, her mother's 'second bustle' – the one in front – had grown so big that her back ached constantly. And she'd become fretful and despondent, which wasn't like her. She spent her days waiting for the post, but was vexed and unsatisfied when it arrived, even if it brought a letter from Papa. Hannah went about her work with a mouth pulled as tight as a drawstring, and muttered about giving in her notice.

In the end, Madeleine realized that it was down to her. She couldn't let her mother go on being so unhappy. She must go to the Forbidden Kingdom and talk to whoever lived there, and then perhaps they could all go to Jamaica, just as Papa was always promising they would, at some future time that never seemed to come.

For herself, Madeleine would much rather stay at Cairngowrie House, for she loved her lonely stretch of beach with its seals and its fulmars and its green-eyed cormorants. But she knew that her parents longed to go back to the land where they were born. Besides, she wouldn't mind seeing a real parrot and a breadfruit tree.

A harsh croak brought her back to the present. The crow was watching her from the gatehouse roof. *Better turn aside now,* it said, *or there'll be trouble.*

She wished she could do exactly that. She didn't want to enter the Forbidden Kingdom. She wanted to be back at Cairngowrie House. She wanted her father. She wanted the scratch of his whiskers, and his spicy smell of moustache wax and Turkish tobacco.

And yet, she reflected, he is the reason that you are here. It isn't fair of him to say 'I forbid it', and then go off to the army for months. He is always leaving us. It isn't fair.

She took a deep breath of the freezing air, and walked through the gates into the Forbidden Kingdom.

Beneath the trees there was a horrible waiting stillness. The snow crunched beneath her boots like broken glass, and her breath sounded rasping and loud. She forced herself to walk slowly, to show the crow that she was unafraid. But it wasn't fooled. It followed her from branch to branch, its harsh laughter echoing through the wood.

She walked for what seemed like hours. Then abruptly the trees were left behind.

She had reached the edge of a vast snowbound park. From where she stood the carriageway swept down past a wide frozen lake, then up a long white hill where a line of marble knights guarded the approach to a huge stone mansion.

Madeleine hated it on sight. Columns barred its front like a great stone cage, and its copper-coloured windows threw back the glare of the sun.

That, she thought, is where the crows go to roost. She pictured them blackening it at dusk in their thousands, then rising to blot out the dawn in a great dark flood.

The crow swept past her and perched on the helmet of the nearest knight. *Last chance,* it croaked. *You'd better turn back now while you still can.*

The blood was loud in her ears; the sense of wrongdoing so strong that she caught her breath.

If her mother were here, she would make a game of this. 'How would you photograph that house, Maddy? How would you show the way it makes you feel?'

The thought of her mother was a kernel of heat. The previous day, they had taken photographs with the new Instantograph, and Madeleine had modelled her mother's green plush evening mantle. Then she'd tried on the hideous stockinette 'abdominal binder' which Dr Baines had insisted her mother must wear instead of stays. As Madeleine had pranced around the drawing-room with a cushion for her second bustle, her mother had mimicked the doctor's rolling Scots tones – 'sup*poort* without *pray*ssure' – and they'd laughed till it hurt.

Halfway up the hill, one of the statues moved.

Madeleine's heart jerked.

It was a knight on an enormous charger. His cloak of draped grey marble was dusted with snow across the shoulders. His mount's long white mane glittered with frost. He was the guardian of the Forbidden Kingdom, come to spirit her away.

With a croak the crow flew off into the forest. *Told you not to go any further!* Then the charger tossed its head and snorted steam, and the statue resolved into an officer on a big grey horse.

Shakily, Madeleine breathed out. Nothing to be afraid of, she told herself. But her heart kept up its jerky rhythm.

The officer hadn't seen her yet. She watched him jump down from the saddle and pick up his mount's near front hoof. The horse arched its neck to watch, while the officer took a scraper from his pocket and removed a stone, then set down the hoof and jumped back into the saddle. Then he turned his head and saw her.

She put her hand in her pocket and gripped Mister Parrot.

'Who are you?' the officer called out sharply. His voice carried through the freezing air. 'This is a private estate. What are you doing here?'

When she did not reply, he put his horse forward and cantered down to her. He only reined in when he was practically upon her. His spurs were at the level of her eyes, and so close that she could see the fine engravings on the cold blue steel.

His horse put down its nose to investigate her, and she

took in a blast of its hot, musky breath. It was enormous, its hooves the size of dessert plates. She had to remind herself of what her mother had once told her: that horses do not care to tread upon children.

She craned her neck to look up at the officer. He had thick fair hair, with darker brows and moustache, and no laughter lines. His eyes were light grey and startling in his sunburned face. Madeleine had never seen a gentleman with sunburn. She had thought only farmers and fishermen got that.

She wondered why he had no laughter lines, and whether he was unhappy, and what he would look like if he smiled. He reminded her of someone. But of whom?

Then she had it. He had the same strong features as the warriors in her *Illustrated Adventures of Ancient Greece*. But she couldn't tell if he was a hero or a villain. He looked as if he might be either: as if he might be capable of great violence or great tenderness in equal measure, and you would never know which was coming next. But curiously, that didn't make her afraid. She felt nervous and uncertain, but most of all she wanted him to like her. She wanted him to smile at her, and be pleased to see her.

All this flashed through her mind as she stood in the snow looking up at him, while he contemplated her with cool grey eyes which held none of the indulgence that grown-ups usually assume on meeting a child.

He had asked her what she was doing in the park. She wasn't sure how to reply. She said, 'I know I'm not supposed to be here.'

'Then why are you?' he said. He didn't seem angry; but nor did he make any attempt to soften his tone.

She pointed at the mansion on the hill. 'I need to see the people who live over there.'

'They are from home. They generally are.'

She was appalled. It had never occurred to her that there might be no-one at home.

'How did you get here?' he said with a slight frown.

'I came with Mr Ritchie,' she replied. 'He's my friend, he's the carter in Stranraer. He's gone on to Kildrochet with a parcel, but he'll be back in an hour to collect me.' She omitted to mention that she hadn't told her mother where she was going; that in fact she'd said that she was going to Stranraer to see the boats.

'Then you had better return to the gates,' said the officer, 'and wait for your Mr Ritchie there.'

She swallowed. She couldn't face going all the way back through the dark woods on her own.

The officer glanced from her to the trees. He sighed. 'It might be quicker', he said reluctantly, 'if you rode my horse.'

'Thank you very much,' she said politely.

He dismounted, lifted her beneath the arms, and swung her into the saddle. Then he drew the reins over the horse's head so that he could lead, and started for the trees.

She was dizzyingly high up, and her legs were much too short to reach the stirrups. As the great horse ambled along, she had to clutch handfuls of mane to keep from sliding off. But the officer did not look round to check if she was all right. She liked him for that. It made her feel grown-up. And she liked the way his long grey cloak whispered over the snow.

It is dashing, she thought. Yes. He is a dashing officer.

She longed for him to turn round and be impressed with her riding. When he did not, she decided to start a conversation. She told him that her father was a soldier too, but that his leave had been cut short, and he'd been ordered to Africa. 'To the Sudan,' she said. 'That's a desert below Egypt.'

He nodded, but did not turn round.

'Papa', she said to his back, 'is a major in the 65th York and Lancasters. To which regiment do you belong, sir?'

'The Borderers,' he said, still without turning round.

'Mm,' she said brightly, for want of more informed comment.

The crow appeared and began to follow them. From the safety of the horse's broad back, Madeleine gave it a cool glance.

'My mother', she went on doggedly, 'generally stays at home with me. She used to go for long walks, but Dr Baines has forbidden them because of my sister-or-brother. She takes extremely good photographs, and she *detests* Scotland, for she can never get warm. But she pretends to like it for my sake. I was born here, you see, so it's different for me.'

By now she was desperate for him to respond. And she was dismayed when the gatehouse rose into sight.

As they emerged from the trees, the sun came out from behind a cloud and the crow took off with an indignant squawk. Madeleine laughed with delight, and at last the officer turned and looked up at her. He didn't smile, but she could tell that he was smiling inside – for his eyes were no longer cold, but warm and vividly alive, like a restless sea with the sun on it.

He swung her out of the saddle and set her on the ground, and she thanked him for the ride. The horse put down its nose to be stroked.

Flushed with the sense that the officer might at last be beginning to like her, Madeleine decided to ask him home for tea. Apart from Dr Baines, they never had any visitors at Cairngowrie House, so it would make a welcome change. She would ask him to tea, and he would make friends with her mother, and she herself would ride the great horse skilfully down to the beach to meet the seals.

'I ought to introduce myself,' she said as she extended her hand. 'My name is Madeleine Falkirk. My parents are Major and Mrs Falkirk of Cairngowrie House. I thought you might care to come to tea.'

The officer had been passing the reins back over his mount's head, but when she said her name he stopped. 'What did you say?' he said quietly.

She had a sudden terrible sense that the sun had gone in. 'M-Madeleine Falkirk,' she faltered. 'I thought you might like to . . .' Her voice trailed off.

The horse nudged the officer's shoulder, but he did not seem to notice. His face was rigid with shock. 'My God,' he murmured. 'How could they do it? To send a *child*.'

She swallowed. 'Nobody sent me,' she said.

Plainly he did not believe her. 'Your name isn't Falkirk,' he said between his teeth. 'It's Durrant.'

'No, Durrant was actually my mother's—'

'Your mother is Rose Durrant. Yes, I know.' He mounted his horse. Madeleine had to step back smartly to avoid his spurs.

She was familiar with grown-up anger from her parents' fights, but this was different. It was no sudden flare-up that was over in minutes, but a deep, slow anger that had no end.

She didn't understand what had gone wrong. She sensed that without knowing it she must have tricked him in some shameful way. She felt hollow and breathless and sick.

'Tell your parents', he said, 'that this will never work.'

'They don't know I'm here,' she whispered, scarcely moving her lips. 'And they wouldn't trick anyone. They are honourable. They—'

'Your parents wrecked lives. Don't you know that yet?'

For the first time since they had met, he looked her full in the face. His eyes were glassy with anger, the pupils black and alarming in the vivid light grey. 'Tell them they're dead to me,' he said in a quiet voice that made her go cold inside. 'And they're dead to the old man. Tell them they ought to have the courage – the decency – to stay dead.'

He yanked the horse's head round and dug in his spurs, and the great hind hooves churned the snow inches from her feet, and the silver tail flicked stingingly across her face.

Her legs buckled and she sat down heavily in the snow. She stayed breathless and unmoving as the officer rode away, as he was swallowed up by the dark beneath the trees. And behind her the crow thudded down onto the gatehouse roof, and filled the air with raucous laughter.

CHAPTER TWO

It was just beginning to get dark when Madeleine climbed down from Mr Ritchie's wagon and started along the coast path.

It was snowing, and the icy wind made her head ache. For the first time in her life her beloved stretch of beach felt unwelcoming. No fat seals greeted her from the rocks. No graceful fulmars wheeled overhead. A trio of cormorants scudded past, but their emerald eyes glanced off her and swept on, like the beam of the Corsewall lighthouse. It felt as if the officer's ill-will had spread to them.

To her surprise, Cairngowrie House was silent and dim when she let herself in. Hannah must have forgotten to turn up the gas. That made it doubly hard to manage the button-hook with her cold-numbed fingers, and by the time she had struggled out of her boots she was fighting back tears of rage. She tugged off her hat and coat and mittens and left them in a soggy heap in the hall, then padded angrily into the drawing-room.

It was empty, and only feebly lit by the dying fire. Muttering, she dragged the piano stool to the nearest gasolier and climbed on top to reach the chain. The drawing-room flared into life. Then she shovelled coal onto the fire, spilling most of it on the hearth. Then she wondered what to do next.

The clock on the mantelpiece said four, but there was no sign of tea. There was no sign of anyone. And she had been counting on tea to make things normal again.

When she thought about the officer she had a horrible churning feeling of guilt and bewilderment and loss. She should never have gone to the Forbidden Kingdom. She should never have told him her name. But why had he been so angry?

She went to the piano and scowled at the photograph of Eden in its tortoiseshell frame. Did Eden have something to do with it? It had certainly landed her in trouble before.

The photograph showed a luminous, ruined house in a jungle of palms and breadfruit trees. Creepers trailed from the broken verandahs. A tree-fern sprouted from a window like a shattered monocle. A graceful double curve of steps swept down into what had once been a garden, and at the foot stood a tall, fair-haired blur which was Papa. He had moved just as her mother exposed the plate.

Eden didn't *look* dangerous, but it was. Madeleine knew, for she had grown up with it: her mother talked of it all the time. Her family, the Durrants, had built it long ago on the edge of the virgin forest, but in the end misfortune had driven them to abandon it, and now the forest was taking it back again.

In Eden everything is wilder and more alive than anywhere else. The sun shines more fiercely, the rain strikes harder, and the leaves are so green that it hurts your eyes. Oh, it's a dangerous place, Maddy. In Eden good and bad and beauty and ugliness are all tangled up together. There are hummingbirds so lovely that you can't look at them for long; and moonflowers which only bloom for a single night, and are so fragile and pale that they're like the ghosts of flowers; and beautiful evil-looking plants whose poison can strike you dumb. And deep in the forest there stands an enormous silk-cotton tree with an entire world in its branches, and the black people say that it's haunted. And the house itself is part of the forest again now, for no-one has lived in it for years and years, so it's fearfully overgrown.

At Madeleine's first and last foray to Sunday School three years before, Miss McAllister had cut short her recital at that point. Oh no, dear, she had said, not overgrown. God would never allow that.

Miss McAllister had told her that what Madeleine called a 'silk-cotton tree' was in fact the Tree of the Knowledge of Good and Evil, and that it couldn't possibly be haunted, as the black people maintained – for the simple reason that there are no black people in Eden.

I believe there are some, Madeleine had cautiously replied. You see, I know about Eden, because it's where I began.

Whatever can you mean, dear, Miss McAllister had said with a frozen smile.

Why, because it's where my parents used to meet before I was born.

That was when Miss McAllister had burst into tears and fled the class.

Her mother was right: Eden was dangerous. Because of Eden, Madeleine's only attempt at meeting other children had been a disaster, and she'd been banished from the rectory for ever. Because of Eden, her mother longed for Jamaica and detested Scotland.

And perhaps, she thought, it's because of Eden that it all went wrong with the officer in the park.

Your parents wrecked lives, he had said. What did he mean? How does one wreck a life? She pictured a broken ferry boat tilting rustily on a beach.

Her parents couldn't have done something like that. It didn't make sense. None of it made sense.

In the glare of the gaslight the ruined house stared back at her with its shattered tree-fern eye. What's so special about you? she thought angrily. You're only a mouldy old photograph. We've got hundreds of better ones in the darkroom.

On impulse she turned it over, undid the clasps, and slid it out of the frame. Then she laid it on top of the piano and with her thumbnail scored a deep, diagonal line across. Her nail scratched the blur that was papa, but she didn't stop. Papa ought to be here to sort things out. Grimly she scored another line to make a giant X.

Upstairs a thump shook the ceiling, and she froze guiltily. The gasoliers' crystal fringes chimed. A moment later she heard her mother ringing for Hannah.

The ringing continued. But no irritable 'Coming, coming' issued from the kitchen.

Wretched Hannah. With an exasperated sigh Madeleine slammed down the photograph and stalked upstairs.

Afterwards, the moment when she opened the bedroom door became fixed in her mind as the point when her life changed.

Until then she had spent her days bickering and laughing with her mother, waging a covert war against Hannah, and wandering on the beach chatting to the seals and the cormorants and Mister Parrot. After she opened the door, everything changed.

Her mother – her elegant, unpredictable, beautiful mother – was crouching on the rug on all fours, panting and baring her teeth like an animal.

She looked as if she had been dressing to go out when she had fallen to her knees. The collar of her walking-coat was twisted, a large rip had appeared under one arm, and her blue velvet bonnet – Madeleine's favourite – had slid down her back and become snarled in her hair.

Then Madeleine saw the great wet patch on the rug. She was horrified. It was inconceivable that her mother could have had an 'accident'. But she couldn't think of another explanation.

Her mother raised her head and saw her. 'Ah, there you are,' she said, bizarrely calm.

Madeleine tried extremely hard not to look at the wet patch. 'Are you unwell?' she mumbled.

'Much better now, thank you, Maddy. Just run and fetch Hannah.'

Madeleine bit her lip. She couldn't let the housemaid see her mother like this. 'You should get up off the floor,' she said. 'You should get into bed.'

'In a minute,' her mother replied. 'Dr Baines said that being on all fours might ease the backache, and although I hate to admit it, he's right.' She gave a mock grimace. 'I know it looks odd, but I—' She broke off with a sudden hiss as some sort of spasm seized her.

Madeleine gripped the doorknob.

'Now here's a thing,' her mother gasped. 'They're coming rather more quickly than I'd expected. You'd better fetch Hannah at once.'

Madeleine fled.

She ran down to the kitchen, but to her dismay it was in darkness. So was the dining-room and the morning-room and her father's smoking-room, and the scullery, pantry, larder, darkroom, cloakroom, downstairs water closet, and cellar. There was no answer to her increasingly shrill cries.

Mewing like a kitten, she raced upstairs. She checked the bedrooms and the bathroom, and finally the attic.

'I can't find her,' she panted when she'd rejoined her mother.

While she was away, her mother had struggled out of her walking-coat, tossed the bonnet in a corner, and climbed into bed. Or rather, she was sitting against a pile of pillows with the counterpane tented over her knees. She looked pale, but much more her normal self.

'I can't find Hannah,' Madeleine said in a calmer voice. 'Her carpet-bag's not there. And her trunk's padlocked with a note on top. I think she's gone.'

Her mother shut her eyes. 'That bloody, *bloody* girl.'

Madeleine was shocked. Her mother never used bad words. To cover her confusion she retrieved the bonnet from under the wash-hand stand and placed it on the dressing-table stool.

Without warning another spasm took hold of her mother. This time she had to suck in her lips to keep from crying out.

Helplessly Madeleine waited for it to end. If only Dr Baines were here. The abdominal binder hung forgotten over the bedpost: a cruel reminder of his absence.

'Don't be frightened,' her mother said at last. 'These pains are supposed to happen.'

Madeleine looked at her in disbelief. 'Why?' she demanded. 'Why are they "supposed" to happen?'

'They simply mean that the baby has decided to arrive a little earlier than we expected.'

'The *baby*?' Wildly she scanned the room. 'Can't you tell

it to wait? It can come tomorrow when I've fetched Dr Baines.'

Her mother's lip curled. 'I'm afraid not. And from the way this is going, I think we're going to need him tonight. You'd better run up the path and tell Mr Ritchie to fetch him.'

Madeleine swallowed. 'Mr Ritchie's not at home,' she said in a tight voice.

'*What?*'

'He went to his daughter's in Portpatrick for a fortnight. He just left.'

Her mother had gone frighteningly pale. When she shut her eyes her eyelids were nearly blue.

Madeleine said, 'I can go for Dr Baines.'

'No you can't. Not all the way to Stranraer.'

'Yes I can. I can take a lantern—'

'Maddy, it's four miles.'

'But I know the way—'

'No.'

'But—'

'It's snowing, it's pitch dark, and you're only ten years old. Absolutely not.'

There was a long silence. At last her mother opened her eyes. She licked her lips. 'Well, Maddy,' she said quietly. 'There's nothing for it. We'll just have to do this on our own.'

Madeleine gripped the bedpost. She had no idea what 'this' actually meant.

'You're going to have to help me. Can you do that?'

Madeleine gave a doubtful nod.

'That's my brave girl. Now in the bottom left-hand drawer of my dressing-table, under the evening corsets, you'll find a little red booklet. Fetch it and bring it to me.'

Madeleine went to the dressing-table and, after some embarrassed fumbling, she found a thin, much-thumbed booklet bound in rust-coloured cloth. Gilded lettering announced it to be *The Wife's Handbook by Dr Archibald Philpott – Or How a Woman Should Order Herself During Pregnancy and Delivery, With Hints on the Management of the Infant, and Other Matters Necessary to be Known to the Married Woman.*

'That's the one,' said her mother. Another spasm took hold, and this time it went on for longer. By the end, Madeleine was swallowing tears.

'I think', panted her mother, 'you had better read it aloud.'

Madeleine's teeth began to chatter. 'I can't.'

'Yes you can. Come on, Maddy. You'll feel better with something to do.'

Shakily Madeleine opened the book. Chapter One swam before her eyes.

Her mother waited, fixing her with a dark, unblinking stare.

'*From – from the first marriage-night*,' Madeleine began uncertainly, '*no woman under the age of forty-five can consider herself safe—*'

To her astonishment, her mother laughed. 'I think we've come a bit further than that! There's an index at the back, Maddy. Find the section headed "Labour", and start reading from there.'

CHAPTER THREE

'*When the pains grow frequent and severe,*' Madeleine read aloud, '*loop a roller towel around the bedpost and give the ends to the woman to pull on, while she braces her feet against the footboard.*'

'We haven't got a roller towel,' panted her mother. 'Fetch a sheet – from the linen cupboard.' Then she was off again on another wave of pain.

Madeleine raced for the linen cupboard.

An hour before, when the pains were not as close together, she and her mother had gone through Dr Philpott's list of *Equipment for the Lying-in Room*. Her mother had tried to make a game of it, but Madeleine hadn't been fooled. They had both clung to the doctor's words with a fervour that would have delighted the Reverend McAllister, had it been aimed at God.

A mackintosh for the woman to lie on had been the first challenge, as her mother didn't own one, and Madeleine's was far too small. The alternatives were *brown paper smeared with pitch*, which sounded horrible, or *oilcloth*. The kitchen tablecloth was pressed into service.

A tablet of soap was easy enough, *a skein of worsted and a pair of blunt scissors* were snatched from the work-stand in the drawing-room, and instead of *lard or cold cream* they took the almond and glycerine face cream from the dressing-table. *Flannels, napkins and baby clothes* were waiting in the linen cupboard – 'top shelf, Maddy, use a chair, and be *careful,'* – and Papa's eau-de-cologne stood in for *a bottle of Condy's fluid*, whatever that was.

'. . . *and finally,'* said Dr Philpott, '*hot water and a brisk fire.'*

The brisk fire was easily managed, for before Hannah left she had obviously suffered pangs of guilt, and filled all the coal scuttles to overflowing. But Madeleine didn't even want to think about the hot water. That would mean braving the geyser in the bathroom, which her mother adored, but Madeleine hated and feared. A fickle cast-iron behemoth, it squatted above the bath, its eerie blue flame for ever aglow. When you turned on the tap it spat steam, scalding water, and, on very bad days, drops of molten lead.

To Madeleine's intense relief her mother said it wasn't time for the hot water yet. Reassuringly, she seemed to have at least some idea of what was going on. She knew the right position she ought to adopt even before Madeleine read Dr Philpott: '*on the woman's left side, with her knees drawn up*', and she knew that '*the woman must refrain from crying out*'. She even managed it most of the time. But she wouldn't let Madeleine help her out of her afternoon gown, and flatly refused to raise her nightgown to her knees, as Dr Philpott said she should. 'No, Maddy, absolutely not. You're far too young as it is. And for goodness' *sake*, look away when I tell you to.'

But there were alarming gaps in her knowledge. She had no idea what most of Dr Philpott's items were for, or even when the baby was due to arrive. And at times, when she thought Madeleine wasn't looking, she would stare wide-eyed into nothingness, as if trying to ward off some malevolent presence.

It was clear that the only person who really knew what to do was Dr Philpott. Madeleine pictured him with ginger eyebrows and a long bushy beard. Like God, but a good deal nicer.

The gaps between the spasms were narrowing, and her mother was beginning to look exhausted. Sweat plastered her hair to her temples, and dark circles ringed her eyes.

'What wouldn't I give', she muttered, 'for a good stiff dose of chloroform.'

'What's chlor— what's that?' said Madeleine.

'It's why I've put up with Dr Baines all these months. A large brandy wouldn't go amiss, either.'

They had a bottle of brandy in the dining-room – Madeleine knew because she'd tried it once in secret – but Dr Philpott strictly forbade alcohol. He said it caused something called *flooding*, which was clearly a very bad thing.

'My poor little Maddy,' her mother said suddenly.

Startled, Madeleine looked up from Dr Philpott.

'You oughtn't to know about any of this. You ought to go on believing that babies arrive in cabbage patches. Or is it gooseberry bushes?'

'I like the one about the stork,' muttered Madeleine.

Her mother wasn't listening. 'You see, I thought I had more time. This wasn't supposed to happen for another three weeks.'

'Is that why it hurts?'

'No. It's supposed to hurt.' Her face twisted, and she sucked in her breath through her teeth. 'If anything happens – don't remember me like this.'

Madeleine shied away from what she meant.

This time the pain went on for longer. Then another one came, and another, and suddenly there were no more gaps. Her mother started crying out bad words, and Madeleine dropped Dr Philpott, and her mother shouted at her to turn away and not look round for *anything* – and to just keep reading, keep bloody *reading*.

Madeleine snatched Dr Philpott from the rug and retreated to the foot of the bed. She couldn't find the right page. The words kept jumping about and getting blurred. 'It says – it says – to bear down and push.'

'I *am* pushing! Ah, Jesus God!'

'*After one final push,*' Madeleine shouted over her mother's cries, '*the head appears, and a minute or two after this, the body.*' She stole a fearful glance at her mother's long white foot pressed against the footboard.

'Turn *away*,' gasped her mother. 'Don't *look*!'

Then she screamed – a terrible, wrenching scream as if she were being torn apart – and Madeleine clapped her hands over her ears and dropped Dr Philpott again. But she could still hear the screams, and the slap of bare feet against the footboard, and the creak of the bedpost as her mother pulled on the sheet.

Then there was nothing. Silence reverberated round the room. Madeleine kept her ears covered and her eyes tight shut.

From behind her came another cry. It was smaller and wilder than her mother's, but just as piercing. It went on and on, rhythmic and unvarying, as if from a pair of bellows being tirelessly worked.

She turned round.

Her mother lay with her eyes closed and her pale lips slightly parted. Her face was shiny with sweat, her eyelids so fragile that they reminded Madeleine of pastry rolled too thin. The nightgown still tented the second bustle – as well as a smaller, twitching lump below it.

The baby, Madeleine thought numbly.

The rhythmic cries came at her in waves, along with an awful smell like chicken innards on the turn. The nightgown was splotched with red. 'Mamma,' Madeleine said in a small voice. 'You're wounded.'

To her bewilderment her mother smiled. It began as a faint stretching of the lips, then widened into a grin – as if, with a little more strength, she might actually laugh aloud. 'It's all right. It's all right.' She paused for breath. She was silent for so long that Madeleine thought she had fallen asleep. How could she sleep with all this noise?

Without opening her eyes, her mother said, 'It was easy. So much easier than the first time.'

Easy? thought Madeleine.

'Pass – the scissors and thread, Maddy. Read the bit about cutting the cord. And – back turned. I mean it.'

Madeleine passed the scissors and the worsted, then stooped reluctantly for Dr Philpott. She didn't want to read any more. She felt shaky and sick. She wanted to put back her head and howl. If the wretched baby could do it, why couldn't she?

Turning her back and wiping her eyes with her fingers, she scanned the page. 'Um. *With the worsted, tie off the cord* – is that the right bit?'

From behind her came a murmur of approval, almost inaudible beneath the baby's cries.

'. . . *t-tie off the cord about two inches from the navel,*' Madeleine read. '*Then tie it off two inches below that and cut, using the scissors.*' She frowned. '*The infant is thus separated from the mother, and lives its own life.*'

Through the shrill rhythmic cries she heard the rustle of the nightgown and the soft flump of her mother subsiding onto the pillows. 'You can turn round now,' she said.

Madeleine didn't want to turn round. She wished the baby would go away. Or at least be quiet. '*Wrap the infant in warm flannel,*' she read aloud.

An exhausted sigh from the bed. 'Sorry, Maddy. I think you'll have to do the rest.'

Madeleine stole a fearful glance at the bloodied night-gown, which was twitching horribly. She would rather jump out of the window than tackle whatever lay under there.

'Go on,' her mother urged. 'Fetch one of those napkins that you left to warm over the fender.'

With a sickening sense of doom, Madeleine put Dr Philpott on the floor and did as she was told. Then she approached the bed.

What she saw when she lifted the nightgown made her recoil in horror. It wasn't a baby; it was a devil. A slimy, spindly, crumpled, blotchy purple, *angry* little devil, smeared with blood and disgusting cheesy-looking stuff, and howling so furiously that she couldn't even see its eyes. And beside it lay a terrible reddish-purple mound of jelly stuff, like a second devil that had followed it out.

Black dots floated before her eyes. Her stomach heaved.

'Go on,' urged her mother, 'don't let her catch cold.'

'Which one?' said Madeleine between her teeth.

'What?'

'Which one do I wrap up?'

Her mother laughed. She actually laughed. 'The one who's crying, of course.'

Madeleine felt a flash of pity. Perhaps her mother hadn't seen it yet. She still thought it was a normal baby.

Grimacing and holding the napkin before her as if she were mopping up a stain, she spread it over where she guessed the 'baby' lay.

'It's all right,' her mother said calmly. 'When you were born you looked just the same.'

'But it's horrible. It's got blood all over, and a worm coming out of its belly-button. I'm sure I never—'

'Yes, you did. The blood is perfectly normal, Maddy. So is the worm. I promise. All babies look like that.'

Madeleine thought about Baby Jesus in His crib, with the Three Wise Men crowding round. She wondered if Miss McAllister had any idea what He had really been like.

'Now give her to me,' her mother said. 'Put one hand under her neck to support the head – carefully. That's it.' She was still smiling. She seemed unable to stop.

The baby smelt awful and was surprisingly heavy. It was an enormous relief to deposit it in her mother's arms.

But the work wasn't over yet. Dr Philpott said that the purplish jelly thing – he called it 'the afterbirth' – *must be caught in a bowl, and burnt as soon as possible*. He made it sound as easy and pleasant as netting a butterfly.

And her mother was no help at all, as she couldn't take her eyes from the baby, which had finally stopped crying. So it was Madeleine who thought of using the warming-pan to carry the 'afterbirth' away, and her idea to throw it out of the bathroom window. The blast of snow on her face felt wonderful, but she was nearly sick as she tipped the monster into the night.

'What *was* that thing?' she mumbled, when she'd wrestled the window shut again and returned to the bedroom.

'I don't know,' said her mother dreamily. 'But the same thing happened with you, and the doctor said it was perfectly normal.'

Madeleine watched her mother hugging the flannel

package which contained the baby. She was smiling and crying, and giving little delighted spurts of laughter. 'We've done it, Maddy. We've done it! You have a sister. A perfect, perfect, *beautiful* little sister.'

Out of loyalty Madeleine forced a smile, but inside she was churning with disgust. How could her mother still think everything was all right? Couldn't she see?

All babies were definitely not like this one. Babies were pink, and they smiled at you and looked about with big round eyes.

'What', said her mother, 'does Dr Philpott say next?'

Madeleine retreated to the dressing-table stool. It was a relief to sit down, but she didn't like being so far away. She wanted her mother to smile and coo at *her*, and forget about the baby.

'*Wash the woman's external geni—*' she scowled at the unfamiliar word, '*geni-talia – in warm water and Condy's fluid, and apply a napkin or sani-tary towel. Change the bed, and bind the woman's abdomen to prevent flooding. There must be no sitting up or talking.*' She threw her mother a doubtful look, but she was lying meekly on the pillows with her eyes closed.

'Don't go to sleep,' Madeleine said sharply. 'Dr Philpott hasn't said that you may.'

Her mother nodded. 'Don't worry, I'm not. But we'll have to ignore the bit about not talking. Read on, Maddy. You're doing magnificently.'

Slightly mollified, Madeleine read on. '*The mother being quietly settled, and the infant having been washed—*'

Her mother's eyes snapped open. They exchanged startled glances.

'I've got to wash it?' said Madeleine in horror.

Her mother studied her, as if gauging how much more she could take. 'I'm so sorry, Maddy. But remember. It's not an "it". It's a "she". Your little sister.'

As if that helped.

Half an hour later, Madeleine grimly draped a napkin over the fender to dry and decided that she deserved a medal. Dr

Philpott himself should be here, telling her she was wonderful.

She had done almost everything he said, except for the bit about washing her mother. (That had been accomplished in secret, while she was out of the room.) She had even made friends with the geyser, which had belched helpfully into life as soon as she turned the tap. Or perhaps she was simply too tired to be scared of it any more.

Somehow, by the time she had refilled the jug and carried it back to the bedroom, her mother had washed herself and struggled into the abdominal binder and the clean flannel drawers, and the flannel nightgown which Madeleine had put out. She had also taken one of the Barnett's Hygienic Wood Wool Diapers for Ladies from the packet which Madeleine had fetched at her direction from the dressing-room bureau. 'How lucky', Madeleine had said, 'that you thought to buy those in advance.' She had been puzzled by her mother's wry smile.

Changing the bed had also been easier than Madeleine had expected. 'Just bundle up the dirty things and throw them out of the bathroom window,' her mother had said. 'Some-one will deal with it tomorrow.'

But washing the baby had been far, far worse. As soon as Madeleine had put it in the washbasin it started crying, and when she rubbed it clean with a handkerchief the crying became an outraged caterwaul. She couldn't bring herself to touch the worm coming out of its belly-button, which was probably why she got soap in the baby's eyes – although it was hard to tell, as its face was so tightly screwed up that she couldn't see. All this trouble, and it wouldn't even look at her.

It was an incredible relief to get it clean and dry and wrapped in fresh napkins – 'Use three,' said her mother, 'the thickest flannel ones, we don't want her catching cold.' And to Madeleine's astonishment and annoyance, the cater-wauling stopped almost as soon as she handed it to her mother, who told her to turn her back while she 'got the baby settled'.

'How did you manage that?' Madeleine said crossly as she was putting the last of the damp napkins over the fender. It seemed the blackest ingratitude for the baby to howl at her for ages, then snuggle up to her mother and behave.

'She's feeding,' her mother whispered. 'She'll be quiet now.'

Setting her teeth, Madeleine picked up the washbasin and stalked off to empty it. Then she stalked back and set it firmly on the wash-hand stand.

Her mother raised her head and gave her a considering look. 'Poor Maddy. You're exhausted. And you haven't eaten a crumb for hours. After everything you've accomplished!'

Madeleine tried not to look pleased.

'Run down to the kitchen and cut yourself the biggest piece of seed cake you've ever seen. Take the whole thing if you like. And pour yourself an enormous glass of milk.'

Obediently, Madeleine went out onto the landing. But she never reached the kitchen, for without warning her stomach began to heave. She barely made it to the water closet before she was violently sick. When it was over she stayed kneeling on the freezing tiles with her elbows on the seat. She never wanted to move again.

Then she realized that she hadn't closed the bathroom door, so her mother must have heard her being sick. A wave of shame washed over her. Her mother had been through much worse, and she hadn't been sick once.

'Sorry,' she mumbled when she returned to the bedroom.

Her mother gave her a dreamy smile. 'You're exhausted, sweetheart. This has been ghastly for you. I'm so sorry you had to go through it. But you've been splendid. Utterly, utterly splendid. I couldn't have done it without you.'

Madeleine sucked in her lips.

'Let's get this little one settled, shall we? Then you shall climb into bed with me, and we'll sleep till the middle of next week.'

That sounded more like her proper mother. But there was still the matter of 'settling' the baby.

According to Dr Philpott, it must be placed in a cot beside

the mother. But the cot was in the new nursery, and far too heavy to drag in. So instead Madeleine emptied a drawer from the bureau and put in a pillow for a mattress, and then her mother's thick Paisley shawl, doubled up. Then she hauled the drawer onto the bed and put it at the bottom, against the footboard. Then she put the baby inside and folded the shawl over it, with the head just showing, like a jam turnover. To her relief, the baby slept through the whole operation. Whatever her mother had given it to eat had obviously worked.

Suddenly, Madeleine was too tired to undress. Fortunately, she was wearing her favourite soft grey jersey sailor frock, with loose flannel petticoats underneath, as her mother didn't believe in corset-waists for children. Yawning, she tugged off her hairclip and crawled beneath the covers.

It was wonderful to burrow into the great mound of bedding, and her mother felt marvellously soft and warm to curl up against. She also smelled reassuringly of soap and eau-de-cologne – although the smell of baby still lingered in the air.

'Sorry I was sick,' Madeleine mumbled.

She felt a gentle breath stirring the top of her hair, as if her mother were trying to kiss her but lacked the strength to reach. 'You were wonderful,' her mother said. 'So grown-up. And *brave*. You're amazing, Maddy. Quite, quite amazing.'

For a while there was silence, and Madeleine thought her mother had fallen asleep. Then once again she felt the breath on her hair. 'Tomorrow,' her mother said drowsily, 'when you've had breakfast and fetched Dr Baines, everything will be back to normal. The doctor will bring a nurse to look after us, and you won't ever have to wash the baby again. And after that, you shall eat nothing but cake all day long, and I'll have the biggest brandy in Christendom – and we'll send an enormous bunch of carnations to Dr Philpott. And then we'll put our heads together and decide how to execute Hannah.'

Madeleine giggled.

She fell asleep listening to the hiss and crackle of the fire, and her mother's deep, even breathing.

She awoke once in the night, when her mother rolled against her muttering 'Cold . . . close the window . . . cold.'

Half asleep, Madeleine got up to check the windows – although she knew they were shut, for Dr Philpott was very stern about draughts. The room was warm but she stoked the fire anyway, then crawled back to bed, and slept.

She was jolted awake by the baby crying. There was no gentle drifting out of sleep. Suddenly she was awake and buffeted by cries.

She lay on her back wondering when it would stop. She could see daylight through a gap in the curtains. She must have slept all night.

Then she became aware of a chilly dampness down her right side, and a strange coppery smell. It must be the baby, she thought in disgust. She wished it had never arrived.

Beside her, her mother still slept. Her face had a waxy tinge, and her expression was strangely absent. It was neither happy nor sad, but simply not there. As if she were dreaming a very deep dream.

Madeleine touched her arm but she didn't wake up. The arm felt hard, like a doll's. Madeleine struggled out from under the bedclothes and knelt beside her. Gently she put her finger to her mother's cheek. The flesh was cool and firm, like an unripe plum.

The baby was still crying.

Madeleine stayed kneeling on the bed. Her frock was cold and damp down the side that had lain against her mother, and when she put her palm to her thigh it came away glistening red. She shuffled crab-like off the bed and peeled back the blankets.

Her mother lay in a great crimson stain that surrounded her like a monstrous butterfly.

A line from Dr Philpott came back to her. *Flooding is a danger, particularly during the first hours after the birth.*

What's flooding? she thought numbly.

This is, came the cold reply inside her head.

The night before, her mother had assured her that the blood was 'perfectly normal'. Perhaps she hadn't known about flooding.

It occurred to Madeleine that she ought to change the sheets. She couldn't get the soiled one out from under her mother, so she left it in place and put a clean sheet on top, then covered that with fresh blankets from the spare room, and the counterpane. She pushed the soiled bedclothes out of the bathroom window as she had done the night before, and watched them land with a *whump* in the snow. Then she took the hot brick from the fender and wrapped it in a flannel and put it beneath her mother's feet, to warm her up.

The baby was still crying. Madeleine ignored it.

Chapter Eight: After the Birth said that *the mother may be given warm milk or beef tea to restore her strength*. She padded out onto the landing, wondering how to make beef tea.

The stairwell was freezing, and when she reached the bottom she couldn't remember what she was doing there. She sat on the stairs, blinking at the pile of mittens, coat and sealskin hat which she'd left on the floor the day before. Jutting from the coat pocket was a corner of Mister Parrot's green felt wing.

The baby was still crying.

On the mat by the front door she saw a letter. She went and picked it up. It was for her mother. The sender's address was inscribed on the back in a tiny, extremely regular hand: *Mrs Septimus Fynn, 24 Wyndham Street, Bryanston Square, Marylebone, London*. She replaced the letter on the mat.

The baby was still crying.

She wondered how to make it stop. She padded back upstairs and into her own room, and changed her frock. She didn't bother about changing her petticoats or stockings or drawers, because the blood hadn't soaked through that far.

Then she went into the bathroom and washed. In the mirror above the basin a white-faced girl with big dark eyes and wavy dark hair stared back at her.

The baby was still crying. But Dr Baines would come

soon, she told herself. Dr Baines would deal with the baby.

She went back into her room and sat on the bed and looked out of the window. It was snowing so hard that she couldn't see the beach beyond the garden wall.

Then she remembered that Dr Baines came once a week on Tuesdays, and that he'd already been the day before yesterday, which meant that he wouldn't come again for another five days.

She thought about going to fetch him. But that would take hours, and she had a feeling that she oughtn't to leave the baby on its own for so long.

She thought about taking the baby with her, but it was far too heavy to carry all the way to Stranraer. So instead she decided to wait in the house until someone came.

Someone would come soon. And they would look after her and the baby, and – and everything. Her thoughts skittered away from what 'everything' meant. She was hazily aware that her mother wasn't going to wake up again, but whenever she started to think about that, a smooth blank wall rose up in her mind, and shut it out.

And the baby was still crying. It didn't sound as if it would stop.

She got up and went to the door of her mother's room. It was cavernous and dim, for she had forgotten to open the curtains, but on the floor by the bed she spotted Dr Philpott, where he had fallen during the night. Keeping her eyes averted from her mother, she crossed the room and picked him up, then retreated to the dressing-table and pulled out the stool. Her mother's blue velvet bonnet lay on the seat, where she had put it the night before. Madeleine put it on the rug at her feet, and sat down.

The dressing-table was covered with the familiar clutter. She looked at the ivory brush set on its little embroidered mat, and the Japanese lacquer ring-tray, the velvet mouchoir case, the jewel casket, the pincushion, and the crystal jar of rice powder that she was sometimes allowed to play with for a treat. She looked at the porcelain pot of almond and glycerine face cream, and the open packet of Barnett's Hygienic Wood Wool Diapers for Ladies.

She pushed everything to one side to make room for Dr Philpott, and turned to the index at the back. After searching for some time, she found what she was looking for: *Infant, Management Of – Page 57*.

She turned to page fifty-seven and started to read.

CHAPTER FOUR

Northern Sudan, 12 March 1884

God, what a country, thought Cameron Lawe as he shouldered his way through the Suakin bazaar.

Mad-eyed hillmen and greasy merchants: fawning over you one moment, and the next, only too ready to slit your throat.

It irritated him to think that in a sense his family's wealth had originated here, in this squalid, stinking little midden of a town. The forebears of these same Egyptians and Berberines had done a brisk trade with Jamaica's first settlers, and for two centuries the cane-fields had swallowed up a steady stream of slaves. So where was the difference between his own forebears and these thieving heathens?

An heretical thought, and one which he had no desire to deal with now. He didn't want to deal with anything. He hadn't slept for thirty-six hours.

Once again he cursed the vagueness of the orders which had brought him here. *Report to the Muhafaza at Suakin with the utmost despatch.* Why? What for? No doubt it was just another glorious army muddle which had sent him on a headlong rush for no reason at all. A freezing overnight train from Scotland, an overcrowded steamer to Port Said and then another through the canal, a dust-choked train across the desert, and finally a cramped and stinking man-of-war along the Gulf.

And then the *coup de grâce*: to be transferred to 'special

duties' with another regiment. Special duties. What the devil did that mean?

He stopped at a saddle-maker's for directions. *Ya sayyid, ayna al Muhafaza?* Which way to the Muhafaza, the Governor's House?

Nihaya as-suq, ya Kabtan, khud al yamtin wa tumma al yasar 'an awwal az-zuqaq. End of the bazaar, Captain, turn right, and down the first alley on the left.

As he said it, the saddle-maker slid him a curious look. It was the middle of the afternoon, and far too hot for Englishmen.

Unless, thought Cameron, giving the saddle-maker a cold stare, one happens to have been born in the tropics.

As he passed a spice-grinder's stall he caught a heady wave of cumin and cloves, and without warning homesickness had him in its grip. Wherever he turned he saw reminders of Jamaica. The dust, the glare, the gaudy robes fluttering in the furnace wind: saffron, crimson, emerald and cobalt. The clamour of voices in a hundred tongues, the teeming black and brown faces. The oiled and intricate plaits of the ebony women.

Why now? he thought angrily. Why here? Hang it all, you don't have time for this.

But if he was honest, he knew why Jamaica was so much in his thoughts. Because on his last day at Strathnaw he had taken a farewell ride in the park, and met a little girl in the snow.

It had taken just one word – Falkirk – and all the anger, the pain, had come boiling to the surface. There is no *justice*, he had thought as he looked down into the child's fearless, eager little face. Your father isn't 'Alasdair Falkirk'. He's Ainsley Monroe. Ainsley Randolph Falkirk Monroe, of the Monroes of Fever Hill, Jamaica. And this isn't some story-book playground for you to explore. It's the ancient seat of the family that your father dragged through the mud.

He had been appalled at the violence of his feelings. For twelve years he had driven Ainsley from his mind. It had been an act of will. A duty. And all it took was a single word to break down the wall.

A butterfly touch on his arm dragged him back to the bazaar, and he glanced down to see an Abyssinian girl shyly offering food, and probably more. She was holding out some infernal mess of stewed goat on dhurra bread, and murmuring in Arabic about the pasha enjoying a 'meal' in her brother's house.

She had large, liquid dark eyes and polished copper skin, and most of his fellow officers would have judged her quite handsome enough for an hour or so. Cameron gave her a look that made her flinch, and pushed on. The thought of bedding a native girl turned his stomach.

At last the bazaar was left behind, and he walked out into the heat and glare of the Keff, the medieval jumble of flat-roofed coral houses where the army was encamped. Skeletal goats trod piles of refuse with delicate hooves. Swarms of flies – the tiny, maddening flies of the Sudan – wavered and settled and rose again.

Beyond the Keff he saw straggling patches of yam and watermelon, and then, with brutal suddenness, the desert: a vast heat-warped plain the colour of dried blood, broken only by sharp-toothed outcrops of stark black rock.

It was a profoundly alien wilderness, and yet he felt a perverse attraction to it. At least out there he wouldn't be fighting homesickness as well as Dervishes.

Down an alley stinking of turmeric and goats, he found the Muhafaza: a run-down old building of battered white coral pitted with bullet holes. Ducking beneath the lintel, he entered the shadowy interior, and came face to face with Ainsley Monroe.

He felt as if he'd been kicked in the chest.

Ainsley had been writing at a rickety little desk by the window, his bright gold head bowed over his papers, and lit by a shaft of sunlight from a half-open shutter. A subaltern stood at his elbow, handing him order slips and clutching a ledger to his chest.

Of course, thought Cameron dizzily. The child in the park had said that her father was a major in the 65th. Why didn't you think of that before?

Ainsley raised his head and saw him, and blinked once. He

45

dismissed the subaltern and rose to his feet. When they were alone he came round to the other side of the desk and put out his hand. Cameron ignored it. Ainsley gave him an uncertain smile. 'My God, Cameron, but this is a fine thing!' His voice shook with emotion. 'You've grown so tall! I quite have to look up to you now.'

Cameron couldn't speak. At one stroke he was a boy again, shocked and bewildered when this man whom he'd loved as a brother had shattered his world. 'Major Falkirk, sir,' he said with a stiff salute. 'Captain Lawe reporting for duty.'

Ainsley gave a startled laugh. Then with an ironic flourish he returned the salute.

It had been twelve years, but he hadn't changed at all. Those warm blue eyes. That wide mouth always ready for laughter. Although perhaps the resemblance to his father had become less marked over time, for he seemed to have lost some of Jocelyn Monroe's straight-backed authority. Or perhaps, thought Cameron, he never had it at all.

He watched Ainsley take a sheet of orders from the desk and hold them out. 'Here you are,' he said, still absurdly smiling. 'These are for you.'

Cameron took the papers in silence. *61377 Cameron Lawe, Captain, 'B' Company, 25th King's Own Scottish Borderers: special attachment to the 65th York and Lancasters under Major Alasdair Falkirk, until such time as the relief of Tokar has been accomplished.*

Ainsley was still smiling. He seemed unable to stop. It made Cameron's skin crawl. What, he thought in disbelief, does he expect? Does he imagine that after what he did he has only to smile, and I'll fall on his neck?

He folded the paper and put it in his tunic pocket. 'Sir, on whose initiative was this arranged?'

Ainsley looked surprised. 'On mine, of course.' He paused. 'I couldn't believe it when I saw your name in the transport lists. It was like a gift from God.'

'I want a transfer back to my own corps.'

Ainsley's smile faltered. 'I'd forgotten how blunt you can be.'

'I prefer to call it straightforward.'

'Indeed. Then I shall be straightforward too. Your request is denied.'

'On what grounds?'

'I need you here.'

'Why?'

'I understand you speak Arabic.'

'A little, but—'

'That's more than most. I need an interpreter.'

'I'd be of no use to you, sir,' Cameron said crisply. 'In this region they speak a corrupt version of the tongue. A sort of – bastard version. If you will.'

Their eyes locked.

Ainsley said, 'You can make this easy for yourself or you can make it hard. It's your choice.'

'What if I simply refuse to serve under you?'

'Then I shall have you court-martialled for insubordination.'

Cameron wondered if he meant it, and decided that he did. Beneath the gentleness Ainsley had always had a ruthless streak. Perhaps he wasn't so unlike his father after all. 'Why are you doing this?' he said.

Ainsley gave him a hooded look. 'I have my reasons.'

The Arabs say that when Allah made the Sudan, He laughed.

They're right. Savage laughter is the desert's natural music. The cackle of hyenas. The bark of jackals. The leathery *thwap* of vultures squabbling over their prey.

But on the eve of a battle, the desert holds its breath.

They had set out from Suakin in the chill of the night, to avoid the blistering heat of the sun, and had joined the main column at an oasis where they struck camp. It was a dreary little place, no more than a well of brackish water beneath a barren bluff – and as the sun rose, the heat quickly became unbearable. They flung up a line of zeribas with walls of thorn-scrub and camel-saddles and camped inside, the officers in tents, the men in what shade they could create from sacking and store boxes. They would rest until nightfall, march by moonlight, and engage the enemy some time after dawn.

It was nearly six in the evening, and stillness reigned: the peculiar taut stillness before a battle. Cameron couldn't sleep. He told himself it was just the pain in his hand, for he'd taken a sabre-cut across the palm in a skirmish during the night, but he knew it was more than that. Something ugly was churning away inside his chest.

Eventually he gave up and went for a walk. He left the zeriba and climbed a goat-track up the bluff, and found a patch of shade beneath a boulder near the top, and sat down. The shadows were lengthening but the heat was still intense. He could feel it beating down on his helmet, pressing on his skin like a blanket.

He sat for an hour or so, and below him the column began to wake up. Blue smoke rose from cooking-fires. Men yawned and stretched in the eerie copper light.

Snatches of talk drifted up to him. After the scrap at El Teb, the Dervishes would have rifles and carbines and Gatling guns. And they sent boys into battle, boys of no more than twelve, armed only with sticks and the love of Allah. But they had to be killed just the same, or they'd snap a horse's legs and be all over the rider like a swarm of flies.

Cameron watched the red men moving about below him in the red light, and wondered how many would be dead by this time tomorrow.

Wherever he looked, the desert stretched to the horizon. The wind whirled tirelessly over the hot, crisp ground. Black sand drifted like infernal snow. This, he thought, is what hell must be like. The world has been blasted to cinders, and this is what remains.

And still that sordid churning in his chest. What, honestly, did Ainsley expect? Forgiveness? An open-armed welcome for the prodigal son?

At the foot of the bluff a group of Hussars crouched in a ring, urging a scorpion into battle against a yellow tarantula. A trio of Egyptian camel-drivers wandered over to watch. As Cameron followed the spider's delicate circling, he was suddenly back in Jamaica, nineteen years before. It was his first week at Fever Hill, and he was six years old, crying beneath the guango tree, for he couldn't understand why his parents had gone away. Where had they gone? When would they stop being dead? He had reached the hiccuping stage when Ainsley had wandered up: a gangly fifteen-year-old, but a god to a small boy. Ainsley had pretended not to notice the tears, and had said simply, Would you care to see my pet tarantula?

Angrily, Cameron got to his feet and threw a stone as hard as he could across the bluff. *God*, why must you think about that now?

He needed to be doing something – anything, so long as it didn't involve Ainsley.

Back at the zeriba he spoke to the officer with the next watch, and negotiated an exchange. Then he retrieved his kit, found a store box to sit on, and buckled on his spurs.

Or rather, he tried to buckle them on, but his injured palm made him clumsy, and he couldn't get them fastened. He cursed savagely, and some of the men turned and stared. None of them laughed. If Captain Lawe lost his formidable temper, you were a fool to get in the way.

'Trouble?' said a voice which made the back of his neck prickle.

'No,' he said without looking up.

Ainsley sat on the store box next to his. 'Those spurs were my father's, weren't they?' he said quietly.

And now they're mine, thought Cameron. For Jocelyn no longer has a son. He flexed his injured hand to make the pain flare. It was a good, clean pain. Nothing like the sick churning in his chest.

'We missed you at dinner,' Ainsley said. 'The colonel asked where you were. He's a bit of a stickler for the conventions.'

Cameron made no reply.

'We pooled our resources,' said Ainsley, sounding amused. 'Sort of a send-off before tomorrow's scrap. Potted meat and tinned sardines, courtesy of Messrs Crosse & Blackwell. Oh, and I believe Forrest has saved you a slice of his aunt's preserved pineapple.'

'I'm not hungry.'

'Indeed.'

There was an awkward silence. Cameron wrestled with the buckle, and wished Ainsley to blazes.

Ainsley said, 'I handled it badly yesterday. You must have thought I was making light of things. I wasn't. I was just so damned glad to see you.'

At last Cameron succeeded with the spurs. He stood up.

'Where are you going?'

'I have the patrol.'

'I'll ride with you.'

'I'd rather you didn't.'

Ainsley gave a lop-sided smile. 'I'm aware of that.'

They rode at the head of the detail, taking the track which Cameron had climbed an hour before. When they were clear of the camp he said, 'I think you ought to tell me what the fellows know about you in the mess.'

Ainsley glanced at him, then turned in the saddle and ordered the men to fall back. When they were out of earshot he said, 'As far as they're concerned I'm Alasdair Falkirk. Have been for the past twelve years. They don't even know I'm from Jamaica.' He paused. 'I thought that best. For the family as well as myself.'

'Indeed,' said Cameron drily. 'Family honour has always been close to your heart.'

Ainsley's cheeks darkened. 'Would you prefer that I made my story known?'

'How could you? They'd throw you out of the regiment.'

Ainsley was silent. Then he said, 'Shall you tell them?'

'Of course not. The old man went through hell to prevent a scandal. I'm not going to ruin that now.' Frowning, he disentangled his mare's mane from the reins. 'He's been ill. I don't suppose you've heard.'

'How could I? You've never answered my letters.'

'I've never read them.' It gave him a sick satisfaction to see Ainsley flinch. It also made him feel ashamed. Once again he tormented his injured hand. 'How could you do it?' he said. 'To break the heart of a fine old man. To desert your wife and child.'

Ainsley let out a long breath. 'When I left Jamaica I didn't know that Clemency was with child.'

'Would it have made a difference if you had?'

Ainsley did not reply.

Behind them the men were casting them curious glances. Cameron quelled them with a look. He put his mare forward, and heard the rattle of pebbles as Ainsley brought his horse level.

'Cameron. Try to understand. I was young. Younger than you are now.'

'You were weak. You've always been weak.'

He gave a twisted smile. 'I can see that you've never been in love.'

Cameron snorted.

'Well, it may surprise you to learn that Clemency at least has forgiven me. Oh, yes, it's true. She wrote to me. Years ago.' He patted his tunic pocket. 'I keep her letter with me always.'

'Whatever for?'

'I suppose – to remind myself that there is such a thing as forgiveness.'

Cameron wondered if that were the whole truth. Why should a man go about with the evidence of his own iniquity in his breast pocket unless he secretly wanted to be found out?

'I suppose I ought to pity you,' he said. 'You never could face up to your responsibilities. You ran off and left your wife and child, and now you've run off and left your mistress.'

'I have not left Rose,' Ainsley said between his teeth.

'You're in the army. It amounts to the same thing.'

Ainsley drew a deep breath. 'You've changed. You used to be able to listen to both sides of an argument, then make your own choice. I always liked that about you.'

'In some things there is no choice. In matters of honour. And duty.'

'You sound just like my father.'

'Well, God damn it,' snarled Cameron, 'he's my guardian, he brought me up!'

He hadn't bothered to lower his voice, and behind them all heads turned.

'I didn't accompany you', Ainsley said quietly, 'to have an argument. I came because I need to tell you something.'

'Then tell me and have done with it.'

Ainsley looked out across the burning plain. 'I have a daughter,' he said. 'A little girl of ten. And God willing, another child on the way.'

Cameron thought about the little girl in the park. 'And what is that to me?' he said.

Ainsley gave him a hard look. 'You just don't give a damn, do you? We used to be like brothers. But as far as you're concerned, none of that ever happened. Did it, Cameron?'

He made no reply.

'Well let me tell you,' Ainsley said, and for the first time he sounded as determined as his father. 'I don't care what you think of me. Do you understand? All I care about is that you help me to help my children.'

'What the devil do you mean?'

Ainsley searched for words. 'Rose has always felt that they'll need the protection of the family if they're to get along in life. I've always felt that it would be pointless to make any kind of approach. Then I saw your name in the lists. It made me think again. I realized that Rose is right.' He paused. 'This campaign should be over in, what, a matter of weeks? When it is, I intend to resign my commission and take my family back to Jamaica.'

Cameron stared at him in disbelief. 'You can't mean that.'

'It's our home, Cameron. It's where we belong.'

'But—'

'Oh, you needn't worry, I shall be discreet. I shan't live openly with Rose. I shall establish her somewhere far away from Fever Hill – near Kingston perhaps. As far as Society is concerned, I shall simply be returning to Jamaica after some years of . . . "delicate health". Isn't that what Father gave out? That I'd gone to some sanatorium on the continent for my health?' He gave a wry smile. 'So you see, there won't be any sort of scandal. One can get away with almost anything as long as one doesn't do it openly. That was always our mistake.'

They began their descent down the bluff, and the horses

jostled for position on the narrow track. Cameron said, 'You seem to have everything worked out. Why bother to tell me?'

'Because I need you to tell my father.'

'*What?*'

'He returns all my letters unopened. Just like you. He doesn't even know he's a grandfather.' He paused. 'I'd rather not have him learn of my return in the *Daily Gleaner*.'

Down in the zeriba the next detail was waiting to relieve them. Cameron watched the red men stalking the red earth in the red light. He felt as if he were trapped in a nightmare.

He wanted to grab Ainsley by the throat and shake him till he saw sense. Couldn't he see that his plan was impossible? Had he no idea what things had been like after he left? Having to watch poor, soft, obedient Clemency cradling her dead baby in her arms, and failing utterly to comprehend the ruin of her life. Proud old Jocelyn humbling himself to buy the silence of her upstart brother. The odious May taking control with unspeakable relish.

He remembered that beautiful little girl in the snow at Strathnaw. Why had Clemency's child died, while the bastard had thrived?

There is no justice, he thought. The wages of sin are a successful army career, a comfortable house in Scotland, and a blossoming mistress and child.

They were nearing the zeriba, and men were coming forward to take the horses. 'We must be civilized about this,' said Ainsley. 'I need you to help me. And by God you shall—'

'*Enough*', said Cameron. 'I've heard enough.' He dismounted and tossed his reins to his man and walked away.

'Cameron, come back. Come back! Damnit, man, that's an order!'

'Go to the devil,' said Cameron.

Chapter Five

Dr Baines never came back to Cairngowrie House. Perhaps he forgot. Perhaps he fell ill. Whatever the reason, the days passed and the snow kept falling, and nobody came.

Madeleine didn't greatly mind. She didn't mind about anything, for she was safe inside her shell. Her smooth, shiny, unbreakable Easter-egg shell, which allowed her to see and hear and smell and taste, but only in a muffled sort of way, as if she were under water.

She didn't like the baby any more than when it had first arrived, but it had proved impossible to ignore. It gazed at her with eyes as dark and deep as a seal's, and when she left the room its outraged howls followed her through the house.

From Dr Philpott she had learned how to look after it. She classified the tasks as easy (bathing) down to most horrible (cleaning up the mess), with dressing, feeding, and making it sleep coming somewhere in between.

Dressing was the easiest because there were lots of baby-clothes, and it was very like dressing a doll. *A flannel binder about the abdomen, a napkin or sanitary towel, a flannel shirt, two substantial petticoats, a muslin dress, bootees and a cap. Nothing tight.* It wasn't *absolutely* the same as dressing a doll because the baby wriggled so much, but that became easier as the layers went on, for they made the baby's arms and legs stick out, which slowed it down.

Bathing was easy too, because the baby liked it. And by now the geyser had become Madeleine's friend. Its trusty blue light burned constantly and never failed to belch into life, although she wondered how long the gas would last.

After washing, Dr Philpott said that the baby must be *dusted with wheat-starch or violet powder to prevent chafing*. To begin with that had been a problem, for there was neither starch nor violet powder in the pantry, so she'd had to brave her mother's room and fetch the rice powder from the dressing-table. But the baby liked being powdered, and generally stopped wriggling – although sometimes it sneezed when she did its face.

To begin with, feeding had been impossible. Dr Philpott said that *If the mother is unable to suckle, the baby should have a few dessert-spoonsful of warm water and loaf sugar every two hours. On the second day, good cow's milk may be added to the sugar-water, or tinned or Swiss milk*. There was plenty of loaf sugar and Nestlé's Condensed Milk in the pantry, but the problem was getting it into the baby.

If a baby is brought up by hand, the feeding bottle must be kept very clean. The first bottle Madeleine chose was a pretty blue glass one which she emptied of syrup of figs and thoroughly washed, then filled with sugar-water. The baby howled and batted it away with both fists. Madeleine tried other bottles, but none of them worked. She tried pouring sugar-water into the baby's mouth from a teaspoon, but it only spluttered and coughed it back again. She was on the point of giving up and dosing it with a sleeping powder from her father's secret drawer when she chanced across Dr Philpott at his most severe: *On NO ACCOUNT should the baby be given anything OTHER than milk or sugar-water. In particular, sleeping draughts or quieting syrups MUST NEVER BE GIVEN*.

Finally she had the idea of soaking a corner of her best handkerchief in the sugar-water. The baby's mouth fastened on it like a magnet. From then on feeding was easy, although it always took an extremely long time.

The section on *changing* puzzled Madeleine at first, but she quickly realized why it came straight after *feeding*. She also learned the truth of the statement that *no-one likes a smelling baby*. This meant another dash into her mother's room to fetch the Barnett's Wood Wool Diapers for Ladies, which she cut into pieces and strapped in place with her father's handkerchiefs. They worked fairly well, although they had a tendency to leak.

The final challenge was to find somewhere for the baby to sleep. Dr Philpott said *in a cot beside the mother's bed*, which wasn't possible, so instead Madeleine dragged the cot from the nursery into the spare room. She slept in the spare room too. She preferred it to her own room.

All this left her with little time for herself, but she didn't mind that. She was safe inside her shell; she didn't need much looking after. There was bread in the pantry and seed cake and a ham, so when she felt dizzy she chewed a piece of ham, or toasted bread on the spare-room fire and dipped it in treacle. She kept the gaslight low for the sake of the geyser, went to bed early to save on candles, and apart from splashing her face and hands she neither washed nor changed her clothes. She began to smell like the Reverend McAllister's retriever, but she didn't care. She found her own smell vaguely comforting.

Sometimes, when the baby was clean, fed, changed and asleep, Madeleine would sit on the spare-room bed and look out of the window. The garden was a white, humped smoothness leading down to the beach. The seals and the cormorants had gone. Everyone had gone. Perhaps there was no-one left in the world except herself and the baby – and her father, of course. But he was away in the desert, so that was no use. He was always away when they needed him. If it hadn't been for the shell, she would have been angry with him.

And she was surprised at her mother, too. Why had she left her all alone like this? Why had she left her to look after the baby by herself? It wasn't fair. Mothers weren't supposed to do that sort of thing. If it hadn't been for the shell, she would have been angry with her mother, too.

On the morning of the tenth day there was a knock at the door.

Madeleine was in the spare room, adding coal to the fire.

When she heard the noise she froze. Visitors never came to Cairngowrie House. That was why Papa had taken it, because it was isolated. So who could be knocking? The postman never knocked. And it didn't sound like Dr Baines's ebullient tattoo.

She glanced at the baby. It was fast asleep after a break-fast of condensed milk, its fists soft and pink and curled, like prawns.

Moving quietly, Madeleine went downstairs and opened the door, letting in a blast of cold, clean air that made her blink.

An unknown couple stood on the porch: a short, plump gentleman with damp jowls, and a tiny rigid lady in a quilted purple cape and a Tyrolean hat adorned with half a dead pheasant.

The lady had a narrow waxy face framed by old-fashioned ringlets of crimped horsehair. Her eyes were close-set and colourless, and they fastened on Madeleine with no dis-cernible expression. 'What', she demanded, 'is your name?' Her voice was as emotionless as her gaze, but she managed to sound as if she intended to disapprove of whatever answer Madeleine gave.

Madeleine said her name, and the lady and gentleman exchanged glances. Madeleine wondered if she had been wrong to open the door. If it hadn't been for the shell, she would have been worried.

The couple walked past her into the drawing-room, and after a moment's hesitation she followed. She hadn't been in the drawing-room since the baby had arrived, and she was careful not to look at the piano, and the piles of *Amateur Photographer* on the sofa.

Briskly the lady divested herself of hat, cape, gloves and muff to reveal a grimly elaborate gown of green and violet tartan. The collar reached to the jawbone, the bodice was punishingly tight, and the skirts were festooned with batteries of bows. A bustle created an illusion of hips, while the top of the stays stood in for a bosom.

'I am Mrs Fynn,' declared the lady. 'You shall address me as Cousin Lettice. This', she indicated the damp-jowled gentleman, 'is Mr Fynn – whom you shall address as Cousin Septimus. Where is your mother.'

Madeleine said her mother was upstairs in her room.

She waited in the hall while the lady and gentleman ascended to her mother's room. Moments later, Cousin Lettice came back onto the landing with a handkerchief clamped over her mouth. Cousin Septimus followed, looking clammy and outraged.

Madeleine felt obscurely at fault.

When they were back in the drawing-room, Cousin Lettice shook out her handkerchief with a snap and tucked it in her cuff. Then she picked up the *Amateur Photographer*s and placed them on the footstool, and sat down rigidly on the sofa. 'When did this occur?'

'A bit more than a week ago,' said Madeleine.

'Where are the servants?'

'We only had one. And she left.'

'Before or afterwards?'

'Um. Before.'

Cousin Lettice looked Madeleine up and down.

Cousin Septimus stood with his hands behind his back and fixed his pale eyes on the ceiling rose. 'The child', he said, 'has not washed for days. Absolute disgrace.'

He made it sound as if it were Cousin Lettice's fault, and a stippling of red appeared on her cheeks. But her gaze never left Madeleine. 'Did not your mother receive my letter?' she said with a frown.

Madeleine wondered what she meant. Then she remembered the letter on the doormat. She went into the hall and retrieved it from the mat, and handed it to Cousin Lettice. It was wet from being trampled, and the ink had run.

Cousin Lettice's colourless gaze went from Madeleine to the letter and back again. 'How', she demanded, 'have you survived?'

Madeleine told her about the geyser, the ham, and Dr Philpott.

'Dr Philpott? So there has *been* a doctor. Where is he now?'

Until then, Madeleine had been holding Dr Philpott

against her chest. Now she held him out to Cousin Lettice.

Cousin Lettice took Dr Philpott and read the title aloud. '. . . *Hints on Other Matters Necessary to be Known to the Married Woman.*' Her head snapped up. 'How much of this have you read? Tell me the *truth*. I shall know it if you tell a falsehood.'

'All of it,' said Madeleine. 'But the first part had nothing to do with babies, so I only read it once.'

Cousin Lettice narrowed her eyes and scrutinized her. Again Madeleine had the impression that she was mysteriously at fault. It reminded her of the Sunday School disaster – although she sensed that Cousin Lettice was more to be reckoned with than poor Miss McAllister. The Reverend's sister might succumb to the occasional outburst of nerves, but Cousin Lettice burned with a deeper, more constant fire.

Upstairs in the spare room, the baby began to cry.

Cousin Septimus forgot about the ceiling rose and turned to Cousin Lettice with a horrified stare. Cousin Lettice went yellowish grey. 'The infant,' she said. 'It survived?'

Madeleine nodded.

This time Cousin Septimus stayed below, while Madeleine took Cousin Lettice upstairs to show her the baby.

They stood together beside the cot, and Madeleine watched Cousin Lettice scrutinize the baby. It was still crying, but with less conviction now that it had company.

Cousin Lettice made no move to touch or comfort it. The stippling reappeared on her cheeks, and she gripped the edge of the cot with hands as shiny and yellow as chicken feet. 'It survived,' she said between her teeth. The ridge of her stays rose and fell. 'It were better', she declared, 'if it had died.'

The baby stopped crying and scowled at her.

With her arms tightly clasped about her middle, Cousin Lettice began to pace up and down. Her mouth was a rigid line. The stippling on her cheeks had coalesced into an angry flush. 'God is *just*,' she muttered to herself. 'God *is* just.' She shook her head.

Then she came to a sudden halt, and turned on Madeleine. 'You', she said accusingly, 'were born with a terrible burden. The infant carries it too.'

Madeleine cast the baby a doubtful glance. How could it carry anything when it couldn't even stand up?

'You', said Cousin Lettice, 'carry a *taint*. You get it from your mother. Your mother was *wicked*. All the Durrants are wicked.' A fleck of spittle had appeared at the corner of her mouth, and Madeleine watched it stretch with each word she took, and re-form into a ball when she paused for breath. 'Your mother', Cousin Lettice went on, 'enticed your father away from his lawful wife. Your mother was *degenerate*. And so are you. Do you know what it means, to be degenerate?'

Madeleine shook her head.

'It means that your blood is tainted.'

Madeleine wondered what tainted meant. She pictured little grey blotches floating in scarlet, like the dust devils she sometimes found beneath the bed.

Cousin Lettice's voice was coming at her in waves: now louder, now receding. 'It *means*', she went on, 'that the wickedness becomes worse with each succeeding generation. Depravity. Insanity. Disease. It is all there. In the blood.' She drew herself up. 'But *God*', she went on with quiet ferocity, 'has delivered you to me. It will be my duty to teach you the life of penitence and obscurity for which you are destined. For God is *just*.' She paused for breath. The fleck of spittle was still there. Madeleine wondered if it was a permanent fixture. 'Henceforth,' declared Cousin Lettice, 'you will live with us. You will take the name of Fynn.'

Madeleine was confused. 'But my name is Falkirk. Madeleine Falkirk.'

'No. Falkirk is a false name.'

'But—'

'Do not interrupt. Your parents were never married. We will never speak of that again. And *particularly* not when we are in public or in company. Do you understand?'

Madeleine shook her head.

'Falkirk', said Cousin Lettice with distaste, 'is merely the name which your father in his wickedness assumed in order to deceive decent, honourable people. You have no name. Henceforth, for the sake of decency, you will be Fynn.'

Madeleine looked from Cousin Lettice to the baby, and back again. She said, 'Miss Lettice, I don't believe Papa will like it if I change my name.'

That brought Cousin Lettice to a halt. She studied Madeleine as if she were a wild animal who might prove difficult to subdue. 'Of course,' she muttered. 'She has not been told.'

Madeleine put her hand on the cot. The baby turned its head and stared at her severely.

'Your father has been killed in battle,' said Cousin Lettice. 'It is a visitation on him. We will never speak of him again.'

Madeleine let go of the cot and sat down heavily on the floor.

Chapter Six

Cameron is riding slowly over the battlefield, picking off the stragglers.

He feels the heat of the sun on his shoulders and smells the bitterness of smoke. He tastes the clinging sweetness of death at the back of his throat. He sees the gutted horses and the sodden scarlet tunics, the fluttering Arab robes and the dead children clutching their bone-crushing sticks.

He doesn't experience any of it. It's happening to someone else. All he really feels, deep inside, is the fierce sick joy of having killed and come through alive.

It's nearly noon, and soon it will be too hot to carry on. His horse picks its way across the bodies and between the jagged black rocks that jut from the sand like dragons' teeth. Around him, the red men move slowly in the blistering sun. Black vultures patiently wait. Greasy black smoke rises from burning flesh.

Some distance ahead, he sees Ainsley leading a small recovery detail. Thank God, he thinks, with a great surge of relief. He's come through it too. Thank God.

Behind him a shout, and he turns to see one of the men bayoneting a wounded tribesman. These Arabs like to fox dead, then rise up and make a last-ditch stand. They like to have company on the way down to Paradise.

When he turns to go on, Ainsley is in trouble. A trio of Dervishes has risen from the dead and butchered his detail to a man, and Ainsley is surrounded. His horse is on its haunches, screaming, its hind leg shattered, but his spur is caught in the stirrup and he can't jump free. He has lost his helmet, and his bright hair is vivid against the smoke as he struggles to right himself, and draws his revolver and drops one of the Arabs. The other two circle behind him to make the kill.

Cameron sees it happening as if through water. He hauls his horse to a halt and levels his revolver, and takes aim into the glare of the sun. He shoots one of the Arabs through the head, and fires again and drops the other with a shot in the throat. 'All right now,' he mutters, 'it's all right now.' His revolver is shaking in his hand, and as he spurs his horse on, he at last understands that the anger of the night before has no meaning; that he would rather be killed himself than watch Ainsley die.

But as he closes the distance between them he sees Ainsley's horse stumble on its shattered leg and struggle to right itself. Ainsley is still fighting to untangle his spur from the stirrup as the horse goes crashing down onto the rocks, with him beneath.

Cameron jumps off his horse and runs to where Ainsley is lying, and drops to his knees in the stinking black sand.

Ainsley lies on his back, his blue eyes wide and astonished. His lips move, but no sound comes. Cameron sees the matted pulp at the back of the head, and the white gleam of bone, and the bright blood pumping out onto the rock and pouring down into the sand. Already the sand is turning to paste beneath him: hot, soft black paste, and a copper-sweet stink, and that brilliant red arterial spurt.

Cameron looks down into the blue eyes and watches the dullness come, like the bloom on a grape.

A small wind tosses a handful of sand across the waxy features, and Cameron tries to brush it away, but it's impossible. The black sand keeps coming, gently sifting into mouth and nostrils, silently sugaring the staring eyes.

Someone is shaking him by the shoulder. 'Captain Lawe. Captain Lawe. Sir. Wake up.'

Cameron woke up.

It was dark in the zeriba, for the moon had not yet risen.

So cold that his breath steamed. The tears were hot on his cheeks.

'Wake up, sir,' said the orderly. 'The colonel wishes to see you in his tent.'

Cameron lay on his back blinking at the stars. He thought, it wasn't a dream. He is dead. He is dead. And now it's too late to make anything right, ever again.

He kicked his way out of his blanket-bag and got to his feet and straightened his uniform. Then he followed the orderly through the sleeping camp. He felt heavy and stiff but strangely fragile, as if one touch would shatter him to pieces. He looked about him at the complicated paraphernalia of war, and thought, how do men live with the knowledge that what they love can be destroyed in an instant?

The lamps were bright in the colonel's tent, and he blinked as he went in. The colonel sat on a canvas stool before a small field desk covered with a tidy litter of papers. An officer whom Cameron didn't know sat beside him with a notebook on his lap and a silver propelling pencil at the ready. He had the clean, unbroken fingernails of a staff officer, but his eyes were pink and inflamed. Perhaps, thought Cameron, he's never seen a battlefield before. Perhaps he's not used to the smell.

He had a vague sense that he was in some sort of trouble. The colonel, a spare, lugubrious man with an extravagantly hooked nose, was studying him in silence, tapping his pencil on the desk.

What have I done now, he thought from a great distance. He was suddenly extremely thirsty. There was a flask of water on the field desk, with a tumbler upended over the top to keep out the flies. He wished someone would offer him a drink.

The colonel cleared his throat. Cameron swayed, and tried to assume an expression of respectful attention.

'A report has reached me', said the colonel, 'that the day before yesterday you disregarded a direct order of your CO. Your CO, the late Major Falkirk.'

Cameron struggled to follow him. The day before yesterday? Yesterday. The late Major Falkirk.

The colonel's voice came at him in waves. '. . . for reasons which pass understanding, Major Falkirk let that go unpunished.' A pause. 'I take it that it was a personal matter. Some kind of – bad blood between you?'

Behind his back Cameron flexed his injured palm, and the new scab cracked. Bad blood. Odd way of putting it. The truth is, there was no blood between us, either good or bad. And yet we always felt like brothers. *We used to be like brothers*, Ainsley had said. *But as far as you're concerned, none of that ever happened. Did it, Cameron?*

Oh, you're wrong, he wanted to reply. I never stopped thinking of you as a brother. I know that now. Why didn't I tell you when I still had the chance?

He dragged himself back to the present. He squared his shoulders. 'Yes sir,' he said. 'Bad blood.'

Again the colonel tapped the desk with his pencil. The staff officer looked up doubtfully from his notebook, as if wondering how to take that down. 'You see,' said the colonel, 'I shouldn't normally trouble myself with what was clearly a matter for Major Falkirk to resolve.' He frowned. 'However,' he went on, 'it is my unenviable duty to investigate a second report. A report of an extremely grave and utterly repellent nature.'

The staff officer bent his head and scribbled furiously.

'Yesterday,' the colonel went on with his eyes on Cameron, 'shortly after Major Falkirk fell, you were seen – you were seen, to put it baldly, despoiling the body.'

Again Cameron swayed. He hadn't thought of that. He hadn't thought.

'You were seen', the colonel continued, 'systematically rifling the pockets, then extracting a piece of paper from the breast of the major's tunic.' He paused. 'Well? What have you to say? Do you deny it?'

Cameron watched the staff officer finish writing with a flourish. 'No, sir,' he said. 'I don't.'

The staff officer looked up and blinked.

The colonel's narrow face was incredulous. 'Are you telling me that these reports are true?'

'Yes sir.'

There was silence in the tent. Outside, the night wind threw sand against the canvas. A horse coughed. An Egyptian hissed at his camels to be still.

The colonel looked so shocked that Cameron almost felt sorry for him.

'This paper,' the colonel said at last, 'this paper which you were seen to – remove. Where is it now?'

'I burnt it, sir.'

The staff officer met his eyes and quickly glanced away.

'You burnt it,' repeated the colonel. This time when he tapped the desk he did it slowly, as if tapping out a dirge. 'What was it? A promissory note? Gambling pledge? Letter from a woman?'

'I'd rather not say, sir. It's a private matter.'

'Not any more,' snapped the colonel. 'Not when it results in one of my officers publicly desecrating the body of a brother in arms – his own CO, God damn it. Not when it leads him to defy the colonel of his regiment. Not when . . .'

Cameron stopped listening. He was back on the battle-field, kneeling by Ainsley's body with Clemency's letter in his hand. The paper was yellow with age, and soft from much folding and unfolding. How many times had Ainsley read it over the years? *She at least has forgiven me. She wrote to me. I keep her letter with me always.*

If the letter were found, the truth would come out. Ainsley would be exposed as a scoundrel who had deserted his wife, disgraced his name, and deceived his brother officers for years. The careful fiction which his father had worked so hard to construct would be in ruins, and the scandal would break.

But if the letter disappeared, then the world would honour Alasdair Falkirk, a good soldier and a pure-hearted man who gave his life for his country. And Jocelyn would know a measure of peace.

'Captain Lawe. Are you listening to me?'

Cameron studied him for a moment. 'Yes, sir,' he said.

'Because I wish there to be no mistake about this. No misapprehension as to the gravity of your position. I am giving you an order. I expect you to carry it out. You shall

66

provide me – now – with a complete explanation of your conduct in this affair.'

The staff officer raised his head and waited, his pencil poised.

'Captain Lawe,' said the colonel, 'I'm waiting. Tell me the truth.'

Cameron licked his dry, cracked lips. The truth, he thought. Why should I tell you the truth? To justify myself? To prove that I'm not the scoundrel you think I am – and to hell with Ainsley and Jocelyn and the whole damn lot? He said, 'Sir, I can't tell you anything.'

The colonel leaned forward. 'Can't or won't?'

'Won't, sir.'

'Captain Lawe. I'm ordering you. Explain yourself at once.'

Cameron met the colonel's eyes. 'No,' he said.

An hour after Cousin Lettice and Cousin Septimus arrived at Cairngowrie House, Madeleine was put to bed in the nursery and told to stay there for the rest of the day.

She lay beneath the blankets, drifting in and out of sleep. She didn't think about her parents at all, not at all. They were outside the shell, and she was inside, where it was safe. She was going to stay inside for ever and ever.

Beside her in the cot the baby slept and woke and cried and punched the air, and sometimes Cousin Lettice came in to see to it, and once Madeleine saw that she carried Dr Philpott in the pocket of her gown. But mostly Madeleine just slept inside the shell.

The next morning she was sent back to her own room, because Cousin Lettice said it was inappropriate to go on sleeping in the nursery. Madeleine stood on the rug, gazing blankly at her things: at the dolls and the dressing gown on the end of the bed, and Mister Parrot. He had been placed on the chair – presumably by Cousin Lettice tidying up – along with her dried-out scarf and sealskin hat and mittens.

It was strange to look at Mister Parrot now. It felt as if he belonged to someone else. He wasn't real any more. He was just a toy which her mother had made out of green and blue felt, with blue glass buttons for eyes. He was outside the shell.

She took off her frock and climbed beneath the covers and slept until noon, then got dressed again and padded into the nursery. She was leaning over the cot, dangling a knotted handkerchief for the baby to scowl at, when Cousin Lettice walked in.

As always, Cousin Lettice spoke without preamble. 'You', she said to Madeleine in her accusatory way, 'will pack your trunk. The day after tomorrow we take the train for London. Henceforth you will live with us. The infant will go to Mr Fynn's sister in Birmingham.'

She continued to say something about schools and head-lice and the desirability of home tuition, but Madeleine stopped listening. When Cousin Lettice had mentioned the baby's going to Birmingham, it felt as if someone had cut a hole in the shell and let in a blast of freezing air. It made her feel shaky and horribly exposed.

The world crowded in on her, and she could no longer keep it out. She felt the cold roughness of the rug beneath her stockinged feet. She heard the loud, stiff rustle of Cousin Lettice's gown as she approached the cot. She smelt the sour smell of the baby, which had just been sick.

The baby belonged to *her*. It was her task to look after it. That was her job. How could it live at Birmingham, wherever that was, if she, Madeleine, lived in London?

It wasn't possible. She couldn't let it happen. Her mind raced. 'Cousin Lettice?' she said at last.

Cousin Lettice stopped talking and fixed her with her colourless stare.

Madeleine improvised. 'Mama . . .' she began, 'Mama wants us to stay together.'

Two red blotches appeared on Cousin Lettice's sallow cheeks. 'What?' she said sharply. 'What is this you say?'

Madeleine caught her lower lip in her teeth.

Cousin Septimus appeared in the doorway, looking irritated. 'Lettice, there is a tradesman at the door who—'

Cousin Lettice silenced him with a glance. 'What is this

you say', she said to Madeleine, 'about your mother wishing you to stay together?'

Cousin Septimus shut his mouth with an audible pop. He looked appalled.

Madeleine glanced from Cousin Lettice to Cousin Septimus and back again. 'Mama wants you to look after us *both*,' she mumbled. 'She said – she said you're the only one who can help us. With the taint.'

She had their full attention now. 'Mama', she went on, developing her theme, 'said that only you can save us – save us both. Together. That's me and . . .' she glanced from the baby to the books on the shelf: *The Water Babies* and *Les Malheurs de Sophie*, 'me and Sophie. That's the baby. Sophie. That's what she's called.'

'Not both of them,' said Cousin Septimus, shaking his head so vigorously that his jowls wobbled. 'Out of the question. We can't possibly—'

Cousin Lettice raised her hand for silence. 'A mother's *wish*,' she hissed. 'It is our duty to pay it heed.'

'A mother's wish?' Cousin Septimus studied her with dislike. 'What would you know about that?'

Cousin Lettice's colour deepened, but she refused to back down. 'A mother's wish,' she repeated like a catechism. 'A mother's *dying* wish. It is a sacred charge, Septimus, you know that as well as I. It is a sacred charge which cannot be ignored.'

Cousin Septimus scowled, but did not demur. It appeared that even he had to agree with that.

Slowly, Madeleine breathed out. The shaky feeling was gone. The shell was whole again.

CHAPTER SEVEN

Letter to Jocelyn Monroe, Fever Hill Estate, Parish of Trelawny, Jamaica, from Captain Cameron Lawe, Carysfort Military Prison, Suakin, 18th March 1884.

Dear Jocelyn,
By the time this reaches you, you may already have seen accounts of an incident arising from the death of my Commanding Officer, Major Alasdair Falkirk, as a result of which I have been the subject of a General Court-Martial. I am writing to report the circumstances in so far as I can, and the sentence of the court, which Her Majesty has today confirmed. (In view of the ongoing campaign, the Court-Martial was convened at great speed, and I regret that there was not time to warn you of it in advance.)

Cameron set down the letter and put his elbows on his knees and pressed the heels of his hands into his eyes.

Discharge with ignominy from Her Majesty's Service. Forfeiture of all field medals and decorations. Committal as a common felon to a public prison for a term of not less than two years.

He remembered Jocelyn's face on the day he had received his commission in the Borderers. He had been so proud. 'For seven hundred years, your family has sent its best to fight for their country. You have the finest of traditions to uphold, my boy. Honour it.'

This was going to tear him apart.

Cameron took his hands from his eyes and stared at the rough coral wall of his cell. A large copper-coloured cockroach emerged from a crack beneath the window. A fly crawled across the notepaper on his makeshift desk. It was an old crate of Nestlé's Condensed Milk which Sergeant Watts, an ill-at-ease gaoler, had dragged in for him the day before. As it was six inches lower than the rough native angareb on which he slept, he had to pause frequently to ease the ache in his shoulders.

He got up and went to the window, and the cockroach withdrew into its crack. Through the shutters came the steady roar of the bazaar. He smelled cumin and palm oil and goat.

Clear and bright and painfully vivid, he pictured the old man receiving the news. He would be on the great north verandah at Fever Hill, sitting in his favourite rattan arm-chair with the frayed old tartan throw trailing on the tiles. At his elbow there would be the usual Scotch and soda, and beside it the tarnished daguerreotype of Kitty, the young wife who had been dead for thirty-five years. The liver-spotted hands would be carefully shaking out his weekly *Times* – his one extravagance – which had just arrived on the mail coach from Kingston. The sunbleached eyes, as fierce as an osprey's, would be scanning the columns with grim relish for reports of suffragists and Baptists and those damned, meddling educationists.

Then the stillness as he spots the familiar names: . . . *A notable casualty of the Battle of Tamai was Major Alasdair Falkirk of the 65th York and Lancasters. It is this correspondent's painful duty to report the horrifying news that one Captain Cameron Lawe, a brother officer on special attachment from the King's Own Scottish Borderers, was observed in the aftermath of the hero's fall despoiling the body . . . persistently refused to explain his actions . . . immediate Court-Martial on grounds of insubordination and conduct unbecoming . . .*

Beneath the window sill the cockroach re-emerged and tasted the air with delicate antennae.

. . . conduct unbecoming an officer and a gentleman, pursuant to Article Fifty-three of the Articles of War . . . disobeying the lawful command of his superior officer in such a manner as to show a wilful defiance of his authority, pursuant to Article Forty-seven of the Articles of War . . .

The hearing had only lasted a morning, but it had felt like a week. It had taken place in the mess hall at Fort Euryalus, the one place in Suakin large enough to accommodate the regulation bench of thirteen officers together with twelve witnesses, three shorthand-writers, and a throng of spectators. The heat was overwhelming, the air thick with the sweet-onion stink of sixty hard-riding men in heavy field uniform. And the flies. God, those flies.

Cameron had found it hard to keep his mind on the proceedings. *Your parents are dead to me*, he had told the little girl in the park. Why had he said that? Why? Had he *wanted* Ainsley dead?

Irrational to imagine that wishes can influence events. But nevertheless he felt that. He felt responsible.

He should have moved heaven and earth to get a transfer back to his own regiment. If he had succeeded, perhaps Ainsley would not have been preoccupied as he rode across the battlefield. Perhaps he would have survived.

Compared with that, what did it matter what they said about him at the hearing?

'You must tell us everything,' Major Forrest had said on his first and only visit to Cameron's cell. An etiolated man with a passion for lists, he had clearly been uncomfortable in his role of prosecutor. And his patience had soon worn thin. 'Damnit, man, the fellows need an explanation! What the devil was it about? A woman? A debt? Just tell us. We've all been through it. We'd understand.'

Cameron had studied the bloodless face and wondered if that were true. 'I'm sorry, sir,' he had said.

'Hang it all, Lawe, you know how this works. You're not some raw recruit, you're an experienced officer. They'll throw the book at you.'

He was right about that. For the army deals in certainties: cause and effect, obedience and disobedience, crime and punishment. His silence created uncertainty, and was therefore the worst betrayal of all.

He had soon given up listening to the prosecutor making his case. Fort Euryalus, he mused. That's an odd name. Wasn't there a Euryalus who fought at Troy?

Jocelyn would know all about that. *The Iliad* was his Bible. When they were small, he used to read them a passage every night as a bedtime story. They didn't understand a word, but they adored it just the same, because it was Jocelyn.

He was the only father they had ever really known, for he had come for them on the day of the accident which had killed their parents. Cameron had been barely six, and Sinclair just a baby.

The white house at Arethusa had been in uproar that day. High rooms echoing to the piercing *ai ai ai* of Negro mourning. Bare feet slapping on hardwood floors. Cameron, forgotten in the chaos, had been discovered on the stairs, and briskly shooed away. *Gwaan back a yuh room, Mas' Camron! Gwaan back a yuh room!*

Instead he'd wandered out onto the verandah, where his mother used to sit with him and watch the rain sweeping the cane-pieces. She would laugh as the grey curtain moved towards them, and clap her hands when the lightning split the sky.

Bewildered, Cameron had stood beside her empty chair and wondered what would happen now. The servants said his mother was gone for ever, but he didn't understand what that meant. All he knew was that he didn't belong here any more. He was a different colour from everyone else.

He wondered if he was old enough to look after himself. He could find plenty of mangoes and guineps to eat, but where would he sleep? And what if there was a hurricane or a cane-fire or a flood?

Then Jocelyn had come. Cameron had watched the tall, unsmiling gentleman riding slowly up the white marl carriageway between the green cane-pieces. The tall gentleman had barked at the servants to get back to work, despatched the baby and its nurse in a buggy, and finally hoisted Cameron before him on his monumental horse, and set off slowly down the carriageway. On the long ride to Fever Hill he never smiled or said a word, but his arm held Cameron fast like an iron bar.

And when they reached the great house on the hill, Jocelyn sat him down on a verandah overlooking a vast rippling valley of cane which stretched to the distant curve of the sea. He introduced Cameron to the two huge bull mastiffs, Castor and Pollux, and made him hold out his hand to be sniffed, so that they would know him for part of the household. Then he had the housekeeper bring out a big tumbler of coconut milk and a bowl of red pea soup. The soup was thick with salt beef and cocos and yellow yam, and Cameron demolished it in seconds, like a puppy.

Then Jocelyn took his hand in a leathery grasp and led him to the library, where they walked the length of the family portraits. Jocelyn spoke of the Monroe who had fought at Falkirk in 1298, and of the Lawe who had distinguished himself at Agincourt, and of the centuries-old friendship between the two families, which had begun in 1655 when Nathaniel Lawe and Benneit Monroe had sailed for Jamaica together, and then carved up the Northside between them: Benneit taking the land to the west of Falmouth, and Nat Lawe taking that to the east.

'Our families are bound together,' Jocelyn told him, 'by ties of shared adversity and marriage and friendship. Your father—' he broke off and blew his nose for quite a long time, 'your father was my best friend. Henceforth I shall be as a father to you. You belong here now. At Fever Hill.'

Cameron ran his fingers over the coral window sill, and the cockroach darted back into its crack. He thought, the old man gave you a home. And see how you have repaid him.

For the first time in his life he saw himself as he truly was. Arrogant. Self-righteous. Intolerant. And with a deep, ungovernable impulse to violence which until now he had never questioned.

He remembered that last ride with Ainsley at the oasis. The

raw, churning anger in his chest. He had been so certain. So sure that he was right.

On the makeshift desk the letter to Jocelyn waited for his signature. The stilted account had taken hours to draft and filled two sides, but he still hadn't found a way to explain or even hint at what he had taken from the body of 'Major Falkirk'. Others would read the letter before it reached Jocelyn, so he must be circumspect in the extreme.

On a separate sheet he had penned a few equally guarded lines about 'Mrs Falkirk' and her children. *A child of ten, I believe, and an infant yet to be born. Needless to say, something must be done for them, as I understand that the major's means were but moderate.*

Hypocrite, he told himself. You don't give a damn about Rose Durrant or her bastards. You can't even think of them without anger.

He knew it was outrageous to blame her in any way for Ainsley's death, and yet he did exactly that. If it hadn't been for Rose . . .

And what would she do now? Would she haul her bastards out to Jamaica and make the old man's life a nightmare of shame?

Another man might come to accept them in time, might learn to overlook the irregularity of their birth. Not Jocelyn. *Death before dishonour* was the ancient motto of the Monroes. It was what he lived by.

'I have no son,' he had declared when Ainsley left Jamaica, and in the years since then he'd never mentioned him again. Time hadn't mellowed him, it had burned him down to his fierce, metallic essence. It would be the final blow to learn that 'that Durrant woman' had produced a brace of bastards to drag his name through the mud. He wouldn't bend. He would break.

But why, thought Cameron suddenly, must he be told of them just yet? Surely that can wait a couple of months? Surely Rose can be persuaded to do that much? After all, she's had no contact with Fever Hill for over a decade. What difference would a few more months make?

He thought about the little girl in the snow. *Tell them*

they're dead to me, he had said. He had frightened her. A despicable thing to do, to frighten a child.

But God damn it, why think of her at all? Why think of any of them? What's the use?

Once again the cockroach emerged and started feeling its way down the wall. Cameron let it go. He was sick of killing.

He went back to the desk and picked up the sheet on which he had written about Rose and her bastards. All he cared about was Jocelyn.

He folded the sheet in half and tore it up.

It was the third day since Cousin Lettice had arrived at Cairngowrie House, and Madeleine was putting the last of her things in her trunk.

If it hadn't been for the shell, she would have been angry. All morning she'd had her mother's favourite song running through her head, and she couldn't get rid of it. *Oh soldier, oh soldier, will you marry me? Oh no, my sweet lady, that never can be. For I've got a wife at home in my own country. Two wives and the army's too many for me.*

At last she understood what it meant. It was yet more evidence of her mother's lies. She had lied about being married, and she had lied about the taint. She had lied about everything. 'Always seek the truth,' she would say when she talked about taking photographs. But all she did was lie.

Were all grown-ups like that? Did everybody lie?

Madeleine thought of Baby Jesus in his crib, so tidy and clean – and of how baby Sophie had actually looked when she arrived. She thought of her mother lying in the scarlet butterfly of blood. Was there always this ugliness underneath, which everybody knew about, but nobody ever mentioned?

Was that why she had found it so easy to lie to Cousin Lettice? *Tell the truth*, Cousin Lettice had told her. *If you tell a falsehood I shall know it.* But she had not known it. She had believed what Madeleine had told her. Even Cousin Septimus had believed.

The Reverend McAllister would have said that Madeleine was wicked for telling lies. Her mother on the other hand had said that she was splendid, magnificent and brave. But Cousin Lettice said that her mother was tainted. So who was right? Was she wicked or magnificent? Who *was* she?

Madeleine had looked up 'taint' in the dictionary. It said, *a defect or flaw. A trace of contamination or pollution.*

A defect or flaw. *It is in the blood.* She pictured the crumbly grey blotches floating in scarlet. Maybe that was why the officer in the Forbidden Kingdom had been angry with her. Because of the taint.

Downstairs the front door slammed. She heard men's voices on the path; the crunch of snow; the creak of a wagon. She went to the window and saw a large, black-curtained carriage moving slowly off down the coast path, followed by Mr Ritchie's wagon, piled high with furniture. It was a brilliantly sunny morning, and the wagon cast cartwheel shadows on the snow.

Madeleine went downstairs to ask Cousin Lettice where the furniture was going.

She found Cousin Lettice alone in the drawing room, which had been stripped of everything but the footstool. This Cousin Lettice had pulled up to the fire, to use as a seat.

She was surrounded by papers stacked on the bare boards, and these she was feeding into the flames, stabbing them savagely with a poker. 'All of it, all of it,' she muttered between her teeth. Her narrow face was flushed, and a coil of false hair had escaped its combs and swung limply against her cheek.

It took Madeleine a moment to realize that Cousin Lettice was burning her mother's photographs. She had dragged in the boxes from the darkroom and was methodically emptying them into the fire. The albums, too, were stacked beside her on the floor. One lay open on her lap. She was neatly gutting it.

Madeleine watched a fresh stack of photographs thrown onto the fire. She watched them curl and smoke and blacken, then flare into brilliant orange, and finally disintegrate into little flakes of darkness which disappeared up the chimney.

The shell began to crack. She started to shake. She tried to keep out the snap of the flames and the chemical smell of the burning photographs, but they kept coming through.

She looked to where the piano should have been, but of course it was gone. She thought of the photograph of Eden, crumbling to darkness in the fire: the beautiful ruined house, the tree-fern in the window; her father's fair head. All carried away in a flurry of darkness.

Cousin Lettice spun round with a start. Their eyes met.

Madeleine's heart hammered in her chest. 'I'm going to tell on you,' she muttered. She turned and thundered up the stairs.

Her mother would know what to do. She would stop this horrible dried-up witch lady from burning the photographs.

She burst into her mother's room. It was empty. Everything was gone. The bed. The wardrobe. The dressing-table. All that remained were bare walls and naked boards and an empty grate.

Her mother was gone.

The shell cracked wide open. The world came crashing in on her. The stink of Lysol and the freezing cold. The footsteps pounding up the stairs.

She screamed.

Cousin Lettice appeared in the doorway, breathless and frightened.

Still screaming, Madeleine pushed past her.

She ran down the stairs and out of the house and through the snow-covered garden and onto the beach.

The chill wind buffeted her screams back to her. The grey seals slipped off the rocks and disappeared beneath the pewter sea.

PART TWO

Chapter Eight

London, March 1894 – ten years later

Ben should of never gone near that shop. If he hadn't, his whole bloody life would of been different. And Robbie's too.

But it's half after six and they're up the Portland Road prossing about in that fog, and it's freezing cold and the black smuts are raining down like dirty snow, and there's bugger all to click – so what's he to do? Here's this nice little empty shop, door unlocked, gas on low, like the shopkeeper just nipped out. *Rennard & Co*, it says in the window, P-h-o-t-o-g-something-or-other. So in they go. And that's his first big mistake.

Queer kind of shop it is, and all. Golden chairs, and this plaster column with red velvet hanging over. 'Lovely,' says Robbie, stroking it. He's always been one for the colours. Last year Ben took him up the Paragon, play about soldiers, penny a go in the gallery. Robbie loved it. All the glittery lights and the colours and that.

But right now Ben's got an eye for a click, and straight off he spots this box, and inside it this little Box Brownie. Get a bob for that at the coffee-house down Endell Street. But then he spots the bowl of apples on the counter, and that's his second big mistake. Should of just clicked the sodding Brownie and cut the lucky *out* of there.

So him and Robbie are stuffing their pockets with apples when all of a sudden this nobby voice goes, 'Stop thief!' and

81

there's this bint behind the counter with a rifle, sodding *rifle*, pointed straight at him. And then this second bint, a little one, pops up beside her.

Ben's never seen a gun before except up the Paragon, so him and Robbie stay put. Next big mistake.

'What have you got in your pockets?' says the bint with the rifle. She's a pretty bit of muslin, nineteen or twenty, cloudy black hair and big black eyes, and a curvy red mouth like a plum; like it'd be juicy if you took a bite. But she puts Ben in mind of his big sister Kate, and that gives him a pain something horrible in his chest, cos Kate's dead, and he swore he'd never think of her again. So now he can't click the sodding Brownie, can he? It'd be like clicking from Kate.

'What have you got in your pockets?' goes Black-hair again.

So him and Robbie put the apples on the counter. Well, she's got the gun, and all.

She frowns. 'What were you going to do with those?'

'Eat them,' snaps Ben. 'What d'you think?'

'But they're rotten. We were going to throw them away.'

'Shows how much you know,' he goes.

Something flickers in her face, like he's hit a nerve. Then she darts a look at the little bint, who's well twitchety, and the little bint gets out this big paper bag and pours out these new apples and pears. 'They're props,' she mumbles. 'We use them for photographs.'

She's ten or so, with long yellow hair. She's nothing like Black-hair, but he can tell straight off that they're sisters. They got that way of talking without talking.

'Take some,' Black-hair tells him. 'Go on. We can buy some more.'

That's when he knows she's not going to shoot; she never was. She's scared of him. Shows some sense, that does.

So now there's nothing to stop him cutting the lucky, except that Robbie's pounced on the apples, and chomping away. His ugly little mug's all scrumpled up, and the bints are staring at him with their mouths open. Well, he's a bit of a sight, is Robbie, with his carroty hair and his greasy old jacket stretched over his hump, and his kicksies that peter out at the shins, and his scabby black feet.

'How old is he?' Black-hair asks Ben.

'Seven,' he growls, 'and he can speak for hisself.' Just because Robbie's one button short of a row, it don't mean he's a sodding idiot.

'How old are you?'

'I dunno. Thirteen? What's it to you?'

He can't make her out. Why don't she just chuck them out or call the bluebottles? What's she after? She curious? Some nobs are. They get a taste for the dirt and the smell and that.

And she's a nob all right. Fancy white blouse with big puffy sleeves. Copper-colour skirt with all black braid and a fancy belt. Nobby as hell. And so clean. He wonders if she's been got into yet, and thinks probably not. Though she could charge the earth, with a figure like that.

He goes, 'You never work in a shop, you're too posh.'

'This is just a hobby,' she says. 'I help out from time to time but I don't get paid. Mr Rennard couldn't afford it. And besides, it wouldn't be respectable for a lady to get paid.' That mouth of hers twists in a smile, like she thinks that's rum.

'Bit early for helping,' he goes. 'Seven in the morning.'

'Sometimes I take my own photographs before we open.'

'And sometimes,' chimes in Yellow-hair, 'as a *special* treat, Maddy lets me come along too.'

Crikey, thinks Ben, that her idea of a treat?

Yellow-hair's not as pretty as her sister, but she'll do – although them eyebrows spell trouble. Not curvy like Black-hair's, but straight and dark. *Watch out*, they seem to say, *or you're in for a fight*.

She hasn't been got into either, Ben can tell. Bet she'd be well narked if he asked. Funny what a fuss nobs make about it. Ben's been getting into bints since he was eleven. So what?

Yellow-hair's got on this red and white stripy pinafore and black stockings and shiny black boots, and Ben wonders if they got studs on the bottom; he always wanted boots like that, so when you skid on the pavement you make sparks. He saw a kid do it once, it was the best thing ever.

'You ought to go now,' says Black-hair. 'Mr Rennard will be here soon.'

'Oh, not *yet*,' goes Yellow-hair.

'Sophie . . .'

'Oh, *please*.' She turns to Robbie, and points at his woolly dog that Ben clicked from the toyshop, and goes, 'What's his name?'

Robbie looks well worried. He's had the sodding thing a couple of years, but never thought to give it a name. 'Dog?' he mumbles.

She nods. 'Dog. Well I'm Sophie, and that's Maddy – Madeleine, actually. Maddy chose my name when I was born, she got it off a book, but we never told Cousin Lettice.'

Robbie's got his mouth open, he can't believe she's talking to him like a proper person. And Black-hair's watching him with this little half-smile; not sneery or nothing, just kind. Ben *hates* that. It makes him go all prickly and hot. So he decides to click the sodding Brownie after all. Just to prove that he can.

'It was my birthday last week,' goes Yellow-hair. She's the talker, her sister's the watcher. 'I didn't have a party, as we don't know anyone. That's why it's so nice to meet you—'

'Sophie, that's enough—' goes her sister.

'– but Maddy gave me black beauty,' goes Yellow-hair, regular chatter-basket, 'it's *brilliant*, I've read it twice already.' She fetches this book from behind the counter.

It's got a horse on it in gold, and Ben goes, 'They got the bridle wrong.'

Yellow-hair's impressed. 'Do you know about horses?'

Robbie pipes up. 'Ben had this job once at Berner's Mews, and—'

'Shut it,' goes Ben. He turns on Yellow-hair. 'So you can read. So what?'

She's taken aback. 'But everyone can read.' Not sneery; just like she never thought about it before.

Black-hair seems to think that's funny, but Yellow-hair puts her clean little hand to her mouth. 'I'm most awfully sorry, I didn't mean – um, can't you read?'

'I know my letters,' snaps Ben. And he does, give or take. He went to school for a couple of weeks when they were giving out soup tickets, and he's a quick learner, but he left before he learnt how to put every last letter together.

'I do apologize,' goes Yellow-hair, and then she's off again ferreting behind the counter. Her sister looks down to see what she's up to, and that's when Ben whips off his cap and stows the Brownie inside, and clutches the cap to his belly like he's just remembered his manners. Nobody sees nothing. Beautiful.

Yellow-hair chucks a questioning look at her sister, and gets the nod, and goes pink and holds out this picture-book to Ben. 'Maddy keeps a few books for clients' children, to keep them amused. I thought you might care to have one. Then you'll be able to read too.'

He's all hot and prickly again, and sick to his stomach. Who the sodding hell does she think she is? *Giving* him things? Who does she think she *is*?

'It's about a cavalry horse in the Crimean War,' she says, 'I thought you might enjoy it, as you like horses.'

He snatches it and shoves it in his pocket. 'I'm not going to read it,' he snarls. 'I'm going to sell it.'

She blinks. 'Um. When you finish it, you can come back, and I'll give you another.'

'You cracked?' he says. 'Why would I come back?'

That's better. Now she looks like she's going to cry. Light-brown eyes with little bits of gold in them, all swimming in tears.

That's when Black-hair shoots him this look. Plain as day it says to him: *Don't you dare go upsetting my sister, Ben Kelly, or I'll have you catting up blood for a week. You understand?*

He glares back at her, but inside he thinks, well, fair enough. He'd of done a lot worse if it was Robbie. And it puts him in mind of Kate looking out for him when he was a nipper, and – just *shut* it about Kate, Ben Kelly. Just shut it right now.

It's high time they was off. 'Come on, Robbie,' he goes.

But they're just out the door when Black-hair knocks him

for six. 'You know, Ben Whatever-your-name-is, you're not as sharp as you think you are.' She hoists the rifle, and twists that mouth of hers in a grin. 'It's just a fake. Made of wood. Gentlemen like to be photographed with it, so that they can pretend that they're lords on a grouse moor.'

Quick as a flash Ben goes, 'And you're not as sharp as you think neither, my girl! Why'd you go blabbing about that to me? Now what's to stop me thrashing the stuffing out of you?'

Course he don't do no such thing, he just cuts the lucky out of there. But it bothers him for weeks that she blabbed about that gun. It's like she was trusting him or something.

Serve her right about the Brownie. Serve her bloody well right.

He tells hisself he's had a lucky escape, but he don't know what from.

So what's he do? He only goes and sees them again.

It's Robbie's fault, as per usual. One day in August they're up their place in Shelton Street, and Robbie's patching over the window with bits of card to keep out the smell of some dead cab-horse down St Giles, and Ben's on the bed, working his way through the last of the book.

'Them posh bints,' goes Robbie. He's been on and on about them for months; keeping tabs on them and all. 'I heard their old man went to smash.'

Ben don't say nothing; he's on the last page. Now that the war's over, Blacky the charger's being sent back home, and Farmer Brown's got this special meal ready for him.

'Their old man,' goes Robbie, 'I heard he croaked and left them stony broke.'

'So?' growls Ben.

'Can we go and see them? See if they're all right?'

'Shut it, Robbie.'

Ben's done all right with the book, except for words with s-h in them. He's not sure what the s and the h are supposed to do to each other.

He's still wondering about that when he gives in to Robbie's badgering and they set off west for Madeleine's

86

place. Just to prove to hisself that she's not his sister or a friend or nothing.

When they get to this Wyndham Street where she lives, and he sees how nobby it is, he gives Robbie a cuff that sends him flying. 'You said they was broke,' he snarls.

Broke? In a street like this? Housemaids scrubbing the steps, and a bloke with a water-cart laying the dust? And Madeleine's house has got these big columns, and railings painted green; steps up to a porch with blue and red tiles, and glassed-in window boxes with frilly plants, and this huge window with all coloured glass: birds and a sun and a wavy blue sea.

But her basement gate's wide open and the kitchen door's ajar, and Ben's shocked, just shocked. Anybody could walk in off the street. He'll have to have a word with her about that.

Robbie says they got no more money for domestics, and sure enough when they nip down the steps, there's Madeleine standing at this big gas range, all in black with her sleeves rolled up, stirring this big stewpan and frowning at the thickest book Ben's ever seen. And Sophie's on the table swinging her legs and chattering nineteen to the dozen. Same pinafore dress as before, but dyed black, though Ben can still see the stripes.

The food smell makes his belly twist something awful. And that kitchen! Gaslights and an indoor tap, and piles of stew-pans that'd keep a tinker happy for a year. Stony broke, my arse.

Him and Robbie go in, and Sophie gives them this big grin like they're long lost friends. 'Maddy, *look*! It's Ben and Robbie!'

Madeleine shoots Ben a cool look and tells him to shut the door, and Sophie asks her sister if she can show them the morning-room. 'There's a stained-glass window which Maddy *detests* as it reminds her of Jamaica, but I think it's stupendous, like in a church.'

Ben's never been in a church, so he takes her word for it.

'No,' says Madeleine over her shoulder, 'they're to stay down here or they'll steal things.'

Ben flashes a grin. 'Now you're learning.'

Robbie's gawping at Sophie, and she asks to see Dog, and they fall to chattering, or Sophie does – though she keeps darting little glances at Ben.

He stays by the door. Says to Madeleine, 'I heard your old man went all to smash.'

'He was our cousin,' she goes, still stirring. 'After he died we learned that he'd been embezzling from the bank where he was a director.' She says it matter-of-fact, like she's not too surprised.

Sophie pipes up. 'Cousin Lettice is in a state of *collapse*, and has taken to her room.'

'Cousin Lettice', mutters Madeleine, 'will outlive us all.' She shuts the book with a thump, and catches him eyeing it, and twists that curvy red mouth of hers. 'I had no idea how to cook or clean, so I thought I should learn. Lettice was horrified; she despises Mrs Beeton. Calls it "the Bible for parvenues who don't know which fork to use".' She and Sophie swap one of their sister-looks that's nearly a smile, then she tells Sophie to lay the table.

Sophie sucks in her lips like she knows Ben's watching, and hops to the dresser for bowls and that. Four of everything, he can't help noticing. He gets that hot prickly feeling again, and stays by the door, so he can cut the lucky whenever he likes.

He watches Robbie sitting at the table, and Sophie fetching a jug of milk keeping fresh in the sink, and Madeleine dishing out the soup. And all of a sudden he's back at Sunday dinner in the old days, with Kate laying the table and yelling at him to run down the pump and sluice or I'll tan your hide.

His chest hurts. He's got to get out of here. But he can't. He watches Madeleine eating neatly like a cat, and Robbie slopping milk in his soup, and Sophie chatting for England. He never met a bint that talked as much as her. If she talked that much in Shelton Street she'd get beaten up.

All of a sudden she hikes her frock up to her knees and goes, 'Look, Ben, I've got a bruise. I fell down the steps and banged my knee.'

'Sophie . . .' says Madeleine, but Sophie twists in her chair and peels back her black stocking to show the cleanest, smoothest knee Ben ever saw. She's frowning and pointing to a faint pink swelling with one clean pink finger.

'That's no bruise,' he sneers.

'Yes it jolly well is,' she flashes back, 'and it hurts, too.'

Crikey, he thinks. I was right about them eyebrows.

The smell of the soup's making him dizzy, so after a bit he sidles over and pulls up a chair where Madeleine's set a bowl for him. It's the best grub he's ever had in his natural. Great big lumps of meat and onions and barley and stout.

Robbie looks up, soup down his chin, and goes, 'Ben clumped a geezer.'

'Shut it,' mumbles Ben.

'This geezer calls me a charlie,' goes Robbie, 'and Ben goes I'll get you, and the geezer laughs 'cos he's a docker and big as a shed. But Ben waits and tips this barrel on him, and the geezer falls under a dray and the wheels go on his legs, and Ben goes, now who's the cripple, eh?' Robbie leans back and roars. Then he sees the bints aren't laughing, and looks worried.

Sophie's staring at Ben with her big brown eyes. 'Didn't you get told off?'

'Who by?'

'Um. Your parents?'

He snorts. 'Dead and gone.'

'That's a coincidence, so are ours.'

They go back to their soup. Then Sophie asks Robbie what their mother looked like, and he's off.

'She had red hair, like me, but Pa's was black like Ben's, and Pa knocked her about so she died. Then Ben took me away and Pa died too and Ben said good riddance. Ma used to send us hop-picking, that's why Ben's so strong, but I had to stop home on account of I was too little. And we had two whole rooms in East Street with a separate bed for the kids, and every Sunday Ben had to fetch the dinner from the bakehouse, brisket and batter pudding and spuds.'

Ben shuts him up with a cuff. Robbie's always pestering him to tell it, but he shouldn't be gabbing to this lot.

Sophie goes, 'I've never seen a picture of my mother.

Cousin Lettice burned them all. But I do have a cabinet card of Miss Sarah Bernhardt, whom Maddy says Mama resembled. Although I'm not sure how Maddy knows that, for she *says* that she scarcely remembers Mama at all.' A sideways look at her sister, like they've had fights about that.

Ben says to Madeleine, 'This Cousin Lettice. She all you got left?'

She nods. 'Mother died when Sophie was born, and Father was killed in the Sudan.'

'What's that?'

'A desert in Africa. He was a soldier.'

Despite hisself, Ben's impressed.

Sophie pipes up. 'His name was Major Alasdair Falkirk and he came from Jamaica and deserted his young wife to run off with our mother. Her name was Rose, but that's all we know.'

Madeleine keeps her eyes on the table, and Ben guesses she knows more than she's letting on.

'We're not supposed to talk about them,' says Sophie.

'Why?' says Ben.

Sophie shoots Madeleine a look. Madeleine gets up and puts her bowl in the sink and smooths back her hair from her temples. 'We're illegitimate,' she says.

Ben don't know what that means, but it's plain that they think it's the worst thing ever.

'It means', says Madeleine, 'that our father never married our mother.'

'Is that all,' says Ben. 'Can I have more soup?'

Madeleine and Sophie stare at him like he's cracked.

So he gets hisself more soup. 'Where I live,' he goes, 'you don't get spliced. In fact, nobody does except toffs. Don't you know that?'

Madeleine shakes her head.

'Think about it. It costs at least sevenpence, and you're prossing about all morning, and for what? Some bit of paper that says you can't get out of it, ever.'

Madeleine is watching his lips like he's talking Chinese.

'Only toffs get spliced,' he goes. 'Cos only toffs got to

worry about who gets the house and the jewels and that.'

She looks at him as if he's said something deep, and in spite of hisself he's pleased.

Robbie asks Sophie if she wants to play stick and goose, and she says what's that, and Madeleine sends them out into the garden, calling after Sophie to put on her hat.

'Proper garden they got,' Robbie shouts down from the steps. 'Grass and flowerpots and a tree.'

When they're gone, Madeleine goes to the dresser and fetches a book and plonks it down in front of him.

'What's this?' he says.

'*The Downfall of the Dervishes*. It's a Jack Hathaway adventure. We thought you might like it.'

He looks at the letters on the front and thinks, so that's what s and h do to each other. Then he realizes she's had that book waiting all along, like she knew he was coming. He *hates* that. He goes, 'I never read the last one. Sold it. I'll do the same with this.'

'Do what you like. It was cheap enough.'

'Cheap?' he snaps. 'Nothing's cheap if you can't pay for it. Don't you know that yet?'

She's leaning against the dresser with her arms crossed. 'I don't know anything,' she says in a funny voice.

What's she on about?

'Sophie knows more than I do,' she goes. 'She's amazing, she reads everything. I'm too stupid and undisciplined. Like my mother.' She bites her lip. 'I don't even know the sort of things you know.'

You got that right, girl, he thinks.

She sits down across from him and puts her hands on the table. 'You think we're rich, but soon we'll have nothing. We've got to sell the furniture to pay off the debts, and I'll have to work to support us.' She pauses. 'Mr Rennard can't afford to give me a job, and no-one else seems to want a photographer's assistant. I can't be a governess because I never went to school, and I can't be a stenographer, I don't know how. I could be a lady's companion or a shop assistant, but that won't keep the three of us alive.'

'So?' says Ben. 'Why tell me?'

She looks at him with her big dark eyes. 'I thought you might be able to help.'

He's outraged. 'Me? I don't help nobody.'

'Then why are you here?'

'That was Robbie's idea.'

She don't say nothing. Just makes patterns on the table with her fingernail.

The answer's as plain as the nose on her face, but she can't see it cos she's a toff. She can read but she can't sodding see. They're all the same.

After a bit he says, 'You could make a fortune on your back.'

She don't even blink. Not even pretend shocked. Just gives him this long, slow look, like she's been thinking the same thing. Bit of a surprise, that is.

'Cousin Lettice', she said slowly, 'would say that it's in my blood.'

'You what?'

'That it's what I was meant to do. Because of who I am.'

Ben don't know about that, but all of a sudden he sees where this could go. She *could* make a fortune. If she was managed right.

He sees her and Sophie set up in a posh little villa in the Brompton Road, appointment only, *if* you please. They got a box at the Hippodrome and a proper carriage, and Robbie's got a new suit of clothes, and Ben's got a pair of boots with studs. And he's their friend, and sees them every day.

Then he goes and screws it up. He says, 'What about your family?'

She goes still.

'If they're in Jamaica, they're rich, yeh?' He knows that cos his brother Ryan was a docker before he got the con, and Jamaica means sugar barons and darkie slaves.

But she's well narked. Shaking her head, with a face like thunder. 'I'm not asking them for help.'

'Why not?'

'For one thing, I don't even know who they are. Lettice would never tell me my father's real name.'

'Get out of it!'

'It's true. We never talk of him. I don't know if he was a Fynn like Septimus, or a Monroe like Lettice, or something else entirely. And I don't care. Why should I? It's not our name. It's nothing to do with us.'

She sounds like she's told herself that over and over, to make it true.

He goes, 'That's not the point. Point is, they're family. They won't want a couple of by-blows mucking things up for them, so they'll shell out a bit to keep you quiet. That's the point.'

But she's still shaking her head. 'They've never done anything for us. Why should that change now? Why should I go begging to them?'

It's his turn to get narked. 'Oh that's beautiful, that is! You say you're broke, but you won't do bugger all about it. Well, I can't be doing with that. You got to help yourself, my girl, cos if you don't, nobody does it for you!'

He grabs the book and yells for Robbie, and they're out the door and up the steps, with Madeleine and Sophie standing in the kitchen looking shocked.

And what really pisses him off is that in among all them stewpans and knives and whatnot, he never clicked nothing. Not even a sodding spoon.

It's the end of September but still baking hot, and the wind's in the south, so there's this choky stink of churchyards and the knacker's yard down Garratt Lane. Ben's on the bed with *The Downfall of the Dervishes*, puzzling out this bit about camels, when in she comes, Madeleine from Wyndham Street, right here in his place.

It's horrible having her here. She's all poshed up in that black dress of hers, with gloves and a hat and a bag and a sun-umbrella, and him in nothing but his kicksies, and Robbie just his shirt. But she don't seem to notice. She looks all in, like she's past minding things like that.

She gives Robbie a bag of cherries and his jaw drops and he's off like a lamplighter into the corner, chomping away. And meanwhile Ben's shoved the book under the bed, so she won't see. He goes, 'How'd you find us, then?'

She brushes that off. 'Robbie told Sophie, then I asked around.'

She paces about and turns, and smooths her hair. 'I did what you suggested, I tried to contact the family. I went to Septimus's attorney. He wouldn't tell me anything except that all this time it was the *family* that's been paying for us, not Septimus. There was some sort of trust, but now there's nothing left in it. No more money. The attorney said there were "irregularities in the accounts".'

'You mean, Septimus nicked the lot.'

She nods.

'So? What d'you want me to do about it?'

She wraps her arms round her waist and takes these deep breaths like she can't get any air. 'Sophie has tuberculosis.'

Robbie looks up from his cherries. 'What's that?'

'The con,' snaps Ben. He starts picking at a scab on his knee. 'So that's that, then,' he says.

She looks at him like she can't believe what he just said. 'It's not consumption,' she says in a shaky voice. 'Her lungs are fine, perfectly fine. The doctor says it's sort of – tuberculosis of the bones.' She swallows. 'Do you remember when she bumped her knee?'

He shakes his head.

'The doctor says that was probably the – the lesion. I think that means where it started.'

He remembers that clean, smooth knee with the slightest of pink bumps. 'How long's she got, then?'

He hears her catch her breath. 'In a sanatorium, with good food and sunshine and a special splint, she might get better, completely better. But if she isn't treated soon – if the disease goes to her lungs – she won't survive the winter.'

He flicks the scab at the wall. 'Poor little cow.'

'Don't you dare call her that, Ben Kelly!'

He looks up and sees that the colour's come roaring back into her cheeks.

'She's not going to die,' she says between her teeth. 'I won't let her die.'

'Oh yeh?' he goes. 'How d'you work that out? A fucking *san*? D'you know how much they cost?'

'Twenty guineas a month,' she snaps, 'with three months payable in advance – yes, you see, I did think to find out, and in case you can't do the sums, that comes to sixty guineas in all. And I'll thank you never to use such language in my presence again.'

Sixty guineas? He can't hardly breathe. Never guessed it'd be that much. 'Well that's that then,' he says again.

'No it isn't. That's why I'm here.'

He shoots her a look.

'You said I could make a fortune on my back. Well that's what I need. A fortune.'

He narrows his eyes. 'So?'

'Help me. Show me what to do.'

'Leave it out.'

'Do it for Sophie.'

'Not for nobody I won't.'

'I'll give you a cut on everything I make.'

'Now you're talking,' he says.

CHAPTER NINE

The pure in heart do not become ill. Disease is a sign of moral turpitude: it comes from bad blood, unwholesome thoughts, and overseas. Lettice was never ill. God is never ill.

When Sophie contracted tuberculosis, Lettice was outraged. For years she had fought to make her charges respectable in the eyes of the world, and now this shameful disease was shouting their vice from the rooftops. Where was the *justice*?

All her life she had struggled to find the justice. She had borne her husband's dislike because that was her punishment for marrying beneath her. That was why her family had severed all ties with her, and she with them. It was just.

She had borne her husband's death and disgrace because that was *his* punishment for dishonesty and vice.

She had even borne her new-found poverty. She had watched in grim silence as Madeleine argued with the tradesmen and sold the furniture and paid off the debts until the money was all gone. And when the last servant was dismissed, she had withdrawn to her room: for, without servants, it would be impossible to answer the door. But Our Saviour was poor, so in a way she could see the justice in it.

All her life she had borne what Fate had thrown at her, because God is just. A decade before, He had given her two misbegotten souls to bring into the light, and she had done it. She had fought to impose her will on a stubborn and recalcitrant Madeleine and an independent and quick-witted

Sophie. She had ensured that they grew up healthy, and knew the importance of concealing what they were.

Now all that had been swept away. Tuberculosis is the mark of vice. Lettice knew that. And the world knew it, too.

The doctor had known it when he had given her the news. The health visitor had known it when she had declared that the house must be washed from top to bottom in Lysol, and the child's linen boiled and blued separately, twice a week. As if Lettice did not already keep an immaculate house!

She was still prickling from the insult as she dressed to go out the following morning. 'Top to bottom,' she muttered as she plunged the final hatpin into her bonnet. 'As if we wallow in *filth*!'

She snatched up her gloves and reticule and her black crape walking-coat, and swept across the landing to the girls' room.

They stopped talking as soon as she opened the door. Sophie lay in bed propped up against the pillows, looking furious. Madeleine was still in her dressing gown, her features suspiciously composed.

Lettice glanced from her to the dyed black walking-costume laid out on the bed. 'You may not go out,' she declared. 'I am going out. You must stay with your sister.'

Madeleine studied her in that distant, contemplative way she had acquired of late – as if Lettice were no longer to be fought, but merely circumvented. 'Mr Rennard', she said, 'is writing me a testimonial. I shall need it if I'm to get a position.'

Lettice wondered if that were true. 'You can collect it later. I must go to Lampleigh's for more Lysol.'

'We still have two bottles.'

'We need more.'

'Mr Rennard said I was to see him at nine.'

'You should have consulted me before making the appointment.'

Again that look. 'I'm sorry,' Madeleine said. 'I'll go next door and see if Mrs Somerville will sit with Sophie. Then we can both go out.'

Their eyes met. Madeleine's were calm and resolved.

Lettice thought, I have become an obstacle. Is that all I ever was? Out loud she said, 'You must not linger at Mr Rennard's.'

Madeleine inclined her head. She was plotting something. Lettice could tell.

As she went downstairs, Lettice took a deep breath, and smelt the smoke of battle. You cannot, she told herself, allow yourself to be circumvented in this way. You must put a stop to this. You must find out what she is up to.

'You're going to see Ben, aren't you?' said Sophie when Lettice had gone.

'No,' said Madeleine.

In the looking-glass she caught sight of the sampler which Lettice had made her cross-stitch when she was twelve. *Fornication Leads to Misery and Hell. Marriage Leads to Happiness and Heaven.* What's fornication? Sophie had asked a hundred times. I don't know, Madeleine would reply. Something bad, I think.

'You're going to see Ben,' Sophie said again. 'Can I come?'

'You know you can't. Dr Wray said you must have complete rest.'

'I had rest yesterday. And the day before.'

'He means for months.'

'But I *can't*. How can I do that? I'm not allowed to read.'

'I know. But I'll read to you when I get back.'

In the distance the bells of St Mary's struck the half-hour. She would have to hurry if she was to meet Ben at eight. She wrenched open the drawer and studied the piles of underclothes. In this heat the cambric combinations would be the coolest, but the silk chemise and drawers were prettier. Would that matter? If she went through with it, wouldn't she have to take everything off?

Her stomach turned over. She didn't even know what 'it' involved.

Yesterday after coming back from Ben's, she had stolen into Lettice's room and sneaked a look at Dr Philpott. To her dismay he was silent on the details of what he called *connexion* – except to say that *the wife must endeavour to think happy thoughts throughout.*

She took out the combinations and pushed the drawer shut. Behind her Sophie plucked at the sheets, her face puffy and mutinous. 'It's not fair,' she muttered. 'I'm being punished and I haven't done anything wrong.'

'I know. It's awful. I do know.' In helpless silence she went behind the screen and dressed. Since Sophie's diagnosis she had felt as if she were living on an edge: a hard metallic edge that swooped down into the cold, wrenching terror of loss.

How could lives change so fast? The month before, she had been contentedly photographing flowers in the garden, while Lettice was planning a trip to Maples to see the latest Electric globes, Septimus voting to ban Americans from his club, and Sophie composing a pamphlet on the plight of the Regent's Park cab-horses. Now Septimus was dead, the money all gone, and her clever, garrulous, infuriating little sister was mortally ill.

'*Why* won't you say where you're going?' said Sophie.

'I did. I'm going to see Mr Rennard.'

'That's just what you told Cousin Lettice.'

Madeleine did not reply.

'You're meeting Ben and Robbie. Aren't you?'

'Sophie—'

'You're meeting Ben and Robbie and leaving me out. You're horrible. I hate you.'

She had been impossible ever since Dr Wray had fitted the splint two days before. A hideous device of steel hoops and bars covered in boiler felt, it encircled her left leg from the upper thigh to a couple of inches below her foot. A patten screwed to the other boot was supposed to even up the difference in heights, and Dr Wray had said that she must practise standing for five minutes a day, to get used to it. He had assured her it was easy. 'He should try it,' Sophie had muttered when he was out of the room. Then she had burst into tears. 'It's just frustration,' she had stammered when she'd brought herself under control. As if she needed an excuse to cry.

She was so determined to be grown-up. When Madeleine

had retrieved her beloved stuffed donkey from his exile in the attic, she had pushed him away for being too babyish. Madeleine had assured her that he wasn't a toy but a mascot, and after that Pablo Grey had been allowed to stay.

The church bells struck the quarter-hour. Madeleine finished buttoning her blouse and came out from behind the screen. 'You're right,' she said. 'I am going to see Ben.'

'I knew it,' said Sophie.

'Just don't breathe a word to Lettice.'

'Only if you promise not to give him any more books without me.' She still hadn't forgiven Madeleine for giving him *The Downfall of the Dervishes* when she wasn't there.

'I promise,' said Madeleine.

Sophie nodded, and picked at the buckle on her splint.

She doesn't look ill, thought Madeleine. Panic rose in her throat. How can she be ill?

It had begun with that bump on the knee, and then a touch of feverishness in the evenings. Lettice had put it down to growing pains, and dosed her with calomel. It was only when she became languid in the mornings that they became alarmed.

Old Dr Bostock had made a brisk diagnosis and said that the leg must come off. Even Lettice had been shocked. Madeleine had thanked him, and found another doctor. Dr Wray, thirty years younger, had confirmed the diagnosis, but prescribed prolonged rest in the famous splint along with plenty of fresh beef, a daily half-pound of mutton suet boiled in milk, and lots of sunshine and fresh air in a sanatorium in the country. The fresh air was critical. Sophie must practically live outside if she was to survive.

He had explained to Madeleine that the disease was not inherited, as Lettice believed, but caused by thousands of invisible organisms called bacilli. That night, Madeleine had lain awake and pictured them as a procession of tiny tombstones in her sister's blood, like the little grey blotches she had imagined as a child.

What if Dr Wray was wrong and Lettice was right? What if the disease *was* the taint, working its way out? What if her parents had made Sophie ill?

She slammed the door on that hard. Slam the door. Don't think about them.

'What are you and Ben going to do?' asked Sophie.

Madeleine took her jacket from the bed. 'We're going to get some money.'

'How? Are you going to rob a bank?'

'Of course not.'

'Are you going to break the law?'

'No.'

'You don't sound very sure.'

'Sophie—'

'Does Ben break the law?'

'All the time, I should imagine.'

Buttoning her jacket, she caught sight of herself in the looking-glass. Her mother's dark eyes stared back at her.

Are you doing this because of her? she wondered. Because you're her daughter, and therefore prone to vice?

But if that were true, did it mean that Sophie was also prone to vice? Or was it like shuffling cards? Had Sophie inherited all the good, while Madeleine had got all the bad?

She kneaded her temples. She couldn't think about that now. Today was Friday, and by Monday she needed twelve pounds. Twelve pounds for food, a month's rent in advance, and a carter to take them to the dingy little rooms she had found in the North Wharf Road.

The *Dictionary of Employment Open to Women* said that waitresses at the ABC started on nine shillings a week, a shopgirl on twelve, a card-leaver twenty-five (with considerable outlay for being 'well turned out'), and a dog-walker (Sophie's favourite) received one and six an hour – provided she could find enough dogs to walk.

In other words, it was impossible to come up with twelve pounds in three days by honest means. But according to Ben, and for some bizarre reason she believed him, they could make *twenty guineas* for her first time ('premium rate in a good house'), and twenty-five a week thereafter.

Sophie was still picking at the buckle on her splint. 'What do dead people look like?'

Madeleine drew a deep breath. 'You know what Dr Wray said about morbid talk.'

Sophie scowled. 'What did Mama look like when she was dead?'

'I don't remember.'

'Yes you do.'

'If I did, I wouldn't tell you. It wouldn't do any good.'

'What will *I* look like when I die?'

'You're not going to die.'

'But if I *do*.'

Madeleine straightened the sheets, retrieved Pablo Grey from the floor, and placed him firmly on her sister's chest.

Sophie was still scowling. 'Will I still be able to see you when I'm dead?'

Madeleine put Sophie's hands one on top of the other on the donkey's fat, furry stomach. 'I don't know. Nobody knows. But you're not going to die. I won't allow it.'

Ben was waiting for her on the corner of Titchfield Street and the Portland Road. He was leaning against a barrel outside a fruiterer's, flirting with a pock-faced little laundress with a basket of washing on her hip.

Madeleine liked Ben. She didn't know why. He was filthy, amoral, foul-mouthed and pitiable. He was like a disgraceful younger brother. Thin as a whippet and quick as a stoat, he wore the stink and grime of the gutter with careless panache. He spat out profanities in a voice still husky with childhood, and his green eyes were sharp with a knowledge gained far too soon. But she liked him. She understood his loneliness and his mistrust, and his passionate attachment to a younger brother who trusted too much.

And she had to admire anyone who had grown up where he had, and survived.

Seeking him out the previous day, she had made her way with increasing trepidation through a warren of stinking courtyards and tenements of unrelenting dereliction. Children swarmed like rats, consumptive and deformed, with grey, pinched faces.

For a ha'penny, a woman had told her where to find him.

In *The Gentlewoman*, the Poor were either good-natured types who made the best of their lot, or murderous villains who coshed innocents to death; but this woman had looked both murderous *and* good-natured. Her enormous breasts lolled unrestrained beneath her sweaty petticoat, and her arms were a patchwork of bruises. But she gave Madeleine a gap-toothed grin and pointed out the Kellys' place, up three flights of stairs, and watch out as there ain't no banisters.

Ben's 'place' was little more than a cupboard, its crumbling walls smeared with generations of bedbugs. The tiny window was stopped with cardboard, the air so fetid that Madeleine's gorge rose.

When she entered, Ben shoved *The Downfall of the Dervishes* under the pile of straw on which he was curled up, and sprang to his feet, as wary as when she'd cornered him with the imitation gun. He was naked to the waist, his skinny chest covered in glistening scabs. She guessed at vermin bites and furious bouts of scratching.

How, she wondered, has he survived?

And now she stood in the sun in the Portland Road, and watched him cracking jokes with the skivvy. She noticed that although he was making the girl screech with laughter, he wasn't joining in himself. In fact, she had rarely seen him smile, and when he did it was just a quick feral snarl, with no mirth behind it.

As she watched, he put his hand behind the girl's head and drew her face close to his, and kissed her. The girl sank her fingers into his greasy black hair, and her body arched against his. Their jaws worked.

Madeleine's cheeks flamed. Was this what Lettice called vice?

When they drew apart, both were breathing fast. The girl's eyes were glittering, her lips moist and bruised. Ben studied her for a moment, his face expressionless and sharply beautiful. Then he looked round and caught sight of Madeleine, and nodded to her, and left the skivvy without a backward glance.

'What's up, Madlin,' he said, wiping his mouth on his sleeve. 'Thought you wasn't coming.'

Her hands tightened on her reticule. 'What do we do now?'

He threw her an appraising glance. 'Little tour. Help you get your bearings.'

They crossed the road, then walked down Riding House Street and into tranquil Langham Place. Stuccoed townhouses frowned down at them with drawn blinds and impeccable black doors. Ben cocked his head at Number Seven. 'One of the better ones.'

She glanced at the well-scrubbed steps, then back to him. 'You don't mean this is a—'

He nodded.

'But it's practically round the corner from where we live.'

'Little story about that. Turns out your Cousin Septimus was a regular.'

She gazed at the blank façade. She ought to be shocked, but she wasn't. She had known since she was ten that there are two separate worlds which coexist side by side, like a ghost-image on a photograph. There is the safe world of the surface, and then the secret world underneath: the world of pain and ugliness, which everyone knows about but no-one ever mentions. The dead woman lying in the scarlet butterfly of blood.

Ben misread her expression for trepidation. 'We're not going in. Just wanted to show you that it's more respectable than you think. Lots of women do it part time, and it don't stop them being respectable again, after.'

She was touched at his attempt to reassure.

They started south, and as they walked he gave her a rapid-fire lesson in geography. At the bottom of the pile were the night-houses in Betty Street, which handled 'the youth trade, that's five and up', and were despised for giving the profession a bad name. Then there were the accommodation houses around Seven Dials, Devil's Acre and the Haymarket, where business was transacted in doorways at sixpence a time. Above that was Great Windmill Street, which had been 'bang-up' a decade ago, but was now well past its best; and above that was Marylebone, and then the pinnacle of Mayfair, where the houses were fearsomely discreet, and the girls never went out unaccompanied. Word would simply go out of a new arrival, and an interested client would have it sent round to his rooms in a cab. No scandal and no disease. All clean and topper and nice.

'Stop,' said Madeleine. They were outside the Coliseum, and she had to raise her voice above the rattle of the trams and the screech of carriage wheels against the kerb. 'I need you to tell me something.'

'Yeh? What?'

'I need you to tell me what this involves.'

He frowned. 'That's what I been—'

'No. I mean what one actually does. What one – does.'

He blinked. 'Shit. You mean you don't know?'

'If I knew, I should hardly be asking you.'

He scratched the back of his neck. 'Well bugger me.'

She waited, but he continued to shake his head. She said, 'Can't you just show me?'

A bark of laughter. 'I don't think you'd like that!'

Just then, a commotion of yelps erupted down a side street. Ben told Madeleine to wait, and ran off. Moments later he returned, grabbed her hand and dragged her after him.

She found herself in an alley lined with shops of the poorer sort. A pawnbroker's, a small shoddy agent for Imperial Gas, Light & Coke. Outside a pub stood a brewer's dray with four black shire horses between the shafts, their ears pricked in mild curiosity at a pair of mongrels mating in the gutter.

The larger dog, a wolfish red cur with a bad attack of mange, had mounted the smaller – which clearly had some greyhound in its ancestry, although not enough to have secured its escape. It was yelping piteously while the larger dog panted and clutched its scrawny flanks.

The commotion was attracting a good deal of raucous laughter. Two respectable women in straw boaters hurried past Madeleine with flaming cheeks.

Ben pointed at the dogs. 'There you are.'

Madeleine looked at him, then back to the dogs. 'That?'

He shrugged. 'Give or take.'

She contemplated the wiry haunches pumping away like some bizarre mechanical toy. It wasn't the first time she had seen two dogs thus engaged, but she had always supposed that such behaviour was confined to animals. She had never imagined it applied to people. Lettice and Septimus? Her father and mother?

Two dogs mating in a gutter. Is that all there is?

But in a way, she thought, what's so surprising about that? If giving birth means blood and sweat and pain, why should 'connexion' be any different?

As they made their way back to the main road, she found herself scrutinizing every man she passed. A telegraph runner in a blue uniform and a pillbox hat; a butcher's assistant with a tray of faggots; a plump, perspiring attorney. She tried to picture herself doing 'it' with them.

I can't, she thought in sudden panic.

Why not? said another voice inside her head. It's in your blood.

I can't I can't I can't.

'I can't do this,' she told Ben. 'Not now. Not – today.'

Ben flicked her a glance. 'I know. Got a better idea.'

'Ben—'

'It'll work. You'll see. You won't have to touch nobody.'

He led her along the Strand and into a narrow street over-shadowed by apartment buildings and criss-crossed with telephone wires. Relief washed over her. The street was silent and respectable. Gas-lamps stood guard like tall police-men, and at the end she could see St Clement's reassuring spire. *Bookseller's Row*, said the soot-encrusted street sign.

Ben snorted. 'Real name's Holywell Street. They changed it to make it respectable, but it's still the same sodding place.'

He stopped outside a little shop whose sign proclaimed it in cracked gold lettering to be *Venables & Co., Specialist Books & Photographs, Domestic & Imported*. The win-dows revealed shelves of dusty volumes and padlocked glass cabinets, while outside a table held secondhand books – *The Perfumed Garden, The Pearl, The Young Wife's Confession* – and a tray of cabinet cards at a shilling a time.

Ben rifled through the cards and pulled out a handful. He passed one to Madeleine.

It showed a girl a couple of years older than Sophie,

straddling a young man. The young man wore the ill-fitting suit of a minor clerk, and an appreciative smirk. The girl wore striped stockings and nothing else. Her expression was preoccupied, as if she had just detected a shred of bacon between her teeth.

Madeleine's heart began to pound. 'You want me to do that.'

'Whoops,' said Ben. 'Wrong picture.' He snatched the card from her hand and gave her another. This one showed a plump girl with wavy blond hair lying on a couch. She was completely naked, and dreamily contemplating a single rose laid across her dimpled thighs.

'Pays well,' said Ben. 'Bloke that runs this place takes the photos. My sister Lily made good money till she got too thin.'

'You want me to take off my clothes and—'

'Well, why not? You don't got to do nothing. And it pays. That's the point.'

She took another look at the photograph. This time, she noticed that the girl had a good figure but rather short legs, which the photographer had disguised by a clever choice of camera angle. Madeleine had used the same trick herself many times. The only difference was that her clients had been clothed.

She swallowed. 'Will I have to take everything off?'

Ben hesitated. 'Like I said, you won't have to *do* nothing.'

The doorbell clanged behind them, and the street was quiet again.

Lettice put her hand on the lamp-post to steady herself. A sharp pain flared in her breast. She shut her eyes and willed it away.

Gradually the pain subsided, and she opened her eyes. She didn't see the street before her. All she saw was Madeleine and that – creature – disappearing into that appalling little shop.

Chapter Ten

'If you need to shave your legs,' said the photographer, 'there's a razor behind the screen. I don't run to soap.'

Madeleine shook her head.

'Good, then we've got time for a cup of tea while we wait.'

She looked round in alarm. 'Wait for whom?'

'Not who, dear. What.' He rubbed his hard little stomach. 'Corset marks. We wouldn't want those.'

He still hadn't met her eyes, which she found increasingly disconcerting.

'Get a move on, dear, tempus is fugiting. We don't want nasty long shadows spoiling the pics.'

She went behind the screen. Over one corner hung a purple robe of imitation silk. It felt greasy, and smelled of cheap scent and stale cigarettes.

She was glad now that she had told Ben to wait downstairs. He had shrugged and said fair enough, and don't worry about Bob Venables, you're safe with him, he's a Marjorie. A what? she'd said, and he'd explained that the photographer had once tried to corner Robbie. When she still didn't understand he'd snapped, 'Oh, leave it out,' and hustled her upstairs.

But whatever he meant, he seemed to be right about the photographer: a plump young man with a bad case of acne and a shock of cherubic blond curls, who nimbly avoided meeting her eyes as he showed her into his surprisingly spacious studio.

Nobody's going to touch you, she told herself as she struggled out of her clothes.

It didn't work. Nobody would touch her, but they would touch her image. And she could not delude herself that it was 'only a photograph'. She knew the power of images. She remembered the photograph of Eden which she had loved and then defaced. And Lettice destroying her mother's work like some latter-day witch.

She had read in *Amateur Photographer* about a tribe of Arabs who believed that the taking of photographs is the taking of souls. Mr Rennard had scoffed, but she had thought it as good a way of putting it as any.

It was hot in the studio, with an acrid smell of chemicals that reminded her of the darkroom at Cairngowrie House. *In a photograph*, her mother used to say, *you can be anyone you want*. Angrily, she pushed the thought aside.

The robe felt horribly insubstantial when she put it on, but when she emerged from behind the screen she was relieved to see that the photographer was still ignoring her. He was busy draping grubby white sheets over the backs of chairs arranged in a semicircle about a couch. The couch had gilded claw feet and upholstery of stained blue plush. It resembled the one at Mr Rennard's which he used for family groups.

She looked at the sheets draped over the chairs and thought, he must be using them as reflectors. And that couch is where I am to sit. Or lie, I suppose.

At length the photographer remembered her for long enough to hand her a mug of black tea which he fetched from a gas ring in the corner. Then he scuttled off and began rooting around in a stack of cartons. He still hadn't looked her in the eye. She wondered why. Ben had told her that she was 'a cut above' his usual models, so perhaps that was it.

She perched on the edge of the couch and sipped her tea. She felt sick. She pictured the photographer's dismay if she spewed tea all over the couch.

To break the silence, she asked what he thought about the new hand-held cameras. She had noticed that he favoured an old-fashioned view camera, with half-size plates and a sturdy tripod.

'Snapshots?' He snorted. 'So now every Tom, Dick and Harriet fancies they're a photographer. I tell you, if I wasn't such an artist I'd be out of the biz.' He scowled into a carton of plates. 'Know a bit about it, do you?'

She told him about helping at Mr Rennard's, and keeping up with developments in *Camera* and the *BJP*. Some of the tension went out of him, and soon he was telling her about the new flash powders he'd been trying out, and his hopes for panchromatic plates – the way of the future, dear, or it would be if it wasn't so bloody *expensive*, pardon my French. For the first time he actually looked at her, and she saw that his eyes were pale blue, and bloodshot from the chemicals.

It struck her as bizarre that *she* was trying to put *him* at his ease, but it also made her feel a little better. So it was a shock when he suggested that she just pop off the robe and lie back on the couch, to get the feel.

She didn't move.

He peered into the viewfinder. 'It's just a *thought*,' he muttered, 'but as the skin texture's so delicate, we might go for a nice, soft, glowing kind of a look? Keep the light flat, pop a bit of muslin over the window?'

'The' skin texture. She appreciated the attempt at distancing, but it didn't stop her breaking out in a cold sweat. She asked if she might have a towel.

'Wouldn't bother, dear. Bit of a gleam adds a certain something? All nice and pearly?' He slotted a plate into the camera. 'Now when you're ready, we can just get rid of that robe. I thought we'd get those hands clasped, or the shaking'll spoil the pics. And a bit of gauze over the face – sort of like a shroud? Be amazed how many of the gentlemen like that kind of thing.'

The girl in the tea shop asked Lettice if she was still feeling seedy, and Lettice replied that she was better thank you, and the girl nodded and hurried off to attend to another customer.

Lettice blinked at her cold tea, and wondered why God had forsaken her.

She had always done His will. Always. When Mama had said how can you think of accepting that Mr Fynn, he is scarcely a gentleman, Lettice had married him, for she had known that she was too plain to turn down the only offer she was likely to get. She had married him, for it was God's will.

When Mama had cut them off without a shilling, and Septimus had cooled towards her, she had borne that too, for it was God's will.

And when, after decades of silence, she had received a letter from Jocelyn – *henceforth I have no son; you will oblige me by never receiving him or entering into correspondence* – she had obeyed without question. For it was God's will.

At the time she had been forty-one, and still happy – or still hopeful that she might *be* happy, if she became a mother. A few years later, all hope was gone. And somewhere along the way she had ceased to think about happiness.

Then one dark February morning, she had opened the letter from Rose Durrant.

The shock of it. To see that infamous name proudly scrawled in bold black script. *Please forgive me for writing, but Ainsley is in the Sudan, and I fear for my daughter and for the little one to come, should anything occur while he remains overseas.* Then the bald request: if 'the worst' should occur, would Lettice care for the children until their father's return? Please, please send an assurance as soon as convenient.

Enclosed with the letter was a photograph of a beautiful woman seated on a chair, with a handsome, fair-haired man smiling down at her, and a lovely little girl on her lap. *Look at me*, said the peerless dark eyes. *All my life I have been wicked. And see how God has rewarded me.*

At that moment Lettice had seen her own life for what it truly was: a cramped existence in a mean little house where she spent weeks without speaking to anyone but the servants; a childless union to a vulgar, unfaithful man who had disliked her for years. Why had God allowed it? Where was the *justice*?

And what must she do about Rose Durrant's letter? To respond would be to disobey the head of the family; but how could she ignore the plea of a woman in distress?

For a fortnight she had agonized. Then she had dashed off a curt response, seeking details of the lying-in arrangements by return.

She had never received a reply. Ten days later she had seen the piece in *The Times*. *Gallant major slain . . . captain held, pending court-martial*. She had overruled her husband's objections and they had travelled to Scotland. *Gallant major slain*. She had been shocked, but also horribly soothed. God had spoken. The world was just.

She had been totally unprepared for the rage which had boiled up inside her at the sight of the children. She had stood beside the cot and stared down at that perfect infant and that huge-eyed, silent little girl. Rose Durrant had been given all this. Where was the *justice*?

Then it had come to her. *This* is the justice. These children before you were born to wickedness – but God has given them to *you*. Rose Durrant died because she was wicked. You have her children because you are good.

For ten years she had clung to that truth as to a rock. But now the rock was crumbling beneath her. God was about to cast her charges into the abyss. He was about to destroy everything she had fought for. It would be as if she had never existed.

All her life she had struggled to do God's will, for He was the only one who had ever loved her. Now He had forsaken her. She didn't know what to do.

She picked up her cup and frowned at it, and took a sip of cold tea. It tasted bitter, but it gave her strength. Surely there must be something she could *do*?

One thing is certain, she told herself. You cannot manage this on your own. You are only a woman. You are not supposed to manage things like this.

She took another sip of tea.

Yes. That is it. You are only a woman. You must find a man to take control.

*   *   *

Madeleine was still tasting bile when she let herself into the house.

On leaving the studio she had retched into the gutter until her eyes watered. Beside her, Ben had been puzzled and disappointed that his efforts had met with such a response. He had left her soon afterwards, and she had found her own way back to Wyndham Street.

Walking the pavements, she had felt as if everyone was staring at her. What did they see? Could they tell what she had just done?

The hall was dim and empty when she let herself in, and her footsteps echoed as she crossed the tiles. The furniture was gone, but darker patches on the wallpaper showed where it had been.

From habit she went to the patch where the looking-glass had hung, and started taking out her hatpins. She felt exhausted and nauseous. She wanted to go upstairs and curl up beneath the covers and think of nothing.

A rustle of skirts behind her made her start. To her alarm she saw that Lettice was sitting on the stairs. Her face was in shadow, but Madeleine could make out the gleam of her eyes. Her bony yellow hands clutched her knees.

Anxiety gripped her. 'Is Sophie all right?'

'Asleep,' said Lettice.

Madeleine let out a long breath. She turned away, and took off her hat and smoothed back her hair from her temples. 'Did you get the Lysol you wanted?'

'No,' said Lettice in a strange, toneless voice. 'I had something else to do.'

'What was that?' said Madeleine mechanically. She wished Lettice would stop watching her and leave her alone.

With a stiff rustle of skirts Lettice rose to her feet. 'Tell me everything,' she said.

'About what?'

'About what you did. With that – creature.'

The hall was completely silent.

'I saw you,' said Lettice. 'I followed you.'

'That was underhand.'

'I followed you quite openly. You were too involved with that creature to notice.'

Madeleine glanced down at the hat in her hand.

'Tell me what you did,' said Lettice. 'Tell me the truth.'

Madeleine did not reply. Lettice didn't want the truth. She couldn't face the truth.

'What', said Lettice, 'did you do?'

'Nothing,' she replied.

'A lie.'

'If you wish it, I'll swear on the Bible.'

'The Bible', spat Lettice, 'means nothing to you.'

Again Madeleine said nothing. Lettice was right.

Sophie appeared at the top of the stairs, balanced precariously on tiptoe to raise herself to the level of her splint.

'Go back to bed,' said Madeleine and Lettice together.

'But—'

'Bed.'

Sophie gave them a mutinous look and hobbled off.

Lettice waited till Sophie had gone. 'For ten years,' she said, 'I have tried to make you decent. Respectable.'

'But I'm not respectable,' said Madeleine. 'You made sure I never forgot that.'

'You can *seem* respectable. You can *pass* for respectable among decent people—'

'I don't know any decent people. You never let me meet any. Except for Mr Rennard, and he's a shopkeeper so he doesn't count.'

'So you blame me when you seek out the dregs? You blame me?'

'No. No. I don't know whom I blame.'

Lettice shook her head, and her horsehair ringlets swung. 'You *long* for the dregs,' she said between her teeth. 'You ache and whine to be down there in the filth.'

Madeleine felt sick. 'Is that what you think of me?'

'How can I think anything else?'

Another silence. Lettice drew herself up. 'I can do nothing more with you. Someone else must try. I have failed.'

'What do you mean, someone else?'

Lettice hesitated. 'There is a gentleman,' she said. 'A churchman. Your grandfather's adopted son. You must apply to him for guidance.'

'My *grandfather*—'

'Did you hear what I said? This man is a churchman. He may be able to save you. If it is not already too late.' She turned to mount the stairs, but Madeleine moved round and blocked her way.

'My grandfather? What grandfather? Why didn't you tell me this before?'

'Because he doesn't want you!' spat Lettice. 'He never wanted you!' Her bony breast rose and fell. Her sallow cheeks were blotched with red. 'Ten years ago,' she said more quietly, 'I felt it my duty to break a long silence. I wrote to him. Jocelyn Monroe. Your father's father. Yes, you see, you and I are related after all. To my lasting shame.' She paused for breath. 'I thought it my duty', she went on, 'to inform him of your existence. He replied that he never wanted to hear of you again. He wished to know nothing about you. Nothing. Save only in the event of your death.'

It was Madeleine's turn to sit on the stairs.

Lettice stood looking down at her. 'His adopted son is a churchman. The Reverend Sinclair Lawe. You must go to him and confess all. I can do nothing more with you.'

Madeleine struggled to take it all in. 'Where does he live?'

'I understand that he has an address in Fitzroy Square.'

'Fitzroy Square? But – that's practically round the corner! Why haven't you ever spoken of him? Called on him. Why hasn't he ever visited us?'

'Because it was my duty to keep you separate!' snapped Lettice. 'The head of the family *commanded* me to keep you separate. And that I have done.' Her hand tightened on the banister. 'Besides, I myself have never met the Reverend Lawe. Indeed I doubt that he even knows I exist.' She paused. 'As you very well know, my contact with my family was all but ended by my marriage.'

Madeleine was silent for a moment. Then she added, 'This Reverend Lawe. What makes you think that he'll see me?'

'What do you mean?'

'If my own grandfather won't see me, why should his adopted son?' She paused, then added with a curl of her lip, 'Or are you suggesting that I should put on some sort of disguise?'

Lettice leaned over her, and Madeleine smelt her sour breath and the musty odour of crape. 'Sinclair Lawe is a *churchman*,' she hissed. 'A man of *God*. Have you any conception of what that means?'

'But Lettice, I can't just—'

'Go to him. Throw yourself on his mercy. I can do nothing more with you.'

Chapter Eleven

What does God *want* from me? wondered Sinclair Lawe in despair.

He took the nailbrush from the washstand and scrubbed his fingers till the water turned pink.

Why had he succumbed, when he had sworn that he never would again? Why had God allowed him to pollute himself?

As he reached for a napkin to dry his hands, his eye was caught by a flash of colour outside the window. He froze. The bathroom was three floors up, and not overlooked – and yet there, on the neighbouring roof, crouched a chimney sweep's boy.

Breathlessly Sinclair took in the inhuman stick limbs and the vivid copper hair; the grotesquely blackened face. The creature had seen everything. Everything. How could he have forgotten to draw the blinds?

He shut his eyes, and when he looked again the creature was gone. And that was worse. Already evil gossip might be spreading about the Reverend Lawe.

He willed himself to be calm. He replaced the napkin on the rail and straightened his smoking jacket. He checked the bathroom to make sure it was in order, then went slowly downstairs to his study, and rang for Mary, and ordered a glass of hot milk. But he could not forget the apparition on the roof.

Perhaps it was some sort of sign? Perhaps God intended

some great change in his fortunes? Oh, let it be so. His life had become intolerable.

Everyone was urging him to do the one thing that he never could. Even the Dean was becoming impatient. 'Now that you have turned thirty,' he had said at their last encounter, 'I presume that you will shortly be delighting us with news of your engagement to an appropriate young lady.'

Then there were the constant invitations to dinners and receptions, where flocks of meek and marriageable young females did battle for his attention. And last but most powerful of all, the letter from Great-Aunt May. *You must marry at once*, she had told him with her formidable singularity of purpose. *There must be no more delay. You are of excellent pedigree and ample means, with a promising career in the Church. Many eligible young females will compete for your attentions. Marry at once. If you do not, I cannot answer for the consequences.*

She had no need to elaborate. *If you do not marry and produce a son*, ran the unwritten message, *Fever Hill will never be yours. Your brother will find some means of worming his way back into the old man's affections, and you will be disinherited. Do not delude yourself that it could never happen. Cameron may be an outcast and a recluse, but he lives in Jamaica. You do not.*

Sinclair went to the window and drew back the curtain and gazed down into the street. The heatwave had broken the night before, and a fine rain was greasing the pavements and making the passers-by hunch beneath their umbrellas.

There was no answer to his dilemma. There could *be* no answer. To gain his inheritance he must marry – and yet he could never marry, for then he would be found out.

With a sense of weary compulsion he returned to his desk. On bad days, he might unlock the secret compartment ten times or more, and take out the little grey booklet and reread the familiar page. It was not that he needed to be reminded of the text, but that he needed to see the words. It was as if he still clung to some hope that this time he might derive a meaning less absolute than he ever had before.

Of course he never did. *Plain Words to Young Men on an*

Avoided Subject was exactly that. *If once a young man succumbs to the imbruted cravings of lust, and wastes his substance in solitary indulgence, the fatal habit is acquired. The clammy hand, the stinking foot, and the haggard countenance are all marks of that vice which – in extreme cases – must end in insanity and death.*

Moreover – and here came the passage which had haunted him for years – *should such a man be wicked enough to marry, he risks passing the dreadful malady to his wife. His progeny are born dead, or else exist only in brief suffering: not born into this world so much as damned into it by the wretch who gave them being.*

He passed a shaky hand over his face. With such a secret, how could he marry? How risk exposure and ruin? He pictured the scene when the truth was laid bare. The outraged father-in-law summoning doctors and lawyers. Jocelyn's face as he cut him out of his will.

At that moment he heard footsteps on the porch. A rap at the door. He sucked in his breath. The chimney sweep? He pictured the creature waiting on the doorstep, rubbing its blackened claws as it plotted blackmail.

When Mary announced 'a lady', Sinclair shuddered with relief.

'A Miss Finlay,' muttered the elderly parlourmaid, her tight lips betraying what she thought of idle young parishioners who couldn't leave the poor young Reverend in peace.

But the girl whom Mary showed in was no parishioner. Sinclair would have remembered her, for she was handsome – although her features were too decided for truly feminine beauty.

Normally, he would have told her to make an appointment and sent her away, but there was something about her that intrigued him. She was in trouble; he could tell that at once. He wondered why.

He offered her a chair by the fireplace and took the one opposite, and ordered tea. He noticed that her manners were ladylike, but that when she drew off her gloves to pour, her fingers were reddened at the tips. Ah. A lady in reduced circumstances. He could always tell.

And she was hiding something. He stopped listening to her commonplace tale of misfortune. 'Forgive me for interrupting,' he said, leaning back and steepling his fingers, 'but I have many demands on my time, and I confess to being surprised that you should come to me for assistance, while concealing the truth.'

A hit, a palpable hit. Her colour fled, her dark eyes widened with shock.

He gave her a brief, reassuring smile. 'I am sorry if I startled you, but my calling has made me expert in these matters. You see, Miss Finlay, you come to me with a tale of a bankrupt guardian and an invalid sister, and an urgent need for guidance, which' – he forestalled her protest with an upheld palm – 'I assure you I do believe. But you make no reference to what prevents you from seeking the obvious solution.'

She looked perplexed.

'Why, marriage, of course. I need hardly point out that a young lady with – permit me – your advantages should not find it difficult to secure a match.'

'Oh no, that's out of the question,' she replied in a forthright, almost masculine tone. 'I can never marry.'

He sensed that they were nearing the secret, and his pulse quickened. 'And why is that?' he said.

She glanced at her lap and frowned.

'Forgive me,' he said, 'I was too direct. It is a failing of mine. But remember, I am a man of God. Whatever passes between us shall be in confidence.'

Some of the tension left her features.

'I suspect', he probed, 'that your concern over marriage derives from some – inherited weakness in your family?'

She did not reply.

Again he sensed that he was nearing the truth. He swallowed. 'Permit to guess. There is some defect in the physical constitution – perhaps of a malignant nature? Or a nervous indisposition?'

'Not exactly.'

'Perhaps – some flaw in the circumstances of your birth?'

She went still.

So that was it. And as he studied her reserved, almost sullen features, he was overwhelmed by a tremendous elation. It came from nowhere, and it shook him profoundly. It was as if he stood on the verge of a great revelation – a revelation which in some mysterious way would alter his destiny. But what could it be? And why should it matter to him if this unknown girl was illegitimate?

He couldn't work it out. And he was gripped by a fear that she would leave before he had discovered the answer.

'Mr Lawe,' she began in her curiously direct yet ladylike way, 'I regret having to ask you this when you've been so kind – but . . .' She bit her lip. 'You see, I need ten pounds. I need it today. If I don't get it, I don't know what I shall do.' She coloured, and he guessed that she knew exactly what she would do.

Money. Of course! Why hadn't he thought of it before?

'My dear Miss Finlay,' he said. 'God has indeed brought you to the right place. I happen to be the trustee of a small charity conceived to help just such unfortunates as yourself – to keep them from the vice to which they are predisposed by birth.'

She took that in silence, but regarded him coolly, as if too proud to accept such a judgement on herself, yet too intelligent to dispute its truth.

That irritated him, so he made her go the final step. 'Ought I to take it from your silence that you do not wish for my aid?'

Her colour deepened. 'I should of course be most grateful for whatever you feel able to do.'

How she hates having to ask, he thought. His excitement was painful. But *why* did he have this sense that she held the key?

Forcing himself to appear calm, he went to his desk and unlocked the money drawer and withdrew four five-pound notes, which he placed on the blotter. 'Will that suit? I have doubled the amount, to avoid your having to remove to those inferior lodgings you mentioned.'

To his astonishment, she was no longer listening. She was gazing at the photograph on his desk: the portrait of Jocelyn, which he kept as a reminder of the inheritance that was right-fully his.

'Miss Finlay,' he said sharply.

Her gaze swung back to him. 'I – I'm sorry,' she stammered. 'I believe I'm a little distracted.'

'To be sure. I was merely enquiring whether twenty pounds would suit.'

She looked at the money on the blotter. 'You are very generous,' she muttered.

He tapped the desk with his fingertips. 'However. I feel it my duty to impose one condition.'

She raised her eyes to his.

'You must return tomorrow, and every day thereafter until such time as I release you. That we might pray together for your salvation.'

She looked from him to the money, then back again.

'Have I your word', he said, 'that you will return?'

She rose to her feet. 'You have my word.'

When Mary had shown her out, he stood at the window and watched her walk away down the street. Now that he had secured her return, he was glad that she was gone. He needed to be alone, to ponder what this meant.

What was the cause of this extraordinary elation? This sense that she held the key to his destiny? He knew it had nothing to do with the hell of carnal attraction. How she looked or talked or behaved was immaterial to him. But God had sent her for a purpose. What was it?

He was turning away from the window when a flash of red on the pavement caught his eye. He forgot to breathe. It was the chimney sweep.

The creature stood on the other side of the road, openly watching the house. It had found time to shed its brushes, and scrub the soot from its evil little face – but its red hair was unmistakeable. And beside it loitered an associate: taller, thinner, with dark hair and sharp, malevolent features.

Slowly, as in a dream, the dark-haired urchin turned its head and looked Sinclair in the eye.

He gripped the curtain.

There could be only one interpretation of that look. The

red-haired imp had told his evil associate what he had witnessed on the roof. And now they meant to tell the world.

The street smelt of rain, wet horses and coal-dust as Madeleine descended the steps of the Reverend's elegant little town house and crossed the road to where Ben and Robbie were waiting on the pavement.

With twenty pounds in her reticule she ought to feel relieved. Instead she felt humiliated. And strangely bereft.

That photograph on the Reverend's desk was the face of her grandfather. She had known as soon as she'd seen it. The hawklike features. The angry, sunbleached eyes. Yesterday he had acquired a name. Today he had a face.

Lettice's words came back to her. *He doesn't want you. He never wanted you.*

She felt again the bewilderment, the ache of loss. She was back in the snow at the gates of the Forbidden Kingdom. The officer's eyes were glassy and cold as he turned his horse's head and rode away.

It was that memory of the Forbidden Kingdom which had prompted her to call on the Reverend Lawe under an assumed name. Because she remembered how it felt to have someone look at you with warmth, only to turn away when you spoke your name.

'So,' said Ben, cutting across her thoughts, 'the parson give you any dosh?'

She told him about the twenty pounds.

He whistled. 'Bugger me. That'll cost you.'

'I don't know what you mean,' she said coldly.

'Oh yeh? Course you do!'

'He wants me to go back tomorrow. To pray with him.'

He spluttered. ' "To pray"? I never heard it called that before.'

'It's not like that. It's perfectly proper.' So why this un-ease? This queasy sense of obligation?

' "Perfectly proper",' Ben quoted drily. Then his green eyes narrowed. 'You're not trying to do me out of my cut, are you?'

'For heaven's sake, Ben, he's a clergyman.'

'So are half the punters in Holywell Street.'

'Yes, well I won't be needing Holywell Street any more.'

He blinked, and she wondered if she'd hurt his feelings. After all, if she no longer needed Holywell Street, she no longer needed Ben Kelly.

They walked on in silence. Ahead of them, Robbie turned and stared at a chimney sweep's boy across the street, who had carroty hair, just like him.

Madeleine said, 'What's the matter, Ben?'

He shrugged. 'Nothing.'

'You were the one who said I should ask the family for help. Well. Now I have.'

'Oh yeh? But I bet you didn't tell him you *was* family.'

There was no answer to that. And she had been shocked by the ease with which she had deceived the clergyman. Of course, she'd had plenty of practice. She had been brought up to lie, and she knew that the best deceptions are the ones that stay closest to the truth. Thus Cousin Lettice had become 'Aunt Letitia', Madeleine Fynn became 'Madeleine Finlay', while Sophie remained her sister, and their parents still fell victim to childbirth and war. All she had done was fillet out any references to Falkirk, Durrant, Monroe and Jamaica.

Ben said, 'So when you going to tell him, then?'

'Tell him what?'

He threw her a look. 'That you're family. So to speak.'

What an instinct he had for the weak spot. 'Soon,' she said uncertainly.

'What does that mean?'

'Ben, please. I just want to get home.'

He turned his head and surveyed the street. 'So what's he like, the parson?'

She wondered how to reply. The first thing that had struck her about the Reverend Lawe was his beauty. His features were pale and narrow and severely well proportioned; the eyes an unblinking cobalt, the lips fine and very red beneath the clipped blond moustache. It was the face of a saint or a zealot or a madman.

Which, she told herself sternly, is absolute nonsense. The

poor man behaved with delicacy, courtesy and great generosity. What more could you possibly ask?

But she still didn't like him. The way his hand had trembled as he counted out the banknotes. And those meaningless little smiles. He was vain, too: she had noticed how his velvet smoking jacket exactly matched the colour of his eyes. And she had a sense that he might be a liar. Being one herself, she could usually tell.

'So what's he like?' Ben said again.

She frowned. 'He's – very correct. And rather secretive, I think.' She told him about the heavy damask curtains which had been closely drawn, even though it was still the early afternoon.

It was a strange room, the Reverend's study: tasteful and sumptuous, but curiously soulless. The gilt-framed watercolours, the Persian rugs, the dark-green morocco chairs were all too pristine and too precisely aligned, like a Household Furnishings display at Shoolbred's. The only thing with any personality was the photograph of the old man on the desk.

Ben was watching her narrowly, as if he guessed that she hadn't told him everything. 'So you'll not be needing me no longer,' he said.

'Of course I shall.'

He spat in the gutter. 'But you're going back there tomorrow.'

'I must. I gave my word.'

'Oh, well, in that case,' he said sarcastically.

They turned into the Portland Road. The pavement was busy with shoppers and afternoon callers, and she had to raise her voice above the noise. 'Will you and Robbie come in and see Sophie?'

He shook his head.

'Please. Just for a moment. I'll give you tea.'

He flicked her a cool glance, then called to his brother. 'Come on, Robbie. Time we was off.'

'Ben – come back. Don't go off in a mood.'

He glanced at her over his shoulder and melted into the crowd.

She told herself it didn't matter, but it did. She needed him. And Sophie needed him, too.

A few minutes later she turned into Wyndham Street, saw the doctor's carriage outside their house, and forgot about Ben. She picked up her skirts and ran. She met Dr Wray coming down the steps, his face grave.

'Is Sophie—' she panted.

'Not Sophie,' he said. 'Mrs Fynn.'

It had taken prayer and mortification, but at last Sinclair understood.

He understood his strange elation over Miss Finlay's illegitimacy. He understood why she alone among females held no terror for him; why he could even imagine touching her, when until now the mere thought had been repugnant. The answer was better than his wildest dreams.

And if any doubts remained, they were quashed by the final proof: the death of the shadowy guardian, the Aunt Letitia. So now Miss Finlay was quite, quite alone. She had no family left – except for the invalid sister, who didn't count. It was proof positive of God's design.

The aunt's funeral took place on an unseasonably cold Thursday afternoon, and, at Miss Finlay's request, Sinclair did not attend. She had said that she did not wish to trouble him, and he was happy to oblige. But when the day came he could not contain his impatience, and went to wait for her at the lych-gate outside the church.

As he had anticipated, she was the only mourner. He watched her black-veiled figure standing by the grave as the vicar rattled through the service. No doubt the old fool was anxious to be away, for after a fetid summer and a week of torrential rain, the churchyard stank. Sinclair himself held a handkerchief soaked in spirits of wine to his nose.

He watched her stoop for a clod of earth and toss it in. She looked down into the grave, her face inscrutable behind her veil. Then she turned and walked away. She took the path which skirted the churchyard, and which would soon bring her to him.

As he watched, he was distracted by a movement at her

back. Beneath the yews at the far end of the churchyard he spied the chimney sweep's evil copper head. And beside the chimney sweep stood the same dark, cadaverous urchin who had stared at him the other day.

Sinclair saw the secret knowledge in their vicious little faces – but this time he was not afraid. Slowly he took the handkerchief from his mouth and bestowed on them a cold and noble smile.

Yes, yes, he told them silently, stare all you wish. I know how to deal with you. I *shall* deal with you. You cannot threaten me now. God is on my side.

At that moment Miss Finlay raised her head and saw him, and quickened her step. He thought how overwhelmed she would be when he revealed his purpose.

How could she not be overwhelmed? The beauty of God's plan was breathtaking. How could he have doubted his Redeemer for an instant?

And yet he *had* doubted. During the long years of darkness he had believed himself polluted and unfit to mate. But he had been wrong. The Lord had given him a creature who, though she might appear pure, had been compromised *from birth*.

With such a creature he need feel no guilt – *for she had already sinned*. With such a creature he need fear no exposure – *for she had no kin*. It was perfection.

As she drew near, she put back her veil to reveal a pale face unmarked by tears.

He took her hand. 'This has been a great shock for you.'

'It was – rather sudden. The doctor didn't hold out any hope after the first seizure, but when the end came it was still a shock.'

Sinclair offered her his arm and they moved out into the street. 'You miss her.'

She thought about that. 'In a strange way I think I do. She was harsh and grim, but you knew where you were with Aunt Letitia.'

They walked on in silence. Then he said, 'Allow me to offer you a moment of prayer before you return home. If you will accompany me to my—'

'You are very kind, but I can't. My sister is alone.'

He repressed a movement of impatience. 'My house is but two steps away. And I have something particular to impart.'

That caught her attention, as he had known it would.

He waited until they were settled in his study, and the tea had been brought and Mary sent away. 'Miss Finlay,' he said. 'It has been – what, eleven days since you first sought my guidance.'

She looked at him with solemn dark eyes.

'And during that time we have prayed together, and I have provided such modest assistance as lies within my power.' He paused to let her recall what that 'modest assistance' amounted to: the initial twenty pounds from the fictitious charity, a further fifteen while the aunt breathed her last, and a rather generous twelve guineas to cover a headstone.

'Mr Lawe,' she said in a low voice, 'I do of course appreciate—'

'No, no' – he held up his hand – 'you misunderstand. It was not my intention to solicit your thanks. I was merely referring to the manner in which our acquaintance has developed.' He leaned back in his chair and passed a hand over his mouth. 'May I speak plainly?'

She nodded, frowning a little, as if unsure whether she would like what was to come. But she would. How could she not?

'With the passing of your aunt,' he went on, 'I believe I am correct in saying that you – and your unfortunate sister – are entirely alone.'

The slightest of nods.

'Until now, I have been loth to tell you something about my own circumstances, for fear of deepening your despondency at this difficult time. But I must now inform you that I intend shortly to take up a living in Jamaica.'

He was gratified to see her face drain of blood.

'I am however troubled', he went on, 'by the thought of what will become of you. You understand that the proprieties would forbid me from continuing to assist you after I have left these shores.' He waited for her to agree, but she made no comment.

'I have prayed for guidance,' he added, 'and the All-perfect has vouchsafed it to me. I believe you will find the symmetry quite beautiful.'

'The – symmetry? I'm afraid I don't understand.'

He smiled. 'Permit me to continue without interruption.'

'I'm sorry.'

He was silent for a moment. 'You will forgive me for raising a painful subject, but remember that I have nothing but your best interests at heart.' Again he paused. 'You have only provided the barest particulars of your unfortunate parentage – and, please, I would not have it otherwise. But we cannot deny that you were begotten in godlessness.'

She coloured.

'Consider then the perfect *circularity* of a scheme whereby the godless one begets the godly.' He waited for her to respond, but she merely looked puzzled.

'I have found a way for you to be redeemed. You shall become my helpmeet.'

'Your helpmeet. I'm sorry, I still don't—'

He silenced her with a glance. 'Understand that I do not make this offer for personal gratification, but for the glory of the Maker. That we may serve together beneath His standard, you and I.'

'You – you want me to go to Jamaica and help in your missionary work?'

He met her eyes. 'Not precisely. It is true that you shall assist me in my work. But you shall do more than that. You shall *be* more than that. You shall be my companion. My fellow labourer.'

'Your fellow—'

'My wife.'

CHAPTER TWELVE

'He wants *what*?' demanded Ben.

He was crouching on the basement steps, watching Madeleine watering Lettice's ferns. 'Oh, *Madlin*. You're never taken in by that!'

'Ben—'

'Give him a bit of snug and he'll make it all right after? That's the oldest trick in the book.'

Madeleine put down the watering can and kneaded her temples. She hadn't slept all night. Her face felt rigid with fatigue, and she was absurdly close to tears. 'It's not a trick,' she muttered.

'Course it's a trick. Think about it. If you say yes, he gets it for nothing. And you—'

'– and Sophie goes to Jamaica,' she snapped, 'where there's sunshine and sea air and a sanatorium up in the mountains.'

'How d'you know all that?'

'He told me.'

'Oh, well,' he sneered, 'then it's got to be true.'

There was an angry silence between them.

Ben took off his cap and furiously scratched his head. 'What's his game, that parson? Toff like him, with a sodding great house in Fitzroy Square. He could marry anyone he wants. So who's he go and ask? A bastard with no money. You tell me how that makes sense.'

She couldn't. As always, he had put his finger on the weak spot. Her only explanation was that the clergyman had developed some sort of regard for her. Which didn't seem very likely.

A gust of wind overturned one of the ferns, and she stooped to right it. It was an ungainly little maidenhair which reminded her of Lettice. That made her feel worse.

'Course,' said Ben, 'soon as he knows who you really are, he'll run a mile.'

She pushed a strand of hair behind her ear and straightened up. 'He won't find out,' she said, 'unless I tell him.'

Ben opened his mouth, then shut it again. 'Bugger me. You're not going to tell him.'

She did not reply.

'Madlin, don't be daft. You'd be play-acting for the rest of your life.'

'And Sophie would stand a chance of growing up.'

'You'd never bring it off.'

'I might.'

'Lying every day? To a sodding parson?'

He was right. What was she thinking of? To deceive an innocent young churchman into wedding the bastard offshoot of his own adoptive family? It was unthinkable. Unconscionable.

But she *was* unconscionable. She knew that already. She had posed for those photographs, hadn't she? What was the difference between that and marrying for money? In the end it all came down to the same thing. Two dogs mating in the gutter. The rest was lies.

Ben got to his feet and put a grimy hand on the railing. 'You'll never do it. You won't. Will you?' For a moment he looked very young, and it occurred to her that if she went through with it he would be alone again, with no-one but Robbie.

She said, 'He's given me until the day after tomorrow to decide—'

'*Given? Given?* Listen to yourself, girl! If you marry him it'll be like that for ever!'

'My God, I do know that!' she burst out. 'But if I don't, what happens to Sophie?'

They stood glaring at one another, while the wind overturned another fern and rolled it across the tiles.

Ben jammed on his cap. 'I got to go,' he muttered.

'Come back tomorrow. I need you to help me decide.'

'Maybe.'

'Promise.'

He shrugged. 'See what I can do.'

When he'd gone, she went into the kitchen and sat down at the table and pressed her hands to her mouth. She longed for Lettice. Not the mute, beseeching invalid of the final hours, but the grim, godly, utterly dependable little martinet who had brought her up.

'Where's Ben?' asked Sophie, when Madeleine took in her milk jelly.

'He had to go. But he's coming back tomorrow.' She cleared a space on the bed and sat down. The counterpane was littered with apple cores, the *Gentlewoman's Magazine*, and *The Children of the New Forest* – the ban on reading having lasted exactly three days. Pablo Grey lay across it, wearing Lettice's old mourning locket on a ribbon round his neck.

On the final night of Lettice's life, Sophie had been allowed into the sickroom to say goodbye. She had asked if Lettice was afraid of dying, and Lettice, too ill to speak, had shaken her head. In case that wasn't quite true, Sophie had left the donkey with her for support.

Had that final act of grace been enough to redeem a life lived without love?

Madeleine felt the sting of tears. Why was everything so mixed up?

Sophie licked her spoon. 'Maddy, are you all right?'

Madeleine shook her head. She longed to tell her sister everything. But she had always protected her from the facts about their parents: it was the one thing on which she and Lettice had agreed.

If she married the Reverend Lawe, that pretence would increase tenfold. *If* she married him.

She found herself hoping fiercely that Ben would come tomorrow. She needed his sharpness, and his flat-on view of the world, to help her decide.

*　　*　　*

It's three in the morning and Ben's just woken up, and for a bit he don't remember nothing, and everything's fine. Then it all comes back in a rush and he wants to die.

He's stiff from sleeping behind the chimney stack, and he's all hollowed out like he's made of glass; like he'd shatter if you touched him. If only he could do that, just shatter and not be there any more, just be dead.

He grinds his knuckles in his eyes, but he can't stop seeing it. Over and over, all the little details.

It was yesterday – only yesterday? Day after he had that row with Madeleine down in the basement. Him and Robbie are round the Garden, clicking a bit of breakfast: couple of greengages, Robbie loves them – and now they're heading off to Madeleine's, just like he said he would.

So they've just cut across Hanway Place when Ben sees Constable Hatch standing on the pavement. He's got his hands on his hips and he's looking about slowly, like he means business. Then he spots Robbie – *Robbie* – and he blows his whistle and shouts, 'Stop thief!' And Robbie's going, 'What? What?' and Ben's thinking, Christ, this is the only time we *ain't* done a bloody click.

So off they go, him and Robbie, up the alley without a word between them. Not a word. Not then, not after. He thinks about that a lot.

So they're up the drainpipes and over the roofs, and Ben's not a bit worried. It's one of his best routes; Hatch hasn't got a chance.

But Hatch won't leave off. He's tracking them on the ground, and he's got two other bluebottles with him, and that's never happened before. And Ben thinks, whatever it was I clicked, it must of been big.

It's tricky on them roofs, and he steps on a loose tile and nearly goes over, shit that was close, and it's all of forty feet down. He calls to Robbie to watch that tile, and there's no answer, so he looks over his shoulder, and Robbie's not there. Stupid little bugger must of taken a wrong turn. He's always doing that. So Ben goes back for him, but he can't find him nowhere. Then he looks over the edge and sees this little crowd on the pavement – and he still don't understand;

it's like he's stupid or something. Then Hatch pushes back the crowd, and that's when Ben sees what's on the ground.

He has to shove his fist in his mouth to keep from yelling out. It's like he's a bird swooping down, he sees it so close and sharp. Robbie's on his back, all twisted like a doll. Dog sticking out of his pocket. Pool of blood round his head. It must be blood, but it's nearly black, and there's these greasy grey splashes all round about.

Robbie's eyes are open, and he's staring up at Ben. *You should of sung out sooner about that tile, Ben. Why didn't you sing out sooner?*

Constable Hatch is looking up at the roof to see where Robbie fell, so Ben edges back. He don't know how long he stays there, fist still in his mouth, but when he looks again, Robbie's gone. Crowd's gone too, and so is Constable Hatch. And someone's sluiced down the pavement, and a costermonger's set up his barrow there, flogging cabbages past their best at a farthing a piece.

All day long Ben stays on the roof, and when it's dark he goes back to Shelton Street. He shouldn't go back, cos Hatch will be watching the streets. But he's got to see it one last time.

On the bed there's Robbie's place, all hollowed out in the straw. And that's when Ben nearly cracks. He's got to get out of there fast.

So he's up on the roof again and this time he heads off east. He keeps going for hours, he just keeps going. And down below he hears the crowds on the doss, shuffling along: nowhere to go, coppers flashing lanterns in their eyes, move along now, no malingering. And he thinks, that's you now, Ben, you're on the doss. Can't get any lower than that unless you're dead.

By now he's come so far east that he don't know the roofs, and all the best spots are already taken. But at last he finds an empty one behind a chimney stack. Soon as he curls up, he feels it rising up inside him: clawing at his gullet, fighting to get out. He shoves it down again, right down deep where it can't get out, till it's just this ache in his chest that he'll never let loose.

He did that when Ma died, and Lily, and Ryan and Kate. And now he's doing it with Robbie. And Robbie's the last of them.

You'll never go through this again, Ben Kelly, he tells hisself. You can't, can you? Cos there's nobody left.

He don't remember falling asleep, but the moon wakes him up and it's three o'clock by the church bells, and he's looking down into this stinking little yard with a water butt and a coalshed and a hut. It reminds him of back home in Shelton Street, and his throat goes all tight.

He can't go on without Robbie. He wants to die.

But you can't, says this voice inside his head. If you top yourself now, who's going to find out where they took Robbie, and make sure he don't get shoved in a pauper's grave without Dog? You got to fix that, Ben. And after that we'll see.

Then he thinks, hang about, there's more. It was that parson as put the coppers onto you. You got to fix him too.

Soon as he thinks it, he knows it's true. He can see just how it went. There's this nobby young parson in his big nobby house in Fitzroy Square, and everything's going along nice and sweet. So one day he asks Madeleine to marry him, and he thinks she'll just fall at his feet. But what's she do? She says she wants time to consider. Nasty shock, that. Nasty. So the parson gets to thinking, and he thinks, ay ay, maybe them two lads I seen in the churchyard been putting ideas in her head. I seen them before, outside my house, and I didn't like the look of them, and I don't now. So I think I'll do for them, I will.

And being a nob, it's easy to fix it with the bluebottles, and that.

The only thing Ben can't understand is why the parson put Hatch onto Robbie instead of him. Cos that's what happened, he's sure of it. When Hatch blew that whistle and shouted Stop thief, he was looking at Robbie.

But why? Robbie never done nothing to the parson. Robbie never done nothing to nobody. He wouldn't know how.

Ben's eyes are hot again, and he stabs them with his

knuckles. Shut it, Ben. Just shut it. You know what you got to do.

First you got to find Robbie and get him settled with Dog. Then you got to see about the parson.

At nine o'clock on Saturday morning, a knock at the door announced the Reverend's manservant, come to collect Madeleine's answer.

She didn't have one. She had fallen asleep fully dressed, and dreamed she was at her wedding. Ben was waiting to give her away, and she was walking up the aisle in her underclothes, and everyone was pointing.

Blearily she told the Reverend's man to wait in the kitchen, and went upstairs to the morning-room – where, among Lettice's few remaining possessions, there was a fountain pen and a sheaf of writing paper.

There was still no sign of Ben. She had waited the whole of the previous day, but he had never arrived. Perhaps he was in some sort of trouble. Perhaps he had given up on her.

It was an overcast October day, and the morning-room was dark when she went in. With the furniture gone, there was nowhere to sit but the window seat, where she had placed Lettice's Bible, her prayer book and her writing-case.

She set up the writing-case on her lap and took out Lettice's fountain pen and a sheet of paper. *Dear Mr Lawe,* she wrote.

She put down the pen. Yes or no? She still didn't know. She didn't *know*.

If she said no, she would be back where she started: wondering where to find the rent, with winter looming and Sophie getting worse by the day. If she said yes, her money worries were over.

And that's what it comes down to, she told herself. Money. It's got nothing to do with deceiving the Reverend. It's got nothing to do with that family in Jamaica that doesn't want you. It's all about money.

In a strange way that made her feel a little better. But she still didn't know what to do.

She picked up the Bible. How many times during her childhood had she longed for it to go missing, so that she wouldn't have to sit through another interminable reading? Well, now let it do its job. Let God decide. She shut her eyes, opened it at random, and put her finger on a verse.

And call upon me in the day of trouble: I will deliver thee and thou shalt glorify me.

That was so apt it was frightening. She tried again.

And the sons of Helah were Zereth, and Jezoar, and Ethnan.

She willed the words to mean something. They did not.

Down in the kitchen, the Reverend's manservant gave a polite, admonitory cough. The Reverend had stressed his desire for a prompt response.

One last try.

This shall be the law of the leper in the day of his cleansing: He shall be brought unto the priest.

She pushed the Bible away as if it were alive.

Outside, the clouds parted. Sunlight blazed through Lettice's stained-glass window. Madeleine glanced at the ruby parrots skimming the emerald jungle beside the sapphire sea. She hated that window just as fervently as Sophie adored it. Sophie called it 'the Jamaica window': she was always giving the parrots names, and trying to find out which exact species they belonged to in *Birds of the World*.

But to Madeleine that window simply meant the family that didn't want them. And the officer who had left her in the snow.

Another cough from the kitchen, this time slightly less polite.

She picked up Lettice's prayer book. Please God, she thought, what should I do?

A letter slipped from between the pages and fell to the parquet at her feet.

It was old, and had been unfolded and refolded so many times that it only just hung together at the edges. The handwriting was large, sprawling, and hard to read, but the signature was clear. *Cameron Lawe.*

Madeleine felt a coldness in the pit of her stomach. She had once asked the Reverend if he had any siblings. 'Only a brother,' he had said with a tightening of the lips. 'It pains me to speak of him. For I am a man of God, but Cameron is a man of violence. He has always been coarse and intemperate, so perhaps it should have come as no surprise when he was discharged from the Service – for a crime too shameful to repeat.' Madeleine had pictured a gambler and a rake: the sort of black sheep who could make a clergyman blanch.

And here was that same Cameron Lawe writing to *Lettice*. Lettice, whom his own brother didn't know.

She wondered why Lettice had kept it all these years: a short note from a disgraced ex-soldier. But Lettice had always admired soldiers. Perhaps she had possessed a hidden streak of romanticism.

The letter was dated December 1886, and it began bluntly and without preamble. *Dear Mrs Fynn, I was surprised to receive your letter – not least because until now I didn't know that I had a cousin in England. But you are right to apply to me: better that than to have written to Jocelyn. As you know, he took the death of his son hard – although you'll appreciate that he would never admit that, even to himself.*

Why not? thought Madeleine angrily. Why shouldn't he admit it? The death of his only son? My God, what sort of family is this?

As you are also aware, Jocelyn wants nothing to do with Ainsley's progeny. Neither do I. But from what you tell me, your expenses are great, so I feel it my duty to contribute what I can. My attorneys will contact you shortly, with a view to amplifying the trust which Jocelyn set up two years ago. I would simply ask that you do not mention this to him, as I see no point in causing him further distress. Yours etc . . .

Clouds covered the sun, and the Jamaica window dimmed. Madeleine sat in the empty room with the letter in her hand.

It was hastily written, and blunt to the point of discourtesy. And Cameron Lawe's distaste for 'Ainsley's progeny' showed in every line. Like her grandfather, he had been only too ready to pay money in order to sweep the inconvenient bastards under the carpet. And like her grandfather, he had thereafter washed his hands of them. What did he care if the trust was emptied by an unscrupulous guardian? What was that to him?

Down in the street, the milkman's pony paused from long habit outside their door, and waited in vain for Sophie to run down the steps with a carrot.

Madeleine crumpled the letter and threw it across the room. She took a fresh sheet of writing paper, and Lettice's fountain pen. *Dear Mr Lawe,* she wrote. *I accept your offer. Yours, Madeleine Finlay.*

PART THREE

CHAPTER THIRTEEN

Jamaica, March 1895 – five months later

Cameron is back in his cell at Millbank prison.

It's the first day of his sentence. He's lying on the planks in the cold and the stink, and the ceiling is pressing down on him and the black sand is blowing in from the desert, and somewhere down a distant corridor a child is crying. Black sand stops his mouth and sugars his eyes. He can't see. Can't find what he's looking for. Doesn't know what it is. And all he can hear is that black sand hissing, and that lost child crying in the dark.

He took a shuddering breath and woke up.

It was dawn. He was lying in his own bed on the verandah at Eden. The sky showed a cool, fresh blue through the hole in the roof. He breathed in, and smelled the metallic sweetness of wet red earth.

He lay listening to the musical ring-ring of the river-frogs, and the buzz of the crickets, and the sugarbirds and grass-quits squabbling in the tree-ferns near the house. Usually this was his favourite time, when he was at his most optimistic, and all things seemed possible. But the dream had left an aftertaste of longing and regret that he couldn't shake off.

He wondered why he'd had it again. It only came when things went wrong. When croptime was late, or there was a fire in the boiling-house. What was it this time? Was it because Sinclair was back in Jamaica? Or was it simply that

Eden was haunted – and, as he'd once heard a cane-cutter say, you can't make peace with ghosts.

He heard the click of claws across the tiles, then felt a blast of hot breath on his shoulder, and Abigail's rasping tongue. She climbed on top of him, he pushed her off, and she clattered away to chase ground doves in the garden.

He rolled onto his side and wrapped the pillow round his head. He was almost as exhausted as when he'd dropped onto the mattress five hours before. For the past three months he'd been racing to get in the cane before the rains made the tracks impassable, and now it was piled high in the works yard, and the mill and the boiling-house were running day and night, and he and his men were red-eyed with fatigue.

A few minutes later, Abigail was back to complete the wake-up ritual. Again she clambered on top of him, and when he could no longer breathe – for she was big even for a mastiff – he pushed her off and sat up.

He pulled on his nightshirt, grabbed the old sheet he used for a towel, and made his way down the steps and through the dripping garden to the river. Abigail bounded ahead of him, startling a flock of white egrets out of the giant bamboo and making the emerald plumes nod and scatter raindrops.

The river was green and opaque and stingingly cool when he dived in. He trod water, and watched Abigail bend one stocky foreleg to drink. Moses was leading the horses down from the stables, with a trio of pickneys skipping behind him in the hopes of a ride. Cameron was dismayed to find that he could take no pleasure in any of it. Again that strange, indefinable sense of loss.

He had bought Eden to make his peace with Ainsley's ghost, but it hadn't worked out that way. Perhaps the blacks were right: perhaps duppies are angry creatures – to be fled, and not appeased.

But he couldn't leave Eden now. He had fallen in love with her. She was beautiful, dangerous and infuriating: a chaotic and wayward nymph. Sometimes, in his black moods, he would ask himself what he was doing here. Why didn't he just give up and let her slip back into the wilderness of sweet-woods and guango trees where she'd been dreaming away two decades of oblivion before he found her? But in the end he always stayed.

Abigail's impatient bark dragged him back to the present. God, why couldn't he shake off that dream?

Back at the house he shaved, flung on clothes, and forced down a plate of ackee and saltfish, which his cook served every morning in the mistaken belief that he liked it. In fact he hated it, for it reminded him of prison, but it was too late to tell old Braverly now. He was as sensitive as a girl about his cooking, and it would only send him off on a ganja-fuelled spree that would land him in Falmouth jail. So Cameron gritted his teeth and ate his saltfish.

After breakfast he left Abigail to guard the house, and rode to Maputah, where Oserius had been supervising the works overnight. He stayed all morning, and dealt with a build-up of trash outside the mill, a broken hogshead in the curing-house, and a fight between warring boilermen.

As the morning slipped away, his frustration deepened. It wouldn't take years to haul Eden into the present: it would take decades. The mill was still powered by the centuries-old aqueduct from the Martha Brae, and completely at the mercy of the weather. Oxen still toiled with agonizing slowness to bring in the cane. Who was he deceiving? Over at Parnassus, old Addison Traherne had laid down a tramway *twenty-five years* before. Even the works at Fever Hill had long since converted to steam.

At midday he returned to the house for a hasty meal of curried goat, then rode over to the western cane-pieces to defuse a row between rival cutting gangs. In the heat of the afternoon, when the rain was a distant memory and the land a parched and dusty red, he rode the eight miles north to Falmouth. He hated going to town, but he'd learned that if he went when it was hot, he rarely encountered anyone he knew.

At Ryle's he ordered kerosene and candles, at Doran's a crate of Scotch and a box of cigars, and then settled his accounts at the saddler's and the farrier's. Finally he decided to make a quick call on Olivia Herapath. She usually helped to put things in perspective.

The 'Closed' sign was up on the studio door, but Etheline let him in and showed him through to the salon at the back. The little room was dim and fugged with tobacco smoke, and littered with yellow-backed novels. Olivia must be having one of her bad days. He decided to stay for as long as it took to lift her mood.

She was on the sofa, manifesting as one of her more alarming past lives: a terrifying old obeah-woman named Juba, who wore a strident blue and orange print robe, a blistering yellow handkerchief, and a tangle of cats' teeth and parrot beaks across her formidable bosom. The contrast between such vivid Negro splendour and Olivia's pasty white face was oddly affecting.

She did not look well. He noticed that the black silk mantle which festooned Hector's photograph had been shakily re-arranged, and that her sharp little eyes were rimmed with red. But the glance which she flung at him outlawed pity.

He asked if she meant to put a spell on him, and she smacked him on the chest with her obeah-stick and scolded him for staying away so long. 'You're on your own far too much up there,' she declared, checking him over as if he were a stallion she was thinking of buying. 'Young fellow like you. Deplorable state of affairs. Simply won't do.'

Cameron gave her a slight smile and moved a copy of *The Heathen Heart* to make room beside her.

'You ought to go out into Society,' she insisted. 'People would accept you with open arms if you gave 'em half a chance.'

'I'm not—'

'They don't care what you did ten years ago. Heavens, man, this is Jamaica!'

'I'm aware of that.'

'Cricket. Bridge. The odd concert. Wouldn't kill you, would it? What on earth's stopping you?'

'I don't know,' he said with perfect truth.

'Well find out. You're becoming just like Jocelyn. Though I know *that's* a forbidden topic. In any event, you should call on me more often. And don't look like that, you know I'm right.'

'Olivia, you're always right.'

She gave a fruity laugh. 'Don't humour me, you wretch.' She poured him a large glass of claret and indicated the humidor on the side table. She herself was smoking Juba's villainously smelly white clay pipe.

'So,' she said after they had both lit up.

'So,' he said. 'Tell me all the gossip.'

She threw him a jaundiced look. She knew very well that he had none of her passion for gossip, but that wasn't the point. The point was, he must do penance for his neglect. So for the next twenty minutes he did, and she made him laugh despite himself. She was shrewd and coarse as only an aristocrat can be, and she knew 'everyone who mattered'. Small wonder that she terrorized every Society matron from Lucea to St Ann's Bay – and that they flocked to her. For where else could they have their photographs taken and their friends dissected by a genuine noblewoman – even if she had dropped her title on marrying a commoner?

'I've been wondering', she said at last, 'how long you think you're going to get away with it.'

'With what?'

'With never mentioning your brother.'

Cameron's heart sank.

'Heaven help us, Cameron, he's been back for nearly four months!'

'So I've heard.'

'And he's acquired a wife.'

'I've heard that too.'

She studied him narrowly. 'You're going to have to do something, you know.'

'What do you suggest?'

With her stick she rapped him on the knee. 'You're going to have to come down out of those hills and *marry* someone.'

'Olivia—'

'That brother of yours means to give the old man a grandson. Adoptive grandson. Whatever that's called. Anyway, he means to cut you out.'

Cameron made no reply.

'Well?' she said. 'Have you seen them yet?'

'Have I seen whom?'

'Cameron, behave. Have you seen your brother and his new wife?'

'You know I haven't. I don't see any of them. Ever.'

She snorted. 'Well, *I've* seen them. Someone had to do it. I left my card on her the morning they arrived.' She bared her small yellow teeth in a grin. 'Sinclair doesn't care for me at all, but he dared not send his regrets. He's such a snob.'

Which, thought Cameron in amusement, was a little rich coming from Olivia Herapath, née the Honourable Olivia Fortescue of Fortescue Hall, who regarded anyone ennobled after Crécy as a parvenu. Sometimes he wondered why she made an exception for him.

There was a pregnant pause while Olivia disentangled her mourning pendant from the parrot beaks and waited for him to speak.

At last he gave in. 'So,' he said. 'What do you think of my new sister-in-law?'

Her eyes glittered. 'Now *there's* a puzzle. Damned good lines, and a tolerable taste in dress – but *no accomplishments*! No French, no German, no music. Can't even ride. Although I hear that Jocelyn's been giving her lessons. But it's frightfully *odd*, don't you think? One wonders where Sinclair found her. And the most provoking thing of all is that she's far too good for him.'

Cameron was surprised. 'You mean you like her?'

'I know, isn't it singular?' She paused to draw on her pipe. 'For one thing, she knows her photography. Oh, yes. She's set up a darkroom in the undercroft – she says it's such a shadowy house that she might as well. Although who knows, perhaps it's a means of getting away from Sinclair.' Another puff. 'Of course, *he* doesn't approve at all, but what can he do, when she buys her supplies from a baron's daughter?' She shook her head. 'Damned intriguing. Can't make her out. Perceptive. Fearfully reserved. Bit of a temper. Prodigiously attached to some sort of invalid sister – whom

148

I haven't yet met. And d'you know, I rather fancy that she's *kind*.' She snorted. 'So not at all like me!'

Cameron maintained a diplomatic silence.

'I cannot imagine why she married him,' she added, 'except of course for the obvious, I suppose.'

'You mean money?'

She inclined her head at the ways of the world.

'Well then,' he got to his feet and picked up his hat, 'it seems he's got what he deserves.'

Usually, seeing Olivia Herapath lifted his spirits, but as he rode out of Falmouth he felt only irritation and an odd sense of betrayal. Olivia was *his* friend, dammit. Why did she have to approve of Sinclair's wife?

He was telling himself not to be so childish when he reached the crossroads over the Martha Brae and turned south for Eden. The heat was intense, for it was still too early in the afternoon for the land breeze, so he kept to the shade beneath the poinciana trees.

He had not gone far when he heard the rattle of wheels behind him, and turned to see a smart new trap crossing the bridge and heading west along the Fever Hill Road.

Sinclair wore a white linen suit and a panama hat – no churchman's black for him – and he drove briskly, staring straight ahead. The young woman at his side wore an all-enveloping dust-coat of russet silk, and a wide straw hat with fluttering bronze ribbons. She was gripping the side of the pony-trap, and, like Sinclair, staring straight ahead without expression. Neither of them saw Cameron.

He only caught a glimpse of the girl as they swept past, but it was a shock. He had imagined any wife of Sinclair's to be slight and blond, with a little pinched mouth for murmuring psalms. This girl had a chignon of rich dark hair, an olive flush to her cheek, and an extravagantly curved red mouth. She would have made a splendid model for Rossetti or Burne-Jones.

It was an unpleasant surprise to find himself admiring his brother's choice. Despite the heat, he kicked his horse to a canter.

As evening came on, his mood steadily darkened. He spent

two hours at Maputah snapping at everyone, then returned to the house for a stiff rum and water and one of Braverly's least successful dinners. The old man's pepperpot was legendary – it had reputedly been simmering for two generations – but tonight his eyes were yellow and wandering after too much ganja tea, and the pepperpot consisted of peppers and very little else.

Still hungry, Cameron went down into the garden and picked a couple of mangoes, and washed them down with another rum and water. Abigail heaved herself off the verandah and followed him.

The night was loud with crac-cracs and croaker lizards and the occasional hoot of an owl. Fireflies spangled the hibiscus, and the air was heavy with the scent of datura and star jasmine. Cameron hardly noticed.

Whenever he thought of his brother it was with a sense of irritation and defeat. Sinclair hated him. Cameron had given up wondering why when they were still at Winchester.

But now Sinclair was back in Jamaica. He was living with Jocelyn at Fever Hill, and driving his handsome young wife about the countryside. He had everything a man could want. He had someone to talk to, to share things with, to work for.

Next to that, what had he, Cameron, achieved in eight years at Eden? What was the point of all his efforts? Who was he doing this *for*?

You're drunk, he told himself in disgust. Just another drunken planter going native out in the bush. It's time for bed.

He turned to go back to the house, and was startled to see that he was not alone. Grace McFarlane stood at the foot of the steps, watching him. Her skirts were still hitched to the knees from the long walk up from Eden, and her children were hiding shyly behind her.

It was a shock to see her again. He wasn't sure if he was glad or not.

Abigail, who tolerated Grace as an erstwhile part of the household, trotted over to welcome her, tail lazily swinging. The children reached out to stroke her ears, and she nosed them as if they were puppies.

'Hello, Grace,' said Cameron.

He caught the brilliance of her smile as she inclined her head in greeting. 'Mas' Camron,' she said. 'Lang time me nuh see you.'

'A long time,' he agreed.

He was not in love with Grace, nor she with him. They had settled that years ago. But they understood each other. Both lived alone and were not at peace, and from time to time they still fulfilled a mutual need for warmth.

But these days she only made the journey from Fever Hill when it suited her: when she was looking for birds' eggs, or visiting one of her countless relations in the hills. He pictured her striding barefoot along the moonlit track: tall, uncompromising and completely unafraid. She was one of the few black people in Trelawny who could walk the Cockpits at night without fear of duppies. And he reflected that Olivia Herapath still had some way to go before she perfected the look of the true obeah-woman – who must be discreet in her attire, since magic was now a flogging offence.

He watched the children becoming more daring with Abigail, who wagged her tail and took their small limbs in her enormous jaws, and finally allowed herself to be chased away through the tree-ferns.

When they were gone, he turned back to their mother. 'How have you been, Grace?'

She tilted her head in a gesture that could have meant anything, and her slanted eyes were full of secrets. 'An you, soldierman? What I hear, you in one a your *black* moods tonight. Not so? Tell Grace why you get vex.'

He made no reply.

She came closer. 'You don' glad you breddah back.' A statement, not a question.

He studied the strong planes of her face. The broad cheekbones, the flaring nostrils, the generous, well-shaped mouth. He thought what a shame it was that he was too dog-tired to do anything about it. A shame for her too, if she'd come all this way with any such hopes.

'You don' glad Mas' Sinclair back,' she said again.

'Glad?' he said. 'What to glad fe, girl?'

She grinned. She liked it when he spoke *patois*. 'Preacher-man fixing to cut you out de fambly.'

'I don't care about that.'

'Hn. I care.'

'Well you shouldn't. I don't have any right to Fever Hill, and neither does Sinclair. It belongs to the Monroes. Not to the Lawes.'

She cocked her head. 'Maybe so. But preacher-man not only ting troubling you. Eh, soldierman?'

No hiding from Grace, not even in the dark. Especially not in the dark.

She drew her finger down his cheek. 'Walk a while. Reason wid I.'

He shook his head. 'I'd be poor company tonight.'

She took the hint and gave him a crooked smile. 'It don' mind. You wait. Preacher-man reckon wid
out Gracie McFarlane. She fix it so he get no boy-child.'

'Grace,' he said sharply. 'Don't go touching him.'

The smile widened to a grin. 'Oh, I don' need fe go *touching* him, soldierman. Don' trouble yourself about dat.'

'That's not what I meant . . .'

But she had gone, melting into the darkness and calling to Evie and Victory as she went.

He stayed in the garden, smoking and thinking, until Abigail's impatient bark reminded him that it was time for bed.

Back on the verandah he poured himself another drink and scowled at it. On the campaign chest beside his bed was a pile of books. On most nights he read a few pages, but tonight he couldn't concentrate. He kept seeing Sinclair in the pony-trap with his pretty young wife.

With a muttered curse he threw the book aside and turned down the lamp.

You're being ridiculous, he told himself. This is *Sinclair*. You wouldn't *want* the sort of woman who'd marry him.

That was the most agreeable thought he'd had all day.

Chapter Fourteen

The Seventh of March, Eighteen Ninety-Five
The West Gallery, Fever Hill Great House
Parish of Trelawny
Jamaica
The West Indies

Maddy has given me this BEAUTIFUL writing-book for my birthday, so I am starting a Journal. I intend to discover:

1) *Everything about Jamaican magic;*
2) *What is troubling Maddy; and*
3) *What Sinclair's wicked brother actually did.*

Dr Pritchard came today and is DELIGHTED with my progress! But he reminded me that staying in bed on the voyage greatly benefited my knee, so I must be patient. (I am glad the voyage did <u>some</u> good, for it was truly horrible and I ran out of books.)

I ADORE Jamaica. It has sugar-cane, magic and alligators, and instead of pigeons they have vultures called john crows. Everything here comes from another country: the mango and banana trees were brought over in olden times, and so were the coffee bushes, the breadfruit, the sugar-cane, the bamboo and the black people. It is exceedingly hot, and there is no rain, for it is the dry season; but there is a sea breeze in the morning and a land breeze at night, which keeps us tolerably cool.

Terrible things have happened in Jamaica, but no-one mentions them, or clears away the mess. At the bottom of the hill on which we live there is a ruined sugar-mill which the slaves burnt sixty years ago in the Christmas Rebellion. They also burnt the original great house (that is Jamaican for mansion), and the Lawe great house on the other side of Falmouth, which is now a sanatorium called Burntwood. Sinclair says that hundreds of estates have since been sold or abandoned. He blames it on when they freed the slaves, which he says was a great mistake.

I don't think Maddy cares for Jamaica. Or perhaps it is just Fever Hill that she doesn't like. I ADORE Fever Hill. Sometimes it smells of rum from the New Works, and always of orange peel from the floor polish, and everything about it is strange. The slates on the roof were originally ballast brought over from Cornwall in the sugar boats; the great pots by the steps are the boilers they used in the olden days for extracting the sugar; and even the cement in the under-croft walls contains molasses!

There is no gaslight, only kerosene lamps and candles, and as it is so very shut in, the house is dark and mysterious even in daytime. The walls are wooden, with slats to let through the breeze, so one can absolutely hear what is said three rooms away. Maddy calls it a House of Whispers.

When we first arrived, she was dismayed to learn that we wouldn't have our own house, but would live here with the family. It is hard for her, as she is only allowed to go for walks at night, for Great-Aunt May disapproves of ladies going out during the day, which they never did when she was a girl. My new friend Evie says that elsewhere things are different now. So does the gazetteer which Maddy bought me in London. It says that in Jamaica, white ladies go about unaccompanied at all times, and it is perfectly safe and respectable. What a shame for Maddy! She says the darkness and confinement are what turned Clemency mad.

Occasionally, however, Maddy does get permission to

visit Mrs Herapath during the day, and yesterday Sinclair took her to see the sanatorium at Burntwood. When she came back, she told me that I won't be going there under ANY circumstances, as it is a pulmonary hospital.

That is a great relief, because my room here is PERFECTION. Actually my _real_ room is just for clothes, I mean the gallery outside it where I live!! A gallery is Jamaican for a verandah which is enclosed by louvres to keep out the sun. This makes it shadowy and hard to see out, but luckily for me, three of the louvres in front of my bed are broken! To begin with, the croton hedge blocked the view, but Maddy cut away some branches with a fruit knife. Her maid Jessie told on her to Great-Aunt May, who was vexed, and so was Sinclair.

My part of the gallery has _my own steps_ down into the garden!!! But of course I mayn't use them yet, and the doors are kept shut to keep out the sun.

Fever Hill was once the greatest estate on the Northside, but now most of the cane-fields are let to the Trahernes, or are left in ruinate. Sinclair says that Uncle Jocelyn has allowed the estate to slide, because he has lost heart. I _believe_ that is because of Sinclair's wicked brother, but no-one will talk of him.

Maddy says she doesn't care to know about the past. But I do.

Ninth of March

Sinclair has just found an egg beneath his bed, and is greatly perturbed. It was only a little pale-blue egg, but he wouldn't touch it and nor would the helpers, and there was quite a to-do. Eventually Daphne took it to the cook-house and threw it in the oven. She said she is too old to be frightened of obeah.

Evie says obeah is Jamaican black magic, and that an egg is a bad obeah sign. I asked what it signifies, but she said she didn't know, which is Jamaican for I'm not telling.

I have just seen my first RATBAT!!! I was so excited I spilt ink on Pablo Grey, but luckily I didn't overturn the kerosene lamp and set fire to the musquito curtains!!

I hope to see more ratbats and an ALLIGATOR. The stream which runs at the bottom of our hill sounds perfect for such beasts. I also long to see a PARROT like the ones in Aunt ~~Lett~~ Letitia's window; however there are no trees near the house for them to sit upon, only the croton hedge. Once I got Maddy to open the door to the garden a crack, and put out a dish of sugar-water to entice hummingbirds, but we only got two beetles and a moth.

Clemency has a cat but it prefers to stay with her, and sadly the dogs (Remus and Cleo) are not allowed in the house. However I have seen many beautiful green lizards, several cling-clings (big glossy blackbirds), lots of john crows and jabbling crows, and some fireflies. In Jamaica these are called peenywallies, and Clemency says that in olden times ladies used to pin them to the hems of their ballgowns, which I think is absolutely disgusting.

Twelfth of March – After supper

Maddy has just gone to dinner. She says the talk is always of sugar and that they freed the slaves too soon, which is embarassing in front of the helpers. Sinclair says they don't understand, but I bet they do. Kean is the butler, and very clever and quiet; Maddy calls him the 'eyes and ears of Fever Hill', as he reports everything to Great-Aunt May. Maddy's maid Jessie is also a sneak, but the others are nicer. There is Daphne the cook, and Rebecca and Susan the housemaids, and Doshey the groom, and Thomas the garden boy, who is extremely old.

I thought Maddy was looking tired tonight. She said she doesn't understand Sinclair, and neither do I. He doesn't like to touch me because of my illness, and I don't care about that, but I cannot forgive that he never compliments Maddy.

She looked BEAUTIFUL in her amber evening gown, and Uncle Jocelyn said so too, so it wasn't just me.

Fourteenth

I can see across the lawn to the duppy tree, but after what Evie told me this afternoon, I wish I couldn't. The English name for it is a silk-cotton tree, but in Jamaican it is called a duppy tree. It is tall and wide like an oak, with creepers hanging down, and spiky wild pines clinging to the branches. In the dark they look like giant spiders.

Evie says that on nights with no moon, all the duppy trees for miles around transport themselves to the deep woods to hold secret conference together. Tonight I woke myself up, to check that our duppy tree was still in place.

Sixteenth

For the first time I have had breakfast with the family! I ADORE Jamaican food. My favourite fruits are mangoes, naseberries, tamarinds and cocoanuts, which Evie calls jelly-fruit. For breakfast I like green banana porridge with muscovado sugar, and fried plantain (which resembles banana and is MAGNIFICENT), and johnny cakes (scones), and bammies, which are made of something called cassava. But this morning I had avocado pear on toast. Uncle Jocelyn calls it midshipman's butter, and has it every single day. I thought it tasted soapy, but extremely nutritious.

Seventeenth – After tea

What a day! I have just had my first walk on the lawns with my new crutches!!!! I was very wobbly and it only lasted five minutes, but I did get a look at the outside of Fever Hill. (I was asleep when we first arrived.)

The house faces north towards the sea, and has two

storeys with galleries all the way round, and a great flight of marble steps down to the carriage-drive. I was surprised to see that on the outside the louvres are peeling, and eaten by termites. It makes the house look ruined, and boarded up.

The ground floor where we live is up the main steps, with the undercroft underneath, where Maddy has her darkroom. In the middle is the huge empty ballroom, and to the east is the dining-room (which is never used), the breakfast-room where the family has its meals, then the morning-room, drawing-room and Uncle Jocelyn's library. That is at the back, with a view of the hills, and has books from <u>floor to ceiling</u> – but I'm not allowed in, as Uncle Jocelyn doesn't care for children. Behind the stairs are the strongroom, cloak-room and the downstairs bathroom, and then on the west side, Clemency's rooms, then mine, and finally Maddy and Sinclair's bedroom and dressing-room, and Sinclair's study.

Upstairs are Uncle Jocelyn's rooms and that of his wife Kitty, who died after they were married just a year. From the upper gallery I am told that one can see the sea, but that is Great-Aunt May's domain.

Through my gap in the louvres I have a good view of the garden, although it is just brown lawns. Clemency says there was once a Rose Walk and an aviary, but when Kitty died Uncle Jocelyn had them all destroyed. Sometimes at night, Clemency goes down onto the lawns, if she hears her baby crying in Hell.

My view looks south-west towards the hills, like Uncle Jocelyn's library. Beyond the lawns I can see the duppy tree, and behind it there is a rise, for our house isn't quite at the <u>top</u> of the hill, but about two-thirds up. On the other side of the rise I understand there is the Burying-place, which has all the family graves. Maddy went there when we first arrived, but returned perplexed. I don't know why.

I <u>wish</u> I could see the Burying-place, for it is the one place at Fever Hill that Sinclair's wicked brother Cameron is allowed to visit. He goes there once a month, but never comes near the house. Uncle Jocelyn used to think the world of him until he did something unspeakable, and got sent to prison. They haven't spoken since. Clemency misses Cameron dreadfully, but Sinclair says it is a great trial to have such a brother. I wonder if Cameron was wrongly accused, like the Count of Monte Cristo.

Somewhere beyond the Burying-place there is a ruined 'hothouse', which is Jamaican for slave hospital. Evie says it is a _very_ bad place, and she wouldn't go there at night for anything, because of the duppies.

A duppy is an evil ghost which appears when someone dies. Evie says that no matter how nice a person was when they were alive, when they die their duppy is always horrid. I asked Evie if I will become a duppy, but she said she didn't know. I don't want to become a duppy and be nasty to Maddy.

Evie says that beyond the hothouse there are cane-fields and cattle pastures all the way to the hills, and on the edge of the estate there is an old hunting lodge called Providence. Beyond that is the Cockpit Country, a terrible place where runaway slaves used to hide, and their descendants still live there. It has no roads, rivers or streams: just ravines and sink-holes, where they used to leave disobedient slaves to die of thirst. White people don't go into the Cockpits any more.

Twentieth of March

I asked Sinclair if white people become duppies, and he became greatly vexed. He said only blacks believe in such nonsense, for they have no moral faculties. Uncle Jocelyn said that black people's magic doesn't work on white people, but Maddy said that she doesn't know enough to say one way or the other, which I think is SO clever and so right.

Uncle Jocelyn is seventy-three, extremely tall, lean and stiff. He has a silver moustache and bushy eyebrows, and his eyes are silvery too. He reads all the time, and calls England 'home', although he hasn't been there since he was a boy. He likes Maddy, and sometimes comes out to the gallery to hear her read aloud. I don't know what she thinks of him.

He keeps a polo-stick by his bed to deal with croaker lizards, which can be noisy at night. I want a polo-stick too, but when I asked him, he said no. He always says no to me and walks away. Maddy says he 'flees'. But I am sewing a pen-wiper for him, and I hope that some day he will allow me in his library.

Great-Aunt May is seventy-six and wears grey kid gloves, for she doesn't care to touch people. Great-Aunt May is in fact Uncle Jocelyn's aunt, the youngest child of his grandfather Alasdair (who died of apoplexy after they freed the slaves). Uncle Jocelyn never calls her 'Aunt', but only 'May'. Everyone else in the family calls her 'Great-Aunt May'. She is narrow and straight and has angry eyes, and wears tight grey gowns and high heels, but she never slips. She often sits in the upper gallery where she watches what goes on, and she used to be a Beauty, but she never married. She doesn't like me. Once she said That Child must have a backboard, and Maddy said that's the last thing she needs, and Great-Aunt May was vexed. Sinclair was too.

Clemency is my FAVOURITE person (apart from Maddy!!!). She is forty-three but still pretty, although she dyed her hair grey when her baby died. She expected her hair to turn grey on its own because she was so grief-stricken, and when it didn't, she dyed it. It is a great shame that she has no other children, for she would have been an extremely good mother.

Clemency is the widow of Uncle Jocelyn's only son, Ainsley. He did something bad, like Cameron Lawe, and no-one mentions him either. Clemency told me she can hardly remember Ainsley, and that she only married him because her brother, Cornelius Traherne, told her to. Clemency always does what she is told. I think that irritates Maddy.

Clemency is frequently unwell, and a great expert on medicines. Her favourites are tincture of henbane, and Dr Hay's Ginger Lozenges for Purifying the Blood. She always wears white in mourning for the baby, and when she laughs she doesn't make a sound. She is scared of everyone (except me), and Sinclair says she is an hysteric. But I do not think that *can be right. Clemency isn't mad. She has just spent too much time in the dark.*

She sleeps with a cat on her bed and basins of water on the floor to guard against centipedes. Once the cat fell in a basin and I heard it sneeze. Clemency takes henbane to make her sleep, and when she forgets, she hears her baby crying in Hell, and walks in the garden. Sometimes she goes all the way to the hothouse, and Grace fetches her back and tucks her in.

Clemency is planning a Journey, which is extremely secret. She has <u>only</u> told me, which is why I must hide this Journal!! I asked where she will go on the Journey, and she said, Why, dear, to Hell, to be with my baby. I asked why the baby is in Hell, and she said that when he was born he had to be baptized quickly, for he would soon die. Clemency wanted to send for the Reverend Fitch who is closest, but Great-Aunt May said no, he is practically a Baptist, it must be the Reverend Grant. But the Reverend Grant arrived too late, so the baby died and went to Hell. Clemency blames herself. The only reason she hasn't gone on her Journey yet is that she doesn't want to inconvenience Uncle Jocelyn.

She spends her days preparing for the Journey. Occasionally when there is no-one about she has a dress rehearsal, but mostly she just prepares by cutting out items from the Gleaner *about sunhats and sleeping-powders, and so on. She lets me paste these into her extract book, and never minds if I put them in crooked by mistake.*

Yesterday I asked her about dead people, and she showed me the funeral photograph of her baby. Uncle Jocelyn arranged for Mrs Herapath to take it on the day the baby died, and Clemency is <u>eternally grateful</u> to him for that, as she was too distracted to think of it herself.

So now I know what dead people look like.

Twenty-fifth of March

Black people are healthier than white people, and have more fun. They wear more comfortable clothes, go about in the sun, sing a lot, and swim in the river – so clearly they are not afraid of alligators. They do all the work and have no money, except for a few who are teachers, vicars, policemen and banana farmers.

Black ladies do not need husbands in order to have babies. For example, Grace who does the laundry has never had a husband. Sinclair says she is an 'abhorrence', but Great-Aunt May keeps her on because the other helpers are scared of her, which makes them easier to manage. Grace has never told anyone who is the father of Evie and Victory. They don't even know themselves.

Black people don't care for Chinamen or Coolies, and they look down on those who are blacker than they. Evie is a lovely caramel colour, and once she called Victory (who is darker) a dutty nigga, and Grace walloped her. Grace herself is the colour of mahogany. She is scary, but I like her laugh and that she smokes a pipe, and I think she is an extremely good mother.

Evie is twelve, and the PRETTIEST little girl I ever saw. Her hair is always in dozens of tiny plaits which are shiny with castor oil. Unfortunately, Maddy won't let me try the same thing myself.

Evie can carry anything on her head, and wears a little charm-bag round her neck to keep away duppies, and she has three names: Evie, McFarlane, and her born-day name, which she isn't telling me. I think she was impressed when I told her that I never knew my mother, and about snow.

Evie is my friend, although not like Ben and Robbie, whom I miss <u>extremely</u>, particularly as they never came to say goodbye. I miss Aunt Letitia, too.

I only got to know Evie a few weeks ago, when Maddy started paying her a quattie an hour to sit with me. Her brother Victory is six, and has curly eyelashes. Maddy says he has a crush on me. He has very white teeth, and he showed me how to make a chewstick out of a twig from a special bush, so that my teeth will be as white as his.

Evie and Victory live with Grace down in the ruined slave village by the Old Works that got burnt. Nobody else will live there because of the duppies, but they don't bother Grace because her family were slaves just like the duppies, and also because she is a witch.

I need to know more about slaves. My gazetteer calls slavery an evil legacy, but Sinclair says that is quite wrong. He says that the Baptists have greatly exaggerated how bad it was, and that the slaves were too _expensive_ to mistreat, and that no-one would ill-treat a four-legged mule, so why would one ill-treat a two-legged one? He says that the blacks were better off as slaves.

Evie also knows a lot about this, for her grandmother _was_ a slave, and when her great-grandmother was six she was given to Uncle Jocelyn's mother-in-law as a wedding present!!! According to my gazetteer, the slaves were freed sixty years ago, and the first of August is now a holiday called Free Come, when the black people sing hymns and hold tea meetings. It seems to me that they would only celebrate being freed if they preferred not being slaves.

Daphne says slavery is long gone and you must let it be, but that some people can't manage that, like Grace.

I don't think Grace cares for white people, but I hope that she likes me. She knows black magic, which is called obeah, and white magic, which is called myalism. Mostly she does good magic, I think.

This morning she returned a handkerchief which Maddy had dropped on the steps. Grace said that one mustn't leave things lying around, even in one's own yard, because they could be stolen, and used to catch a person's shadow.

I asked Evie about this and she explained that Grace didn't mean the normal sort of shadow, but a different one, _inside_ the person, that only a witch can see.

Evie says that when a person gets sick, it's because someone has stolen their shadow and nailed it to a duppy tree. After that, the only way to get better again is to catch the shadow and put it back inside the person.

She says that someone must have stolen _my_ shadow, which is why I am so ill.

But Evie doesn't know _everything_. It isn't as if she is a witch, like Grace. Besides, why would someone steal my shadow?

Last night I saw someone at the duppy tree. They were hunched and creeping, and the dogs didn't bark. It wasn't Clemency.

After that I didn't sleep, in case it was a duppy. I heard Great-Aunt May pacing in the upper gallery, and also an owl, which Jamaicans call Patoo, and are afraid of.

I need to tell Maddy, but I can't. More and more it feels as if she is far away, even when she is reading to me, or making Pablo Grey have arguments. And at times she looks so oddly at Uncle Jocelyn and Clemency and Sinclair.

Clemency says Maddy is like any newly wed lady who is hoping for a child. And to be sure, when I asked Maddy, she said she is hoping for a child, as it would be such a relief for her and Sinclair. But she didn't sound happy about it.

Sophie put down her pen and listened to the crickets' afternoon rasp.

Around her the house lay dreaming in the heat. Maddy was downstairs in the darkroom, Uncle Jocelyn in his library, Great-Aunt May and Clemency were resting in their rooms, and Sinclair was writing in his study. Evie and Victory were still at school.

Since the wedding, Maddy had changed. She didn't talk as much, and she took two or three baths a day, as if she never felt clean. But when Sophie asked, she said she was fine, and it had been worth it, hadn't it, now that Sophie was getting so much better?

Perhaps Maddy found the secrecy tiresome. It must be hard, always having to remember that not even Sinclair must know that their parents came from Jamaica, or that their father's name was Falkirk. Sophie found it hard too, although she had grown up with secrets, for Cousin Lettice had always forbidden them to mention their parents to anyone.

Then it occurred to her that perhaps Maddy had secrets from her too. The thought made her skin prickle. They never had secrets from each other.

Very late

Everyone is asleep, and in the moonlight the lawns are almost as bright as day, although the light is blue. The crickets are singing but they sound different, and the duppy tree is still there. So far, no-one has visited it tonight.

I don't think Evie can be right about my shadow. I don't see how someone could have taken it and nailed it to a duppy tree, because I became ill <u>before</u> we came to Jamaica, and there are no duppy trees in England.

Next week, if Dr Pritchard lets me, I shall make my first visit to Falmouth. If Sinclair doesn't come with us, I shall ask Maddy what she thinks about all this. Also, Mrs Herapath was an obeah-woman in a previous life, so if I get the chance, I shall ask her too.

CHAPTER FIFTEEN

On the morning of the visit to Falmouth, Madeleine awoke before dawn, to find that her monthly courses had begun.

Oh no, she thought as the familiar ache took hold. No, *no*.

Once again she would have to tell Sinclair that she would not be giving him a son. That their uneasy peace was ended, and they would have to do *that* again.

He slept beside her curled in a ball, with his fists clenched beneath his chin. Even in sleep he was not at peace; and since the episode of the egg, he had taken to dosing himself with a sleeping-draught every night. She wondered what dreams he had; what shadows haunted the creases of his mind.

She lay back on the pillows and tried to doze. She dreamed that the mosquito curtain was collapsing on top of her. She lay watching the billowing whiteness sinking softly, softly towards her. And as she watched, a red stain began slowly to appear in the white. At first it was no more than little blotches far apart, like blotting paper soaking up ink; but gradually it coalesced into a larger stain. A scarlet butterfly.

She awoke with a start.

What was happening? Why that dream again?

She drew aside the gauze and slipped out of bed and crept to the dressing-room. She needed to be by herself, if only for ten minutes in the darkroom.

'Are you *sure* this means you are not with child?' Sinclair had demanded the last time her courses had arrived.

She was sure. A vague recollection from Dr Philpott had

been confirmed by discreet enquiry of a startlingly frank Clemency.

But Sinclair had remained suspicious. 'I've never heard of a woman *bleeding* like this. Every month? That cannot be natural. There must be something wrong with you.'

She didn't think there was. But on the other hand, she didn't know why she bled every month, either. Lettice used to call it a reminder of the Original Sin. She used to say that as Madeleine already had sin in her blood, it was only to be expected that she should manifest it early, at the shamefully young age of thirteen. But beyond that, Lettice hadn't been any the wiser as to why it occurred.

Once, Madeleine had suggested to Sinclair that they should ask Dr Pritchard.

'Ask him what?' he had snapped. 'Why my wife is un-clean?'

Unclean, unclean.

The word rang in her ears as she finished dressing and slipped out into the gallery in her stockinged feet. She let herself out onto the steps and paused to put on her shoes. The light was grey, but the air already warm with the promise of the day to follow. Out on the lawns, the pea doves were cooing their melancholy refrain. *What-am-I-to-doo? What-am-I-to-doo?*

She went down the steps to the undercroft, opened the darkroom door and took a deep, reassuring breath of the familiar chemical smell.

Unlike the main floors of Fever Hill, the undercroft was built of thick blocks of the local cut-stone. The floor was rough-cut coral, the rafters of bulletwood, the door of mahogany dashed with sand to keep out the termites. It was rougher than the upper floors, but more genuine. And it was her place. Nothing could reach her here. Not Sinclair, not Great-Aunt May. Not those nagging dreams about her mother.

She lit the kerosene lamp, and shadows flared. Faces leapt from the prints pegged up on the line to dry.

Sophie and Pablo Grey ('I know it's babyish, but he's more of a mascot, really . . .')

Jocelyn in the library with his books and his great framed map of the Northside, and his daguerreotype of Kitty.

Clemency, luminous in cloudy white, with Evie standing shyly at her side.

A stark, unforgiving profile of Great-Aunt May.

Madeleine walked slowly down the line, choosing prints to show to Mrs Herapath that afternoon. As she was shuffling them into a pile, there was a scratch at the door, and Remus the mastiff put in his nose. He was too well behaved to intrude any further, but a moment later she heard the familiar tap of Jocelyn's cane across the flags.

When she emerged blinking in the light, the old man turned his head and saw her, and made a tolerable job of appearing surprised. They had an unspoken convention that he would never disturb her in her sanctuary, but would simply make his presence known if he happened to pass by on one of his walks, just in case she cared to exchange a few words.

'Rather early for you,' he remarked.

'And for you,' she replied.

'Curse of the old. Four hours' sleep. That's my lot these days.'

'I couldn't sleep either. So I thought I'd choose some prints to show Mrs Herapath.'

'Ah yes. The long-awaited expedition to town.'

She bit back a smile. 'Sophie will be gone all afternoon. How shall you bear the peace and quiet?'

The corners of his mouth turned down. 'I can scarcely imagine. May I see what you've chosen?'

She held them out.

He took his spectacles from his breast pocket and scrutinized each print with a careful frown. Then he gave them back to her, shaking his head in baffled admiration. ''Straordinary. You've caught Clemency to the life. And the way you've included the little pickney – very fine. Very apt.'

'Wherever Clemency goes, a child usually appears.'

'To be sure. But you were the one who brought it out.'

Remus put his muzzle under the old man's hand and gave it an impatient nudge.

'Yes, yes, my dog, to be sure.' He glanced at Madeleine from under his brows. 'He wants his breakfast. Shall I see you later? For morning tea?'

She nodded. 'I'll be up soon.'

She watched him go: a tall, unbending figure in old-fashioned frock coat and narrow grey trousers. Impenetrably courteous and impenetrably withdrawn – as if, after all the loved ones he had lost in his long life, nothing could really reach him now.

It still surprised her that she liked Jocelyn. Sometimes she had to remind herself who he was: not just a proud, lonely old gentleman who admired her and was wary of Sophie, but the grandfather who had dusted off his hands and forgotten them.

At first she had tried to be angry with him. It hadn't worked. *Your parents wrecked lives*, the officer in the snow had said. And here at Fever Hill she was living among the wreckage. Jocelyn hadn't asked for his family to be torn apart. And he had responded to what had happened in the only way he knew. By denying it.

But how strange that he could look kindly on a photograph of the illegitimate Evie, while wanting nothing to do with his own grandchildren.

There were so many questions that she wanted to ask him. Did you mourn your son at all? Why isn't he buried with the rest of the family, at the Burying-place? Do you ever think of your grandchildren in England? Do you ever think of us?

She went back into the darkroom and shut the door and leaned against it. But for once, it didn't give her the sanctuary she needed. She felt tired and edgy and afraid. Afraid of what? Was it the monthly indisposition, or something else? What was happening to her?

When she'd first arrived at Fever Hill, the past had been easy to ignore, for she'd been caught up in the exhausting business of concealment. The enquiries about her 'people'; her education; how she had met Sinclair; whom she had known in London.

But those had soon subsided as she ceased to be the

newcomer and became part of the family, and then she'd had more time to think and to look about her. To notice the baleful Monroe serpent on the Wedgwood dinner service, and the huge, smoke-blackened oil painting of Strathnaw in Jocelyn's library. That was when she had begun to dream of her mother and Cairngowrie House for the first time in years.

But Cairngowrie House, she had told herself fiercely, has nothing to *do* with you any more. This is your life now. You are a normal married woman living with your normal husband in the house of your normal father-in-law.

She looked down at the prints in her hand. In the steady glow of the lamp she caught a trace of her mother in Sophie's wilful mouth. Her father gazed out through Jocelyn's hooded eyes.

Go *away*, she told them silently. I don't want you. I never wanted you. Why can't you leave me alone?

But not even her sanctuary was safe any more. They had followed her in.

She had given Sinclair the bad news just after luncheon, when he had withdrawn to his study to work on his monograph.

He had looked at her steadily, then suggested that she might care to have a bed made up on the gallery until she was clean again. It wasn't a choice but a command, and they had parted with polite ill will.

She went to their bedroom, intending to lie down until it was cool enough to start for town. But as soon as she shut the door behind her, she knew that she had to get out.

She hated their room. She hated the high mahogany walls that felt like a coffin, and the huge old armoire of blackened walnut with the door that swung open at night. And most of all, she hated the oxblood hangings on the enormous bed, with the Monroe serpent woven into the damask. Great-Aunt May had unearthed them from some ancient press, and they still smelt faintly of mildew and long confinement in the dark.

She couldn't stay here a minute longer. She rang for Jessie

and told her to lay out her afternoon gown and her dust-coat. She would risk universal disapproval and go to see Mrs Herapath now, in the blazing sun.

For once, luck was on her side. By the time she and Sophie were ready to leave, Sinclair was closeted in the library with Jocelyn, and Great-Aunt May had gone upstairs to rest. The only people about were Clemency, who had taken an opiate for her spinal irritation and barely understood that they were leaving, and Doshey the groom, who brought round the trap and helped install Sophie on the seat with a sleepy lack of curiosity.

The royal palms lining the carriageway gave little shade, and as they started off the heat was like a wall. The cane-pieces lay stunned beneath the onslaught: shaven and ugly now that croptime was over, and dotted with muck-spreading gangs and brilliant white egrets, and meandering Indian cattle.

Already Madeleine could feel the sweat collecting beneath her corset. She felt earthy and indelicate. *Muliebrous*, to use Lettice's favourite word, which she had employed with grim disdain whenever she encountered a particularly buxom female. Once, Madeleine had looked the word up in the dictionary. *Muliebrous: the condition of being a woman*. It sounded like a disease.

Sophie was unusually quiet on the drive, but for once Madeleine didn't try to talk her out of it. She had too much to think about.

Five days, she thought. Six at the most. Then I'll be 'clean', and we'll have to do it again.

Four times in as many months, and each time as messy and humiliating as the wedding night.

The wedding night. Whenever she thought of it her spirits sank.

Neither of them had known what to expect, and in their different ways they had both been profoundly shocked. Not by the act itself, but by the blood.

Sinclair had been terrified. '*Blood*', he had whispered, his face grey with shock, his lips taut with disgust. He had retreated to an armchair and drawn up his legs beneath his nightshirt, like a small boy after a nightmare. Nothing she had said could persuade him back to bed.

It had been different for her. One look at those scarlet blotches on the sheets and she had been a child again, staring at her mother's body in the crimson butterfly. She had felt again the yawning disbelief, the bewilderment of loss.

The following month they had tried again. This time there was no blood, but by then the damage had been done. Sinclair couldn't forget that scarlet stain any more than she could, and he couldn't forgive. She was unclean. She had tricked him into marrying her, and then cheated him of the son who was rightfully his.

Unclean, unclean.

The pony-trap swept across the Martha Brae, and the faded Georgian elegance of Falmouth rose into view. The little town was still slumbering away the afternoon. Goats picked their way through the refuse in the gutters. A trio of pickneys played cricket with a green mango and a bamboo bat. A john crow hitched itself off a fence and flew away.

They were passing the parish church of St Peter's when Sophie turned her head and gave the ancient silk-cotton tree in the churchyard a dark stare. 'I didn't think they'd allow one so near the church,' she said.

'Why not?' said Madeleine.

But Sophie only frowned and shook her head.

Madeleine threw a glance at the churchyard. When she'd first arrived at Fever Hill, she had made a search for her father's grave. She hadn't wanted to do it, but she'd needed to know. Lettice had told her years before that his remains had been repatriated to Jamaica, so it had been a shock to find no trace of him at the Burying-place. And no trace of him at St Peter's, either. The waters had closed over Ainsley Monroe with shocking completeness. He had simply disappeared.

All she had found in the churchyard were the Durrant graves: a clump of crazily tilting tablets encrusted with lichen. And the only one she could read was the tomb of her grandfather – her other grandfather. *Aristide Durrant, 1813–68. Of Your Charity, Pray for His Soul.*

Angrily, she flicked the whip across the pony's rump. It had been a mistake to come past the church. The coast road would have been quicker. Why hadn't she thought of that?

And why was everything conspiring to remind her of the past?

They found Mrs Herapath in the salon, two-thirds of the way through a bottle of Manzanilla. She wore an empire-lined gown of painted turquoise muslin liberally sprinkled with snuff, for she was half-heartedly manifesting as an attendant of the Empress Joséphine. She greeted them in French, but switched to English when she remembered that Madeleine didn't understand.

At least, that was the charitable explanation. The less charitable one was that she was in a bad mood, and wanted to vent some spleen by needling her guest.

Madeleine busied herself settling Sophie in an armchair, with a footrest for her splint.

'I'm sorry,' muttered Mrs Herapath after she had poured Madeleine a glass of sherry which she didn't want.

'Why should you be sorry?' said Madeleine.

'For being perfectly horrid. I'm afraid I'm in one of my moods. Wretched day. Wedding anniversary. Twenty-fifth.'

'Oh no. We shouldn't have come.'

'No, no. I invited you. And we had a good innings, Hector and I.' Blinking furiously, she quoted under her breath, '*Rangy Hector of the flashing helm.*'

Madeleine glanced at the stout gentleman in the photograph above the desk. The eyes held a dry intelligence, but the whiskered cheeks suggested a hamster.

'Did Mr Herapath become a duppy?' asked Sophie.

'Not as such,' said Mrs Herapath. 'He ascended to a higher state of being.'

Sophie considered that. 'Mrs Herapath, do you know about shadows?'

'Sophie . . .' said Madeleine.

'It's quite all right,' said the older woman. 'Sweet child. I take it you mean the Jamaican kind?'

Sophie nodded.

'As it happens I don't. But you might find a book in the studio, if you care to look. That is,' a questioning glance at Madeleine, 'if she's allowed to move about?'

Madeleine nodded. Dr Pritchard had said that since the knee was so much better, Sophie should start learning to use her crutches, although she must still wear the hated splint at all times, to keep the joint immobile.

'Then run along,' said Mrs Herapath tactlessly. 'And you may borrow two books to take home with you. But not the Oscar Wilde. I don't think you're ready for it.'

When Sophie had been helped to her feet and had hobbled laboriously out, Mrs Herapath turned back to Madeleine. 'You seem out of sorts, my dear.'

'Not at all,' lied Madeleine. 'I'm fine.'

'What's the matter? Some sort of spat with Sinclair?'

Madeleine shook her head.

Mrs Herapath gave an ill-tempered smile. 'Ah, young love! Strongest force in the world. And the most destructive. You just ask that twisted lot up at Fever Hill.'

'I'd rather not,' said Madeleine.

Mrs Herapath threw her a curious glance. 'I'd noticed that. Whenever I get anywhere near the Scandal About Which We're Not Supposed to Know, you close up like a limpet. If that's what limpets do.'

Madeleine did not reply.

Mrs Herapath drained her glass and put it unsteadily on the side table. 'It's just that it *bothers* me to see that old man mouldering away up there, missing poor dear Cameron so terribly – and he does, you know, though he'd never admit it – and doing nothing about it!'

Madeleine turned her head and studied the portrait of Hector.

'And you see,' said Mrs Herapath, relentless, 'I've always believed that if we could just get the two of them *together*, just once, then at least that part of the wretched muddle could be sorted out.'

'They're grown men,' said Madeleine stiffly. 'I'm sure they can sort it out for themselves.'

Mrs Herapath gave a mirthless laugh. 'My dear, how little you know about men!'

Madeleine did not reply.

Out in the square a dog barked. A Chinaman rattled by on his bicycle. A horse snorted and shook its bridle.

Mrs Herapath heaved herself to her feet and refilled their glasses. 'I knew Rose Durrant, you know. Oh yes. I suppose you've heard of Rose?'

Madeleine kept her eyes on the sherry glass in her hand. The pale gold Manzanilla was very slightly shaking, but if she concentrated, she could make it go still.

'She used to help me in the studio,' said Mrs Herapath. She subsided onto the sofa and leaned back and gazed at the ceiling. 'Quite a talent for composition. But wild, of course. All the Durrants were. Impulsive. Passionate. And such a temper! Still. I adored her. *Such* a blow when she ran off like that. Why, my dear, you've gone quite pale.'

'I'm fine.'

Mrs Herapath put her head on one side and studied her with narrowed eyes. 'You know, it's a part of the family history. Your history now. You ought to take more of an interest.'

Madeleine felt herself growing hot. 'Why should I want to know about something that happened twenty years ago? What's it to me?'

Mrs Herapath looked startled. 'But— I'm sorry. I had no idea that you felt so strongly.'

'I don't.'

'Then you *are* out of sorts.'

'Not in the slightest,' said Madeleine coolly.

'Oh, what rot!' snapped Mrs Herapath.

There was an irritable silence between them. Mrs Herapath picked up her glass and scowled at it. Madeleine thought about apologizing, and decided against it.

'I'm sorry,' they both said at the same time.

Madeleine put down her glass and smoothed her skirt over her knees. 'You're right,' she said, 'I am out of sorts. I'm a little – indisposed.'

Mrs Herapath leaned over and patted her hand.

To her horror, Madeleine found that she was close to tears. She rose quickly to her feet. 'Sophie's been awfully quiet. I ought to go and see—'

'Oh dear, now I've chased you away.'

'No you haven't. It's time we were off.'

'Shall you come again? Soon?'

'If I'm permitted.' She leaned down and kissed Mrs Herapath on the cheek, and hurried out to find Sophie.

Sophie wasn't in the studio at the front of the house, but the door onto the verandah was open, so she must be outside, watching what was going on in the square.

Madeleine hung back in the studio. She needed to be alone. It had been horrible to hear her mother spoken of with such easy familiarity. It made her feel shaky and exposed: as if someone had peeled away a scab and blown on the raw flesh underneath.

'Oh *yes*,' came Sophie's voice from outside, 'I do so agree.'

Oh no, thought Madeleine. Just for once, she wished her sister hadn't managed to strike up an acquaintance with whomever she happened to have met in the street.

Softly she moved closer to the door, and saw Sophie leaning against the balustrade, stroking the nose of a large bay gelding. It wasn't clear if she was addressing the horse or its owner, a tall European at the bottom of the steps.

He was tying the reins to the hitching-post, and Madeleine couldn't see his face, but from his clothes she guessed him to be a planter of the not so profitable kind. His topboots hadn't been polished in years, and his riding breeches and shooting jacket looked as if he'd slept in them. His thick sandy hair was unkempt and in need of a cut.

In no mood for new acquaintances, she drew back into the shadows.

'His name is Pilate,' said the gentleman.

'Pilate?' said Sophie. 'You mean, like Pontius Pilate in the Bible?'

'I suppose so, yes.'

'But that's not fair. Pontius Pilate was horrible. Your horse doesn't deserve a name like that. He didn't *do* anything.'

'You're right,' said the gentleman. He had an agreeable voice, and Madeleine could tell that he was smiling. 'But you see, he was called that when I bought him, and horses don't care to have their names changed.'

'Like people,' said Sophie.

'Like people,' agreed the gentleman. 'Did you see how he twiddled his ears? That means he knows we're talking about him.'

Pilate twiddled his ears again, then bent his sturdy neck and nuzzled Sophie's chest. She squealed with delight, and would have toppled over if the gentleman hadn't put out a sunburned hand to steady her. As she regained her balance, she glanced indoors and spotted Madeleine. 'Oh look, there's my sister! Maddy, do come out and meet Pilate the horse!'

Madeleine's heart sank. But it was too late to escape now. Straightening her shoulders and assuming a social smile, she moved out into the light.

The gentleman turned to face her, and the sun went in as she recognized the officer at Strathnaw.

Ten years fell away in a heartbeat. She was back in the snow, in that final moment before he realized who she was and it all went wrong.

He hadn't changed. Perhaps he was a little more lined than she remembered, and considerably less well groomed. But the vivid grey eyes were the same, and the brief lightening of the sunburned features that was almost a smile.

Her heart was thudding against her ribs. He doesn't recognize you, she told herself. You can see it in his face. He has no idea who you are.

It was true. His features had stiffened before her continued silence, but his manner showed nothing more than the courtesy which any gentleman might extend to any well-bred young woman whom he had only just met.

Sophie sucked in her cheeks and announced, 'Maddy, this is Mr *Cameron Lawe*. His estate is called Eden, isn't that a lovely name? And it's only eight miles away from us, up in the hills just before the Cockpits, and he has a dog called Abigail, and *parrots* in the garden, and I'm to go there for tea and meet Abigail and the parrots . . .'

Madeleine stopped listening. She was falling from a great height. Cameron Lawe. The officer at Strathnaw. How could she not have seen this coming? How could she have been so stupid?

She realized that the silence was becoming embarrassing, and that he was offering her his hand. When she didn't respond, he withdrew it, and his face became carefully expressionless.

She cleared her throat. 'I'm Madeleine Lawe. That is, I'm Mrs Sinclair Lawe.'

'Yes, I know,' he said bluntly.

'How? Did Sophie—'

'I saw you with him. With my brother.'

'When?'

'A few weeks ago? You were out driving. I'd – just come from town.' He frowned, aware that that sounded as if he'd been spying on them. 'You went past before I had time to call out,' he muttered.

'Indeed,' she said. 'Sinclair will be sorry to have missed you.' That was such a blatant lie that he made no reply, and she felt herself colouring.

He doesn't look anything like Sinclair, she thought, watching him take his wide-brimmed hat from the bench and frown at it. He was taller and broader, and he lacked his brother's delicacy of feature.

At that moment he threw her a glance and then looked quickly away, and she wondered with a stab of alarm if something had jogged his memory.

With his hat he gestured towards the studio. 'I wonder, do you know if Mrs Herapath is—'

'Indisposed,' she replied. 'I don't believe she'll see anyone today.'

'I'm sorry to hear that.'

'Yes.'

He nodded. 'Well. Perhaps you'd tell her I called?'

'Yes.'

'I would leave a card. But I don't have any.'

'Of course.' He didn't look like the sort of man who carried cards.

'Well,' he said again. 'I should be on my way.'

'Of course.'

He raised his head and studied her face for a moment, narrowing his eyes a little, as if it hurt to look. Then he gave her a curt nod, and went down the steps to untie his horse.

'You were *so* rude to him,' said Sophie as they were driving home. She sat with her leg propped up on the cushions, clutching her chosen volumes to her chest: *A Folkloric Monograph on the Island of Jamaica,* and *The Count of Monte Cristo,* which she had decided to reread.

'I was not rude,' said Madeleine, giving the reins an admonishing snap. They were still a few miles from the gates of Fever Hill, on the section of road which giant bamboo had turned into an airless, mosquito-ridden tunnel. Above their heads the great canes creaked and shifted like a ship on a stormy sea.

In the green light Sophie's face looked sallow and peevish. 'Does that mean that I can go to Eden and see the parrots?'

'Of course not. We're not going anywhere near Eden.'

'Why not?'

'You know perfectly well. Uncle Jocelyn would never countenance it. He and Mr Lawe haven't spoken since – well, not for years.'

'I bet they would, though,' said Sophie, 'if they only met just once.'

That was an uncanny echo of Mrs Herapath, and it occurred to Madeleine that the older woman had probably chosen that particular day to invite them to tea in order to engineer a meeting. It would be just like her. It would appeal to her sense of drama.

'You *were* rude,' said Sophie.

'In what way?'

'You didn't smile, you hardly said a thing, and you *refused* to shake hands.'

'I didn't refuse. I forgot.'

'Just because he went to prison. It's not fair.'

'That has nothing to do with it.'

'He didn't think so.'

179

'How do you know?'

'I could tell. Anyone could. You practically cut him dead. I bet he thinks it's because he was a convict.'

'Oh, do be quiet, Sophie, and let me drive!'

They emerged from the bamboo, and the cane-pieces opened out all around. After an uncomfortable silence that lasted nearly twenty minutes, the gatehouses loomed into sight.

Like most of the estate buildings, they were of the golden local cut-stone, and covered in creepers and strangler fig. As they passed, Madeleine caught the baleful glare of the Monroe serpent between the leaves. Another reminder of Strathnaw. As if she needed one.

In retrospect it struck her as extraordinary that in all the years since that encounter in the snow, she had never once asked herself who the officer might actually be. It was as if he couldn't possibly have a name like an ordinary man. He was simply the 'officer in the snow': a statue who had come to life, and been kind to her for a while, and then turned against her and ridden away.

It was impossible to think of him as Sinclair's brother, the infamous Cameron Lawe. The author of that brusque, un-feeling little note in Lettice's prayer book.

And he lived at *Eden*, of all places. What had possessed him to go and live there?

That doesn't matter, she told herself firmly. What matters is that he didn't recognize you.

And he didn't, did he?

She found herself going over everything he had said, every nuance and expression. The more she thought about it, the more she wondered. That final look had been so searching.

Oh God, she thought. Don't let him have recognized me.

CHAPTER SIXTEEN

She didn't tell Sinclair of her encounter with his brother, but by the time she had settled Sophie in the gallery, and taken a bath and dressed for dinner, he already knew.

The ice beneath her feet had begun to crack, and the fracture lines spread with alarming speed. Dinner was eaten in uneasy silence, and Jocelyn withdrew to his library when it was over. Clemency looked frightened, Sinclair treated Madeleine with impenetrable courtesy, and May surveyed the proceedings with icy calm.

After dinner Madeleine asked Sinclair what was wrong. Nothing was wrong. What could conceivably be wrong?

She gave up, and went to say goodnight to Sophie. She found her wide-eyed and anxious, convinced that it was all her fault. It turned out that Sinclair had questioned her while Madeleine was taking her bath.

That night she slept in the gallery. The north wind howled through the house, and behind her in the bedroom she heard Sinclair pacing the boards. Around midnight he came to the door, and she felt him watching her. She pretended to be asleep, and after an uneasy silence he returned to bed.

The next morning she waited for the inevitable dressing down, but it never came.

A day passed. And another, and another. Cameron Lawe was due at the Burying-place that afternoon. The house crackled with tension, but nothing was said. Madeleine stayed in the gallery with Sophie, forcing herself to concentrate on the gazetteer she was reading, and trying not to think about what Cameron Lawe might or might not have remembered about his brother's new wife.

The following day she made another attempt to clear things up with Sinclair. If she could only make him understand that she'd scarcely spoken two words to Cameron Lawe, then surely this ludicrous farrago would be at an end. He cut her short and walked away. Where his brother was concerned, it seemed that only he was permitted to open a conversation.

Two nights later, they made a fifth attempt to conceive a son. It was a disaster.

'I can't! I can't!' gasped Sinclair, collapsing beside her.

They lay side by side, staring into the darkness, while outside the young owls hooted and the crickets rang in their night song.

'It's this confounded heat,' he muttered. 'It saps my vitality.'

'Yes,' said Madeleine. 'The heat is very trying.'

'Ever since we arrived I have been out of sorts. The overseasoned food. That filthy Negro charm.'

Madeleine turned to look at him. 'It was only a bird's egg. I'm not sure what it could have—'

'You never try to understand. Your only response is to contradict and to ridicule.'

He got up and went to the looking-glass. His reflection was pale and drawn, and when he passed his hands over his throat he left faint red marks. 'This is your fault,' he said without turning round.

She made no reply.

'I should have known it would turn out like this,' he said. 'You are just like him.'

'Like whom?'

But she already knew. These days, his brother was never far from his thoughts. It was as if her encounter at Mrs Herapath's had reawakened all his boyhood fears.

'You are coarse,' he said, still regarding his reflection in the looking-glass. 'You have no life of the spirit.'

She sat up and pushed her hair behind her ears. 'So this is my fault. Because I spoke to your brother. Once. A week ago.'

He raised a hand for silence.

'Sinclair—'

'We will *not* speak of it again.'

'I think we must.'

'No! You will do me the courtesy of obeying. In this if in nothing else.'

The following day, it was as if their talk had never happened, except that the atmosphere of unspoken censure was even worse than before. Great-Aunt May looked quietly pleased, Clemency retired to her bed with a sick headache, and Jocelyn affected not to notice anything amiss. Clearly he was reluctant to interfere.

At last the rains came. Every afternoon, great silver downpours rattled the slates, pounded the lawns, and made the carriageway run red. In the humid shadows of the great house, Madeleine and Sinclair circled each other with a cold courtesy that set her teeth on edge.

Four interminable weeks dragged by. Four weeks of silences and denials, and little pained smiles. Eventually she could stand it no longer. She must have it out with him or go insane.

She chose a teatime when Jocelyn was in his library and Sophie was asleep, but Clemency and May would both be present. She needed witnesses. That might make it harder for Sinclair to evade her as he had always done before. It might also help to keep her temper in check.

The weather was blustery, so tea was laid in the drawing-room, a dim mahogany chamber dominated by a Winterhalter portrait of the eighteen-year-old May in presentation dress. On a sofa beneath it sat the present-day version: nearly sixty years older but no less narrow and uncompromising, in a savagely tight gown of rigid dark-grey moiré, and the ever-present grey kid gloves. Clemency, an insubstantial shadow in white muslin, sat on her right, and Sinclair on her left. They reminded Madeleine of a woodcut she had once seen of the Spanish Inquisition.

'I'm not sure what crime I'm supposed to have committed,'

she said as she stirred her tea, 'but I really do think that this has gone on for long enough, and that I should be given a chance to lodge a defence.'

Clemency froze with her cup halfway to her lips, her extraordinary young-old face a mask of fright.

May serenely finished pouring, and handed Sinclair his tea.

He nodded his thanks to her, then gave Madeleine one of his meaningless little smiles. 'There is no question of a *defence*,' he said.

'Good,' said Madeleine. 'Then we are agreed that I've committed no crime.'

Clemency threw her a horrified look and shook her head. May's gaze slid from Sinclair to Madeleine, and back again.

'You know,' said Madeleine, 'I didn't *intend* to speak to your brother. At first I didn't even know who he was. It was a chance encounter. And one which I've no desire to repeat.'

In fact, that was a lie. Today was Cameron Lawe's day for visiting the graves, and all morning she had been wondering whether to go and confront him. She knew it would be the height of folly, but over the weeks the suspicion had grown that he had seen something in her face which had jogged his memory. She kept picturing him alone up there at Eden, with all the time in the world to think and to remember. One way or another, she needed to know.

Sinclair put his cup to his lips, then replaced it in the saucer and set it on the side table. 'My brother', he said, 'is not a respectable man. *That* is the reason for my objection.'

'I thought he'd served his sentence,' said Madeleine. 'I thought it was our Christian duty to forgive.'

'Thank you for reminding me of my duty,' said Sinclair. 'And it might interest you to learn that we *have* forgiven him. That we pray daily for him to mend his ways. Sadly, that has not come to pass. Therein lies my objection to your conduct.'

'I don't understand. You mean he's done something else?'

'Of course you do not understand. That is why I had hoped that you would trust my judgement in this matter.'

'Can't you just tell me what he did?'

He hesitated. Then he turned to May and Clemency. 'My

apologies for trespassing on a matter of some indelicacy.'

May inclined her head. Clemency looked up from her teacup in bemusement.

Sinclair turned back to Madeleine. 'Something happens to the white man when he cohabits with the Negress.'

She was startled. 'What do you mean?'

'If you will permit me to continue?'

She folded her hands in her lap and waited.

'The nature of the white man', he went on, 'becomes coarsened by such an association. Animalized by the imbruted cravings of the creature with whom he has thrown in his lot.'

'I'm sorry,' said Madeleine, 'but this sounds a little trumped up. Are you asking me to believe that you object to my having talked to your brother for five minutes because he has a black mistress? As I understand it from Mrs Herapath, that rules out conversation with three-quarters of the planters on the Northside.'

Sinclair pressed his red lips together. 'The wife of a man of God', he said quietly, 'can never be too vigilant when it comes to her character. I had hoped that you might understand that.'

'Of course I do. But a few words on a verandah don't—'

'You were seen with a compromised individual. You *contaminated* yourself. I see nothing "trumped up" in that.'

His cobalt gaze locked with hers, and she read in it the coded meaning. *And remember how especially vulnerable you are to contamination, by virtue of your birth.*

'Contamination', she said between her teeth, 'is too strong a word.'

He gave a merry laugh. 'I had not appreciated that you were so learned in doctrinal matters! I had believed that *I* was the Doctor of Divinity with the cure of souls.'

She felt herself growing hot.

'You did wrongly,' he said. 'You injured yourself, and you injured me. Moreover, you—'

'This is ridiculous, I didn't *injure*—'

'Moreover,' he went on, raising his voice to drown out hers, 'you injured your sister.'

'Sophie? Oh now really, I can't agree with that!'

'Which matters not at all, since you are not her legal guardian.'

Alarmed, she met his gaze. His blue eyes were glittering. He was enjoying himself.

She glanced down at her hands, tightly clenched in her lap. She saw now that she hadn't *done* anything wrong, and that he knew it as well as she. It wasn't about that. It was about control. It was about ramming home the fact that he was the husband, and she the wife – and, as he was fond of pointing out, 'when Man and Woman ride the same horse, Woman must always ride behind'. Until he had her public acknowledgement of that, he would never let up. He would go on and on until she was as mad as Clemency.

'Well then,' she said, struggling to keep her voice steady. 'Let's bring this war of attrition to an end, shall we? I apologize. Wholly and without reservation. There. Is that better?'

May folded her ringless fingers in her lap. Clemency laughed her noiseless little laugh and clapped her hands.

Sinclair gave Madeleine a considering look. '*Thank* you,' he said. 'Henceforth we will speak no more of this. I would simply ask that in the future you exercise greater discretion.'

She couldn't trust herself to speak.

He rose, and turned to his aunt. 'I shall be writing in my study for the rest of the afternoon. It would be a *great* indulgence if I were not disturbed.'

After he had gone, Clemency gave Madeleine her propitiating smile. '*There*, now! Saying sorry wasn't so very difficult, was it?'

Madeleine did not reply. Her hands were still clenched in her lap. In the dim brown light they looked yellow and sere and prematurely aged.

She heard a stiff rustle of silk as Great-Aunt May rose to her feet. 'Sinclair', she remarked, 'has the most perfect respect for the proprieties of any being I know. One might go so far as to call it a reverence. Others would do well to emulate him.'

Madeleine raised her head and met her eyes. They were ice-blue and startling, with rims of angry red. 'What sound advice,' she said crisply, rising in her turn. 'I think I shall take a turn about the lawns, the better to reflect upon it. That is,' she added, 'if I am permitted to leave the house during daylight hours?'

Something flickered in the ice-blue gaze. 'I was not aware', said Great-Aunt May, 'that you were subject to any restriction.'

The wind had dropped by the time Madeleine made her way out onto the lawns, still buttoning her dust-coat in her haste to get away.

After the shadowy great house it was like walking into a furnace. She didn't care. She felt a perverse satisfaction at the thought of the 'crime' she was about to commit. Sinclair would be outraged. How he would enjoy that.

Over the Cockpits she could see a thick bank of slate-grey cloud, and distant lightning flashing, on-off, on-off, like a lamp flaring in a darkened room.

Storm on the way, she thought. Good. Let it come.

She glanced back at the house, and caught a glint of sunlight on the upper gallery. That would be Great-Aunt May, donning her steel-rimmed spectacles. The old witch had lost no time in regaining her post.

Take a good long look, Madeleine told her silently. This ought to give you something to talk about.

She turned and made her way across the lawns. There was no-one about. The helpers were all in their quarters down by the river, the dogs dozing in the undercroft. Only a john crow lazily circled overhead.

She made her way up the rise and over the other side to the Burying-place. It was a peaceful, sunny clearing: untended and seldom visited, except by Clemency. Tall coconut palms and wild lime trees enclosed a dusty green hollow, where a dozen raised barrel tombs dreamed away the decades in the long silver grass.

It was deserted. Cameron Lawe had not yet arrived. Or perhaps, thought Madeleine with a start, he's already been and gone. What a fine irony that would be. You decide to brave universal condemnation, only to find that you've missed your chance.

She waded through the grass to the poinciana tree which shaded the tomb of Jocelyn's young wife Kitty. Beside it, a low slab of blue slate – robbed of its inscription by the weather – made a convenient seat. A gap in the trees gave her far-reaching views to the south: down past the tangled ruins of the old slave hospital, over the emerald expanse of the nursery cane-pieces, to the cattle pastures and the distant treetops of Providence, and the blue-grey Cockpits beyond. And somewhere up there, hidden among the trees, lay Eden. With an effort of will she pushed the thought aside.

She took a deep breath, and smelt lime blossom and spicy red dust, and the sharp green tang of the asparagus ferns among the graves. Around her the long grass buzzed with crickets. Above her head the poinciana was brilliant with vermilion flowers and alive with sugarquits.

Some of her anger and frustration seeped away, leaving in its place a distant sadness. To her right stood the little white marble tomb of Clemency's baby, lovingly adorned with fresh flowers every night. *Elliot Fraser Monroe, died 1873, aged two days*. Her half-brother. The last remaining trace of her father at Fever Hill.

And before her she could just make out the deep Gothic inscription on her grandmother's tomb. Time had dulled its edges, but not the pain behind it. That still shouted to heaven.

Here lies Catherine Dorothy Monroe, née McFarlane
1831–1850
and with her the blasted expectations of an adoring husband.
Death, thou hast obtained thy victory.

She thought about the love which had made Jocelyn stay faithful to a memory for a lifetime. She thought about the love which had compelled her parents to forfeit everything they had in order to be together. She thought about her cramped and haunted existence with Sinclair.

A breeze stirred in the coconut palms to a pattering

mockery of rain. An egret sped across the sky, shining white against deepening grey.

She put her hands by her sides and felt the hot, smooth slate beneath her palms.

You *chose* this life, she told herself. You went into it with your eyes open. Now you must make the best of it.

Yes, but how?

She plucked a grass stem and turned it in her fingers. She had never felt so alone.

A movement at the edge of her vision made her start. She turned to see Cameron Lawe standing at the edge of the trees, watching her.

What was he thinking? Was he remembering that long-ago meeting in the snow?

She rose to her feet and stared back at him across twenty feet of silver grass and barrel tombs. Her heart was hammering against her ribs. 'I'd quite forgotten', she lied, 'that it's your day for visiting.' Her voice was steady, but she had to clasp her hands together to stop them shaking.

'That's all right,' he said.

'I expect you'd rather be alone.'

'No, no, I—'

'But you've come all this way, and brought flowers.' She coloured. That sounded bizarrely like a hostess greeting an unexpected guest.

He frowned at the flowers in his hand: an artless bunch of large spiky white blooms and heliconia, its great scarlet claws tipped with gold. The white ones were ginger lilies. A memory surfaced of something her mother used to say. *At Eden there are ginger lilies as big as your hand, and moonflowers that only bloom at night . . .*

Not *now*, she told herself fiercely. She was horrified to feel her throat beginning to tighten.

'In fact,' he said, still frowning, 'I did rather wonder if you'd be here.'

A cold wave washed over her. 'Why? What do you mean by that?'

'I suppose – only that I hoped you might be.' He tossed his hat and riding-crop in the grass and ran a hand through his hair. 'I'm sorry, that wasn't very proper. But it's the truth.'

She didn't know how to take that. What did he mean? Had he recognized her?

He was looking down at the flowers in his hand, his face unreadable. Over the past ten years he seemed to have learned how to hide his feelings. But she still sensed in him that capacity for violence and tenderness that she had sensed as a child. If he knew her secret, he would be a formidable enemy.

To break the silence she said, 'How did you get here? I didn't see you arrive.'

He gestured over his shoulder towards the old slave hospital. 'There's a track down there. It joins the road up to my estate. That's where I left my horse.'

'Ah.' She realized that she was twisting her hands together, and that he had noticed. She thrust her hands into the pockets of her dust-coat. She said, 'Sophie tells me that I was rude to you the other day.'

'No, no,' he said unconvincingly.

'She says that I practically cut you dead.'

For a moment some of the tension left his features, and he gave her that incipient smile which seemed habitual to him. 'Your sister has strong views.'

'Yes. Yes, she does.'

He hesitated. 'Those crutches of hers. What is it, polio?'

'Tuberculosis of the knee.'

'Ah. And – is she—'

'Getting better. Oh yes.' But she sounded more certain than she felt. Over the past weeks, Sophie's progress seemed unaccountably to have slowed.

She watched him approach the tomb on the other side of Kitty's, and cast last month's shrivelled flowers into the asparagus ferns, and place the ginger lilies at the head. He seemed ill at ease. Was that because he had been having doubts about her? Or was it more innocent than that? Had he simply lost the habit of polite conversation?

She watched him studying the tomb. The inscription read: *Alice Amelie Monroe, née Vavasour, 1821–83*. What, she wondered suddenly, had Jocelyn's mother to do with Cameron Lawe?

'She was my great-aunt,' he said as if she'd spoken aloud. 'When I was a boy, she was a widow, living up at Providence. She used to swoop down and snatch us away from our lessons, and take us for long rides in the hills. I adored her.'

'So does that mean – was your mother a Vavasour?'

'Yes. I'm sorry, I thought you knew that.'

'Sinclair never speaks of his parents.'

'Ah.'

Vavasour was a Huguenot name. Like Durrant. It was an unsettling feeling to know that they both came of the same stock.

'In Jamaica,' he explained, 'everyone's related to everyone else. For instance, Jocelyn married a McFarlane, whose grandmother married a Traherne, whose daughter married a Barrett, whose cousin married a Durrant—' He broke off.

'And the Durrants', she supplied, 'bring us neatly back to the Monroes.'

There was an awkward silence. She shut her eyes. What self-destructive madness had prompted her to blurt that out?

When she opened them again, it was to find him studying her face. Here it comes, she thought. She lifted her chin and met his eyes. Let's get this out in the open, she told him silently. I dare you to remember.

Not a trace of recognition showed in his face. Only puzzlement, and something else that she couldn't fathom. The relief was so great that her knees nearly gave way.

'Are you all right?' he said, putting out a hand, then withdrawing it.

'I'm fine,' she muttered. 'Perfectly fine.'

A gust of wind stirred the feathery leaves of the poinciana tree. A flock of wild canaries swooped down onto it, squabbling noisily, and put the sugarquits to flight.

Cameron Lawe glanced up at them. 'Rain on the way. I should be going.' He thought for a moment, then held out the heliconias to her. 'I wonder, would you mind? These are for Ainsley.'

The ground tilted in front of her. '*What?*'

He gestured at the blue slate behind her. 'Ainsley Monroe? Jocelyn's son. That's the grave. – I'm sorry, I thought you knew.'

She pulled in her skirts from the slab on which she'd been sitting moments before. 'B-but – there's no inscription,' she stammered. 'Nothing at all.'

'It's underneath.'

'What?'

'The inscription. The old man had it turned over, so that he wouldn't have to look at it.'

She put her hand on Kitty's tomb to steady herself.

'You're not all right, are you?' he said. 'You've gone quite pale. You really should sit down.'

The buzz of the crickets was loud in her ears, the sun fierce on her back. She felt sick. 'His own son. He did that to his own son.'

He moved round to her side, careful to keep some distance between them, and went down on one knee and placed the heliconias on the hot blue slate. 'You'll soon find out', he said, 'that forgiveness isn't a very marked trait in that family.' He paused. 'I suppose you know the Monroe motto? *Death before dishonour*. Poor old Ainsley got it the wrong way around.'

'"Poor" Ainsley? But I thought you were terribly angry with him.'

He threw her a curious look. 'Why would you think that?'

She remembered the officer's cold, unforgiving eyes as he had stared down at her in the snow. *Tell them they're dead to me*, he had said, before he had turned and ridden away.

'Why would you think that?' he said again.

She swallowed. 'I don't know. I suppose – because everyone else is.'

'Twenty years is a long time to stay angry,' he said. He glanced at the heliconias, and to her surprise his lip curled. 'Those were his favourites. When I was little he used to tell me that they were dragon's claws. And of course I believed him. I always did.'

It had never occurred to her that he had grown up with

her father. That he might have cared about him. The thought threw everything into disarray.

She watched him silently contemplating her father's grave. He no longer looked threatening. He looked dusty and tired, and he had cut himself shaving. There was a raw scrape along his jaw, and a smudge of dried blood on his collarless shirt.

As she looked at him, she felt a lightening inside her, as if something tight had worked itself loose. This man had loved her father, and her father had loved him. In the end that was all that mattered. It was as if, at last, the officer in the park had turned his horse's head, and ridden back for her.

She cleared her throat. 'You know,' she said, 'I didn't really come up here by accident.'

He kept his eyes on Ainsley's grave. 'I did wonder about that.'

She put a hand to her temple and smoothed back her hair. 'Sinclair made a fearful row when he heard that I'd spoken to you at Mrs Herapath's. It's too ridiculous for words. So I thought I'd really give them something to row about.'

He turned his head and looked at her, and his light-grey eyes were warm. 'That wasn't a very good idea.'

'No. I don't suppose it was.'

They exchanged tentative smiles.

Above the Cockpits a thick, straight cord of lightning split the sky. A few seconds later there came a terrific, rippling crack of thunder. The canaries rose in a cloud and flew away. A grey curtain of rain moved towards them across the emerald cane.

Cameron Lawe stood up. 'It's strange,' he said, 'but you're not at all what I expected of Sinclair's wife.'

'What did you expect?'

'Oh. Someone little and blond and pious, I suppose.' He thought about how that sounded, and coloured. 'I'm sorry, I didn't mean to imply that you're not pious.'

'That's all right,' she said, biting back a smile. 'I'm afraid I've never cared very much for the Bible.'

He looked at her for a moment. 'That's very direct.'

She made no reply.

Another ripple of thunder. He glanced up at the sky, then back to her. 'You should go in or you'll get wet.'

'I don't care about that.'

'Well. I do.' He stooped to retrieve his hat from the grass.

Suddenly she didn't want him to go. She wanted him to stay and talk to her about Eden. And she found herself wondering about the 'Negress' with whom he'd cohabited, and what dreadful crime he had committed to get sent to prison. She said, 'According to Sinclair, you did something "unspeakable". Can that really be true?'

He turned his hat in his hands. Once again his face had become unreadable. 'Quite true, I'm afraid.'

'What did you do?'

'Surely Sinclair's told you by now? I'd have thought he'd rather enjoy that.'

'He never talks about you. Nobody does. But – sometimes I get the feeling that you're all they think about.'

He rubbed a hand over his face. Suddenly he looked very tired.

She knew she shouldn't press him, but she couldn't help it. She wanted him to stay and tell her everything. 'Why don't you tell me what you did?' she said again.

'Why? To satisfy your curiosity?'

She bit her lip. 'Mrs Herapath thinks there's been some kind of misunderstanding between you and Jocelyn. She thinks that if you were to meet, just once, you might be able to sort it out.'

'That's rather a naïve way of looking at it,' he said.

'What do you mean?'

He sighed. 'Some people need outrage in their lives. It helps them screen out what they're too afraid to confront.'

'Which is what?'

'Isn't that obvious? What happened between Ainsley and Rose Durrant, of course.' He paused. 'As long as the family has me to condemn, they can go on forgetting about those two.'

There was another ripple of thunder, this time much closer. The sky had darkened to pewter. In the stormy light the feathery leaves of the poinciana glowed preternaturally green.

'But what did you *do*?' she said. 'Why don't you just tell me?'

'Why should I?' he said sharply.

'Because – I want to know.'

He blew out a long breath. Then he stooped and picked up his riding-crop, and studied it with a frown. 'I was in the Sudan,' he said without looking at her. 'Ainsley was my CO. I—'

'You were in the Sudan? With him? You saw him die?'

'Well, of course. My God, hasn't Sinclair told you anything?'

'I told you, no. That's why I need you to tell me now.'

He cast around for some means of escape. 'We were on the battlefield,' he said shortly. 'Ainsley had just been killed. I despoiled the body. I rifled through the pockets while he was still warm.' He looked down and spread his hands, as if to let something fall. 'Conduct unbecoming. Discharge with ignominy. Two years at Her Majesty's pleasure. There. Now you know.'

Chapter Seventeen

28th June 1895
To Cameron Lawe Esq.
Eden Estate
Parish of Trelawny

Dear Mr Lawe,

I am extremely sorry but I shall not be able to come to tea at Eden, for my sister says that Uncle Jocelyn would not approve. Please be assured that at some future date I should <u>very</u> <u>much</u> like to visit Abigail and the parrots. And of course yourself.

In the meantime, I should like to ask your opinion on a matter of some concern. There is a silk-cotton tree in our garden, which as you know is also called a duppy tree. I have heard that if a person falls ill, it is because their shadow has been stolen and nailed to the trunk, and that only a shadow catcher can restore it and make them well again. Is this true? Does Jamaican magic work, and does it work on white people as well as black people?

I await your opinion most earnestly.
Yours with great respect,
Sophie Lawe.

P.S. I hope that this reaches you soon. Evie McFarlane

has promised to deliver it, but I hope that is not another of her inventions.

2nd P.S. In prison, what did they give you to eat?

2nd July
To Miss Sophie Lawe
Fever Hill Estate

Dear Miss Lawe,
Evie was as good as her word, and your note arrived with commendable speed. As regards your questions, I'm afraid I must be brief, for we're having trouble with the distillation apparatus, and my time is limited.

First, does Jamaican magic work? My answer is that it only works on those rare souls who believe in it implicitly. Thus if an obeah-woman tells a particularly gullible cane-cutter that she has 'put hand on him', he may feel unwell simply because he expects to do so. However this is rare, and only occurs among black people who have been brought up to believe in magic. It has no effect on white people who are predisposed by religion and education to disbelieve it.

You also asked whether people fall ill because their shadows are stolen and nailed to duppy trees. Emphatically not. People fall ill because of poor nutrition, infectious agents, or inheritance. Not because of trees. Your silk-cotton is merely an imposing plant; nothing more.

I hope this helps, and trust that Evie will be as prompt as before. However I think it would be prudent to pass any future correspondence by your sister. As you know, relations between Eden and Fever Hill are somewhat strained. I wouldn't like you to get into trouble.

With best wishes for the swiftest possible recovery,

Cameron Lawe.

P.S. *In prison we ate salted herrings, suet pudding and cold Australian meat. I grew accustomed to it surprisingly quickly, but found the constant cold less agreeable, and the fact that I never saw the sky.*

Ninth of July – written while Maddy is at luncheon

I have had a slight cough for the past three days, and Maddy has imposed strict inactivity and <u>taken away my books</u>. I am therefore writing this in secret.

Maddy has been out of sorts since she met Cameron Lawe at the Burying-place – although I do not see why, for that was two weeks ago, and by her own admission she got off astonishingly lightly, with no telling off from Sinclair. She says that he doesn't know what to do when one simply defies him, then owns up to it and apologizes straight away.

It vexed me greatly that she didn't tell me before she met Cameron Lawe, for if she had, I could have met him too.

Tenth of July

Cough no better. Maddy is worried, although she tries not to show it. She apologized for being preoccupied over the past two weeks, which was nice.

Dr Pritchard came, and said she was right about the strict inactivity. He told Maddy that we must guard against the <u>slightest</u> shadow on the lungs, which in my weakened state would prove fatal. I wasn't supposed to hear that, but I did.

So now I know that white people have shadows as well as black people – although it is puzzling that Dr Pritchard thinks it so important to keep mine out of my lungs.

I wonder what Cameron Lawe would say about this. I should like to write to him again, but I don't think Maddy would let me; and Evie is too busy to take another note, for she has to work at their 'ground' after school. Their ground is a patch of land on Clairmont Hill behind the New Works, where they grow callaloo and chocho and all sorts of bread-kind such as yams and sweet potato. I wish I had a ground, and could grow things and keep fowls, like in The Children of the New Forest.

Eleventh of July

Cough persisting. Maddy very worried.
  I have been thinking a great deal about why this is happening to me. When I first became ill, Maddy told me about the little bacilli, which she said are the cause of the disease. (I think they must be what Cameron Lawe calls 'infectious agents'.) It seems clear that the bacilli are indeed A *cause, but I do not think that they can be the complete explanation. The question is,* WHO SENT THE BACILLI?
  I asked Maddy about this at tea, and she said that no-one sent them: they simply came. I have thought about this a great deal, and I don't believe that it can be right. I think someone stole my shadow and nailed it to the duppy tree. I think that's why the bacilli came.

Twelfth of July

Cough seems to be lessening, but I'm still feeling extremely seedy. To cheer me up, Maddy has given me back my books.
  Mrs Herapath's folkloric monograph is excellent: SO detailed about obeah and myalism, even though it was written by a Reverend. It appears that black people some-times give duppy trees presents of rum if they want a favour. Surely it can do no harm for me to give our tree a present of rum? Evie says that if I give her my pocket money, she will buy me a bottle of rum at Pinchgut market. That is nice of her. I think things may be taking a turn for the better.

Cough very nearly gone!

Everyone is busy with preparations for the Trahernes' ball on the twentieth. Even Clemency is busy, although she isn't actually going. She is helping Maddy to take in her ball gown, as she has lost flesh since she had it made. Maddy doesn't care to go at all, but Sinclair says that they must, for the Trahernes' July Ball is THE event on the Northside. Even Uncle Jocelyn will be going, for although he calls Cornelius Traherne a parvenu (when Clemency isn't there), he is obliged to be nice to him. I don't know why.

Clemency dislikes Cornelius Traherne, even though he is her older brother, because after her husband died and she refused to re-marry, he wanted to send her to the nervous clinic at Burntwood. It is now a sanatorium for pulmonary cases, but Clemency says it is still the same place, and if you are a difficult patient they tie you up in restraining sheets, and in hot weather if they forget to untie you, you die.

Clemency was only saved from being sent to Burntwood when Uncle Jocelyn said that she could stay at Fever Hill. That is another reason why she is eternally grateful to him.

Later

I had an argument with Sinclair. Occasionally Uncle Jocelyn comes to my part of the gallery for tea (which is a <u>great</u> treat, for usually only Maddy and Clemency care to sit with me), but unfortunately whenever Uncle Jocelyn comes, Sinclair comes too.

I asked Sinclair about the paragraph in my gazetteer on the branding of slaves. I said that branding must have hurt a great deal, and is surely <u>proof</u> that slavery was a bad thing. Uncle Jocelyn looked at Sinclair and made a strange hee-haw noise that may have been laughter, and Sinclair was vexed, and said I was misinformed. As proof he fetched a small silver branding-iron which he keeps for a paperweight on his desk. He said that if the iron were heated until red-hot in a *flame of spirits of wine, and then applied to skin previously anointed with sweet oil, the pain was minimal and fleeting. He said he has many historical accounts which confirm this, and that children as young as six used to submit to the brand quite willingly, and without ill effect.*

I had no answer to that, but I mean to test it for myself.

Fifteenth of July

Sinclair is wrong. Last night I anointed my forearm with cocoanut oil procured by Victory, and then held a quattie in the flame of my lamp, using tongs also procured by Victory. Then I applied the hot quattie to my forearm. It hurt <u>extremely</u>, and I now have a nasty red burn, which still hurts. I can't show it to anyone. Maddy would be distressed, and Sinclair would only say that I didn't do it correctly, or some such thing.

I have sworn Victory to secrecy, and I believe implicitly that he won't tell, for he says I am his favourite buckra (which means white person). I think that's because when we play guessing games, I sometimes let him win. Evie never does.

Sixteenth of July

Evie has procured the rum, which is hidden under the croton bush by the steps. Tonight I shall give it to the duppy tree and ask it to make me well again.

Later

I got caught by Grace.

I waited till extremely late, and went across the lawn on my crutches. It took ages, but there was moonlight, and Remus and Cleo came and sniffed at me, which was a help, for if I had met an alligator or a duppy they would have chased it away. The duppy tree was enormous and scary with creepers, and then I saw a shape, and dropped the rum in fright and nearly screamed, but it was Grace. Evie had told on me. She is a _sneak_.

Grace was EXTREMELY angry, she said I had no business messing with powers I didn't understand. She grabbed my arm and I cried out, and that's when she saw the burn where I'd put the hot quattie. She said what is that? So I told her how Sinclair had said that branding didn't hurt, but that I'd tried it and it jolly well did. At that she absolutely laughed, and said of _course_ it hurts, Master Sinclair was lying!!

After that she was quite nice, and took me back to bed and said we wouldn't tell Maddy, and that she would take the rum, so that I wouldn't get into trouble about it. Then she fetched an aloe leaf and split it and put it on my burn. It REALLY helped, which is proof that she is a good witch.

But when I asked if she would fetch my shadow back from the duppy tree, she said no – BECAUSE IT ISN'T THERE.

But if the duppy tree doesn't have my shadow, then where is it? I have to find it. Whatever Maddy says, and Dr Pritchard and Cameron Lawe, if I don't get my shadow back, I shall die.

Sugar and slaves, sugar and slaves. Another over-elaborate dinner in the stifling heat, with the wind carrying up the dizzying smell of rum from the New Works, and the worry about Sophie eating away at her until she wanted to scream.

Sophie had been drowsy all day, for she said she hadn't slept much during the night. Madeleine had summoned Dr Pritchard, who had advised against sleeping powders in one so young, and instead prescribed a liqueur-glassful of cognac after supper.

Please let it work, thought Madeleine. Please give Sophie a peaceful sleep. She needs it so much.

At last the dinner drew to a close. Great-Aunt May folded

her hands in her lap and glanced about the table, and finally rose. Shortly afterwards, Madeleine pleaded indisposition and went to check on Sophie.

The cognac hadn't worked. Sophie was wide awake and frighteningly pale. She had seen the duppy tree move.

Madeleine went across the lawn to check, and came back and assured her that it hadn't moved an inch. As additional proof she cited the fact that neither Remus nor Cleo had barked. And they would have, wouldn't they? Being guard dogs, they would have spotted a thing like that.

Sophie agreed that the dogs hadn't barked, and pretended to be reassured.

That wretched, wretched tree, thought Madeleine. When she'd first arrived at Fever Hill and been told that the strange, buttressed hulk was a silk-cotton tree, she had been astonished and dismayed. It was nothing like the miraculous Tree of Life of her mother's stories. It was stark and ugly, and so old that some of the branches had cracked under their weight and rotted away.

But for some reason it was profoundly disturbing Sophie. Even Dr Pritchard had remarked on it. That had prompted Madeleine to go to Jocelyn and ask him to have the wretched thing cut down. To her astonishment he had declined. 'Worse than breaking a mirror,' he said somewhat sheepishly. 'Bad luck in perpetuity, don't you know? Of course it's all a lot of tommyrot. But the thing is, the helpers wouldn't stand for it. They'd leave. All of 'em. That's the thing.'

She drew back Sophie's mosquito curtain, and made room on the bed beside Pablo Grey. 'What would make you feel safer?' she said. 'Would you like to move to another part of the gallery, where you can't see it?'

Sophie shook her head. Clearly that would only make it worse – presumably because then the tree might creep up on her unawares.

'Then what?' said Madeleine gently.

Sophie's bony fingers tightened on the bedclothes. She looked as if she was wondering how much to reveal. 'A charm-bag might help,' she said. 'Like the one Evie wears round her neck?' She paused. 'Grace made it for her. It's got spirit weed and rosemary and Madam Fate.'

'I'll get one tomorrow. I'll go and see Grace.'

Sophie looked doubtful. 'I don't think she'll make one for a white person.'

'Yes she will,' said Madeleine.

Evening-time, and Grace is taking her ease out on her step, and everything going silk.

She's been cooking up fufu for supper, and waiting for the children to come home after their chores. Smoking little pipe, drinking little bush tea, with a drop of that rum in it of Missy Sophie, to warm up the blood.

Yes, Grace, she tells herself. Everything going silk.

Mosquitoes humming a hive, but Grace don't mind, for they dislike how she taste. And Patoo going hoo hoo up in that old calabash tree, but she just tells him to get out a her damn yard, and he go. He no fool, that Patoo.

She looks around at her place, and it all tidy, tidy-sweet. Hogs and chickens fed; good bamboo fence roundabout; lot, lot a fine trees in her yard: cashew, guava, alligator pear and mango; paw-paw, breadfruit and garden cherry over by Mother Semanthe and Grandmother Leah tombs.

And she got a good stone house behind her, too besides. Two rooms strong-built from slave time, which Grand-mother Leah mortared with powdered bones and molasses, and ash from the old great house that got burnt in the Rebellion, together with a spell or two. And it got a good steep roof on it of thatchpole that Mother Semanthe weave. No weakly cane-trash that last couple a years, then rot away to black and blazes.

Hn. Why she thinking of the family, long dead? Why they creeping into her head at this time? Grace never did even *like* Mother Semanthe, even though she was her own self mother. Always talking, talking about how she born a slave. How she worked in pickney gang since six year old, carrying trays of dung out to the cane; and how that stinking sour brown dung-juice always running, running into her eyes – year in, year out, until by Free Come day, she total blind.

All those stories about slave time. When Grace a girl, she use to yell at her mother, why I should *care* about slave time? It done! It gone! We free now!

And Mother Semanthe used to say, it never done, girl. Don't you know that yet?

Jesum Peace!

But the funny thing about it, as Grace grows up and becomes a woman, she starts to think about slave time too. And now she thirty-seven years old, and she thinks of it more and more. All these black confusion feelings churning away in her head, about slave time and Mother Semanthe and everything.

Ember cracks, and Grace reaches out and settles it down under the coalpot, and checks on the bake bananas.

Reverend Mayeau over at the Baptist Church at Salt Wash, he says, Grace, you got to find a way to get *along* with those feelings of yours, or you never be free.

And she try. She try everything. Try Bible-talk and myalism and Revivalism and obeah. Try black lover, white lover, yellow, brown. Nothing help. Still those black confusion feelings churning away in her head.

Maybe she got to work out *who* she is, before she can work out how to live. But who she is? She Negro, mocho, Jamaican, nigger, black, Congo and Koromantyn. She all those things. But she still don't know who the hell she is.

Only time these mix-up confusion feelings go away is when she looks at Evie and Victory.

She's growing them up straight and strict, and they shooting up fast, like love bush scrambling over house. Skin smooth and brown; eyes bright and black like ackee seeds.

Grace leans back and blows smoke-ring at the sky. Raise up you spirits, Gracie girl, she tells herself. Things could be worser. You got two fine children. You got the best place in the village. Hell, you got the *only* damn place in the village!

That always make her crack a laugh.

She still laughing when the chickens start up a squabble, and she sees a figure coming down the path from the aqueduct. But what is this? Jesum Peace. Is Miss Maddy walking quick, quick, with her skirts trailing out behind her like a fishtail. What in hell she doing down here?

Grace dislikes Miss Maddy. Oh, she speaks nice and sweet, and she seems soft and weakly, like all buckra woman. But she different. She hiding something. Grace can't make out what.

And right now she's got some worry-head in her, Grace can see that straight. She's like a piece of tight-stretch elastic, like she's got trouble in head and heart.

'You walking late, Miss Maddy,' says Grace, getting to her feet. She behaves respectful, but not too respectful. She may be only a helper, and Miss Maddy up-class Society lady – but hell, Miss Maddy's in Grace own self yard.

'I don't have much time,' Miss Maddy says. 'I need to get back, to dress for dinner.'

Now why in hell, thinks Grace, Miss Maddy come all this way down the hill this night, when she could a sent for Grace up at Master Jocelyn house at any time? Grace only been up there at the wash-house the whole damn day.

Then Grace says to herself, hn. Maybe Miss Maddy don't want that husband of hers to know. That Master Sinclair with the lock-purse mouth and the trickified ways. Cho! To see him walking round Master Jocelyn place as if he the original proud thing, it makes Grace spit.

'I need something from you,' says Miss Maddy, simple straight.

'I know it, ma'am,' says Grace.

'I need you to make one of those little charm-bags. Like the ones your children wear?'

Grace give Miss Maddy the blank eye. 'I don't know, ma'am,' she says.

'Yes you do. It's a little bag with rosemary and spirit weed and Madam Fate. And probably other things besides.'

Now Grace getting on suspicious. How Miss Maddy know a thing like that? 'You fooling me up, Miss Maddy,' she says. 'Black people medicine for buckra lady? Cho!'

'I'll pay you a shilling,' Miss Maddy says.

'Oh, I don't know, ma'am,' says Grace again. But in her

head she thinking, hn. White people always calling black people magic 'witchcraft', and saying it *bad*. But then they go right along and make their *own* self magic! They turn wine into blood, and eat up God himself every Sunday sabbath! And now this buckra lady she wants a piece of *black* people magic, too besides. Grace considers that powerful strange. Out loud she just says again, 'I don't know, ma'am.'

'It isn't for me,' says Miss Maddy. 'It's for Missy Sophie.'

'Missy Sophie, ma'am?'

She nods.

Grace spits. 'That child sick bad, ma'am. She flaking away. Needs strong tea, and maybe a bush-bath. Then she go pick up again.'

'Perhaps. But right now what she thinks she needs is that charm. Will you make her one?'

Grace swallows her spit and considers a while. Not all buckra bad. Master Cameron and old Master Jocelyn now; and poor Miss Clemmy. And that little Missy Sophie, she all right, too. Course, she always got to be making some kind of noise, that one, like it hurt her to stay silent for a moment. She got to be talking a stream, or singing, or argifying with that jack-mule of hers. But she all right. Grace says, 'I think pon it a while, ma'am.'

'Think on it quickly,' Miss Maddy says sharp.

Grace scratches her headkerchief. Decides have a little fun. 'You come from foreign, ma'am, but you understand potwah good. I know some buckra ladies, live here roundabout long time, never understand as good as you.'

Miss Maddy colours right up, like she just been found out. She hiding something. Sure as sin.

Grace takes a pull on her pipe. 'You bring trouble to the house, Miss Maddy. You not who you say.'

Miss Maddy tight up her hand, but not turn way her eye. She not to frighten easy, that true to the fact. She says, 'You're impertinent, Grace. You should watch your tongue.'

Grace takes a next pull on her pipe and decides have little more fun. 'You understand potwah,' she says. 'Well, I speak buckra talk, you know.' She straightens up and says in buckra talk, 'That is, when I have a mind to do so.' She cracks a laugh. 'Oh yes. Master Cameron teach it to I.'

But look me trouble, what all this? Soon as Grace says soldierman name, Miss Maddy she opens her mouth like she got a sudden thought, and dislikes how it taste. What the hell this all about?

Then it comes to Grace. Miss Maddy finding out that marriage have teeth, and bite hot. And maybe that old charm of Grace did its work on Master Sinclair and struck out him manhood, and he getting vex and blaming it on her, like men always do if they get the chance. And Miss Maddy young, and her blood calling out loud and natural, even if she not know it yet – and she *dislikes* the notion of Gracie McFarlane and soldierman together. And maybe, maybe she got an eye for him herself.

Certain sure, Miss Maddy she looking at Grace like she burning to ask something more about it, but can't, for she too damn proud. 'One shilling,' she says, strict and sharp. 'Bring the charm tomorrow. Bring it to me and no-one else. Do it for Missy Sophie.'

'We see about it, ma'am,' says Grace.

She watches Miss Maddy go, and she thinks, well all right. I bring the charm tomorrow for the little girl child, so maybe her blood thicken, and she pick up some.

But you, Miss Maddy. You better watch out, now. Gracie McFarlane and Master Cameron they gone their separate ways from long, long time – but Gracie still watches out for him.

Don't you go make trouble for him, Miss Maddy. Or I make trouble for you.

Chapter Eighteen

Excerpt from the *Pall Mall Gazette*, 22nd March 1884 (in the personal files of Mrs Olivia Herapath)

. . . No incident at the Battle of Tamai was more distressing than that which followed the death of Major Alasdair Falkirk, a gallant and much-decorated officer who was cut down by Dervishes in the immediate aftermath of the conflict. Shortly after the unfortunate hero's fall, one Captain Cameron Lawe, a junior officer, was seen rifling through the dead man's pockets and extracting a piece of paper therefrom, which he straightway destroyed.

Captain Lawe has since declined to explain his extraordinary conduct, or indeed, the nature of the altercation which was seen to take place between the two men on the eve of the battle.

What was the paper he destroyed? A promissory note? A letter from a lady? We may never know, for the Captain persists in his silence – which is said to have weighed heavily against him at his recent Court-Martial . . .

Proceedings before a General Court-Martial held at Fort Euryalus, Suakin, on the 18th day of March 1884, on Captain Cameron Anthony Lawe, 61377, 25th King's Own Scottish Borderers.

. . . Throughout these proceedings you have persistently, I might say wilfully, declined any assistance in your defence,

and pleaded guilty to the charges arraigned against you. For
the last time, do you wish to alter your plea?
Prisoner: No.
Prosecuting officer: *Do you wish to bring evidence as to*
the nature of the altercation between yourself and the
deceased?
Prisoner: No.
Prosecuting officer: *Do you wish to bring any evidence what-*
soever in your defence?
Prisoner: No.
Prosecuting officer: *Do you wish to exercise your right to*
cross-examine the witnesses for the prosecution?
Prisoner: No.
Prosecuting officer: *Do you wish to bring evidence as to your*
character?
Prisoner: No.
Prosecuting officer: *Do you wish to exercise your right to*
address the Court?
Prisoner: No.
Prosecuting officer: *Do you wish to bring evidence in miti-*
gation of punishment?
Prisoner: No.

Madeleine closed Mrs Herapath's blue morocco folder and
tied it up again with the pink satin ribbon.

She tried to picture the court-martial in the stuffy little fort
at Suakin. She could almost hear Cameron Lawe infuriating the prosecutor with his blunt, unhelpful replies.
Wilfully, almost perversely calling down on himself the full
wrath of the army. As if he no longer cared what became of
him.

She kneaded her temple. What was she doing here, sitting
on Mrs Herapath's sofa with this lovingly assembled file of
cuttings on her lap? What good did it do? What was she
hoping to find?

She didn't know. All she knew was that in the weeks since
she had seen him at the Burying-place, she had found herself
going over and over every word, every expression, every

glance that had passed between them. He had been so honest with her; even at the end, when he'd clearly hated every minute of her relentless questioning. And he'd made no attempt to cast himself in a favourable light.

Perhaps that was why she was here now. Because in some strange way she felt she owed it to him to find out the truth behind the stark facts he had given her.

And if she was honest, there was another reason too. Perhaps, in talking to Mrs Herapath, she might discover whether he and Grace McFarlane were lovers.

'Well?' said Mrs Herapath, dragging her back to the present. 'What do you think?'

Madeleine coloured, glad that the older woman couldn't guess her thoughts. 'What do I think?' she said. 'I think – he kept quiet to protect Ainsley. That's it, isn't it? So that the world wouldn't discover that Alasdair Falkirk, the "gallant officer", was in fact Ainsley Monroe, the man who deserted his wife.'

'And didn't it work *splendidly*,' said Mrs Herapath, handing her a cup of tea. Thankfully, she wasn't 'manifesting' this afternoon – having entered, as she put it, 'a little patch of calm'.

'But surely', said Madeleine, 'people guessed that Alasdair Falkirk was Ainsley Monroe? I mean, people in Jamaica. It's not much of a disguise. Falkirk's the family name.'

'Oh, doubtless a few of them did,' said Mrs Herapath, 'but that's hardly the point. The point is, Cameron made it possible for people to behave as if they *hadn't* guessed.'

Madeleine watched her briskly despatching a buttered scone with guava jelly. All these rules, she thought. They weren't her rules. She had been born outside them. She felt like an interloper in an alien tribe.

With her forefinger she traced a circle on the blue morocco folder. 'What about the piece of paper he took from – the body. What was it? Do you know?'

'Letter from Clemency,' mumbled Mrs Herapath through a mouthful of scone. 'Granting Ainsley absolution. As it were.'

How like Clemency, thought Madeleine. Clemency with her breathless little laughs and her startling outbursts of truth. 'Oh, I didn't at *all* care for being married,' she had once confided. 'But I did so *adore* being with child. I felt so *significant.*'

And how like Cameron Lawe to have thrown away his career and his good name for the honour of the family which had brought him up. It seemed a curiously old-fashioned gesture. And it made Madeleine feel more of an outsider than ever, and obscurely angry with him. After all, she was the one with the Monroe blood – and yet it was he, the adopted son, who had done the honourable thing. It was an unwelcome reminder that she was not only a bastard but a liar, and dishonourable through and through.

'How do you know all this?' she asked, stirring her tea.

'Why, Cameron told me, of course,' said Mrs Herapath. 'A few months after Hector died.' Her glance strayed to the photograph above the writing desk, and she shook her head. 'Desperate time. Desperate. But that darling boy used to come down out of the hills every week, just to see me. He was the only one I could tolerate. He didn't *pussyfoot*. We just sat and smoked and talked about Hector. Such a tonic. And that glorious voice.' A flush rose to her cheeks, and she blinked rapidly. 'You know, I've always believed that he told me his story as a sort of *distraction*. To "take me out of myself", as one's maid might say. And it worked beautifully. For of course, as soon as he told me the bare bones, I simply had to know every last little thing. That's why I sent for the transcripts.' Her tone implied that transcripts of military proceedings could be obtained as easily as a mail-order catalogue from Whiteley's – which, if one was a baron's daughter, they presumably could.

'But I still don't understand,' said Madeleine. 'Why won't Jocelyn see him? Surely he of all people must have guessed why Cameron did it?'

'Oh, undoubtedly.'

'Then why?'

Mrs Herapath spread her tapered fingers. 'Disgrace is disgrace, my dear. Discharge with ignominy. Incarceration. Scarcely the sort of career which Jocelyn had planned for him.'

'But – Cameron did it to protect him. I can't believe that even Jocelyn—'

'Believe it, my dear. There's granite in that old man.'

And perhaps, Madeleine reflected, Cameron had been right in what he had told her at the Burying-place. *Some people need outrage in their lives. It helps them screen out what they're too afraid to confront.*

And it was certainly true that no-one on the Northside seemed to want to remember Ainsley and Rose. Even Cameron himself didn't like to talk of them. She thought of his taut face at the Burying-place when she had questioned him.

And Mrs Herapath, despite professing to have adored Rose, had expunged all trace of her from her cluttered, picture-lined little drawing-room. Earlier that afternoon she had told Madeleine that she'd destroyed all her photographs of Rose. She had been so *angry*, she said. So angry and so let down.

It reminded Madeleine of Cousin Lettice burning her mother's photographs in the grate at Cairngowrie House; and Jocelyn overturning his son's gravestone. It was as if they all believed that by destroying the image or the graven word, they could somehow erase the person.

She glanced down at the folder on her lap. Strange. She had expected to feel the old, familiar anger towards her parents. After all, here was yet another life which they had managed to wreck. Instead, she felt only pity and dismay.

'I suppose', she said, 'none of this would have happened if Ainsley hadn't married Clemency. But from what she's told me, he wasn't in love with her. Or she with him. So why did they marry? Why did they marry if they weren't in love?'

Mrs Herapath gave a bark of laughter. 'My dear! What an astonishingly naïve question.'

Madeleine flushed.

'And remember, Ainsley wasn't even twenty. I'm rather afraid that poor dear Jocelyn practically forced him into it.'

'Forced him? I – didn't know that.'

'Didn't you?' She shrugged. 'But you mustn't blame the old man. He genuinely believed that he was acting for the best. As indeed he was.'

'But why should he want his son to marry a Traherne? He detests the Trahernes.'

'Well of course he does. We all do. But they're still vastly preferable to the Durrants.'

'The D— I don't understand.'

'Why, my dear, if it hadn't been for that marriage to Clemency, Ainsley and Rose would have eloped.'

'*Eloped?* But – I thought the affair with Rose began *after* he married Clemency.'

'Good heavens no! Ainsley and Rose had been in love since they were children.'

At that moment there was a knock at the door, and Etheline came in with fresh hot water and scones.

In a daze, Madeleine watched Mrs Herapath briskly fielding the refreshments, thanking the helper, and waiting for her to leave, all with that suspenseful air which people assume when they're keen to go on with a choice piece of gossip.

She offered Madeleine the plate of scones, then helped herself to another. 'Eighteen sixty-six,' she said, reaching for the butter dish. 'That's when they met. Of course, they'd met before. Dozens of times. But that was the first time they actually *saw* one another, if you know what I mean. Fever Hill great house. Boxing Day Masquerade.'

'You – were there?'

'Oh, everyone was there. It may be difficult to credit now, but in those days, Jocelyn was really rather sociable.' She stopped buttering her scone, and looked back into the past. 'Ainsley arrived late, as I recall. Caused quite a stir in his costume. Banquo's ghost. Completely white. Immensely striking. And there in the ballroom was Rose as some sort of

– *signorina*, I believe. I dare say it was simply got up, with just a few scraps from her grandmother's clothes-press, for they never had any money to speak of. But she *did* look enchanting.' She shook her head. 'They must have been – what, sixteen? So terribly *young*.'

On the bookshelf, the ormolu clock struck half-past five. Out in the square, a street-seller went past, touting her wares. '*Ripe pear gwine past! Ripe pear! Ripe pear!*'

Mrs Herapath's gaze returned to the portrait of Hector. 'I must say, I did feel rather sorry for them,' she said. 'You know what it's like when one falls in love for the first time. It's as if there's a current simply pulling one along. One can't escape it. One can't swim against it. All one can do is follow it, and hope that one doesn't drown.'

Madeleine made no reply. With great care she placed her teacup on the side table at her elbow. 'But if they were so much in love,' she said at last, 'why didn't Jocelyn let them marry?'

Mrs Herapath's dreamy expression vanished. 'A *Durrant*? Two hundred years of dissolution and *crimes passionnels* and goodness knows what else besides? Oh no, my dear. That would never have done.'

'But – from what I've heard, there's no family on the Northside that hasn't had its share of that sort of thing. Including the Monroes.'

'Well, the odd indiscretion, of course. But the trouble with the Durrants was that they always went too *far*.'

It was Madeleine's turn to look back into the past. She remembered her father saying something similar to her mother during one of their passionate arguments.

She turned back to Mrs Herapath. 'Did you ever correspond with Rose? I mean, after she went to England?'

Mrs Herapath looked outraged. 'Good heavens, no!'

'But I thought she was your friend.'

'She *was*. But she forfeited all that when she ran off with Ainsley.'

There was an uncomfortable silence.

Mrs Herapath moved the sugar basin a fraction to the

right, then moved it back again. 'She knew the rules, Madeleine. But she didn't *respect* them. That was always her mistake. It would have been perfectly possible for her to have carried on seeing him after he married Clemency, so long as they'd been *discreet*. Happens all the time. No-one causes a to-do about it – because no-one is forced to *know*. But Rose couldn't do that. Oh, no. She had to run off with him. She had to make it impossibe for us all to ignore.'

So that was her crime, thought Madeleine. It wasn't that she broke the rules, but that she broke them in such a way that it was impossible to ignore.

It struck her as strange that Mrs Herapath should have reserved all her opprobrium for Rose. It was as if in such affairs the man were merely the passive victim, and only the woman was guilty.

For the first time in a decade, she felt sorry for her mother. It seemed a terrible punishment, to be cut off for ever from everyone she had known, and exiled from this lush, ruined, bewitchingly beautiful island where she had spent her whole life. After Jamaica, Cairngowrie House must have seemed so bleak.

She watched Mrs Herapath buttering another scone with some ferocity. 'You still miss her,' she said.

'I do not,' snapped Mrs Herapath.

There was an uncomfortable silence.

'It's just such a *shame*', Mrs Herapath burst out, 'that the whole wretched muddle had to whiplash onto Cameron. Confounded waste. Attractive boy like that.' She plucked a crumb from her lap and frowned at it. 'You want to be careful about that, my dear.'

Madeleine was startled. 'What do you mean?'

'This sudden interest in transcripts and whatnot. I'm not at all sure that it will do.'

She felt herself colouring. 'You were the one who suggested I should learn more about the family.'

'This isn't what I meant.'

'Yes it is. He's family, isn't he? I don't see the harm.'

'That,' said Mrs Herapath, 'is rather my point.'

Evie has found out where my shadow is. In return for my silver crucifix that Cousin L gave me when I was confirmed, she went and asked a great many black people (not Grace of course), and finally learned that my shadow is in the hothouse – where I can't go. I had suspected it was there, for the hothouse is full of duppies, as it was once the slave hospital.

Victory has offered to go and fetch it for me. He said it would be safer if he went, as I might not be able to keep the duppies at bay. I think that is SO brave, but of course I said no. Victory is only six; it wouldn't be fair. Besides, he wouldn't know which shadow is mine.

Despite what Evie says, I bet I CAN get to the hothouse on my own. I can move about quite well now on my crutches, and I wouldn't have to go all the way up the rise, for Victory says there is a path that goes around it, if one knows where to look. That would be much easier. And for protection, I have the little charm which Grace made for me, and Victory has brought some extra rosemary, which I've put in a glass of water by my bed. But I wish I had my crucifix as well.

The best time to go will be extremely early in the morning, when nobody has woken up, and the duppies are still asleep. The morning after the Trahernes' ball will be the best, for then everyone will stay in bed until very late.

Out on the lawns Remus barked twice, and then fell silent.

Sophie stopped writing and drew back the mosquito curtain. She turned down the lamp, and moonlight streamed through the broken louvres. The lawns were bleached to silver. The duppy tree was a pillar of darkness, with great outstretched arms.

Sophie listened for a long time, but Remus didn't bark again. All she could hear were the crickets and the distant hoot of Patoo, and the slow creak of the floorboards as Great-Aunt May walked the upper gallery.

Sophie wondered if she would have the courage to brave

the hothouse on her own. That afternoon, when she was talking it over with Victory, it hadn't seemed too daunting. But here in the dark, it seemed impossible.

As she was pondering that, a sharp cry echoed through the sleeping house. *I can't! I can't!*

Sophie caught her breath. She pulled the sheets up to her mouth and waited. But the cry didn't come again.

Someone had been having a nightmare. She couldn't tell who it was, except that it had been the voice of a grown-up. A grown-up having a nightmare. A terrifying thought. She had never imagined that grown-ups could be so scared.

'I can't! I can't!'

Sinclair collapsed beside his wife and rolled onto his back, shuddering and staring up into the darkness. After a while he drew a deep breath. 'This cannot go on,' he said.

His wife raised herself on her elbow to look at him. Her face was grave, but he knew that inside she was laughing at him. Why was she forever laughing at him?

He sat up and poured himself a glass of water from the decanter on the bedside table. The chloral made it bitter, but he drained it with a grateful shudder.

In the glow from the nightlight his wife had an unwholesome beauty, and he felt again the deep, dirty pull in his loins. He wanted her, but whenever he tried to take her, he couldn't. His flesh wilted. His skin prickled with dread.

It was all her fault. Sometimes when he was alone, he would take one of her camisoles from the dressing-room and press it to his face. And always beneath the milky scent of her skin he would catch that faint, impure sweetness: the smell of blood. It didn't matter how many baths she took. He would always detect it now.

Why was God punishing him? Why had this affliction struck him, an innocent man?

He had been so hopeful when they had first married. Surely, he had reasoned, the dying sister must be the only one afflicted, and his wife almost pure – or at least, pure enough to bear his child?

Beside him, his wife lay back on the pillows. 'You should

try to get some sleep,' she said, her voice falsely gentle.

'What an original idea,' he snapped.

She ignored that. 'Perhaps,' she said, 'if you stopped taking the chloral for a while—'

'If I require medical advice,' he said, 'I shall consult Dr Pritchard.' He turned on his side so that he wouldn't have to look at her.

'Goodnight, Sinclair,' she said.

He did not reply.

Long after she had fallen asleep, he lay watching the ethereal glimmer of the nightlight through the gauze. It looked so pure. So spiritual. Small wonder that his wife detested it. She said it disturbed her to have a jar of fireflies slowly dying through the night.

He gazed into the soft, pulsing light, and waited for the chloral to carry him away.

He awoke drenched in sweat, and throbbing with a desire so strong that it hurt.

It was nearly dawn. The fireflies were dead. He lay on his back, wondering what to do. This was becoming unbearable.

At length he slid out of bed and crept to the dressing-room, moving softly so as not to alert his wife. He needed to be alone. He needed to pray. He needed to get away from his wife.

He crossed the lawns and began to climb the rise. The sky was lightening in the east when he reached the top, and below him Fever Hill still slumbered in a light morning haze. He took a deep draught of cool, fresh air, and some of the tension within him began to subside.

This is what matters, he told himself as he looked out over his inheritance. Not some female sullying your bed. But this.

Below him lay the great house, and beyond it the New Works and Clairmont Hill, and the ruins of the Old Works, and the cane-pieces of Alice Grove all the way to the road. To the west lay the cane-fields of Glen Marnoch and the Queen of Spains Valley and the distant works at Caledon. To the south-west lay the hill-pastures of Corner Pen and the treetops of Providence, and to the south-east, the lush young cane of Bellevue and Greendale and Bamboo Walk, stretching all the way to the Martha Brae. To the edge of Eden.

Eden. As always, the thought of his brother brought an upsurge of bitterness.

The *injustice* of it. He, Sinclair, was the beautiful one; the godly one deserving of praise. And yet simply because he had been born a few years later, none of that mattered. Despite court-martial, incarceration and disgrace, people respected his brother more than they did him. Men measured their actions against his. Women sought his protection and regard. Even now, Clemency missed him, May feared him, and Jocelyn loved him the more. And why? Simply because he was the *elder*.

A gust of wind cooled his face. He shut his eyes. Calm yourself. Calm. *Cain killed Abel and was cast out, and Seth the third son of Adam found grace in the eyes of the Lord, and from his loins all men descended.*

You *shall* come into your inheritance.

He pictured that day just as he had as a boy, when Great-Aunt May had first read him the story of Cain and Abel and Seth. He would be riding a white horse up the carriageway, and people would be lining up to honour him. His brother would be destitute and friendless, and Sinclair would lean down and extend the hand of charity. Perhaps.

Already the sun was burning off the mist, and the birds were beginning to stir. But he wasn't ready to go back yet. He couldn't face the same torture all over again. Wanting her, and being repelled by her; feeling her sapping his strength, depriving him of his manhood.

He turned and set off down the other side of the hill.

He walked without seeing, but after a while a stink of rottenness brought him back to his surroundings, and he saw that he had reached the ruins of the old slave hospital. He was standing in a dank, shadowy little dell, where broadleaf trees and ironwoods blotted out the sky. Thick cords of strangler fig trailed over the tumbled cut-stone walls. The rasp of crickets rose and fell like the swell of a dirty sea.

Before him stood the windowless cell where the less viable

slaves had been sequestered. Its bulletwood door still hung firm on its hinges.

Once, when he was eight, he had trapped his brother inside that cell. The aim had been to frighten him, but it had failed. Cameron had become so angry that when his shouts had drawn a garden boy and he was freed, Sinclair had had to run all the way to Great-Aunt May for protection. And it had been Cameron she had asked Jocelyn to thrash, as punishment for frightening his younger brother.

As his eyes became accustomed to the gloom, he noticed a plant growing on the threshold of the cell. Its great glossy leaves were speckled with sickly grey, like some loathsome disease. That, he thought, is what the blacks call dumb-cane; because a few drops of its milky juice on the tongue of a recalcitrant slave caused hours of choking agony.

Once again he felt the dark, dirty tug at his loins. It was as if the evil thing were calling out to him.

No-one crosses this threshold, it whispered. *Even the blacks don't venture in, for fear of their filthy heathen spirits. But you need not be afraid, for you are a white man. You could penetrate this darkness. And here you could ease the intolerable pressure building inside you.*

He felt the sweat break out on his forehead. His breath came fast and shallow. You could do it, he thought. And no-one would ever know.

Perhaps. But God would know. *And God*, as Great-Aunt May used to tell him, *has a special Eye for what is done in the dark*.

He turned and ran. He crashed through the undergrowth: raising clouds of midges, startling ground doves, and tearing his clothes. He didn't stop until he was back at the top of the rise.

'What am I to *do*?' he whispered to the empty sky. 'Why did You give me that woman and then deny me a son? How am I to come into my inheritance? Help me! For I am innocent!'

But no answer came.

He looked down at the great house, and felt a sudden horror at what his life had become. Soon he must go back down there and bathe and shave and dress, and sit at breakfast opposite that mocking, disobedient creature whom he had the misfortune to call his wife.

Why do women exist? he wondered. Weak, passive, unreflecting creatures, whose only purpose is to kindle vile appetites in the flesh of men, while they themselves – the *injustice* of it – remain coldly inert to carnal desire.

CHAPTER NINETEEN

I speak buckra talk, Grace McFarlane had said, looking Madeleine up and down with her lovely, insolent eyes. *Oh yes. Mas' Camron teach it to I.*

Beautiful, independent, knowing Grace, with her polished mahogany skin and her frank, uninhibited ways. Of course she would appeal to a man like him. Wouldn't she?

It was a wildly inappropriate thought to be having at the Trahernes' July Ball. But then, Madeleine hadn't expected Cameron Lawe to be there, drinking cognac in the billiard-room.

She had been with Mrs Herapath, crossing the marble entrance-hall towards the ballroom, when she had seen him, standing silently amid a throng of gentlemen.

As if suddenly conscious that he was being watched, he had turned his head, and their eyes had locked. She had known by his stillness, and by some deeper sense that she couldn't explain, that he was sharply, intensely *aware* of her, as she was of him.

The next instant the moment was broken. One of the gentlemen clapped him on the shoulder, and for a second he was distracted. Madeleine seized her chance and swept on towards the ballroom.

He isn't supposed to be here, she told herself fiercely. He never goes into Society. It isn't fair.

For she had decided that Mrs Herapath was right. It just wouldn't do.

And now she stood, as she had stood all evening, in the Trahernes' enormous, shimmering ballroom, longing to be safely back home with Sophie, where she wouldn't have to think about anything. Least of all Cameron Lawe.

It was one o'clock in the morning, and Sinclair had declared it their duty to stay until three. So far she had danced with him once, and once with Cornelius Traherne, and once with Jocelyn. She had smiled until her cheeks were stiff, and seen enough beaded trims and chiffon overdresses to give Clemency an exhaustive account of the latest importations. She had heard her first orchestra, and been astonished that they all managed to play the same tune without getting lost. She had listened to a river of Mrs Herapath's imperious gossip, and wondered what her friend would say if she learned that she was talking to a bastard who had once posed for photographs in the nude. And she had kept a silent watch for Cameron Lawe, and been relieved and disappointed when he did not appear.

And underneath it all, she had felt a creeping unease. Looking about her at the Trahernes' bought-in sophistication, she'd had the strangest feeling that this whole glittering masquerade might at any moment be swept away by the darkness waiting at the edges. The delicacy of Strauss might fill the ballroom, but outside the air rang with the crickets' harsh song. In the galleries, Italian finches sang in little filigree cages, but out in the moonlight it was Patoo who haunted the trees. And through it all the soft-footed helpers glided among the guests in impenetrable silence.

But no-one else seemed to notice anything amiss, least of all their host. And why should he? According to Mrs Herapath, Cornelius Traherne had just crowned himself emperor of Northside Society by betrothing his elder daughter to an Irving of Ironshore.

And he had clearly spared no expense to celebrate his triumph. Parnassus, the first great house in Trelawny to be wired for electricity, was a blaze of light. The grounds had been newly landscaped by English gardeners, the cinnamon and pimento trees clipped to release their fragrance, and the pergolas planted with roses, stephanotis and mignonettes.

The state rooms had been repanelled in satinwood, the ball-room newly floored in black and white Carrara, and the band of the West India Regiment replaced by a thirty-piece orchestra shipped out from Vienna.

An army of French chefs had been drafted in to create *tortue claire, foie gras à la gelée, filet de boeuf hollandaise*, and *charlotte à l'italienne* – and, for the traditionalists among the guests, baked black land-crabs, fricassée of ring-tailed pigeon, and lobster pepperpot. Silent helpers dispensed Margaux, Lafitte, and Pommery Extra Sec.

It was very perfection. Although, as Mrs Herapath remarked to Madeleine between the gavotte and the polka, 'It takes more than a liveried footman to make a gentleman.'

And Cornelius's great-great-grandfather had known all about that, for he had been a blacksmith. 'Yes, my dear, a *blacksmith*. Isn't it killing? His name was *Owen*, I believe. Sailed for Jamaica in 1714, bought a swathe of cheap Government land, and set about "bettering himself", as these people do. Kowtowed to the Monroes, the Lawes and the other first families, sent his sons home to become gentle-men, and purchased slaves by the shipload. And imported fresh batches every three years.'

And when he died, his son had left the estate with an over-seer and gone back to England to live off the revenue, and his heirs had followed suit. It was only in 1832 that the Christmas Rebellion had summoned Addison Traherne back to Jamaica, to view the blackened ruins of Parnassus, and four thousand acres of cane turned to ash.

At 'home' the Government had pushed through the Emancipation Bill, and in Jamaica the slump had set in. And as blacks could no longer be forced to work for nothing, the columns of the *Gleaner* had filled with notices of bank-ruptcy. Soon estates could be had for the price of a dinner service.

And Addison had looked about him and seen that the only men to prosper were the money-lenders, so he had become one himself. The family motto was *Deus mihi providebit*: God will provide. 'But in the meantime,' as Mrs Herapath paraphrased behind her fan, 'I intend to help myself. And if that means profiting from other men's ruin, then so be it.'

Once he had risen to the top of the pile, Addison had set about consolidating his grip on Jamaican Society. By now his one mistake was some years in the past, when he'd over-reached himself by offering for the foremost Beauty of the island, the imperiously lovely May Monroe, and been summarily rejected. 'My dear, of what can he have been thinking? His people were *blacksmiths*, for heaven's sake! Can you imagine her consternation? I don't believe she ever forgave him. Or any of the Trahernes. Indeed I'm not at all sure that she hasn't been blaming poor silly Clemency ever since.'

But Addison had worn his rejection lightly, and made a brilliant marriage to a Barrett of Cinnamon Hill and then to a Palairet of Greendale – finally expunging his youthful humiliation by betrothing his daughter Clemency to May's great-nephew Ainsley. He'd survived to see his oldest son Cornelius marry a Hall of Tryall, then a McFarlane of Caledon (both of whom died conveniently young), and finally the enormously wealthy Rebecca Sammond of – 'of Lombard Street, I'm very much afraid. And they do *say* that her grandpapa absolutely changed his name. *From Salomon*.'

But although Mrs Herapath might deplore the 'aquiline' turn of Rebecca Traherne's nose, not to mention Cornelius's 'rather vulgar' penchant for very young girls of whatever class or shade, her disapproval was voiced discreetly, behind her fan. There wasn't a Society household in Trelawny which was not in debt to the Trahernes, and that included herself.

'But the *singular* thing', she went on, shaking her head so that her startling dragonfly headdress seemed about to take wing, 'is that young Irving seems actually to have fallen for little Davina. Isn't that killing? I hear old Meredith wasn't too keen at first, but his boy absolutely threatened to run off and join the Legion, so what could he do? Oh look, there they go now. She's underbred, of course, and that figure won't last, but one must admit that they're rather sweet.'

Madeleine gave her a strained smile. She knew it was ungenerous, but she had no desire to gaze fondly upon a young couple who were 'so very much in love'. Davina Traherne was only two years younger than herself.

The waltz ended, and Madeleine watched the Irving boy leading his fiancée to a little gilt sofa, and bringing her a rose-water ice and gazing into her eyes, and generally getting as close as he could before a score of watchful relations.

Suddenly an image came to her of Ben Kelly kissing the little skivvy in the Portland Road. It was disturbing and inappropriate, but she couldn't shake it off. She remembered the way their jaws had moved. The glitter in their eyes when they drew apart.

She turned to find Sinclair watching her from across the room. His gaze was cool and unsmiling, and she returned it in kind. In his dress coat he looked severely beautiful, but there were shadows beneath his eyes. Despite the chloral he had not been sleeping well, and there were nights when he awoke ten times, and knelt on the floor to check beneath the bed for charms. And in some way that she didn't understand, he blamed her for his malaise, although when she asked him, he always professed not to know what she meant.

What was it about her that horrified him? Why had he married her?

Suddenly the music was loud in her ears; the ballroom hot and airless. She had to get out. She muttered an excuse to Mrs Herapath and went through into the gallery.

It was almost as crowded as the ballroom. She descended the steps to the lower terraces. They were quieter, but the ladies and gentlemen among the potted orange trees were not eager to be noticed. Tonight, everywhere she looked she encountered courting couples. She left the terraces and finally reached a pergola which opened onto the lawns, and was mercifully empty.

She took a deep breath, but still felt breathless. The air was warm and still, and heavy with the scent of cinnamon and stephanotis, and the bitter haze from the Spanish braziers that kept the mosquitoes at bay. Across the lawns, banks of white tea-roses glowed in the moonlight, and strings of lanterns flickered in the trees. The night-song of the crickets was a clear, pulsing ring.

Above her head, through gaps in the pergola, she glimpsed the people on the upper terraces. They seemed a world apart: golden and unreal, like some glittering *tableau vivant*.

She snapped off a stephanotis flower and crushed its waxy white petals in her palm, staining her white kid evening glove, and releasing a heavy, funereal perfume. Again that image came to her of Ben kissing the girl in the Portland Road. The glitter in their eyes. The way their jaws had worked.

Then another image took over. Grace McFarlane. Beautiful, independent, knowing Grace.

She shredded another flower and ground its petals beneath her dancing slipper, and wondered what it would be like to be kissed by a man.

I wish I was old, she thought savagely, with everything behind me. I wish I was old and terrifying, like Great-Aunt May.

Like a sorceress summoned by an incantation, Great-Aunt May appeared on the upper terrace. She looked magnificent, in a forbiddingly tight gown of pewter *peau de soie*, with an aigrette of jet crowning her iron-grey hair, and long, narrow gloves of glacé kid.

'Brought up to snare a duke,' Mrs Herapath had told Madeleine at supper. 'Punishing childhood. Punishing. Backboards. Tight-lacing. Governess used to make her practise walking across a ballroom for hours. Sandbag on the head. New dancing slippers. And you know how treacherous those satinwood floors can be. *How* she didn't break an ankle I'll never know. But you see, it was all part of the plan. Her destiny. To be presented at Court and become a Beauty, and snare a duke. And in the end, she managed everything but the duke. Turned out they were in short supply that Season. Or some such thing. At any rate, she didn't "take".'

Looking up at her now, Madeleine caught a glimpse of what had shaped the old despot. The predestined match had failed to appear, so she had resolved to have no-one. The world had robbed her of her birthright, and she had decided to despise the world. Everything she did expressed her disdain. The savage tight-lacing. The collars boned to the jaw. The rigid adherence to form. All taken to such extremes that they became an act of contempt for the very conventions she purported to honour.

I wonder if I'll end up like that, thought Madeleine. A fearsome old witch who hasn't touched another human being in fifty years.

Her throat tightened. Her eyes grew hot. *One must admit that they're rather sweet. And so very much in love.*

She ground another flower beneath her heel, and left the pergola and went out onto the lawn.

About thirty feet ahead of her, a man was walking up and down in the moonlight, smoking a cigar. She knew him instantly by his height and his fair hair and the set of his shoulders.

He turned his head and saw her, and for a moment they faced one another in silence.

She had wanted to see him again, but not like this. Not when she was in this strange angry mood, on the brink of tears. Slowly, not wishing to appear in retreat, she turned and walked back into the shadows beneath the pergola.

Then it occurred to her that far from indicating rejection, her behaviour might be taken as provocation. The unhurried turn, the bared nape of the neck. Rapunzel, Rapunzel, let down your hair. Was that what she had become? An unhappy wife ineptly flirting with her own brother-in-law?

Setting her teeth, she quickened her pace through the pergola, across the lower terrace, round the west wing, and into the gardens at the front of the house.

A flight of shallow steps led down into a sunken parterre overlooking the carriageway. She found a bench near the steps, and sat down. The parterre was bordered with clipped lime trees and planted with English lavender and yellow allamanda. From where she sat, an avenue of stately royal palms led down to the sea, with torches staked in between. In the distance she could just make out the pale glow of the beach, and beyond it the lights of a steamer approaching Falmouth.

Apart from the torches, there were no illuminations. There

didn't need to be. Moonlight flooded the parterre with silver-blue radiance. She was not invisible.

She wondered if he would follow her; if he thought that she wanted him to. Well she did, didn't she? That was why she was here. It was a sordid parody of the sort of coy hide-and-seek in which a courting couple might innocently indulge, but which this time was being played out between a married woman and her less than respectable brother-in-law.

Again she felt the pressure of unshed tears. Not *now*, she told herself.

She turned and watched him appear at the corner of the house, as she had known he would.

He made no pretence of finding her by chance. He walked swiftly through the garden and down into the parterre, halting at the foot of the steps about six feet from where she sat.

'Please go,' she said. 'I don't wish to talk to you.'

'Then why did you come out here?' he said in a low voice. 'You could have gone back into the house. But you didn't. You knew I'd follow you.'

She did not reply.

She watched him put his hand on the balustrade, and run his fingers over the lichen-crusted marble.

He was better groomed than before, but not by much. Sophie had told her that he kept his clothes in his old campaign chest 'because it's Abigail-proof. Abigail, that's his dog. Otherwise she sleeps on them.' His dress coat did indeed look as if it had spent several years inside a chest, his waistcoat seemed to date from the previous decade, and he had mislaid his gloves.

Somehow that made it harder. If he'd been impeccably elegant like his brother, it would have been easier to tell him to leave.

He glanced up to find her watching him, and for a moment they regarded each other in silence. Then he said, 'You ought to be careful, you know.' He realized how that sounded, and frowned. 'I mean, there aren't any braziers out here. If you were bitten, you might catch a fever.'

'I'm fine,' she said.

'No. I don't think you are.'

She was horrified to feel her eyes growing hot again. She drew a ragged breath. 'And *I* really think that you should go.'

'I don't want to go.'

'That's not gentlemanly.'

He gave her his incipient smile. 'You know the answer to that.'

She couldn't look at him any more. She glanced down at her fists clenched in her lap. If it weren't for these wretched evening gloves, she could dig her nails into her palms and really give herself something to cry about.

'Madeleine—'

'I'm *fine*,' she said again. And nearly broke down.

'Please *don't* feel sorry for me,' she said, when she had brought herself under control.

She was asking the impossible. Watching her fighting back the tears had been horrible. He had never felt so powerless.

She wore a gown of amber silk with a low, square neck edged in black. No jewels. Just a ribbon of amber satin in her hair. And when she turned away, he saw the little smooth bumps at the top of her spine. It was a physical effort to keep from reaching out and touching her.

'Do *not* feel sorry for me,' she said again, wiping her eyes with her fingers.

'I can't help it,' he replied. 'I should feel sorry for any woman married to my brother.'

There was a moment of appalled silence.

He shut his eyes. What had *possessed* him to say that? It might be the truth, but it sounded facetious and cruel. Like a bad imitation of Wilde.

'I suppose', she said, 'you think you can get away with remarks like that because of your past.'

'You're right. I apologize. I left my manners in prison.'

'How convenient for you. But I didn't think that ex-convicts attended balls.'

'Only this one,' he said. 'Cornelius likes to hedge his bets.'

'I don't understand.'

Now that they had shifted to neutral ground, she seemed calmer, and more inclined to talk. Perhaps she wanted to prove that she had not, a few moments ago, been on the verge of tears.

'I once obliged his father', he told her, 'by taking Eden off his hands. As there's still a chance that I might make a go of it, I always receive an invitation.' And I always send my regrets, he thought, and stay away. Until tonight.

My God, he thought, what are you doing? This is Sinclair's wife. His *wife*, for heaven's sake.

But that argument hadn't worked before, and it didn't work now. He had been thinking about her for months. Wondering what she thought of him, and why in God's name she had married Sinclair.

And that strange, edgy conversation at the Burying-place had raised more questions than it answered. At first she had been frightened of him, he was sure of it. But why? Then had come that moment when she'd looked into his eyes and seen something there, he didn't know what, and after that she hadn't been frightened any more. Again, *why*? She had the most expressive face. But strangely, although she wasn't good at hiding her feelings, she was extremely adept at concealing the reasons behind them. Such an astonishing mix of secrecy and directness.

And she'd cross-examined him mercilessly about Ainsley, forcing him to tell her the worst of himself. He ought to resent that, but he couldn't. He could only remember the way she had smiled at him. *That wasn't a very good idea*, he had said. *No*, she had replied with a slight smile, *I don't suppose it was*. In that moment he had felt a flash of pure recognition. There was no other word for it. He had *known* the person she was. He had known that they should be together.

She brought him back to the present by remarking that she hadn't appreciated that the Trahernes had once owned Eden. 'I thought it was the Durrants',' she said, smoothing her amber skirts.

It seemed an odd topic to pick. Why should she want to

know about that? Or was she still making uneasy small-talk to regain her composure?

He decided to play along with it. 'It was indeed the Durrants',' he told her. 'But they weren't too good at being planters, so they mortgaged the place to the hilt, and it ended up with old Addison Traherne. A couple of decades later I bought it.'

'Why?'

'Why did I buy it?'

She nodded.

He hesitated. He didn't want to mention Ainsley. 'It was cheap,' he said. 'It had been a ruin for twenty-four years.'

'Why in ruins?'

By now he was convinced that this wasn't small-talk. Beneath the generalities she had more personal concerns. He longed to know what they were. And he had the sense, too, that she was circling some taboo subject; some question that she wanted to ask. 'Oh,' he said lightly, 'the usual story. The price of sugar collapsed and the slaves were freed.'

She gave a slow nod. 'And you live there on your own?'

'Yes. Well. I have a cook, and a stable boy.'

Another nod. 'And you love it there.'

'Yes.' He frowned. 'How did you know that?'

She threw him a glance. 'It's not hard to tell.'

They were silent. Then he said, 'Why don't you ask me what you really want to ask?'

Again she flicked him a glance. Then she turned and gazed at the distant lights of the steamer. She laid her black silk fan in her lap, and put a hand to her temple and smoothed her hair. 'Very well,' she said. 'Is Grace McFarlane your mistress?'

Jesus Christ.

There was a taut silence. A gust of wind rustled the lime trees, and carried the scent of English lavender and cinnamon.

He cleared his throat. 'No,' he said. 'She isn't.'

She opened and shut the fan, and smoothed its black silk tassel over her knee. 'Was she your mistress in the past?'

He swallowed. 'Yes.'

Her profile remained impassive. He had underestimated her ability to conceal. Was she shocked? Presumably she would be. Wouldn't she? He wished she would turn and look at him.

'When?' she said, still looking down at her lap.

'About five years ago.'

Colour rose to her cheeks. 'How long did it last?'

'About a year.'

'Who began it?'

'Grace.'

'Is Evie your daughter?'

It was his turn to colour. 'Of course not. She's twelve years old.'

'Is Victory your son?'

'No. He's six years old.' He was beginning to feel giddy. It was bizarre and unwomanly of her to question him like this. He didn't want it to end.

'She's beautiful, isn't she,' she said. ' Grace, I mean.'

So are you, he told her silently.

'Isn't she?' she repeated, frowning slightly.

'I – suppose so. Yes.'

Still she wouldn't turn and look at him. He wished she would. He needed to see her eyes.

'Why are you always so honest with me?' she said at last. She sounded almost accusatory.

He ran his hand over the balustrade. 'I think', he said, 'that's one question too many.'

For the first time she turned and smiled at him. Not her meaningless social smile, but a proper one that made him catch his breath and want to do anything, anything in the world, to keep her from harm.

He told himself that he ought to leave right now, this very minute. Instead he went and spoilt it all. 'I think', he said, 'that it's my turn to ask a question.'

She inclined her head in silent assent.

'However did you come to marry my brother?'

Her smile faded. She looked as wary as she had at the

Burying-place: as if there were more behind his enquiry than mere unforgivable curiosity. 'He lived in the parish next to ours,' she said. 'I went and asked him for money.'

God, she was blunt.

'Our guardian had died,' she went on. 'We had nothing. I didn't know what else to do.'

'So you applied to the Church. And the Church asked you to marry him.'

'Yes.' She frowned. 'I still don't know why.'

Cameron stole a glance at her face and thought, Well, I could hazard a guess.

A breeze stirred the lime trees. The torchlight made the shadows leap in the royal palms.

She raised her chin and met his eyes. 'I married Sinclair for his money,' she said. 'That's what you wanted to know, isn't it? Well, that's the reason. That's the truth.'

But not the whole truth, he thought. She hadn't mentioned her sister. She seemed to be trying to shock him: to present the absolute worst of herself. He said, 'Why do you make yourself out to be worse than you are?'

'I don't.'

'Yes you do.'

She rose to her feet. 'You don't know enough about me to have an opinion. No-one does.'

'What does that mean?'

She pressed her lips together. 'Please, I think you should go now. And this time I really mean it.'

Standing, she came no higher than his chin. He had an urge to lift her and place her on the step next to him, so that they could look one another in the eye. But he knew that it wouldn't end there. He needed to kiss her, and he could sense that she wanted him to – although if he tried, she would push him away.

'Cameron,' she said. It was the first time she had spoken his name. 'This isn't helping.'

'I know,' he said. 'I do know.' The urge to touch her was almost overwhelming.

She said, ' You'd better go in first. I'll follow in a little while.'

He nodded, but didn't move. There was one last question he had to ask her. He knew that if he didn't ask it, it would haunt him for weeks. 'About Grace,' he said. 'Are you – shocked?'

She glanced down, turning the black silk fan in her fingers. 'I don't know,' she said at last. 'I suppose I must be.'

It wasn't the answer he wanted.

He turned on his heel and left her in the parterre, with the shadows leaping in the royal palms, and the wind from the sea stirring her amber skirts about her.

He went back through the garden almost at a run, and fought his way through the throng on the upper terraces, and took a hasty leave of Rebecca Traherne. Then he went out to the stables and called for his carriage, and wished to God that this infernal fancy dress hadn't forced him to bring the pony-trap instead of his horse. He wanted to put his spurs to Pilate and take him down the carriageway in a flat-out gallop, and to hell with them both if they broke their necks.

Why had he told her the truth about Grace? Why hadn't he had the sense to lie?

At that moment he saw his brother making purposefully towards him. Sinclair was pale, and there were red patches on his chin as if he'd been rubbing it.

God damn it to *hell*, thought Cameron.

'Off so soon?' said Sinclair.

'It's two in the morning,' snapped his brother. 'I've got to be up at five.'

Yes of course you must, thought Sinclair. For you are the man of action, aren't you, my brother? The soldier, the planter, the lover of Negro whores. The defiler of other men's wives.

He smiled. 'How commendably hard you work. I have no doubt that you shall reap your reward.'

His brother snorted.

In his mind Sinclair saw again what he'd just witnessed in the parterre. His wife and his brother together. Close, but

236

not touching. Although they wanted to touch. Sinclair could tell.

He felt better than he had done in weeks. Clearer in his mind and more certain of his purpose – for at last he understood what had been going wrong. He understood why he had been unable to possess his wife. It was because she was unfaithful. Therefore, God would not *allow* him to possess her. *It was God's way of keeping him pure.*

Looking back, he realized that she had seduced him into marrying her. She had concealed her true nature and made herself appear innocent and in need of protection, when in fact she had no true feminine softness about her, no natural obedience or desire to please. She was not a proper woman.

He turned back to his brother. 'I am glad', he said, 'that you decided to brave your critics and attend tonight. It is the dearest wish of my heart to effect a reconciliation between yourself and the old man.'

'I wouldn't put money on that happening any time soon,' said his brother.

Oh indeed? thought Sinclair. So you are *not* plotting your way back into his affections? You are *not* scheming to cheat me of my inheritance? That is merely an idle fancy of mine. Of course.

A stable boy ran up with the pony-trap, and his brother went round to the other side to check the harness. Sinclair watched the horse turn its head and nuzzle its master's shoulder. His brother gave it an absent caress.

That single gesture seemed to sum up everything Sinclair loathed about his brother. The physicality. The lack of reflection. The ease.

He licked his lips and forced himself to appear calm. 'It is a great pity', he said, 'that this evening you did not have the chance to become acquainted with my wife.'

His brother did not reply.

'I had particularly hoped', Sinclair went on, 'to introduce you to her.'

His brother adjusted the farthingale. 'We've already met.'

Yes indeed, thought Sinclair. And what legions of untruths are concealed behind that simple statement. 'Because you see,' he said as if his brother hadn't spoken, 'my wife requires – protection. Yes. Protection.'

'From whom?'

'Why, from herself.'

His brother straightened up and looked at him across the horse's back. His face was expressionless, but Sinclair was suddenly glad that they had the animal between them. 'What do you mean?'

Sinclair hesitated. 'There are aspects about her character,' he said, 'and about her background, which are – little short of indelicate.'

His brother opened his mouth to protest, and Sinclair raised his hand. 'No, no, do not ask me to elaborate. It is too painful. Suffice to say that I know her somewhat better than you.'

His brother threw the reins on the seat and came round to his side. He was a good head taller, and Sinclair was forced to take a step back. 'All right, Sinclair,' he said, 'let's stop circling, shall we, and tell the truth.'

Sinclair blinked.

'You saw us together,' said his brother.

'"Us"? Who is "us"?'

'Come along, little brother. I know a jealous husband when I see one.'

'*Jealous?*' Sinclair could hardly breathe. '*Jealous?* You could scarcely be more wrong!'

'Indeed. Well, be that as it may, you have nothing to fear from me.'

Sinclair was still struggling for self-mastery. '*I* have never had anything to *fear* from you. I came out here to warn you, brother.'

'About what.'

Again he licked his lips. 'About my wife. She is not – not as innocent as she seems.'

His brother's grey eyes became glassy. 'You mustn't speak of her like that.'

Sinclair took another step back. 'And you', he said, 'must not speak of her at all.'

For a moment they faced one another in silence. Then his

brother dropped his gaze. He opened his palm and studied it, and Sinclair felt a shiver of alarm. He remembered the way his brother had used his fists when they were at Winchester together. Once, Cameron had taken on a trio of prefects for 'greasing' his younger brother: for spitting in his face until he was covered in slime and screaming for mercy. Two of those prefects had ended up in the infirmary for the rest of the term, and Cameron himself had come very close to expulsion. And Sinclair had hated him. For being stronger. For protecting him.

His brother raised his head and met his eyes, and looked at Sinclair as he had once looked at those prefects. Then he turned, and put his foot on the board and jumped up into the pony-trap. 'You're right,' he said shortly. 'But it was my fault that I met her tonight, not hers. I sought her out. She didn't want to talk to me. It won't – it won't happen again.' He snapped the reins on the horse's rump and the trap moved off. He did not look back.

Sinclair had to draw back sharply to avoid being spattered with dirt. Yes, go, he raged at his brother's departing back. But you cannot run from me for ever.

Jealous? Jealous of you?

It won't happen again, you say. Ah, my brother, in that you are more correct than you can imagine. I shall see that it never happens again.

The pony-trap swept down the carriageway and out onto the coast road, and for a moment, as the boy waited in the shadows by the gatehouse, his heart lurched, for he thought he'd spotted the parson at last.

Then he realized his mistake, and swore under his breath. It had only *looked* a bit like the parson. Same fair hair and that. But this bloke was bigger, and drove his horse at a lick that'd rattle a churchman's teeth. And his face was anything but godly. The boy knew that look, he'd seen it back home on the faces of dockers and costermongers. It meant, get out of my way, for I'm in a mood to break heads tonight.

Spitting with disappointment, the boy settled down to wait.

Still, he told himself, drumming his thin fingers on his knees. There's no rush. You only come to look, remember? Not going to do nothing tonight. Just mark your target; that's what they call it. Mark your target. And watch and wait.

And waiting was something Ben Kelly knew all about.

Chapter Twenty

It was four in the morning by the time the carriage swept through the gates of Fever Hill and started up the carriageway.

'At least that's over for another year,' said Jocelyn, drawing off his gloves.

Madeleine, sitting opposite, glanced at his liver-spotted hands and thought how old he looked. He was usually so upright and authoritative that one forgot that he was in his seventies. But tonight every line showed.

Beside him Great-Aunt May turned her head to survey the darkened cane-pieces. 'I could not but remark', she said, 'that Cameron was among the guests.'

At her side, Madeleine felt Sinclair tense.

'Did you speak to him?' May asked Jocelyn.

'Of course not,' he replied.

Serenely, May resumed her study of the fields. 'I cannot imagine', she said, 'why Cornelius thought it appropriate to invite him.'

Madeleine said, 'Someone told me that it's because Cameron is doing rather well with his estate, and that Cornelius likes to hedge his bets.'

'Doing rather well, is he?' said Jocelyn, his face studiedly blank.

'That's what I heard.'

Sinclair's gloved hands tightened on his cane. 'You should not believe everything you hear.'

She made no reply. It gave her a quiet satisfaction to repeat what Cameron had said, and to add a little positive twist of her own.

A moment later, her spirits plunged. What was the point? A petty rebellion that could never come to anything. What on earth was the point?

She turned her head and watched the dark cane-fields whipping past. She felt exhausted and fragile; hollowed out by that conversation in the parterre.

He had been so painfully honest. Too honest. What right had he to tell her such things, simply because she asked? Why hadn't he lied? She did. She lied to him every time she saw him. It was simple. All you have to do is withhold the truth.

She felt Sinclair's breath on her cheek. 'Your colour is rather high,' he said. 'Parnassus has always been prone to putrid airs. I trust that you have not taken a fever.'

'I'm just tired,' she said without turning her head.

'Ah. Tired. To be sure.'

With a spurt of irritation she wondered what he meant. Why could he never say what he meant?

When they had reached the house and said their good-nights, and attained the relative privacy of their room, Sinclair sent Jessie and his man away. He folded his arms across his chest, and paced up and down. 'I was right,' he said. 'You have over-taxed yourself. I can tell.'

Madeleine unbuttoned her gloves and drew them off and laid them on top of the bureau. 'I don't feel at all unwell,' she replied.

Another lie. Her face felt stiff, her eyes hot and scratchy. She wanted to go to sleep and never wake up.

'You have over-taxed yourself,' he repeated. 'You need rest, or you will bring on a brain fever.'

She met his gaze, and wondered where this was leading. If anyone were feverish, it was he. His face was clammy and pale, and his eyes had an unhealthy shine. He seemed agitated and unable to keep still.

'It would be best', he said, 'if you were to stay on the

property for the next few months. Yes. Very quietly. To regain your strength.'

She moved past him into the dressing-room and sat down at her dressing-table, and began letting down her hair. She withdrew each pin and set it beside the others in the little lacquer tray. 'As you wish,' she said.

In the looking-glass she saw him blink. Perhaps she had surprised him. 'No more visits to town,' he said.

'Very well.'

'And you must make your excuses to Mrs Herapath.'

'I shall write to her forthwith.'

No doubt he was longing for her to protest, so that he could explain in elaborate detail why he felt this new measure to be his duty. But for once their wishes were the same. She would miss her outings to Falmouth, and she would miss Mrs Herapath's intolerant wit, but it was time to make a clean break. No more driving about the country-side pretending she was free. No more talks in the moonlight. She was not free. Trying to pretend otherwise only hurt. A clean break. That's what you need.

She took off her dancing slippers and began to unfasten her bodice, and asked Sinclair if he was coming to bed.

In the looking-glass she saw him take a deep breath, as if he couldn't get enough air. 'Later,' he said. 'I need to take a turn about the lawns. Yes. I need a turn about the lawns.'

What I need, thought Madeleine, is chloral.

No thinking. No dreaming. Just sleep.

On the river bank something rustled in the ginger lilies, and Abigail growled. She gave a low warning cough, and trotted down to investigate.

A flurry of barks and crashing through undergrowth, and she returned, wet and smelling of the river, to lean against Cameron's calf.

He drew her silky ear between his fingers. 'What was that,' he said, 'a mongoose?'

She answered with an indignant cough.

They were sitting on the steps which led down into the

garden: Cameron in shirtsleeves and riding-breeches, with a bottle of Scotch at his elbow. It would be dawn soon, and he would regret the Scotch, but he didn't care. He didn't care about much any more.

No. That wasn't true. He *wanted* not to care. He wanted it to be croptime again, so that he could work round the clock and not think about anything except rum yields and striking points and how many hogsheads per acre.

He had driven home at a furious pace, and the horse had been lathered and trembling when they swung into the yard. Cameron had untacked it himself and rubbed it down. He should have woken his groom, for Moses would fret about that in the morning, and require assurances that he wouldn't be sacked. But Cameron had needed to be on his own.

Still in his evening coat, he had flung himself onto his camp bed, and fallen immediately into a fitful sleep – and the dream had come. The black sand sugaring the wide blue eyes. The prison ceiling bearing down on him. The child in the distance, crying for help.

He'd woken with a shout that had brought Abigail clattering across the tiles. Further sleep had been impossible.

Again the ginger lilies rustled, and again Abigail barked.

'All right, girl,' he told her. 'Settle down.'

He took another pull at the bottle, and felt the whisky's clean, cauterizing burn.

He wished there were some kind of draught he could take that would wash away the last twelve hours from his mind. Everything. The way she had smiled at him. Her face as she'd admitted that she was shocked. And most of all, his brother's pale, feverish features as he'd slandered her. *She is not as innocent as she seems.*

In the instant after he'd said it, Cameron had wanted to grab him by the hair and beat out his brains on the carriage wheel. It wasn't a fleeting impulse: he had seen himself do it. Hammering that narrow head again and again onto the iron-rimmed wheel until it split open like an egg.

He set down the bottle and put his elbows on his knees and studied his palms.

How could you think it, even for a moment? Your own

brother. You played together as boys. You shared a cabin on those interminable trips to England. You protected him from bullies, and he resented you, and you pretended not to notice. Your own brother.

He got to his feet, and the bottle overturned. Whisky leaked out onto the steps. Abigail put down her head and sniffed, then tentatively lapped.

Cameron pushed her away. 'Not for you, Abby. And not for me either.' He stooped for the bottle and lobbed it as hard as he could into the bushes.

To the devil with everything, he thought.

Sinclair knelt in the darkness of the hothouse, gasping and shuddering with relief.

In the distance a mule brayed. The dumb-cane trembled in the pre-dawn breeze.

He leaned back against the mossy wall and shut his eyes. He felt light and clean and calm again. He felt immensely powerful.

He turned his head and gazed at the faint grey rectangle of the doorway, at the dumb-cane on the threshold. Not devilish as he had supposed, but beneficent. Keeping him from harm.

He had been wrong about it, as he had been wrong about so many things. But at last he understood. What he had just done was not self-pollution. It was self-*purification*. God does indeed have a special Eye for what is done in the dark – and God had seen this and permitted it, *for God approved. It was keeping him pure.*

What a difference an hour makes, he thought, shutting his eyes again.

In the carriage he had been in torment. The thought of them together. Taking their pleasure. Laughing at him. He had felt the pressure building inside him until he'd wanted to scream.

Then in the dressing-room, watching her take down her hair. That knowing way in which she'd uncoiled it and laid it over one shoulder: a dark, monstrous serpent, leading him on.

He had read once of a medieval belief that a woman's womb is a separate creature: a toxic presence to be feared and confined. How well the ancients had understood. He had only to look at her to sense the poison cradled within.

And to think that there had been a time when he had wanted her. Thank God that was all in the past. Thank God he had been shown the way.

He flexed his shoulders, luxuriating in his new-found ease. He drew a deep, calm breath, and opened his eyes. And met the gleam of another's in the gloom.

A child was crouching in the furthest corner of the cell. It was a pickney: a small boy pickney, very dark, and huddled into a ball. The creature was not moving; not even blinking. The whites of its eyes glistened with fright.

For a long, appalled moment they stared at one another.

It was in here all the time, thought Sinclair, his heart hammering in his chest as the implications came crashing in on him. *It had crouched in that corner and seen everything – everything* – while he, in his ferocious need, had stumbled in and fallen to his knees, oblivious of all but the fire in his loins.

Dear God, he thought. What do I do now?

Through the doorway the sounds of a new day wafted in. The rattle of a woodpecker. The crickets gathering force.

With his back against the wall, Sinclair got slowly to his feet.

The pickney watched, but didn't move. It seemed to be holding its breath.

Keeping his eyes on it, Sinclair brushed the dirt off his knees and straightened his linen. Then he backed out of the cell.

Still the pickney watched, but didn't move.

Sinclair paused in the doorway.

The pickney watched with huge, unblinking eyes.

Sinclair took a step back, and beneath his heel he felt the dumb-cane snap. He took another step, and grasped the heavy bulletwood door, and swung it shut.

After a moment he put his ear to the door and listened. No sound from within. He pictured the pickney crouching in the

246

darkness. Silent. Obedient to its fate. Sinclair liked that. It confirmed that he had done the right thing.

The sun was nearly up, and the darkness was beginning to drain from the dell. Vapour rose from the long grass. Ground doves cooed.

He drew a deep breath. The air had never tasted so clean and pure. A new dawn.

Nothing to fret about, he told himself. Have faith. God will not allow you to come to harm.

He looked about him and found a lump of cut-stone, and wedged it under the door.

As she watched Sinclair wading away through the long grass, Sophie swayed on her crutches and nearly fell.

Her heart was still thudding from the fright of seeing him emerge from the hothouse. What had he been doing inside?

She had been so sure that everyone was asleep before she'd ventured out. She had lain awake and listened to them returning from the ball. The snort of the horses, the rattle of harness. The murmur of the helpers, and the slap of their slippers across the floors. The creak of the stairs and the closing of doors.

She had pretended to be asleep when Maddy came out to check on her, and drew aside the mosquito curtain to feel her cheek, and dropped a kiss on her forehead. And she could have sworn that they were all in bed and fast asleep, even Clemency and the cat, by the time she had let herself out of the gallery and hobbled down the steps, heart thumping wildly.

To her dismay, Remus and Cleo had not come bounding across the lawns to keep her company. And it had taken for ever to find the path. Several times she had stumbled, and once she had nearly cried out when something slithered across her slipper.

The hothouse was a well of darkness when she reached it, and she hung back beneath an ironwood tree, one hand clutching the creepers for support, the other gripping Grace's charm about her neck.

That was when she'd seen the duppy emerge from the

doorway. *A duppy*. Leaving its lair to come and get her.

Then the duppy had turned, and resolved into Sinclair. The relief was like a wave of warm water washing over her.

But something was wrong with him. His face was pale and glistening, his eyes vacant. What had he seen in there? *Why had he shut the door?*

There could be only one answer. He had seen a duppy. Perhaps a whole nest of duppies. That was why he'd looked so terrified as he'd closed the door and wedged it shut.

And now she was all alone with a nest of duppies not ten feet away.

She peered through the gloom at Sinclair's fast-retreating form. She opened her mouth to call him back. Then shut it again. Sinclair didn't like her. Even if he heard her cry, he wouldn't turn back. He would just go on to the house, and tell on her to Maddy.

There was nothing for it but to hobble all the way back to the house as quickly as she could, and hope that Sinclair had shut the door securely enough to stop the duppies getting out.

As she started off, she blinked back tears. Once again she had tried to recover her shadow, and once again she had failed. Perhaps after all it was time to ask Victory for help.

CHAPTER TWENTY-ONE

Tuesday 23rd July – Teatime

Victory has run away, and has been gone for three days. At first Grace was vexed, but on the second day she asked Great-Aunt May to have the helpers make a search. Great-Aunt May said No, that pickney is always wandering off and will surely return when he is hungry. Sinclair agreed with Great-Aunt May, and so did Uncle Jocelyn, but Maddy said But surely we must do all we can, what if it were Sophie?

After that Uncle Jocelyn sent a field-gang to search Clairmont Hill and Pinchgut and Caledon. They even dragged the pond below the Old Works. But they didn't find anything.

Nobody talks about Victory, but there is a horrid feeling in the house. I asked Evie if she knows where he went, but she said no, and this time she was telling the truth. And the night before last, Clemency heard her baby crying in Hell, but much louder than before. Clemency said it is a bad sign, but Maddy was vexed, and told her to keep her fancies to herself, did she want Grace to hear?

I think that when Sinclair was at the hothouse he failed to lock up the duppies securely enough, and they escaped. Maybe they chased Victory away. Maybe they got him.

But Victory can run extremely fast, so I am hopeful that he got away and is hiding somewhere, afraid to come out.

*　　　*　　　*

Sophie awoke in the middle of the night with her journal digging into her cheek.

She pressed her face against the calfskin binding and breathed in its familiar smell as she listened to the noises in the house. Steps on the stairs. Hushed voices in the ballroom. Something was wrong.

Moments later, Maddy came out onto the gallery. She wore her russet walking-costume but no hat or gloves, and her hair was pinned up in a hasty knot.

Sophie asked what was wrong.

Maddy's gaze was distracted, as if she hadn't expected Sophie to be awake. She said, 'You'd better sleep with Clemency for the rest of the night.'

Sophie struggled to sit up. 'Why? What's happened?'

'I don't want you out here on your own.'

Sophie glanced at the sprig of rosemary on her bedside table. 'Did they find Victory?'

Maddy shook out Sophie's slippers and dressing gown, and put them on the bed.

'He's all right, isn't he? Maddy?'

Maddy sat down on the edge of the bed and placed her cold hand on Sophie's wrist. 'No,' she said. 'He isn't. He got trapped in the hothouse and couldn't get out. I'm afraid, Sophie – he died.'

She left a shocked and silent Sophie with Clemency, and set off down the hill for the old slave village.

On the steps, Sinclair had tried to stop her. 'This is preposterous,' he said, 'there's no need for you to go. These people do not feel as we do. You should leave that woman to her own kind.'

'Her own kind', said Madeleine, picking up the basket which Daphne had prepared, 'are too frightened to go near her. And it'll be tomorrow before any of her relations arrive.'

Sinclair compressed his lips, but to her surprise he made no further objection.

She turned to go, then brought herself up short. 'There's something I ought to tell you,' she said.

'Indeed.'

'I sent for your brother. I thought it might help Grace.'

'Indeed,' he said again. 'And no doubt sending for him was your first thought when you learned of this – occurrence.'

'No. My first thought was for Grace.'

He ignored that. 'Is this how you honour your promise to obey me and live a retiring life? Three days, and your promise is broken.'

'A child is dead, Sinclair. That changes things.'

'I do not see why. The fate of the deceased was the will of God. The will of God. If the mother accepted that, she would know peace.'

Madeleine bit back a retort. Looking at his serene and resolute countenance, she thought how he had changed over the past few days. No more twitchiness. No more incessant inspections in the looking-glass. She wondered why.

She kept to the carriageway until she reached the bottom of the hill, then found the track that branched off to the left, and followed the old aqueduct towards the slave village. It was eerily quiet. Only the slow creak of the bamboo canes, and the low ring-ring of the crickets, and an occasional grunt from Grace's hogs. Madeleine wondered what was missing, then realized it was the birds. There never seemed to be any birds at the slave village.

In the darkness, her passage through the ruins was slow. She went past ruined slave-houses open to the sky, their walls mounded with creepers, their doorways blocked by wild mango trees like uninvited guests. She smelt stagnant water and the sweet odour of decay.

She thought of the little boy who had died. The focus of so much of his mother's fierce, resentful pride. *These people do not feel as we do.* What a convenient lie.

As on her previous visit, it was a shock to come upon Grace's orderly yard amid the tangled wilderness. She couldn't see anyone about, although a glow of lamplight came from the open doorway.

In the outdoor hearth by the steps, a fire still flickered. But the old iron cooking pot had been knocked on its side, and was leaking a mess of stewed vegetables into the ashes. The yard was littered with shards of pottery. It looked as if Grace had stood on the steps and dashed down every cup and plate and yabba she possessed.

As Madeleine climbed the steps to the door, the sweet, alien smell of death hit her like a wall. Dark spots darted before her eyes. She fought the urge to retch.

The room looked as if a storm had blown through it. More shattered earthenware on the floor; and shredded lizard skins and bright, mangled feathers, and the tiny crushed skulls of birds. Grace must have destroyed her entire stock-in-trade.

The black woman crouched on the floor beside a low wooden bedstead on which lay her son. He was curled into a ball, his skin a bluish-grey, his belly marbled greenish-purple, as if the blood vessels had risen to the surface. He looked much smaller than he had in life.

Grace's face had a similar blue-grey hue to her son's. She wore a sheet of undyed osnaburg tied haphazardly under the arms, and a plain white headkerchief. *The head tied across*, thought Madeleine. The sign of mourning.

'Is who dat?' said Grace without turning round.

Madeleine set down the basket inside the door, but didn't go in. 'It's Miss Maddy,' she said. 'I've brought you some things for the laying-out.'

Grace turned and looked at her. Her eyes were dry and swollen and her blink was slow, as if exhausted by grief and rage. 'Go way, ma'am. Please. Get out a me yard.'

Madeleine hesitated. 'Daphne packed the basket,' she said. 'I believe it has everything you need. Jackson's making the coffin.'

'Why you come to I house, ma'am? Why you bring dese tings?'

'The helpers are too scared.'

Grace spat on the floor. 'Frighten? Of what to frighten? Of duppy chile?'

'Of you, I think.'

That seemed to put a little spirit into her. 'They *should* to frighten. Who done dis, die soon. I self gwine see to dat.' She glanced at Madeleine. 'Tink me not tell de trute, Miss Maddy?'

Madeleine shook her head. 'Not at all. I know you mean it.'

She was not surprised that Grace had assumed that her son's death had been no accident. The garden boy who'd found the body had said that the hothouse door had been blocked from the outside.

But surely, looked at dispassionately, it must have been an accident. No-one would do such a thing to a child. Somehow a stone must have become dislodged, and rolled in front of the door.

But it was no use telling his mother that. She wanted blood, and who could blame her? If it were Sophie, Madeleine would want it too.

Grace gazed at her with swollen, exhausted eyes. 'Why you not frighten too, ma'am?'

'I've seen death before.'

For a moment the black woman held her gaze. Then she turned back to the body on the bed. The dismissal was clear.

But as Madeleine went down the steps and out into the yard, Grace called after her. 'Ma'am?'

'Yes?'

'Evie ran off when she heard the news. If you see her, would you please tell her to come to I?'

'Of course,' said Madeleine.

She couldn't find Evie in the yard, or by the aqueduct, or anywhere in the ruins. Tired of searching, she rested for a moment on a block of cut-stone.

Away from Grace's chickens and hogs, the old village seemed even more mysteriously hushed. Only the eerie, infrequent creak of the bamboo sounded in the shadows, like a ship setting out into the dark.

It was a cool night, and damp air wafted off the stagnant aqueduct. Madeleine shivered. Above her head, an old ackee tree spread its branches. She could just make out the bright coral fruit, bleached dark grey in the darkness. According to Sophie they were poisonous until they split to reveal the glossy black seeds. 'Jamaica poisoning', they called it. It seemed that everywhere she looked she encountered death.

My God, she thought, what if it had been Sophie?

Jocelyn had told her that from the condition of the body, the boy must have died some time that morning. 'It was probably thirst that killed him,' he had said, shaking his head. No wonder Grace had smashed everything she owned.

'I told you I heard crying,' Clemency had said to Madeleine in her matter-of-fact way when she'd heard the news. Then she'd taken Sophie into her bed and given her the cat to hold, and reached for her excerpt book and a jar of ginger bonbons. *I told you I heard crying.*

Hoofbeats on the path brought Madeleine back to the present. She turned to see Cameron reining in his mount at the entrance to Grace's yard. The horse's breath steamed as it threw down its head to cough.

She wondered what to do. She hadn't planned to be here when he arrived.

The next moment she knew that was a lie. It was true that she had sent for him for Grace's sake, but she needn't have brought the basket down herself. That could have waited till morning, when one of Grace's cousins from the Cockpits could have taken it.

You're despicable, she told herself. Despicable. She got to her feet and started forward to meet him.

He was tethering his horse to the bamboo fence when she approached. When he saw her he took off his hat, and wiped his forehead on his wrist, and waited for her. It was too dark to see his expression. 'Doshey told me what happened,' he said. 'But I don't understand. He said the boy was shut in.'

'Yes.'

'How?'

'We don't know. Some kind of accident. A stone rolled in front of the door.'

He put his hands on his hips and scanned the yard, as if the darkness might provide an answer. Then he glanced down at her. 'You look cold.'

'I'm all right. I came out to find Evie.'

'I'll find her. You'd better go back up to the house.'

She didn't move. She said, 'He was six years old.'

'I know.'

'He died within a stone's throw of the house. Clemency

heard him crying, but I didn't believe her. I told her to be quiet, in case Grace heard and became upset.'

He put out his hand to touch her shoulder, then withdrew it.

For the first time in her adult life, she wanted to be close to a man. She wanted to put her arms round his waist and lean against him and bury her face in his chest.

Grace is allowed to do that, she thought. A flash of pure jealousy went through her.

My God, she thought, you really are despicable. You would begrudge that poor woman her only comfort, because you want him.

'Madeleine,' he said.

She looked up at him.

'You did a good thing, sending for me.'

She shook her head.

'Go on up to the house. I'll find Evie and take her to Grace.'

Two days after the pickney was found in the hothouse, Jocelyn drove Sophie to Falmouth.

They made good speed from Fever Hill, and were already within sight of the sea: trotting along through the dappled shade of Bulletwood, with the glare of the beach just coming into view up ahead.

Jocelyn flicked the reins on the horse's rump, and decided that his idea of cutting through to the coast road had really been rather inspired. The child needed sea air, for the iodine. It was gratifying to see a little colour coming back into her cheeks.

Above them, a flock of emerald parakeets exploded from the trees and flew away, furiously beating their stubby little wings. Sophie's jaw dropped. 'Those were real parrots,' she said. Still with her mouth open, she gazed at him from beneath her sunhat.

He felt irrationally proud, as if he had conjured up the parakeets especially for her.

Madeleine would be pleased. She had approached him after breakfast as he was preparing for the magistrates' meeting, and asked if, as a special favour, he would take the child with him into town. 'I can't go myself,' she had said, and explained Sinclair's wish that she should remain on the property.

Jocelyn had been surprised. Madeleine was not the woman to be cowed by a weaselly little fellow like Sinclair. But perhaps she had lost confidence after this dreadful business of the pickney. In that she was not alone. The whole estate still lay under a pall.

'I'm worried about Sophie,' she had said. 'She won't talk about it, but I know it's all she thinks of. She needs distraction; something to take her out of herself.'

She needn't have told Jocelyn, for he had already noticed the unaccustomed silence in the house. He had never known a child who loved talking as much as Sophie. And when she wasn't talking she was singing, humming, or reading aloud to one of the pickneys, or Clemency's cat, or that stuffed animal of which she was so fond.

Her voice had become one of the background noises of the house, like the crickets and the crows. And when it had fallen silent, Jocelyn had been surprised and a little dismayed. He wouldn't go so far as to say that he missed it; the absence was simply disconcerting, that was all.

'You know how she admires you,' Madeleine had said. 'And she'll be no trouble. You can leave her with Mrs Herapath, or if she isn't at home, just put her on the bench outside the courthouse; she'll be in her element. There's always plenty to see on market day.'

And since it was Madeleine who asked, of course Jocelyn had given in. 'I should be delighted,' he had said. And Madeleine had given him a wry smile, for she had known that he was lying.

The prospect of being alone with Sophie filled him with apprehension. He knew that he was not good with children. And this child alarmed him more than most. She did not at all conform to his notion of what a little girl should be.

The first time they had met, she had managed to stay silent for no more than two minutes before politely asking why bamboo grows so much bigger than other grasses, and how did the Cockpits get their name, and what is the plural of mongoose?

He had fled. He had feared for his books and his privacy, and perhaps also for himself, in some way that he did not entirely understand.

But now he was worried because she was not bombarding him with questions. She sat very straight, with her splinted leg sticking out in front and one thin hand clutching the guardrail, while the other held a book on her lap. Tucked beneath her arm was the ever-present toy donkey.

He felt a pang of concern. Over the past few weeks her face had regained the invalid sallowness which he had hoped was gone for good. But how was he, an old fellow of seventy-three, to draw her out? A girl of eleven? What did he know about such a being?

Madeleine had told him that Sophie was passionate about nature, so he tried to think of something to say about alligators. In vain. Then he remembered that question about the Cockpits.

'I wonder if you know', he said, looking straight ahead, 'why the sanatorium on the other side of town is called Burntwood?'

Out of the corner of his eye he saw her turn and look up at him. 'Um. Because it got burnt in the Christmas Rebellion?'

'Precisely. Well done.'

She sucked in her lips.

A guessing game, thought Jocelyn. Yes, good show. Capital. 'What about Alice Grove?' he asked.

She frowned, looking suddenly very like her sister. Then shook her head.

He told her it was named for his mother, who had been sweet and kind but also extremely determined, and had made her husband build a schoolhouse for the helpers' children.

A little more colour returned to her cheeks, and Jocelyn felt an absurd sense of triumph. 'What about Fever Hill?' he said, giving the reins a jaunty flick. 'How d'you think that got its name?'

'I don't know,' she answered promptly, 'but I've been wanting to find out for ages.'

Jocelyn told her how the estate had originally been called Monroe's Pen, after old Benneit Monroe, but after the great hurricane of 1712 a fever had swept the Northside – and at that point Jocelyn realized with horror that this was the last story he should be telling. But Sophie was waiting, so he floundered on. 'And I'm rather sorry to say', he said with a wince, 'that old Benneit's youngest daughter, er, perished. Of the fever. So he decided to change the name in her memory.'

Sophie took that in silence. Then she asked, 'What was the daughter's name?'

'I believe it was Catrion,' he muttered.

'How old was she?'

'D'you know, I couldn't say.' The child had been eleven.

He threw her a worried glance, and wondered what she was thinking. There had been times during the drive when she had looked as if she were puzzling something out: something awful, and far too big for her to manage. And once, she had asked him a question which clearly mattered enormously. But she had framed it in that bewildering way that children have of asking something which gives no clue as to why they need to know.

'Will the policemen come about Victory?' she had asked, and Jocelyn had said no, for it had been an accident, and since he himself was a magistrate he could sort things out on his own.

He wondered whether his answer had laid to rest whatever childish anxieties were secretly plaguing her. He doubted he'd ever find out. With Sophie he felt the same baffled helplessness he used to experience with his son.

And for the tenth time he wished that he didn't have to go to Kingston the following day. Of all the times to be needed at the Assembly. This dreadful affair of the pickney, and now this child beside him, clearly in need of help.

She was gazing solemnly ahead of her, thinking heaven knew what disquieting thoughts. In desperation he asked the title of the book on her lap.

'*The Gods of Ancient Greece*,' she said. She explained that she was returning it to Mrs Herapath, from whom it had been borrowed.

Now he really did feel bad. Thousands of volumes at Fever Hill, and she was compelled to borrow one from Olivia Herapath. It wouldn't do. How could he in all conscience persist in keeping the library out of bounds?

Although of course if he did let her in, it would mean putting Catullus and Fielding out of reach. And de Quincy and Ovid. And those Brontë girls. In fact it would require a wholesale reorganization.

To his surprise, he found that he could contemplate the prospect without too much displeasure. Hang it all, it was about time the old place was sorted out.

They reached the village of Salt Wash, and the press of traffic became so great that they slowed to a walk. Higglers dragged handcarts piled with mangoes and paw-paws and yams. A group of women in strident print gowns strode past with trays of hard-dough and cassava pone on their heads. A sugar wain turned off for the quay, and as it passed, Jocelyn noticed that the sacks bore the Eden mark.

Damn and blast it to *hell*. Since that confounded ball at Parnassus he'd been coming across reminders of the boy wherever he went. Well well, he told himself. Nothing to be done about it now. All water under the bridge.

He was relieved when they left the quays and turned inland for the market square, but as soon as he saw it his heart sank. Usually he enjoyed market day, but this morning all he could see were the pickneys: dodging in and out of the traffic, hitching rides on tailgates, pestering their mothers for quattie dolls and chocho pie, and that sickly scarlet syrup they all adored.

He saw Sophie gazing at them, and silently cursed.

'Uncle Jocelyn?' she said in a small voice.

'Yes?'

'How will they stop Victory becoming a duppy?'

Good Lord. What could he say to that? Dismiss the whole notion of duppies as balderdash? The trouble was, after seventy-three years on the Northside, he knew that it wasn't. Or rather, that if enough people believe in a thing, it acquires a reality of its own.

'They can't,' he said. 'The trick is to stop the duppy

walking. Stop him, er, bothering people. D'you see?'

'How do they do that?'

He blew out a long breath. 'Well. They put slices of lime on the, er, eyes. Rub the body with lime juice and nutmeg. Sew up the pockets.' He glanced at her, hoping he'd said enough. But she was waiting for him to go on.

He cleared his throat. 'They fill the pillow with parched peas and corn, and put it in the coffin along with all sorts of other things to keep the duppy quiet. Salt. Madam Fate. And something called "compellance powder". No idea what that is.'

She nodded.

'Rum on the grave,' he went on, 'and more corn and salt. And often they plant pigeon peas nearby. And then, nine days after the, er, passing, they hold something called a nine-night. That's like a wake, when they do all sorts of things to send the duppy to sleep. Sing songs. Tell stories. Have a decent supper. Can be rather jolly, I believe.'

But Sophie was not to be deflected by jollity. 'Does it work *every* time? Does the duppy always go to sleep?'

He paused. The answer was no, or why would there be duppy stories? But he was dashed if he was going to tell her that. 'It does when Grace McFarlane has anything to do with it,' he said. 'Very powerful woman, Grace. Extraordinarily good at nine-nights. Never been known to fail.'

He wondered if he had laid it on a bit thick, but to his relief some of the tension left the small face.

They pulled up outside Olivia's studio. More pickneys. More gleaming ivory smiles and plump, shiny black limbs.

Lord help us, he thought. That poor little boy. What a ghastly, lonely death.

And it was your fault, Jocelyn Monroe. All you had to do was have that confounded ruin made safe. But no. You were so wrapped up in your own affairs that you allowed a death-trap to remain on your land.

Well dammit, man, you'd better do something to prevent it happening again. When you get back, you're going to have words with that manager of yours, and order a thorough review of the entire property. Hang it all, children are curious. It's no good telling the little tykes to stay out of trouble. It's in their nature to get *into* it.

A thorough review. Yes, that's the ticket.

He glanced at the solemn little girl beside him and thought, God help me, what if it had been her?

Chapter Twenty-Two

There's something about markets that gives Ben the hump. Maybe it's all them darkies laughing and chattering and calling each other 'sistah' and 'breddah' and 'muddah', like they're one big sodding family. Or maybe it's all that sodding fruit.

Ben *hates* fruit; and it's everywhere in this country. Hills, gardens, side of the road. Whole bloody country never stops growing. Right now, on the main road to Falmouth – the one they call the Fever Hill road – there's these three fat darkie women up ahead with great big piles of fruit on their heads. Mangoes, bananas, jackfruit, shaddock; guavas and paw-paws and coolie plums.

Robbie would of loved it. He would of been in clover. Ben don't know exactly what clover is, except that it's something topper that everybody likes, and Robbie would of been in it.

So what with the fruit and the darkies and that, Ben could do without this sodding market.

He's hot and dizzy on account of being off his feed, and his chest is all tight after that dream. Last night he was kipping out on this beach past Salt Wash – it's nice there, peaceful, with just the little waves for company – and that's when he had that sodding dream.

Him and Robbie are having larks on the beach. The sea's like blue glass in the sun, and the sand's so bright you can't hardly look. And him and Robbie are all clean, not a louse between them, and they're running along grabbing sea-grapes and chucking them at each other. Laugh! Do they laugh!

When Ben wakes up he's making these little jerky moans like he wants to cry. He *hates* that. When Robbie got killed he never cried once, not once. And he's not going to start now.

He's coming into Falmouth, and the streets are looking all right, with their fancy pink and blue houses and the trees with the yellow flowers hanging down. Couple of john crows prossing about on a fence, and he thinks about chucking a stone at them. Decides not to bother. They're outsiders, like him. Raggedy black wings and ugly red heads, and that ruff round their long skinny necks, like a dirty ha'penny collar. And like him, they're getting ready to work the market, and see what they can click.

Streets are filling up with darkies and coloureds and Chinks and that. Not many whites about, but Ben don't mind, cos he knows he blends in all right. He's got his dungarees and his calico shirt and his tatty straw hat, and them rope-soled shoes that round here they call bulldogs. So to the darkies he's just another walkfoot buckra what can't afford a jack-mule. He learnt some of the darkie talk from this cook on the boat coming out, and that helps with the blending in, and all.

He's in Duke Street now, and as he goes past the church he spits it a good one, but through his fist, so that nobody sees. These days he always spits at churches; cos churches mean preachers, and preachers mean the parson what killed Robbie.

When he thinks of the parson he gets this cold feeling in his belly, like he's swallowed a stone. He's only seen the parson once since he got here, just a flash as the carriage rattled past, but it was enough. Parson sitting inside so upright and proper in his chimney-pot hat, with his hands on his cane and his little red screwed-up mouth. Soft as shit and twice as nasty.

Ben goes hot and cold just thinking about him. And about that gun, too. He's left it tucked up safe in that tree out on the Eden road – but even now, when he's miles away, he can feel it watching him. It's like it owns him or something. And he's only had it a week.

He was padding the hoof a few miles to the south when he come upon this village, and seen this pony-trap stopped under a tree. Nobody about; must be a doctor on his rounds or something. And he wanders closer, and there's this little handgun poking out from under a cushion, just asking to be clicked. He can't hardly believe his luck. So over he goes, and stuffs it down his front in a brace of shakes, and cuts the lucky out of there. And when he's well into the bush, he gets it out for a look.

He's never held a gun before in his natural, and his heart's thumping so loud he can hear it. He's never killed nothing before, neither. Never got the chance. But now he points the gun at this john crow in a tree and pulls the trigger. And gets nothing but an empty click. Bloody gun's got no bloody *bullets*, has it? That doctor must of kept it just for show. Bloody marvellous. No bloody bullets in your gun.

So now it's off to the sodding market for Ben Kelly, and maybe this time he can click a *loaded* gun, thank you very much – or at least a few sodding bullets.

He passes a couple of darkie women sitting under a bean tree. Bright cotton headkerchiefs like all the darkie women wear, and green and red print dresses hitched to the knees, and their stuff all spread out on the ground around them. Big stacks of hard-dough, and necklaces of black-eyed seeds, and paper twists of wangla nut brittle that he can smell from here.

'Eh, bwoy!' the big one calls out to him. 'Buckra bwoy! You too *meagre*, bwoy! Need feedin up! Come buy likkle candy from Cecilia, nuh! Come buy likkle hard-dough, bwoy!'

Ben don't say nothing. Just shoots them a look.

The other one waggles her finger at him; great big grin on her face. 'You mind Cecilia, nuh! You eat plenty hard-dough, an drink good cerasee tea – an no time at all, bwoy, you grow big and muscle-strong. An then, mm-*mm*,' she smacks her lips, 'you be handsome-to-pieces!' They slap their thighs and roar with laughter.

Ben still don't say nothing. He just walks on, and leaves them laughing. He's decided he don't much like these Jamaican darkies. Back in Shelton Street he never paid darkies no mind. They had a bad time of it in London, and all. But out here they're so happy and polite. *Tank you, me breddah, tank you; me bery well, tank you, sistah!* What they got to be so happy about? They're just as poor as the ones in Shelton Street.

He's thinking on that as he reaches the square, and the market crashes over him like a wave. Spicy dust-smells and horse-shit and sweat; cocoanut milk and pickled mangoes and greasy saltfish fritters. And all them people yelling and joking and haggling: darkies and Chinamen and Syrians; coloureds looking down their noses at everybody; and coolie girls in bangles and brilliant floaty prints.

Robbie would of loved all them colours. Yellow and green and red, purple and blue and orange. He wouldn't of known the *names* for half of them, but he'd of loved them just the same.

Shut it, Ben tells hisself. You shut it right now. Just click the sodding bullets and cut the lucky out of here. Sodding darkies with their sodding colours and all their fruits and their big happy sodding families.

But deep down, he knows it's not the darkies he hates. It's him. Ben Kelly. Cos here he is, walking along in the sunshine, all warm and clean, so fucking clean – and Robbie's dead.

It's got a lot worse since he come this side of the island. On the *Marianne* he had to work so hard that he never got the time to think. And in Kingston he was just so glad to get back onto dry land, and so busy staying alive. But then one day he got wind of the parson's family, and *bang*! All of a sudden it's real.

And for the first time he thinks about what it'll be like to kill the parson. What it'll be like, really. And every time a pony-trap goes by, his chest gets all tight in case it's Sophie or Madeleine. Course it never is, and he's well narked at hisself, cos he don't want to see them again, not ever. She went and married the parson, didn't she? She's the enemy now.

But still. He can't help wondering what'll happen to them when he kills the parson. She'll be a widow. What if the parson's family chucks her out, and she's poor, and Sophie gets worse and dies, and it's all on account of him?

Everything's so mixed up. He can't get it straight in his head.

And so far, no sodding bullets at this sodding market. Just bunches of chickens hanging by their feet, and darkie girls with trays of hog plum jelly on their heads, and darkie men with baskets of swamp oysters and parrotfish and turtles lying on their backs and waving like drowning men.

He's pushing his way through the commotion, and picking up speed past the courthouse, when somebody calls his name. *His* name, 'Ben, Ben!', right out loud above the din.

Something in his chest shifts painfully.

He looks up and there she is on the verandah, not ten yards away. Long yellow hair pulled back in a black velvet ribbon. Frilly white pinafore over a tartan frock. Black stockings, shiny black boots, a couple of crutches, and that clumpy iron thing still on her leg. And she's waving her big straw hat with this green ribbon fluttering, and yelling, '*Ben! Ben! Over here!*' and nearly toppling off the bloody verandah, she's waving so hard.

It's like he can't hear nothing, can't see nothing but Sophie on the verandah, waving at him. Nobody's been pleased to see him since Robbie got killed. But Sophie is. He don't know what to do.

'Ben! It's me! Sophie!'

He shoves his hands in his pockets and hunches up his shoulders. No harm in saying hello, is there? And it'll stop her yelling. Which is all to the good since she's outside the bloody courthouse. Not that he's actually clicked nothing yet. But still.

He pushes his way through the crowd and jumps up onto the verandah. Takes off his hat and sits down at the other end of the bench. 'What's up, Sophie,' he goes.

She sits down too – more like falls down, on account of her splint and the crutches and all – and she's laughing and crying, and so glad that she can't hardly breathe. 'Ben, you've grown so tall! And brown! And you've got new clothes – and, and everything—'

'And I don't pong no more,' he puts in, seeing as she's too polite to mention it.

She giggles.

And again that something shifts in his chest, and makes him wince. 'And look at you,' he goes. But then he can't think what else to say, cos up close she looks so done in that it fair gives him a turn. She's nothing but a bag of bones. Face like a skull, lips all pale; big blue shadows under her eyes.

She says, 'Oh, Ben, I thought I'd never see you again. You never came to say goodbye.'

'Couldn't. Got into chancery, didn't I?'

'What's chancery?'

'Trouble. Bluebottles after me.'

'Bluebott— oh, you mean policemen. I guessed it must have been something like that. Is it all right now?'

He turns away and looks out over the market. No, he thinks. It'll never be all right now.

Then she says what he hoped she wouldn't. 'Where's Robbie?' she says.

His chest goes tight again and he sucks in his breath to keep from crying out. 'He's not here,' he goes.

She shoots him a look, and don't ask no more. She's all right, is Sophie.

For a bit they don't say nothing. Then she goes, 'How did you find us, Ben? How did you get to Jamaica?'

He looks at her funny little face and wonders how much to tell her. How he was on the doss for days after Robbie got killed, and he clicked enough for a proper burial, and got Robbie settled, and then just wandered off, and fetched up at the docks. No reason, just fetched up there. The stink of sugar so thick you couldn't hardly breathe; the quays all brown and sticky with it. Then he spotted that mark on one of the sacks, *F-H*, and a ganger said that's the Monroe mark. The Monroes of Fever Hill, big name in sugar, or used to be, top quality muscovado. That's when he got the idea. Sugar boats leaving every day of the week. Always needing extra hands.

But he can't tell Sophie all that. It'd only get them round to why he's come after the parson, and straight back to Robbie again. So he just shrugs and says, 'I worked on a boat.'

'Gosh, how exciting. Did you get seasick?'

He shakes his head.

'I didn't either. Or Maddy. But Sinclair did, a little.' She twists her hands together in her lap.

Something's up, he thinks.

He watches her take the little beaded purse on her wrist and snap it open. 'We're quite rich now,' she says, talking too quick. 'I get pocket money and everything. Here. This is a present.' She holds out two silver crowns. 'I'm sorry it isn't more, but it's all I have until next Tuesday.'

Angrily he pushes it away. 'I don't want your sodding money.'

'Don't be silly, Ben. You need it—'

'I said no!'

She blinks. 'I-I'm sorry. I didn't mean to offend you.'

She's missing the point. Point is, he's narked at *hisself*, not her. Who does he think he is, turning down good money? But he can't take it from her. Silly little cow. Silly, crippled little cow.

She shuts the purse and puts it in her lap, and clutches it in her bony fingers.

She's holding on too tight, he thinks.

'Oh, Ben' she says, 'I'm so glad you're here.' Then she bursts into tears.

Shit, but it's horrible watching her cry. He hates it. *Hates* it. What's he supposed to do?

He touches her arm, but he's all dusty and her sleeve's too clean, so he brushes it off. 'What's up, Sophie,' he goes.

After a bit she stops sobbing. Just hiccups for a bit. Nose pink, eyelashes all spiky. Then she just ups and tells him. That's Sophie for you. First she's blubbing away, then she gets herself together, then she spits out what's bothering her. No mucking about.

To begin with it's hard to follow, but soon he gets to the meat of it. And he can't hardly believe it. First the parson done for Robbie, and now he's gone and done for this little darkie that was Sophie's mate. *Why?* It don't make no sense.

But she's not making it up. She may be a nob and a bint and that, but Sophie's sharp. She knows what she saw.

'I'm sure he didn't *mean* to do it,' she says, twisting her purse in her fingers. 'He couldn't have done, could he? He couldn't have known that Victory was inside.'

She searches his face with her big brown eyes, but he don't say nothing. No point scaring her, is there?

Then he gets a thought that makes him go cold all over. As long as the parson thinks nobody seen him shut that little darkie in the lock-up, everything's fine. But if the parson gets wind that Sophie was there, then – well, Ben don't like to finish that particular notion. 'Here, Sophie,' he goes. 'Who else d'you tell about this?'

'No-one. Only you.'

'You sure?'

'Positive.'

'Good. Keep it like that.'

She looks puzzled. 'I don't—'

'I mean it, Sophie. Don't go breathing a word to a living soul. And don't tell nobody about me, neither. You never seen me, all right? Just like you never seen the parson shut that door.'

'Can't I even tell Maddy?'

'You cracked, or what? She's *married* to him! He'd worm it out of her in no time.'

'What do you mean? I don't understand.'

Keep it that way, he thinks. 'Listen,' he says. He takes her arm. She's so thin, it's like grabbing a cat. 'Your mate. The one that got killed.'

'Victory.'

'Yeh. Well, he's dead, all right? Nothing won't bring him back now. So you got to forget about him and start thinking about you. You got to start getting better, girl.'

To his surprise she shakes her head, and all of a sudden she looks well grown-up. 'It's not that easy, Ben. I was getting better. But then someone took my shadow.' She bites her lip. 'I think that's why Victory – I think he was trying to get it back. I *told* him not to go there on his own, but I bet he did. He was always trying to impress me.' Her eyes fill with tears.

He gives her another shake. 'Stop that.'

'Sorry.'

'Right. Now just tell me what you're on about.'

She takes out a little lawn handkerchief from her purse and blows her nose. Then she tells him this queer little story about shadows and darkie magic and that. When she's finished she gives him this worried look, like she don't know what he'll make of it.

Truth is, he don't know *what* to make of it. He learnt a bit about darkie magic off of Amos the cook on the *Marianne*, and as far as he's concerned it's a load of bollocks. But Sophie don't think so. And if she don't watch out, she'll fret herself to an early grave.

That's when he pulls hisself up short. Whoa, Ben, whoa. Don't you get mixed up in all this. It ain't your problem. She's doing all right, is Sophie. She's got plenty of dosh, nice clothes, plenty to eat, and a topper big sister to look after her. She's in clover, she is.

Only she's not.

'Right,' he says, sounding a lot cockier than he feels. 'You leave it to me. I'll get your shadow back, and I'll sort it out about the parson, too. But you got to do your bit. All right?'

She nods. 'What do I do?'

'You don't say nothing to nobody, you stop fretting, and you start getting better.'

Sinclair picked up the little silver branding-iron from his blotter and turned it in his fingers, and wondered what this unsettling news from town could possibly mean.

He told himself to stay calm, and to have faith. Hadn't God protected him from the menace in the hothouse? Hadn't God so ordered events that all he'd had to do was wait and keep silent, and wonder how long it would take?

But this report from Kean was peculiarly disturbing. 'A white boy,' Kean had said, 'cheaply dressed and very meagre, with black hair and a sharp, wicked-looking face. He seem to know Missy Sophie well.'

It was impossible. Inconceivable. Those urchins in London had been seen to; the officer had assured him of that.

And yet – if it hadn't been the urchin from Fitzroy Square, to whom had the sister been talking? And why?

A soft knock at the door.

'Enter,' he said.

Kean came in and bowed low. Missy Sophie, he said, had been awakened, and was expecting Master Sinclair. She would be alone, as Master Sinclair had requested. Miss Maddy was taking her bath.

Sinclair replaced the branding-iron on the blotter and rose to his feet. 'Very good,' he said.

The child was sitting up in bed when he went out to her. She was still dazed with sleep, her sallow face creased from the pillow. After the visit to town, his wife had insisted that she should go straight to bed for a nap.

Sinclair stood looking down at her for a moment. Then, in a low, gentle voice, he said, 'You were seen outside the courthouse, talking to an undesirable.'

A hit, a palpable hit. He watched her face drain with shock.

'You appeared to know this individual,' he said. 'Can that be true?'

She shook her head.

He gave her a kindly smile. 'A wastrel and a no-account, and yet you knew him? I think you ought to tell me who he was, and what was said.'

She did not reply.

He repeated the question.

Another silence. She was watching him like an animal, scarcely daring to breathe.

'I think', he said, 'that you really ought to tell me everything. You will feel a great deal better when you do.'

She swallowed. 'He was asking the way,' she said. Her lips barely moved.

'He was asking the way,' repeated Sinclair. 'For a quarter of an hour.'

She nodded.

He leaned over her: close, but not so close as to inhale the effluvium of her disease. 'I am surprised that you, of all people, should attempt to deceive a man of God with a false-hood. You must know that you have not long to live. You could go to hell for that.'

Beneath the dressing gown her bony breast rose and fell.

He straightened up. 'I think I ought to leave you, to reflect upon what you have done. And when you decide to tell me the truth, you shall find me an attentive audience.' He walked down the gallery, then paused at the door to his study. 'In the meantime,' he said, putting a little hardness into his voice, 'do not imagine that you shall go unpunished.'

The effect on her was immediate and astonishing. She sat up so abruptly that she jarred the bedside table and sent her glass and the water jug flying. 'Oh no please!' she cried. 'Don't lock me up! Don't, I couldn't bear it, I should go mad!'

Lock her up? Whatever did she mean?

He swayed. Dear God. What did she mean?

'I won't tell anyone ever,' she cried, 'I swear on the Bible! Just don't lock me up in the hothouse!'

He forced himself to take a deep, slow breath. Calm, calm. Trust in the Maker.

He walked back across the gallery, and drew up a chair beside her and sat down. 'Tell me,' he said very gently. 'Tell me what you think you saw.'

CHAPTER TWENTY-THREE

With luck, no-one would see her leave. Jocelyn had gone off to Kingston early that morning; Great-Aunt May was taking her afternoon rest; Clemency's spinal irritation had kept her in bed in a fog of laudanum; and Sinclair had gone to town on business of his own. Sophie was fast asleep in the gallery. Yesterday's trip to town with Jocelyn had been an enormous success, but since then she'd become silent and withdrawn, and was clearly worn out. Madeleine had given her one of Dr Pritchard's new sleeping powders, and told Rebecca to sit with her until she returned.

By the time the house was finally quiet, it was four in the afternoon. Madeleine calculated that it would take her about an hour to ride to Eden. That should leave her with just enough time to say her piece to Cameron, and make it back before Sinclair returned.

She told Jessie to run to the stables and have Doshey saddle her horse, but to wait for her in the stable-yard, rather than coming round to the front of the house. Then she went to her room and changed into her riding habit. She was astonished that she could act so calmly, when inside she felt hollow with apprehension.

Nearly a week had gone by since the ball at Parnassus, and with every day that passed she felt worse about deceiving him. She had tried to tell herself that he deserved to be lied to. Hadn't he written that note to Cousin Lettice?

Hadn't he washed his hands of Ainsley's children? Hadn't he?

It didn't work. He had been honest with her, and she must be honest with him. She must tell him who she was. Then he could make of it what he would, and she could put it all behind her, and begin again.

She finished pinning on her hat, and grabbed her dust-coat and riding-crop from the bed. She cast a last glance round the room. From the oxblood hangings, a baleful Monroe serpent met her eye.

When I next see you, she told it silently, someone else will know the truth. She wasn't sure if that made her feel better or worse.

She slipped out through the back of the house and took the walkway past the cook-house to the stables, attracting curious glances from the helpers, which she ignored.

Doshey was waiting in the stable-yard with Kestrel, the little grey mare which Jocelyn had given her when he'd taught her to ride. The groom was shaking his head. 'You better hurry wid dat ride, Miss Maddy. Rain go come in a hour or so.'

He was right. The air was hot and heavy, the eastern sky thickening to a dirty grey as she put Kestrel into a trot along the track that led south, along the muddy little stream they called the Green River. The track was narrow and uneven, but sheltered from prying eyes by giant bamboo. Not even Great-Aunt May would see her leave.

After a mile or so, the track emerged into the open cane-pieces of Bellevue, on the south-eastern borders of the estate. On any other day she would have enjoyed the ride: the wind in her face; the young cane shivering in the breeze; the mare's smooth-running power beneath her. This afternoon she scarcely noticed. She kept wondering what Cameron would say when she told him. What he would think of her.

After half an hour she saw the ancient guango tree which marked the turning into the Eden road, and reined in sharply. She had the strangest feeling that so long as she remained on Fever Hill land, she could still turn back; but that once she was out on the Eden road, her path would be set.

She glanced back over her shoulder. Then she put Kestrel forward again.

But as she was nearing the guango tree, a figure stepped away from the trunk and moved out into the road. It stood there unmoving, waiting for her.

She was still too far away to make out his face. He looked like a field-hand, in dungarees and tattered straw hat – and yet something about him was sharply familiar. More than a boy but not quite a man, the thin face was wary and unsmiling as he watched her approach.

Her stomach turned over. No, she thought. It can't be.

'Hello, Madlin,' said Ben.

She's not pleased to see him like Sophie, he can tell. She's horrified. Or maybe scared. Maybe she thinks he's after money; that he wants paying, for not telling no-one about them photos.

He should of stayed hid. She's a grand lady now, with a feather in her hat and her glossy white horse. What's she want with him?

And she's in a hurry, too, like she's off somewheres important. Out of breath, horse in a lather; quick look up the road, quick frown at the sky. Ben Kelly's just in the way.

He'd hoped that maybe she'd be a little bit glad to see him. Course, she's got no reason to be. Just like he's got no reason to be seeing her, neither. In fact he's got every reason *not* to be seeing her, what with her being married to the parson and all. But he couldn't stay hid and let her ride past. Not Madeleine.

He watches her bring her horse about, and jump down. '*Ben,*' she says in that low voice of hers. 'God. *Ben.*'

Without thinking, he takes the bridle from her and calms the horse down a bit, and ties it to a tree root. Makes a pig's ear of that, and all. Fingers shaking so much he can't hardly tie a knot. It's like he's got the jitters or something.

'Ben,' she says again. 'What are you *doing* here?'

He chucks his hat under the tree where the horse can't get at it, and shoves his hands in his pockets and shrugs. 'Sophie didn't tell you nothing, then.'

'Sophie? What do you mean?'

'Saw her in Falmouth, didn't I? Outside the courthouse.' He tries to grin. 'Ben Kelly sitting on a bench outside a courthouse. Fancy that.'

She don't smile back.

'Anyway,' he goes, 'what was Sophie doing there in the first place? I never thought to ask her, and all.' He knows he's talking too quick, but he can't stop hisself. He feels like he's got to keep talking, it don't matter what about, or he's going to crack wide open.

She's watching him with her big dark eyes, and maybe she guesses why he's rabbiting on, cos she goes along with it for a bit. 'She was waiting for Jocelyn,' she says. 'He was at a magistrates' meeting. But tell me about—'

'Jocelyn. That the old bloke? The one she calls Uncle Jocelyn?'

She nods.

'Is he your grandpa, then?'

She shoots a glance over her shoulder, like she thinks there might be someone watching her or something. 'Yes,' she goes. 'My father was his son. Ainsley Monroe.'

He spits. Scuffs dust over it with his foot. 'Only that grandpa of yours don't know that yet. I'll bet.'

'Nobody knows.'

'Not even Sophie?'

She shakes her head.

Behind them the horse is kicking up a fuss, like a hornet's got at it or something, so he goes over and talks to it to calm it down.

A rumble of thunder up ahead. They're in for a storm. He watches her looking up at the sky. She wants to be off. It gives him a turn to see how much. Cos he don't want her to go. He *really* don't. It's like he's a nipper again, and scared of the dark; scared of being left all alone. Sod it, what's wrong with him? She's not his big sister or nothing, she's just some toff who went and married the parson.

'Ben?' she goes. 'Where's Robbie?'

He opens his mouth to fob her off, but no sound comes out. Nothing. Sod all. Just opens and shuts his mouth like a bloody fish.

'Ben? What's the matter? What happened? Where's Robbie?'

He backs away from her and trips on this tree root and sits down hard. The horse puts down its head and gives him a sniff, and he just sits there gaping like a fish.

She gets down on her knees beside him in the dust. She don't seem to care about her posh riding-frock and her shiny riding-boots, and that. And up close, she's not the grand lady no more, she's just Madeleine.

He takes this big gulp of air to steady hisself, and then he tells her everything. Funny, that. Right up until he starts, he don't know that he's going to do it. But she's Madeleine, she's a big sister – not *his* big sister, but *a* big sister – so out it all comes.

He tells her how the parson paid this bloke to follow him and Robbie back to Shelton Street, to see where they lived, and then called the bluebottles and fingered them for a click: a big one, with silver plate and all. When he gets to the bit about Robbie getting killed, he can't look at her no more. He just looks at this tree root, all knobby and twisted, with these little brown ants running up and down, and he hears his voice telling her what happened, and it's like it's not Ben Kelly talking, but somebody else.

And then he's past Robbie, and out the other side to the docks and the *Marianne* and that. But even then he can't stop, it's like he's a train or something, chugging along. He tells her about the gun and the bullets and the plan. The only thing he don't tell about is that little darkie that was Sophie's mate and died, in case it gets Sophie into trouble.

When he gets to the end he's shivering like it's the middle of winter, even though it's stinking hot. She tries to put her hand on his shoulder but he twitches away. If she touches him he'll crack into pieces. That's what it feels like. Like he'll smash into little pieces in the dust.

Gently, like she's talking to a baby, she says, 'Oh, Ben. I'm so terribly sorry.'

He spits. 'Well,' he goes. 'Way of the world.'

There's a silence. High above them a john crow does a circle in the sky, then pushes off. The horse puts down its head to cough.

'Ben,' she goes, and this time she sounds different. More grown-up. 'The gun. Show me the gun.'

He don't even think about refusing. Gets up and goes to the tree and finds the special place, and takes it out. Unwraps it and lays it between them in the dust.

She looks at it without touching. 'Do you know how to use this?'

He nods. He's got the bullets now. Even done a bit of target practice down by the river. That pigeon, it just dropped down dead out of that guinep tree. No squawk, no nothing. Just dropped down dead.

'You can't, Ben,' she says in her low voice. 'You can't do this.'

'Yes I can. I—'

'No. No. Listen to me. I'm not thinking about Sinclair, God forgive me for that. I'm thinking of you. You'd be caught, Ben. They'd hang you for it.'

He tries to shrug. 'Who cares?'

She fixes him with her dark eyes. 'Robbie,' she goes. 'Robbie cares.'

He jerks back like she's hit him in the face. 'Robbie's dead,' he snarls.

'But what if he weren't? What if it were the other way round, Ben? What if you were the one who'd fallen from that roof, and he was the one who'd survived?'

'What you on about?'

'What if Robbie had lived, Ben, and found his way out here? Would you want him to stay alive and make something of his life? Or would you want him to get himself hanged?'

Ben don't answer. He can't, can he? He's got something stuck in his throat. Great big lump of something, like a bit of crust, stuck in his throat. 'R-Robbie', he blurts out, 'would

278

of never *got* out here. Not on his own. Silly little b-bugger.'

She puts her hand on his back and smoothes it up and down, and he wants to tell her to lay off, but he can't. He can't say nothing on account of that lump.

And all of a sudden it comes so strong upon him that he can't hold it back no more. Right up from deep inside him it comes, and cracks him wide open. It's like a butcher's taken a chopper to his chest and split him right down the wishbone, and out come these great big jerky hee-hawing sobs, over and over, till his ribs ache something awful, and his throat's all sore, and he can't stop for nothing, he just can't, and it *hurts*, ah fuck but it hurts.

Madeleine wrapped the revolver in her scarf and stowed it gingerly in her saddlebag. She had no idea what she was going to do with it; give it to Cameron, perhaps. All she knew was that it was imperative to get the thing away from Ben. His strange, half-baked, suicidal notion of murder would only get him killed.

He had finally stopped those terrible wrenching sobs, and was sitting hunched on the ground, clasping his knees, and still shaking, his long black eyelashes still spiky with tears. He looked thin and young and utterly spent: his face pale beneath its tan, his eyes a watery emerald.

She could understand how he had fastened on Sinclair as someone to blame. He'd needed to make sense of his brother's death, and couldn't bring himself to accept it for what it really was: a terrible accident. But this bizarre notion of 'paying back the parson' could get him killed or deported, or thrown into prison at the very least. She wondered if she'd managed to talk him out of it.

Hunched amid the tree roots, he looked so alone, and so completely out of his depth. How could she ride off and leave him?

But she could hardly ask Jocelyn to give him a job at Fever Hill. That would be the worst possible thing for him, given his strange delusion about Sinclair.

She had tried to give him money, but been snarlingly rejected. He was doing all right, he told her. This country was easy pickings. Plenty to click. Even the odd job here and there. He was in clover, he was.

She didn't believe a word of it. He looked as if he hadn't eaten for weeks. And what was worse, he looked as if he didn't care.

A flurry of wind stirred the Spanish moss in the guango tree. She glanced up at the sky. The rain was approaching fast. If she didn't go soon, it would be too late, and she'd have to turn back.

'Here,' she said. She knelt beside him and took her card-case from her pocket and wrote a few words on the back of one of her cards. 'This is the address of a good friend of mine in Falmouth. Mrs Olivia Herapath. Go and see her as soon as you can. She'll find you a job. I'll send her a line, so that she'll know to expect you.'

He wiped his nose on the back of his hand, and took the card and scowled at it.

'She knows everyone,' Madeleine said. 'She'll find you a job. Perhaps something in a stable, where you can work with horses.' The inadequacy of that made her flush with shame. But she couldn't think of anything more to do.

She watched him read the card to himself, his lips silently moving.

'Ben,' she said. 'Promise me you'll go to see her.'

He glanced up, his eyes unfocused.

'Promise?'

He nodded.

She wondered if he'd even heard. 'I have to go now,' she said. She stood up and dusted off her skirts.

He stayed where he was.

'Ben? Would you help me onto my horse?'

That seemed to bring him back to himself, as she had hoped it would. He struggled to his feet and pocketed the card, then untied Kestrel and helped her into the saddle.

'Rain coming,' he said. To her relief he sounded almost his old self. 'Where you off to, Madlin, in such a hurry?'

'Just making a call,' she said.

He glanced up the road. 'Not much up there,' he said.

She did not reply.

A moment later his face changed. 'Bloody hell. Bloody *hell*. The brother.'

Dear God, he recovered fast.

'That's it, isn't it? You and the parson's brother.'

She flashed him a look, but he wasn't quelled. He was shaking his head and gazing up at her with new respect. 'Sodding hell,' he said. 'What a sodding mess.'

She gave him a twisted smile. 'As you say.' She gathered the reins and turned Kestrel's head. 'Look after yourself, Ben Kelly. If not for you – then for Robbie. Yes?'

He did not reply. But as she was putting Kestrel forward, he called out after her. 'Madlin?'

She reined in.

'The parson. If I *had* of shot him. Would you of cared?'

She looked at him standing there in the dusty road, so young and so alone. She wished there was more that she could do for him. 'Stay away from Fever Hill,' she told him. 'Don't get mixed up in this.'

The first spots of rain were pitting the red dust as she cantered south towards the Martha Brae.

The foreman of a field-gang confirmed that she was on the right road. Just head on up, ma'am, and once you cross the river you're on Eden land. Mas' Camron's in the first cane-piece just past the bridge.

He said something more about a broken axle, but she was already too far ahead to hear.

The road climbed steadily, darkened by tall cedars and wild almond trees with huge, wind-tossed leaves. Over the Cockpits, lightning flared in a purple-grey sky.

She crested the hill and made a muddy descent towards a moss-covered bridge across the river, where she brought Kestrel to a skittering halt.

The Martha Brae slid silent and opaque between banks of heliconia and thick, purple-flowered creepers. On the other side, in a clearing of ironwood and giant bamboo, lay a cluster of ruins. She knew them at once. The old slave village at Romilly. It had often featured in her mother's stories.

She had a powerful sense that nothing had changed since

her parents' time; that on the other side of the river lay the past. Cut-stone dwellings stood open to the sky. Thick, corded creepers laced the tumbled walls.

Once again she was poised at the edge of the Forbidden Kingdom. But this time there was no baleful marble serpent, no sharp-eyed crow mocking from the trees. The only sound was the pattering of rain on the leaves, and her own uneven breathing.

She hadn't expected it to be so difficult. She'd thought only of seeing Cameron and telling him the truth; not of where she was going. Seeing it now, the Forbidden Kingdom just a few paces away, she felt shaky and exposed and obscurely frightened. Even the rain seemed threatening. A rainstorm in July? Who ever heard of that? It felt as if the hills themselves were warning her to stay away.

Another crash of thunder. Kestrel snorted and side-stepped. She gathered the reins and put the mare forward, and cantered over the bridge and down into Eden.

She kept her eyes on the road as she passed the ruins, and cantered between the trees. Suddenly the woods were left behind. Cane-pieces opened out on either side of her, acid green in the stormy light. Up ahead, the hills loomed shockingly close: the start of the Cockpits.

Some distance away, in a cane-piece to her right, a little group of field-hands clustered about a wagon leaning drunkenly into an irrigation ditch. She saw Pilate tethered nearby, and Cameron's fair head. He was by the wagon, stooping to examine the damage. As she reined in, he straightened up and saw her.

At that moment the wagon gave a shuddering jolt and sank further into the ditch. Everyone sprang back.

Cameron turned to speak to a tall Negro beside him, and reached for his hat, and went round the back of the wagon to untether Pilate.

'I have to talk to you,' she said when he'd ridden across. She had to raise her voice above the noise of the rain.

He gave her a concentrated look that she couldn't read. 'That', he said, 'isn't a good idea.'

'I know, but— I know.'

With the back of his hand he wiped the rain from his face. 'What about Sinclair? Does he know you're here?'

'Of course not.'

A terrific peal of thunder. Their horses sidestepped in alarm.

He glanced over his shoulder at the men by the wagon, then back to her. 'Come up to the house.'

CHAPTER TWENTY-FOUR

By the time they reached the house, the rain was coming down in force.

They went in the back way, so Madeleine saw nothing of the exterior except rain-pummelled creepers and broken fretwork eaves. Then they were in the hall, and he was showing her into a dim and shuttered 'spare room', then leaving her without another word, to go and see to the horses.

She removed her hat and her sodden dust-coat and threw them on a chair. Her hair was wet, her riding habit damp but not soaked through. Nothing to be done about that now. Besides, it was too hot to catch a chill.

As her eyes adjusted to the gloom, she made out more of her surroundings. A thick, soft covering of dust, and a musty smell of neglect – but the room must once have been beautiful. The walls were panelled in amber sweetwood, the windows hung with the remains of blue and white shantung, the floor tiled in cool terracotta. But the hangings were mildewed, the panelling worm-eaten, and the canopied bed had collapsed into a pile of mouldy planks. Rain rattled into a washbasin through a hole in the roof. The chair on which she'd thrown her dust-coat had lost one of its legs.

She remembered the haunted ruin in the photograph on the piano at Cairngowrie House. The tree-fern in the window like a shattered monocle; the steps curving down into the jungle garden. She was inside the house which her own forebears had built. Inside the past.

A crash of thunder and a brilliant flare of lightning, and the rain on the shingles became deafening. She moved to the window.

Against the broken louvres the fronds of an enormous fern trembled in the rain. She looked down over a steep slope of wind-tossed trees: palms and wild almonds and tattered philodendrons, their huge leaves dipping and swaying beneath the onslaught. At the bottom of the slope she made out stables and a cook-house, smothered by creepers and bougainvillaea and great scarlet bursts of ginger lilies. It was hard to tell whether the buildings supported the greenery, or the other way round.

Everywhere she looked she saw dilapidation and decay and abundant life. *In Eden everything is wilder and more alive . . . the sun shines more fiercely, the rain strikes harder, and the leaves are so green that it hurts your eyes . . .*

No, she told herself. Don't think about that now.

On the wall near the door hung a shattered looking-glass, still with a silvered fragment in one corner. She went to it and set about unpinning her hair and combing it through with her fingers, and putting it up again.

The rain ceased with tropical suddenness. Blue sky began to show through the hole in the roof. Sunlight limned the ferns with gold, and a haze of vapour rose from the slope. Grassquits twittered furiously amid a ringing chorus of frogs.

She opened the door into the hall and looked out. It was empty. Cameron must still be down at the stables. She emerged into a large central space made airy by high open rafters, louvred fanlights, and several more holes in the roof.

The house seemed to be smaller than Fever Hill, but was clearly much older. Mrs Herapath had told her that it was the oldest on the Northside, and one of the few to have survived the Christmas Rebellion – for by the standards of the time, the Durrants had been good to their slaves. 'Too good,' Mrs Herapath had muttered darkly. 'Too many little black and brown unofficial Durrants scurrying all over the place.'

The hall was empty of furniture except for an enormous

and very dusty mahogany table which was clearly a dumping ground: a trio of hurricane lamps with cracked glass shades; a tottering stack of *Gall's Weekly Newsletter*s from the previous year; three large tins of Everett's Patented Harness Cleaner; a crate of Glenfallock Highland Whisky, Gibbon's *Decline and Fall of the Roman Empire*, and a tattered copy of Cassell's *Book of the Horse*. From what she could see of the rooms that led off the hall, they too were in a similar state of neglect.

How can he live like this, she wondered. *Where* does he live?

She moved through to the sitting-room, which was empty except for an ancient, battered chest of drawers on top of which lay a belt with a broken buckle, a watch-chain and a pile of loose change. She resisted the temptation to look in the drawers, and went forward to the louvred doorway, which presumably led into some sort of gallery.

She never forgot that first moment when she opened the doors. She had expected a dim, shuttered chamber like the gallery at Fever Hill. Instead she found herself on a wide, open verandah in a blaze of light.

A flock of parakeets exploded from the trees, and filled the sky with emerald wings. The sun shone green through tree-ferns dripping beneath the eaves. Purple grenadilla invaded the broken fretwork balustrade, and white bougainvillaea, and papery red hibiscus. At her feet a double curve of creeper-choked steps swept down into a steaming wilderness. She saw mango trees and cedars and palms; lime trees and wild cinnamon, powder-blue plumbago and purple thunbergia, and the vivid orange and cobalt of strelitzia. At the foot of the slope, the opaque jade-green river slid by beneath water-heavy plumes of giant bamboo, the banks aflame with torch ginger and the scarlet claws of heliconia. Across the river, the road cut a rust-red slash through the shimmering cane-pieces, and far in the distance lay the grey-blue glitter of the sea.

The air was rich and hot and buzzing with life. The rasp of crickets, the piping of frogs, the twittering of sugarquits and wild canaries. She took a deep breath and smelt the mineral freshness of wet red earth. *In Eden everything is wilder and more alive . . .*

She ran to the end of the verandah and leaned out as far as she could. The house was set in an amphitheatre of forested hills, their slopes dark in the glare of the sun. *And deep in the forest there stands an enormous silk-cotton tree. That's where we used to meet, your father and I.* She scanned the hills, but it was impossible to see for the glare.

Then, as she watched, a haze passed across the sun, and for an instant, far in the distance, she thought she saw it. Taller than any oak, its great outstretched limbs supported a separate world above the canopy: a world of strangler fig and Spanish moss and orchids like little darts of flame. The Tree of Life. *The creepers hang down to the ground, and at night after a rain they're speckled with fireflies; and there are moonflowers as big as your hand, so fragile and pale that they're like the ghosts of flowers; and with each breath you take in the scent of cinnamon and lime and sweet decay . . .*

She blinked back tears.

A sound of footsteps behind her, and she turned to see Cameron coming out onto the verandah.

He saw her taut expression, and misread it. 'It used to be a proper gallery,' he said, as if he felt he must apologize, 'but the wood-ants got into the louvres. It seemed simpler just to open the whole thing up.'

She crossed her arms about her waist. 'It's beautiful.'

There was an uneasy silence. She noticed that he remained by the doors, a safe distance away. He stood with his hands in the pockets of his shooting jacket, awkward and on edge.

Then two things happened at once. An enormous mastiff hurtled up the steps and launched itself at Cameron, and an ancient black man with unsteady yellow eyes emerged from the house bearing a tray with an earthenware pitcher, two tumblers, and a bottle of rum.

Helper and mastiff narrowly missed one another, and Madeleine, grateful for the diversion, found a rickety cane chair near the steps, and sat down. She took a tumbler from the helper's tray and held it on her knees with both hands.

There wasn't much furniture on the verandah, but the

question of where Cameron lived was finally solved. He lived out here. Behind him was a cot-bed hastily covered by a moth-eaten grey blanket, and flanked by an elderly wash-stand and a large, iron-bound campaign chest. On the chest was a stack of battered ledgers, an ancient kerosene lamp, and a corner of silvered mirror-glass. She thought, no wonder he cuts himself shaving.

He caught the direction of her glance, and coloured. 'Sorry about this. You must think I've gone bush.'

She shook her head.

'It's just that there's always so much to do on the estate. I haven't had time for the house.'

'Why do you sleep out here? Is it because of prison?'

He dismissed the helper, and watched till he was gone. Then he turned back to her. 'How did you know that?'

'Oh. Just a guess.' She paused. 'Was it awful?'

'Um. Yes.'

'Did it change you?'

'I think so.'

'How?'

He frowned at the floor. 'Made me more tolerant, I suppose. I mean, I had some good friends in prison, but they weren't the sort of people with whom I'd have associated before.' Again he coloured, and she guessed that he was thinking about Grace.

She wanted to tell him that she wasn't the least bit shocked that he'd had a black mistress. How could she be shocked, when right now her photograph was probably gracing the trays outside Bob Venables' grimy little shop in Holywell Street?

The mastiff trotted over to investigate her, and sniffed her hand, then trotted back to Cameron and slumped at his feet.

She said, 'I take it that's the famous Abigail.'

'Sophie told you about her?'

She nodded. 'She'll be annoyed to have missed the introductions.'

Another awkward silence, while they both thought how unlikely it was that Sophie would ever be allowed to visit Eden.

Madeleine took a sip of her drink. It was freshly pressed cane juice: pearl-grey and fragrant and wonderfully steadying.

'Would you like some rum in that?' said Cameron. 'You must have got rather wet.'

'No. Thank you. But you go ahead.'

He poured a measure of rum into his own glass and added a splash of cane juice from the pitcher, then took a chair by the campaign chest. She noticed that he only used his right hand, and that his left remained in the pocket of his shooting jacket, where a dark blotch was beginning to soak through. She said, 'You've hurt your hand.'

'I caught it on a nail, that's all.'

She remembered the moment when he had seen her in the cane-piece. The wagon's lurch and his quick recoil. He must have been concealing it in case she was squeamish. 'You ought to see to it,' she said. 'Go on. I've seen blood before.'

Looking slightly embarrassed, he took his hand out of his pocket, and she saw that the handkerchief he'd wrapped about it was mostly scarlet. He unpeeled it to reveal a messy cut across the palm. Abigail raised her head and sniffed, and he pushed her nose away.

Madeleine said, 'Does it hurt?'

'No.' He shrugged. 'Yes.'

They exchanged slight smiles. He went inside and came back with a clean handkerchief from the chest of drawers, and sat down again.

She ought to tell him now why she had come. Just tell him and get it over with. But she couldn't do it yet. Let him bandage his hand and have a drink. Yes, let him have a drink. He was going to need it.

Behind him on the campaign chest stood a leather travelling frame containing a pair of photographs. In one of them she recognized a younger Jocelyn, much less rigid and hawk-like. In the other, a young man with wavy fair hair. He looked happy and handsome and unafraid. He was her father.

Cameron said something, but she didn't hear.

She had forgotten what her father looked like when he

289

smiled. How could she have forgotten something as important as that?

'Madeleine? What's wrong?'

She dragged her gaze away. 'Is that Ainsley?'

'I'm sorry? Oh. Yes, that's Ainsley. Abby, go *away*.'

'He looks young.'

'He was twenty-two when it was taken. Just before he took off with Rose.'

'What was he like?'

He picked up the bottle and splashed rum over his palm, hissing as it began to bite. Abigail lapped blood and liquor off the floor until he shoved her aside with his boot. 'He was clever,' he said without looking up. 'Imaginative. Enormously self-critical. Which could be infuriating at times. And kind.' He paused. 'I think that's why he could never be happy after what he did. Because of all the people he'd hurt.'

At Cairngowrie House when her father had been home for more than a few weeks, he would become pensive and quiet, and her mother would say that he was beginning to feel guilty about being with them.

'Have you really forgiven him?' she said.

He glanced at her in surprise. 'Of course. He was so young when it happened.'

'Have you forgiven Rose?'

'She was young too.'

'That's not an answer.'

He considered that. 'I was thirteen when they left, and a little bit in love with her myself. But yes. Of course I've forgiven her. Poor Rose. One can't be angry for ever. But it's strange. I still—' He broke off with a frown.

'What were you going to say?'

'It's just that I still dream of him. Ainsley. And they're not peaceful dreams. I don't know why.'

Don't you? she thought. He had never once mentioned Ainsley's children. He seemed to have driven them from his mind. Strange that such a perceptive man should be able to deceive himself for so long.

She said, 'Do you still miss him?'

He laid the handkerchief across his knee and folded it to form a makeshift bandage, and began winding it round his palm. 'Imagine how you'd feel if Sophie went away and never came back.'

In the garden a flock of crows settled squabbling in a mango tree. Abigail gave a gruff bark and hurtled down the steps to see them off.

Madeleine said, 'You know, I read the transcripts of your court-martial.'

He raised his head and stared at her. 'Why?'

'To find out what you did.'

'I told you what I did.'

'No, I mean really. I wanted to know everything.' She looked down at her lap. 'Mrs Herapath told me about Clemency's letter.'

With his teeth he pulled the knot tight. 'Olivia Herapath talks too much.'

'I don't think so.' She paused. 'Why have you never tried to make it up with Jocelyn?'

'Why should I?'

'Because you could.'

He made no reply.

'I think', she said, 'that you've become accustomed to living like this. It's become a way of life. Just as it has for Jocelyn. You're so alike. You could be father and son.'

She watched him pour himself another drink and look at it, and put it down untasted.

His hair was still damp, and as he wasn't wearing a necktie she could see the droplets of rainwater trickling down his neck. Heat rose to her cheeks.

'Madeleine, ' he said, 'why did you come here?'

'I needed to see you.'

'It only makes things worse.'

'Yes. I know.' She spread her hands on the rust-coloured serge of her skirt. Now was the time to tell him. Just tell him and have done with it.

She tried to imagine what he would say when he knew that she had been lying to him from the beginning. She looked at him sitting there with his elbows on his knees and his injured hand held a little stiffly, and his damp hair curling on his neck like a boy's. He seemed so capable and strong, but he could be hurt. Especially by her. How could she do it? She couldn't hurt him. All she wanted was to keep him from harm.

'I needed to see you,' she said again.

'Why? What good does it do?'

She shook her head. She couldn't tell him. It was cowardly and wrong, but she couldn't do it.

He rubbed his good hand over his face and gave her a look that she couldn't read. 'That night at the Trahernes',' he said, 'I wanted to kill Sinclair. My own brother. And I wanted to kill him for what he said about you.'

'What did he say?'

'He said you're not as innocent as you seem.'

She got up and went to the balustrade. 'He's right,' she said. 'I'm not.'

'I don't believe that.'

'It's true.'

'What do you mean?'

She shook her head. She heard him get to his feet and come to stand beside her.

They stood together in silence, looking out over the steaming garden. Again she felt herself growing hot. She wanted to touch him, to put her fingers to the base of his throat and feel the cool rainwater and the warmth of his skin.

He said, 'If things had been different, we'd be living here together, you and I.'

'Don't say that.'

He turned to her. 'Leave him. Leave him and come to me.'

'I can't.'

'Yes you can. You don't have to follow the rules, you can break them. I know, I've done it.'

'Well, I can't. He's Sophie's guardian.'

'Bring her with you. She'd love it here. She'd get better.'

'He'd come and take her away. He could do it. He'd have the law on his side.'

'So you have thought about it?'

'Of course I have.'

'So what are you saying, that there's nothing to be done?'

She paused. 'The only way out', she said, 'would be to run away. Leave Jamaica and forget about everyone else. Just like Ainsley and Rose. But that would only start the whole wretched cycle over again, and I won't do it. So yes, I am saying that there's nothing to be done. And you know it, too.'

He opened his mouth to reply, then shut it again. She was right.

Rainwater dripped from the eaves. An egret sped upriver, brilliant white against searing green. In the garden, Abigail rooted around in the undergrowth.

She glanced at his hand on the railing. He had rolled back his shirtsleeve to deal with the cut, and she looked at the broad wristbone and the fine fair hairs and the thick vein snaking up his forearm. Why couldn't she touch him, just once, so that she'd have something to remember?

She reached over and put her fingers on the back of his hand, just above the bandage. She felt his grip tighten on the balustrade; the muscles moving beneath the skin. She felt the tension in him, the holding back.

She put her hand on his shoulder and raised herself on her toes and kissed him. She had meant to reach his mouth, but in her nervousness she missed, and her lips found the roughness of his cheek. He smelt of rum and horses and cool, rain-washed skin.

He put one hand on her waist and the other on the nape of her neck, and bent and kissed her mouth. Softly at first, just finding her lips. Then more deeply.

Startling, unfamiliar, strange. She was spiralling down into heat and strength and otherness; warmth and closeness, unbelievable closeness; no barriers, no holding back, no more being alone.

She put her arms round his neck and felt the heat of his skin against her wrists, and his damp hair, and his grip about her tightening. She didn't want it to end. She wanted to drown in him and never wake up.

At last they had to draw apart for breath. They stood with their heads together, taking in each other's scent. She was shaking and so was he.

'I don't understand you,' he said. 'Is this what you came to tell me? That you want to be with me but can't?'

'Yes,' she said. 'That's why I came.'

'You know I'll never accept that.'

'You don't have a choice.'

'There's always a choice.'

She put her hand on his chest and felt his heart beating beneath her palm. Why must it be like this? she thought. Just when everything's so clear, it has to end.

'Madeleine—'

'It's getting late,' she said. 'I've got to go back.'

His arms tightened about her. 'You can't go. Not after this.'

'Cameron—'

'You can't just leave.'

'Let me go. I'm sorry. Let me go.'

'I don't understand you. It's always as if there's something missing.'

'I know. I do know.'

'Why won't you tell me?'

She put both hands on his chest. 'I have to go,' she said again. 'It's late. Please. Fetch my horse.'

'Madeleine, you can't just—'

'Yes I can.'

She had promised herself that she would not look back, but of course she did. She was halfway down the track to the cane-pieces when she reined in.

Already Eden had slipped back into the past, but she could still see Cameron standing on the steps, watching her go.

She hated herself. She had told him nothing and achieved nothing, except to hurt him and make everything a hundred times worse.

She turned and put Kestrel into a canter, and rode blindly through the cane-pieces and across the sliding river, and down the muddy road towards Fever Hill.

It was six o'clock by the time Sinclair returned from town, greatly calmed by his interview with Dr Valentine. But he was granted no time to dwell on that, for as he brought the pony-trap to a halt outside the house, Kean descended the steps with a note from Great-Aunt May.

I must speak to you. The west grounds, forthwith. We must not be overheard.

A cold sweat broke out on Sinclair's forehead. What could possibly be so momentous that Great-Aunt May would break the rule of a lifetime and go into the grounds in daylight?

Without stopping to wash or change his clothes, he hurried round to the back of the house.

In the shade of the great, half-dead silk-cotton tree, two straight-backed chairs had been set on the hard brown grass. In one, beneath an enormous black sun-umbrella, sat Great-Aunt May: rigid, unmoving, and armoured against the sun by a floor-length dust-coat of flint-grey silk, the ever-present grey kid gloves, and a wide-brimmed hat swathed in veils of pewter chiffon.

Trembling with nerves, Sinclair took the chair beside her.

She turned her head to regard him, and through the veils he caught the gleam of her inflamed blue gaze. Her imperious ivory features were as inscrutable as ever.

He licked his lips. 'I confess, Great-Aunt, that I do not understand what—'

'Indeed you do not,' she said coldly. 'But you shall.'

He passed his hand over his throat and chin. She did not seem to be angry; at least, not with him. If he hadn't known her better, he would have said that she was excited. Or perhaps grimly satisfied. His pulse quickened.

'This afternoon,' she began, 'Kean overheard an exchange between two persons on the Eden Road. Your wife and another. An undesirable.'

He opened his mouth to protest, but she quelled him with a glance. 'Regrettably,' she went on, 'Kean did not hear all, for he was disturbed by field-workers and forced to move on. But he heard enough.' She paused. 'Your wife has not been honest with you, Sinclair.'

'That I know,' he said hotly.

'No,' she said, 'you do not.' She folded her long narrow hands in her lap. 'Your wife,' she said evenly, 'is not who she says she is.' She glanced down at her hands. 'Your wife is Jocelyn's granddaughter.'

Chapter Twenty-Five

Power and knowledge fizzed in Sinclair's veins as he rode out in the early morning to see his brother.

He looked about him and relished everything he saw. The young cane glistening after yesterday's rain; the blacks weeding the rows with brute, unthinking vigour; the pick-neys scurrying for the quatties he tossed in the mud. Yes, everything knew its purpose in God's grand design.

And now his own purpose had fallen into place with startling grace. *The old man's granddaughter!*

When Great-Aunt May had first told him, he had been stunned. But she had cautioned him not to act rashly, and she had been right. So he had kept his silence and spent all night in prayer, seeking to grasp the full glory of God's plan for him.

And now at last he understood. He understood why God had given him this woman to wife. He understood the trials which God had made him undergo. *They were to prove his worthiness for the great office which was his destiny.*

Looking about him at the rain-washed cane, he thought, who on earth can stop you now? It is all so clear. Dr Valentine will cure her of her condition, and she will be a proper wife to you at last. She will gratify your needs and bear you a son, and when the time is right you will tell the old man the truth, and watch him dandle his great-grandson on his knee. And your inheritance will be secure.

The old man's granddaughter.

How strange to think that only days before, he, Sinclair, had been frightened to touch her. But he knew better now. For this was no ordinary woman. This was Ainsley's child. This was his inheritance made flesh.

It no longer mattered that she was intransigent and unwomanly, *for that was not her fault!* He understood that now. He understood from yesterday's providential visit to Falmouth that she was simply *ill*. Dr Valentine had explained it all most fully.

'Women, my dear Mr Lawe, are closer to the infantile state than men. And as such they are impulsive, emotional, and extremely prone to disorders of the nerves. I can well understand your dismay at your wife's behaviour – but be assured that her condition is not uncommon. That self-will which you describe, that persistent flouting of authority, are, to an experienced physician, merely the familiar symptoms of acute neurasthenia; what one might in layman's terms call an exhaustion of the nerve power.'

An exhaustion of the nerve power. What a relief to have it laid bare in cool scientific terms, and to learn that it could be cured! 'There is much room for hope, Mr Lawe, oh yes indeed. For there is a regimen, well established and of proven efficacy, which I myself have used for many years to treat just such cases as this. Depend upon it, my dear sir. After three months of the isolation cure – that is to say, of bed-rest, seclusion and sedation – in short, no stimuli whatsoever – your wife will be a different woman. Obedient, well regulated, and properly eager to take her place at your side as your helpmeet and comforter.'

The track narrowed, and Sinclair reined in. He could see nothing but empty cane-pieces, and beyond them the eerie grey-green cones of the Cockpits, looming startlingly close. He wondered if he was lost. But just then he spotted a pickney in the distance. He hailed the boy, and tossed him a quattie to lead the way to Master Cameron.

'Mas' Camron at de works yard, sah,' said the pickney, pointing up the track with a grimy finger. 'Mile or so up ahead. But him have a *short* heart dis morning, sah, dat true to de fact! Swearin, sah! Swearin like half past midnight! An nobody cyan say why.'

Well well, thought Sinclair, putting his mount forward to follow the boy. So my brother is not in the best of humours.

He recalled his wife's altered features when she had returned from her ride the previous evening. A lovers' tiff, no doubt. Well, well. It was of no consequence now. Once his brother learned the truth about her, all that would be at an end.

He pictured them together in the squalid old ruin he had just glimpsed in the distance. How often had they met? What was it like? Did she divest herself of *all* her garments? He pictured her in poses he had seen on his visits to Holywell Street . . .

A chicken hawk exploded from the trees, making him start. He passed a shaky hand across his brow. Calm, calm, he told himself. It doesn't *matter* what sins they have committed in the past. Nothing matters but your destiny. You will take her to Providence for the isolation cure, and Dr Valentine will make her well again, and she will be a proper wife and bear you a son. And when your inheritance is secure, your brother will know the bitterness of eternal defeat.

Smiling, he looked about him at Eden's shimmering cane-pieces. Yes, yes, my brother, you may toil all you wish, but it will always be in vain. You can never surpass me now.

He rode on up the muddy track, and at last the pickney pointed out the works yard, fifty feet ahead. Sinclair reined in. So this was what his brother did with his time.

A sprawling, untidy compound populated by the usual gaggle of blacks. In the foreground a jumble of workshops and storehouses; at the far end, an enormous cut-stone boiling-house with a towering chimney, and an aqueduct behind it, and a mill; a curing-house, a distillery, and at the furthest remove, a long, low trash-house surrounded by piles of sickly yellow cane-trash spread out to dry in the sun. Croptime was long over, but there must be a tail-end of milling in progress, for the ground was white with trampled trash, and the air thick with the stench of burnt sugar and rum.

How can men live like this? wondered Sinclair in disgust. How can they blind themselves to all that is good and noble and pure?

He dismounted and gave his horse to the pickney, and strolled over to wait at the entrance to the yard.

He could see his brother outside the distillery, supervising a group of blacks unpacking some piece of equipment from an ox-wain. He was hatless and in shirtsleeves, his hair unkempt and curling with sweat. Sinclair was disgusted. This, he thought, is what happens when the white man consorts with the black. The darkness may not rub off on his skin, but it stains his soul.

At last his brother saw him and crossed the yard. He made no attempt to conceal his displeasure.

Sinclair took off his hat and put on a jaunty smile. 'Hail, brother, and well met!'

His brother wiped his forehead on his arm. He looked tired, his eyes red-rimmed, as if he hadn't slept. 'What are you doing here?'

'And a good morning to you too,' said Sinclair gaily. 'Working on a Saturday? However did you prevail upon our dusky brethren?

'I paid them,' he snapped. 'Now what d'you want?'

With his riding-crop, Sinclair indicated the track. 'Walk with me. I have something to impart.'

'I don't have time.'

'I assure you, it will not take long.'

'All the same, I—'

'Indulge me, brother. I have come all this way.'

His brother glanced at him, then back at the yard, and sighed.

They started walking up the track. It was overhung with poinciana trees, some of them still in late bloom. Sinclair studied the vermilion petals underfoot. 'Brother,' he said, 'I have something to tell you.'

'So you keep saying,' his brother said irritably. 'Why don't you just—'

'Please.' Sinclair held up his hand. 'This is of some moment. Indeed, I should call it little short of a revelation.'

'Really,' said his brother, sounding unimpressed.

'Yes. Really.'

'Concerning?'

Sinclair turned and met his eyes. 'Concerning my wife.'

The dogcart clipped smartly along beneath the giant bamboo, and Sophie hugged Pablo Grey and thought what a difference a day could make.

Everything was going to be all right now. Ben would find some way to retrieve her shadow, and she would start to get better at last. And the accident with Victory had, after all, been exactly that: an *accident*. Sinclair had explained it all in great detail.

As soon as she had told him what she'd seen at the hothouse, he had changed completely. He had been really quite nice, and had explained that he'd only been stern with her before because he was worried at her telling a falsehood. Which, considering that he was a churchman, was understandable.

It had been an *accident*. Of *course* he hadn't known that Victory was inside. In fact, he'd closed the door to *stop* little children from wandering in and getting into difficulties.

It was such a relief. She'd wanted to tell Maddy straight away, but Sinclair had said no, we shall wait until we're all at Providence together, and then you can tell her.

It had been his idea to arrange the holiday to Providence as a surprise for Maddy. That morning, after he'd returned from his ride, he had suggested to Maddy that she might care to go into town to see Mrs Herapath, and Maddy had jumped at it, for she had been very much out of sorts since her ride the previous afternoon. Then, while she was gone, they had packed Sophie's valise, and left for Providence – for it was Sinclair's idea to take her there a day ahead, so that she could supervise the housekeeper in making the house nice for Maddy, as part of the surprise.

As the dogcart clipped along beside the Martha Brae, Sophie's pulse quickened. Maybe this was the day when she would see an alligator. Certainly there seemed to be plenty of wild creatures about. So far she had seen a large pale-yellow butterfly, a flock of bald-pates, and possibly a mongoose, although Sinclair had said that it was only a cane-rat.

The next moment, her spirits plunged. Victory hadn't been dead a week, and here she was spotting wild animals as if he'd never existed.

She dreamed about him every night. She wondered if it was lonely being dead, and if it had hurt to die. Maddy had said that he would have become sleepy through lack of water, and not known what was happening. Sophie hoped that wasn't just a white lie to reassure her.

The afternoon was wearing on, and she began to wonder if they would ever reach Providence. She decided not to risk asking Sinclair. He had been nice about the hothouse, but she hadn't forgotten what he had told her about going to Hell. With Sinclair, you could never tell.

The road became steeper, and they left the river behind. The hills were suddenly much closer. The Cockpits at last? She longed to consult the little volume in her valise which Clemency had given her as a present: *Tales of the Rebel Maroons of the Cockpits*. The very thing for a holiday in the hills.

She would miss Clemency. She had helped with the packing, and fussed and not wanted Sophie to leave, just like a proper mother. To cheer her up, Sophie had told her about Ben, and made her swear to keep him secret, and Clemency had been touched. She'd cried when they left, and promised to visit Sophie very, very soon – but Great-Aunt May had said No, that would be inappropriate, and Clemency had backed down. She always backed down, and Sophie really wished that she wouldn't. Real mothers do not back down where their children are concerned.

At last they came to a pair of tall iron gates, and Sinclair reined in and spoke to the gatekeeper. The gates swung open, and they trotted up the carriageway between ranks of rigid yokewood trees.

As the house rose before them, butterflies started up in

Sophie's stomach. She knew that Providence was a hunting lodge, so she'd been expecting something cosy and rustic, like the cottage in *The Children of the New Forest*. But this house was even larger than Fever Hill, and slightly frightening. It had pointed gables like a witch's dwelling, and blank, unfriendly louvres painted dark grey. And worst of all was the huge wedge-shaped structure with blind stone walls which jutted from the west wing like the prow of an enormous ship.

Sophie asked what it was.

'That's a cutwind,' said Sinclair. 'In the old days, they used to shelter inside it from hurricanes. And perhaps also', he added with a curl of his lip, 'they used it for locking up naughty little children when they were especially bad.'

Sophie told herself that he was only joking. But she didn't think it funny in the least. Not after Victory.

Helpers in grey uniforms ran down and took charge of the dogcart and Sophie's valise, and one of them picked her up and carried her up the steps and set her down in a shadowy gallery with her crutches. The gallery was extremely clean, with a floor of brown linoleum like the scullery at Wyndham Street, and it stank of Lysol. It was screened off on either side, but Sophie sensed that there were people behind the screens, although she couldn't hear a sound. The whole place was eerily quiet, and she realized that there weren't any dogs, which was unusual for Jamaica.

As she waited for Sinclair, a helper emerged from the house, bearing a tray of small brown phials, and drew aside the screen and disappeared inside. Behind the screen, Sophie glimpsed a woman lying in a bathchair. She was so thin that her chest beneath the sheet was flat like a boy's, with jutting collarbones. Her face was turned towards Sophie: the nose sharp, the cheeks sunken but curiously flushed. A rope of pink phlegm hung from the corner of her mouth and looped all the way down the side of the bathchair; her bright, indifferent eyes gazed through Sophie as if she weren't there.

Sophie wondered who she might be. The housekeeper, perhaps? The sick housekeeper being nursed back to health?

Then Sinclair mounted the steps and swept past her and

told her to hurry, and she saw no more of the woman, for she had no choice but to start after him on her crutches, with Pablo Grey swinging from her wrist by the new red and yellow halter which Maddy had plaited from embroidery silk.

She asked Sinclair about the sick housekeeper, but he told her sternly to be quiet. He was back to the old, disapproving Sinclair who didn't like her, and she wondered if she'd done something wrong.

As they hurried along the Lysol-smelling corridor, someone upstairs, possibly a man, began to cough. Sophie had never heard anyone cough like that: a thick, wet, wrenching sound that went on and on, as if the man were coughing up his insides. When it stopped, the silence was deeper than before. Sophie wondered if the man were better or worse.

At the end of the corridor a door opened, and a tall lady came out and ushered them into a study with an enormous desk and two hard black leather visitors' chairs. Sinclair declined tea for both of them, although Sophie was by now extremely thirsty.

The lady was deferential to Sinclair, but clearly not a servant. She wore a grey silk dress like Great-Aunt May's, only plainer and without the gloves; but her face when she glanced at Sophie wore a similar expression, as if she would have *liked* to be wearing gloves. She took the crutches from Sophie, along with Pablo Grey. 'This will have to go,' she said, holding the donkey by one ear. 'Toys are not permitted. They harbour dust.'

'Oh, he's extremely clean,' said Sophie. 'When I first became ill, Maddy soaked him in Lysol overnight. It took ages to dry him out. And now I brush him every single day.'

The lady did not reply. She crossed to the other side of the room and laid the crutches and Pablo Grey across a chair. Then she gave Sophie a book and told her to study it in silence while she talked to the Reverend Lawe.

By now Sophie was convinced that she was missing something. She didn't like this place, and she was sure that Maddy wouldn't like it either. And the lady was wrong about Pablo Grey.

Sinclair and the lady were talking in low voices about 'registration', so Sophie stopped listening and opened the book. In fact it wasn't a book, but only a single page of thick grey paper bound between two sheets of olive-green pasteboard.

RULES, it said in large black letters. *Patients must be silent at all times. Patients must not move or indulge in ANY exertion without Doctor's permission. Patients must not read, write, draw, sew, indulge in music or conversation, or otherwise make ANY noise whatsoever. Patients must not indulge in unnecessary coughing. Patients . . .*

Sophie began to feel sick. She raised her head and cleared her throat. 'Excuse me?'

Sinclair and the lady stopped talking and turned to her.

'Excuse me,' she said again, 'but is this place called Providence?'

The lady tightened her lips, and did not reply.

Sinclair regarded Sophie with distant calm, as if she were no longer his concern.

Sophie looked down at the book in her lap. The cover said: *Rules for Patients. Burntwood Private Clinic for Afflictions of the Lungs.*

Chapter Twenty-Six

'She's *where*?' said his wife.

Quietly, Sinclair repeated what he had just said, and invited her to sit down.

He could not have planned this better himself. His study was where he felt most powerful, and she had chosen to burst in upon him here, while he sat at his desk: the patient churchman enduring yet another onslaught from his increasingly unstable wife. 'Be seated,' he said again, 'and calm yourself.'

'No I will not "calm myself"! Not until Sophie's back where she belongs.'

'She belongs where I choose to place her.'

'Nonsense. She—'

'I say again, calm yourself!' This time he allowed the steel to enter his voice, and it had its effect.

His wife sat down. Her face was pale and altered, and he could see the effort it took to restrain herself. 'Sinclair,' she said in a low voice shaking with emotion, 'whatever you feel about me, don't take this out on Sophie. She's done nothing to you.'

'You misunderstand. I have only her best interests at heart.'

She opened her mouth to protest, but he raised his hand. 'Your sister's condition requires constant nursing. That has made you ill. Yes, ill. It is futile to deny it. I have taken medical advice. I know I am right.'

'This is because of Cameron, isn't it? You've sent Sophie to that awful place to punish me.'

He leaned back in his chair and studied her face. She clearly had no idea that he knew her secret. He could bring her down any time he wished. 'There is no question of punishment,' he said. 'It is a matter of rest and recuperation. For you *and* your sister.'

'Sinclair, listen to me.' She put her hands on the desk and leaned forwards, and for one alarming moment it seemed that Rose Durrant's unfathomable dark eyes stared out at him. 'Sophie cannot stay at Burntwood. It's a hospice for consumptives. People go there to die. I won't allow you to do this. I—'

'*You* will not allow *me*?' He gave an incredulous laugh. 'Have you forgotten that I am the husband and you the wife? Do you have any conception of what that means? It means that you have given yourself into my care. Do you understand? You have given yourself spiritually, legally and bodily into my care.'

Ah, now he had her attention.

'You ought to be grateful to me,' he went on. 'If I were a less forgiving man, I might do as many a wronged husband has done before me, and have you committed to an asylum.' He paused to let the word reverberate around the room. 'I could have you committed right now,' he said. 'One stroke of my pen is all it would take. Dr Valentine has confirmed that, and so has my attorney.'

She licked her lips. 'Dr Valentine? And who is he?'

'Dr Valentine is my physician.'

'He's never even met me. How can he say that I'm mad?'

With weary patience he kneaded his temples. 'He predicted that you would react like this. He warned me that contentiousness is one of the symptoms.'

'Symptoms of what?'

'Exhaustion of the nerve power.'

She snorted. 'What nonsense. There's nothing wrong with my nerves.'

'Dr Valentine would disagree. And since he is the

physician and you are not, it is his opinion which decides the matter.'

She sat back in her chair, and he watched her struggling to take it in. Just as he had watched his brother that morning, struggling to master his shock.

'I did try to warn you,' Sinclair had told him as they walked beneath the poinciana trees. 'That night at Parnassus. Do you remember?'

But it was doubtful that his brother heard a word. His face was taut, his gaze turned inward. Perhaps he was recalling all those stolen moments with his mistress which were now revealed as lies.

'It was a shock to me too,' Sinclair assured him. 'Indeed, I remain in a state of utter disbelief.'

Still that silence.

'So tell me,' Sinclair said gently, 'for I would have a brother's counsel on this. What ought I to do?'

At last the grey eyes met his. But they were distant and unfocused; still trying to comprehend.

Sinclair felt a stab of jealousy. What right had the lover to take this harder than the husband? 'Tell me,' he repeated, 'what ought I to do? Should I go to the old man and tell him that the woman he has come to esteem is in fact his bastard granddaughter, an adventuress who duped his adopted son into marriage, for who knows what vengeful purpose of her own? Or should I, as her husband, feel duty-bound to keep her secret – even if by doing so, I become complicit in her deception? Tell me, brother. What ought I to do?'

But his brother had only blinked and shaken his head, and walked away.

Sinclair had felt cheated. As always, his brother had disappointed him.

In the study, the grandfather clock struck seven. Sinclair pushed back his chair and rose to his feet. 'You must hasten', he told his wife, 'and dress for dinner. We must not keep Great-Aunt May waiting.'

She was shaking her head in disbelief. 'But can't you see that this is pointless? In a fortnight Jocelyn will be back from Kingston. He won't allow her to stay at Burntwood.'

'Yes he will,' he replied. 'He will respect the wishes of her legal guardian.'

'Not when he learns where she is.'

'Oh yes, even then. Remember, the old man lives by his principles. Not by his affections. He would never come between a man and his wife. Or between a man and his legal charge.'

'I don't believe that.'

'Yes. You do. Remember his conduct towards his only son.'

He was gratified to see how she flinched.

'The old man', he added, 'may not *like* my decision, but he will most certainly respect it. You may depend upon it.'

At last she saw the force of that. Yet still she opened her mouth to protest.

'*Enough!*' he cried. 'Understand that in this I am not to be moved! Now for the last time, do as you are told and dress for dinner. And after dinner you shall pack your trunk, for tomorrow morning, directly after church, we leave for Providence.'

'*What?* But I can't possibly—'

'And I warn you, any attempt to defy me, and I shall have you sedated.'

'Sedated? But Sinclair—'

'If you defy me,' he repeated, raising his voice to conquer hers, 'I shall have you sedated. But if you obey me, and if you do all that Dr Valentine requires, then I may decide, in time, to permit your sister to join us. Think carefully. The choice is yours.'

That found its mark. No more protests. No more resistance. At last she had grasped that further disobedience would only delay her sister's return. And delay was not something she could afford, for the child was among consumptives, and would not last long once the disease had taken hold of her lungs.

In fact, he was counting on it.

The Reverend Grant was not known for the brevity of his sermons, but this morning he outdid himself. He spoke until

Madeleine's jaw was knotted and she wanted to scream. A quarter past ten o'clock, and she still had no plan for getting Sophie out of Burntwood.

She sat in the family pew, flanked by Sinclair and Great-Aunt May like two highly respectable gaolers, while around her gentlemen coughed and children squirmed, and ladies fanned themselves and buried their noses in handkerchiefs sprinkled with Florida water, and the coolness of the great stone church gradually gave way to a scent of packed bodies and eau-de-cologne.

She had lain awake all night, and the thought of Sophie in that place had been a physical pain in the chest. Wild schemes whirled through her mind. Steal a horse and make her way across country. Send for the police. Kill Sinclair. She could do that, couldn't she? She was a Durrant; wasn't that what Durrants did?

But when morning came, the hopelessness of her position became apparent. She was watched constantly, and the helpers had orders not to let her anywhere near the stables. She had no allies at Fever Hill. Clemency was too frightened to help, and her maid reported straight to Great-Aunt May. Olivia Herapath wouldn't dream of interfering in what she would regard as a purely family affair; and although Ben Kelly might be prevailed upon to help, she had no idea where he was.

Which left Cameron. But how could she get a message to him? He never came to church, didn't observe the Sabbath, and was probably in some distant cane-piece right now, with no idea of what had happened.

At last the sermon ended, and the final prayers were said. Gentlemen stretched, nursemaids hissed at their charges, and ladies sought parasols beneath the pews. With agonizing slowness, the congregation filed out.

Sinclair preceded Madeleine into the porch, and paused to say a few words to the Reverend Grant. Great-Aunt May drew down her veil and put up her parasol to protect herself from the sun on the way to the carriage.

Madeleine went out into the glare, and stared blankly at

the little groups of parishioners talking in the churchyard; at the carriages jostling each other in the street; at the pickneys trotting along beside their mothers in their Sunday best. This couldn't be happening.

She turned, and saw Cameron standing beneath a cassia tree on the other side of the road.

He was in his work clothes, as if he'd decided on impulse to ride down and see her, and he was looking straight at her. No pretence that he had come for any other reason.

Relief washed over her. It'll be all right now, she told herself. He'll get her out. It'll be all right now.

She went to Sinclair and touched his arm. 'Your brother is here,' she whispered.

He glanced across the street. 'Ah, to be sure,' he murmured. To her surprise he did not look dismayed, but quietly pleased.

'I must speak to him,' she said. 'I need – to—'

'To say goodbye?' he supplied. To her astonishment, he inclined his head in assent. 'But you seem surprised,' he said. 'Why? I am not your gaoler, you know. I have no objection to your speaking to your brother-in-law after church.'

She didn't wait for him to change his mind. Ignoring the curious glances of her fellow parishioners, she crossed the street almost at a run.

Out in the open, the heat was intense. She could feel the perspiration breaking out between her shoulder blades.

'I haven't much time,' she told Cameron as she drew near.

'Walk with me,' he said.

They started slowly up Duke Street, keeping to the shade beneath the trees. Acquaintances nodded at them, then murmured behind their backs.

'I need to speak to you,' he said when they were out of earshot. 'I need to—'

'Sophie's in Burntwood,' she broke in. 'Sinclair took her there yesterday when I was in town. You've got to get her out.'

He stopped and turned to her. His expression was strangely withdrawn, and she felt a prickle of unease.

'Just get her out,' she said, 'and bring her home. Or better still, keep her at Eden until Jocelyn returns. Just until then, when the whole thing can be sorted out.'

Still he did not reply. Still that unnerving scrutiny.

'Cameron? What is it?'

He glanced up and down the street. When there was no passer-by within earshot he said, 'Sinclair told me who you are.'

Outside sounds receded. She felt herself sway. Sinclair knows, she thought. God. Sinclair knows.

She thought back to their talk the evening before. His chiselled features so calm and so assured; his serene blue eyes. She glanced back at the churchyard and saw him standing in the porch, watching her. 'He knows,' she said aloud.

'Which, I imagine, is why he let you come and talk to me. It's his little game. Letting you find out from me.'

She turned and met his eyes. He seemed neither angry nor reproachful, but simply withdrawn.

He said, 'You were going to tell me at Eden, weren't you? That's why you came. But you didn't trust me enough.'

'I didn't want to hurt you.'

He took that in silence.

They started walking again. She fiddled with the clasp of her reticule: open, shut, open, shut. She wondered how to reach him.

He said, 'I feel as though I don't know you any more. But I suppose the truth is, I never did.'

'Cameron—'

'I always knew there was something wrong between us. I mean, something more than just Sinclair.' He gave a little half-smile that was painful to see. 'I still can't believe it. Ainsley's daughter. The little girl in the park. You know, I always felt bad about that. I felt such a blackguard for frightening a child.'

'I know. I never blamed you for it.'

He put his hands behind his back and studied the ground. 'You see, if that were true, I think you'd have told me sooner.'

Oh God, she thought. He doesn't believe me. She said, 'You think I'm saying it now to persuade you to help Sophie.'

'I think you'd do anything for your sister. Yes.'

'Cameron—'

'Tell me,' he said, 'why did you marry him? I mean really. Why?'

'What does it—'

'It wasn't some kind of – I don't know, some kind of revenge? Revenge against the family?'

'Of course not. You asked me before, don't you remember? And I told you the truth. I married him for money. For Sophie.'

He looked unconvinced.

'We had no money, Cameron. Can't you understand? Oh, I know there was a trust, but Septimus took it all, and when he died there was nothing left. Then Sophie fell ill, and suddenly we needed a great deal of money, very soon, or she wouldn't survive.' Again she snapped open the reticule: open, shut, open, shut. 'What was I to do? If I'd been a man I'd have got a job, or robbed a bank or something. As it was, the only plan I could come up with was to become a prostitute.'

She saw his shock, but it was too late to pull back now. 'Then Lettice told me where Sinclair lived, so I went to borrow money from him instead. It all happened just as I told you. I wanted to borrow money, but he asked me to marry him. So I did.'

'You were planning to sell yourself?' he said.

'Yes, but I never—'

'How could you even think it?'

'Well my God,' she flashed out at him, 'what was I supposed to do, let Sophie die? Do you *know* how much a sanatorium costs? Do you *know* what a "respectable" position for a lady actually brings in? And it's no good looking at me like that, you won't make me feel bad about it, I'd do it again if I had to. What choice did I have? And has it occurred to you', she added, unable to stop, 'that if you and Jocelyn hadn't been so damnably eager to slough off the black sheep's monumentally inconvenient bastards, none of this would have happened? But it did happen, and I was left to sort it out on my own, so I did.'

She drew a deep breath, and forced herself to be still.

An Indian rattled by on a bicycle, trailing a plume of red dust. A black woman and her daughter went past in their Sunday best: ruffled pink parasols in one hand, polished Sunday shoes in the other.

'You're right,' said Cameron. 'This is our fault, not yours.'

She shut her eyes. 'I didn't mean to blame you. That's over, it's in the past.'

'Are you sure about that?'

She turned her head away. 'I lied to you. I admit that. I lied to everyone. I married a man I despised for his money. But Cameron – women do that all the time. We marry for money, or position, or because some man tells us to, because we're not allowed to do anything else. Look at Clemency. I don't see you condemning her.'

'I'm not condemning you,' he said quietly.

'Are you sure about that?'

He did not reply.

A planter on a glossy bay mare trotted towards them and raised his hat, then replaced it with an uncertain look when he received no response.

Cameron said, 'What about the old man? Does he know?'

She shook her head. 'Not unless Sinclair told him; and I don't think he has. I was going to tell Jocelyn myself. When the time was right.'

'Yes,' he said. 'As you were going to tell me.'

She shot him a look, but his face gave nothing away. She said, 'Try to understand. The only reason I lied was to protect Sophie. Is that so different from what you did at your court-martial? You kept quiet to stop my father's story coming out.'

He studied her for a moment. Then he said, 'We should turn back. They're waiting for you.'

Madeleine began to feel sick. None of this mattered next to Sophie, and he had brushed that aside as if he didn't care.

They turned and started walking back, and she saw that

while Great-Aunt May was waiting in the carriage, Sinclair was still in the churchyard, standing slender and straight with one gloved hand on a tombstone, watching them.

In a few minutes they would reach the carriage and Cameron would leave, and nothing would have been achieved except damage and more damage, and Sophie still at Burntwood.

'All right,' she said, 'don't forgive me. Forget about me. But don't make Sophie pay for what I did. I'm the one who lied. Not her. She doesn't know anything about this. She doesn't even know that she's Ainsley's daughter.' She paused. 'His daughter, Cameron. Think about that. For eight years you've been up there in the hills in your self-imposed exile, having those nightmares about him and wondering why. You say you've forgiven him, but have you? Don't you think that if you'd really forgiven him, you wouldn't have visited his sins on his children by denying their very existence?'

'Madeleine—'

'Because that's what you did, isn't it? You sent off a cheque and made sure that we'd never trouble you again. You washed your hands of us.'

He looked appalled.

'She's his *daughter*, Cameron. She's eleven years old, she's never done anything wrong, and she's stuck in that dreadful place among a whole lot of dying people. And you're the only one who can get her out.'

They were almost within earshot now. She could see Great-Aunt May sitting rigid and straight in the carriage, and Sinclair standing beside it, waiting to hand her in.

'For God's *sake*, Cameron. Here's your chance to make amends. Don't throw it away.'

He rubbed a hand over his face, and gazed about him at the churchgoers moving in the street. Finally he shook his head. 'What do you imagine I can do?' he said in a low voice. He didn't meet her eyes, but she could see the emotions warring in him. Pain and frustration, and anger at herself, and pity for Sophie.

She said, 'You could get her out. You could—'

'He'd only put her back again. He's her guardian, Madeleine. He has the law on his side.'

'But—'

'No.' He put up a hand as if to ward off some imaginary blow. 'I'm sorry. I'm sorry. I can't help.'

Chapter Twenty-Seven

So this is Fever Hill, thinks Ben. Bugger me, what a pile.

It gives him the jitters all right. All them shutters peering down at him. And so sodding quiet.

This is where the parson lives, actually lives. He could be in there right now, writing sermons at his big gold desk. What if he gets wind that Ben's out here? What if he has him chucked in the clink? Then how's he going to even things up for Robbie?

Evie hisses at the guard dog to 'sit', and it sits, sweeping the grass with its tail. Big brown guard dog with big yellow fangs; it scared the hell out of Ben when it jumped out the bushes and followed them up from the river. Only right now, the big brown guard dog's turned into a big brown puppy, and Evie's wagging her finger at it and telling it to 'stay'.

She cocks her head at Ben to follow, and he's only too glad to get up the steps and away from all them fangs. In the gallery he looks out for Sophie, but she's not there. Oh well. Maybe she's having her tea. Besides, she's not why he come. This 'Miss Clemmy' has got a job for him; that's what Evie said. And a job at Fever Hill gets him closer to the parson, and that's the point.

It's been three days since he seen Madeleine, and he's still narked when he thinks about it. Ben Kelly crying in the road. Crying like a baby. It makes him want to spit.

Bloody Madeleine. And it's all very well her telling him

what Robbie would of wanted. 'Get on with your life,' she said. All right. But how?

He's thinking on that when Evie pulls him into this sitting-room and hisses at him to wait while she fetches 'Miss Clemmy', and not to take nothing while she's gone. Ben gives her a look. She think he's daft, or what? Rule is, you do a click, and you cut the lucky straight off. You don't pross about while they see what's missing. So he's not likely to click nothing yet, is he? Not till he's on his way out the door.

Queer sort of room he's in, and all. Golden couch and lots of silky cushions, but they're all just purple and grey, like in a coffin. And everywhere these little black bows, hundreds of them, even round the photos on the walls. He goes and takes a look at the biggest photo, over the couch. Curly golden frame with all curly letters at the bottom. *Secure the Shadow Ere the Substance Fade; Let Nature Imitate What Nature Made.* What the sodding hell's that supposed to mean?

Hang on. They're all photos of babies. No – just the one baby. And come to that, it's just the one photo, too. Oh, *all* right, now we're getting somewhere. Baby's dead, that's why all the black bows and the coffin colours and that.

He wanders through into the bedroom. More black bows and coffin colours, and this great big bed, and in the middle of the bed, this cat. Fat little marmalade job. Cat glares at him, he glares back, and it knows when it's licked, and shoots under the bed.

Then he sees this frilly little desk with all silver pots and brushes on top, and he perks up a bit. Nice little something to click, when he gets the chance.

Footsteps, and in a trice he's back in the sitting-room, and in comes Evie with this old lady. No, she's not old – buggered if she isn't *young* – or at least, youngish. No wrinkles, nice figure on her – but she's gone and dyed her hair *grey*, he can see the actual yellow growing through at the roots. Now why would she want to go and do a thing like that?

And it's not just the hair, neither. She's got this necklace of pearls that loops all the way down below her waist, and this floaty white frock that makes him think of something drowned. And her face is all waxy yellow; and them eyes. Big, staring blue eyes that go right through you, and then skitter away.

'You must be Ben,' she whispers, with a queer little smile that's more like a wince.

He whips off his hat.

'I'm Mrs Monroe,' she whispers, 'but you shall call me Miss Clemmy.' She shoots a look over her shoulder, like she might of been followed. 'I take it that no-one saw you come in?'

He swallows and shakes his head.

'Good. Good.' Another painful little smile. 'Because you see, Great-Aunt May doesn't care for me to have visitors, oh no, not at all. It would never do if she were to learn that you were here.'

That whispering's giving Ben the jitters. Has she got a slate loose, or what? But then he thinks, well I suppose you've got to whisper in a place like this, if you want to keep a secret. All them holes in the doors and windows. It's like the whole sodding house is listening in.

Which don't do much for his jitters, neither.

So Miss Clemmy's peering at him with her barmy blue eyes, and behind her he can see Evie lounging against the door. So to give hisself a lift, he catches her glance and rolls his eyes, but she just glares at him, like he's done something wrong. He's narked about that, till he remembers that her brother was the little darkie that the parson killed. Course, Evie don't *know* what the parson done to her brother; the less people know about that the better. But still. It's no wonder that she's not up for a laugh.

Miss Clemmy sits herself down on the couch, like she thinks she'll be safer down there, and grabs this big pale-green china jar from a table, and holds it out to him. 'Ginger bonbons,' she whispers with her scary little smile. 'Take as many as you wish.'

He don't know what to do. In the end he just grabs the jar and mutters 'thanks', like Kate used to go on at him about.

She tells him to 'be seated', so he looks round and picks this little footstool. It's better than one of them golden chairs with the coffin cushions.

So he's sitting there with the jar between his knees, munching away on a sweet, and she's watching him and twisting her hands in her lap.

Then it comes to him. She's scared. Miss Clemmy of Fever Hill, grand lady with all pearls and that, and she's scared out of her wits. But scared of who? Not of Ben Kelly, she can't be. He's too far beneath her for that.

He's puzzling this out when she takes this deep breath and tells him what she wants. Well, more or less she does. It's in a right old muddle, all rushed and that, but after a bit he gets the picture. The parson's put Sophie in a san. A san for lung jobs; the kind where they carry you out in a box. Sod it. *Sod it.*

'Of course,' whispers Miss Clemmy, leaning towards him so that he can see deep into her skittery blue eyes, 'I'm *convinced* that Sinclair only meant the best for her. Oh yes, to be sure.'

Oh, I'll bet, thinks Ben. It's plain as a pikestaff what's going on. Somehow, the parson's got wind that Sophie knows about the little darkie, so he's packed her off to the san. So no more Sophie.

'. . . and there's a doctor's certificate and everything,' goes Miss Clemmy, 'and Great-Aunt May *thoroughly approves*, and she says that Jocelyn does too, so there can be no conceivable objection . . . And yet,' she bursts out, 'I cannot *bear* to think of that poor child in that dreadful place!' She beats her soft white hands in her lap, and her face goes pink.

So now he knows why she's running scared. She's gone behind their backs. Got a bee in her bonnet about Sophie – and good for her – but she's frightened silly of this Great-Aunt May, who must be the scary old cat with the gloves that Sophie told him about.

Oh, she's scared witless, she is. Red spots on her cheeks, and her eyes all skittery; and she keeps looking over her shoulder, like she'll be put away just for talking about it. Bloody hell, he thinks. All them pearls and silver brushes and that, and she's in bloody clink. Only difference is, you can't see the bars.

'What about Madeleine?' he pipes up, going red for talking out of turn. 'She got something to say about this, or what?'

'That's the *thing*,' whispers Miss Clemmy. Then she tells him how the parson's taken Madeleine off into the hills, and she's not coming down again for months and months. 'Sinclair says she's neurasthenic' – Ben guesses that's posh for mad – 'but I don't know what to think, for you see, he once said the same about me, and I'm rather sure that I'm not.'

Don't know about that, thinks Ben, shifting uneasily on his footstool. And sure enough, what she says next only goes to show. Barmy idea she's got, barmy, about him, Ben Kelly, padding the hoof all the way to this Burntwood, and 'rescuing' Sophie; all on his lonesome – or maybe with that brother of the parson's, Miss Clemmy's not too clear on the details.

In fact she's not too clear about nothing, except that they've got to get Sophie out sharpish, cos she's been in there since Saturday, and it's Monday now, and it's no good waiting till grandpa gets back in two weeks' time, cos by then it'll be too late.

He thinks about Sophie in the san. Lung jobs all around her: coughing; catting up rubies. It's a shame, and that. Sophie's all right.

But what's he supposed to do about it? Spring her from the san on his own? How's that going to work? Apples to ashes he'll just end up in the clink. Besides, he can't let hisself get distracted. He's got Robbie to think of.

So he picks up his hat and gets to his feet and tells Miss Clemmy he can't do nothing about it.

She's not expecting that. Hands start going all a-flutter, big blue eyes all staring. 'B-but – Sophie *said* – she said you were her *friend*.'

Sophie, he thinks angrily, should of never told nobody nothing.

He looks about him at the golden chairs and the silver

brushes – too late to click one now – and he thinks, see sense, Ben Kelly. Sophie don't need you. You try anything, and *you're* the one that gets into chancery.

Besides, it'll all get sorted without you sticking your nose in, you wait and see. Either this barmy young-old bint will come to her senses and get the grandpa back sharpish from Kingston, or else that brother of the parson's will get it sorted, or else Madeleine will.

Come to think of it, Madeleine's the best bet of all. Bloody tiger she is, when it comes to Sophie. Yeh, Madeleine'll get it sorted. No doubt about it.

Excerpt from *A Discourse on the Treatment of Nervous Exhaustion (Neurasthenia) through a Variant Form of the Weir Mitchell Isolation or Rest Cure* by E. St John Burrowes.

As we have seen, the elements of the isolation cure are seclusion, sedation, inactivity, massage, overfeeding on a milk diet and, where available, the administration of electrical shock. The patient is confined to bed for at least two months, and forbidden to sit up, read, write, sew or use her hands in any way. No visits, books or letters are permitted, and the sickroom is rendered devoid of stimuli by the use of whitewash, plain white bedclothes and blinds.

It is impossible to overstate the importance of enforcing the patient's complete obedience to, and dependence upon, her supervising physician. Indeed, this is the critical element of the cure, for it effectively suppresses the patient's personality and makes her a child again, thereby allowing the physician to 're-create' her anew. Moreover, as the cure approaches its conclusion, this dependence may gradually be transferred to the patient's husband, father, brother, or other appropriate guardian, to lasting and beneficial effect.

The above is the cure in its standard form. However, over the past two decades it has become apparent that a sub-population of patients often proves resistant, and requires such lengthy periods of isolation that psychosis may result. It is with such patients in mind that this physician has, over many years, developed a variant regimen, which he has employed in numerous cases with almost consistently positive results.

In accordance with this variant regimen, the patient is kept comatose for an initial period of a day or two, by means of laudanum, veronal, or a similar soporific. This suspends the cognitive faculties, allowing regeneration of the nerve power to commence apace. After this initial period of profound rest, the patient is allowed gradually to recover consciousness, and tends to awaken in a highly confused but peaceable state. She may then be kept sedated but conscious, in order to facilitate feeding and handling . . .

She is at Cairngowrie House, curled up on the window seat, watching the snow covering the garden. Smooth white garden. Soft white sky. White surf glowing on the beach. Everything peaceful and soft.

The window seat begins gently to rock. A man's voice says, *Mrs Lawe. Mrs Lawe. Wake up. Open your eyes.*

She doesn't want to open her eyes. She wants to stay on the window seat, where it's peaceful and safe.

'Still unconscious,' the man's voice says.

No I'm not, she thinks drowsily. I can hear you perfectly well. It's just that I don't feel like opening my eyes.

The door shuts, and the footsteps fall away. She drifts back into the snow.

When she wakes again, it is to a nagging sense that something is missing. All is soft and peaceful, so peaceful that her eyelids are too heavy to lift; but she's hungry and thirsty, and something is missing.

She doesn't know what it is, except that it has something to do with parrots. If only she could smooth out her thoughts; but they're tangled up, and she can't remember. What was it about parrots?

The next time she awakens, it's with a start, as if she's fallen off a step; and this time she knows exactly what's missing. But it's not 'what'. It's 'who'.

Sophie is in Burntwood. Oh dear oh dear oh dear. Burntwood is a bad place. *Naughty* Sophie. Come out of there at once.

Sophie is in Burntwood. But where are you?

She opens her eyes and sees only white: a perfectly white room. No looking-glass, no pictures on the walls, no furniture except for this bed.

Fragments of memory return. Sinclair sitting at his desk: his cobalt necktie exactly matching the colour of his eyes. *You are ill. I have taken medical advice. I know I am right.*

Cameron looking down at her with that distant expression. *I feel as though I don't know you any more. But I suppose the truth is, I never did.*

But Sophie's in Burntwood, and that's a bad place. *Bad* place. And there's no-one to get her out. Oh dearie me.

And you're not helping, are you, Maddy? Everyone's so cross with you. Cameron. Sinclair. Even Mrs Herapath; Sinclair saw to her too. *I regret*, she had said in her curt, shaky little note, *that in view of what your husband has told me about your extraordinary deception, I must decline all further communication.*

So everyone is cross with you and no-one will help, and it's all down to you, Maddy, oh yes it is. You shall just have to sort it out on your own.

Don't want to sort it out. Don't know *how* to get to Burntwood. Don't know *how* to get away from Sinclair.

What about killing him? Now there's an idea. Lettice always said you were bad. And remember, you've still got Ben's gun. It's in the bottom of the trunk, rolled up in a pair of combinations. The eau-de-nil ones with the rosebuds round the hem. Heigh-ho.

The door opens. She shuts her eyes and pretends to be asleep, and listens as someone comes in and stands by the bed. It must be a man, for its tread is heavy, and she can hear it breathing noisily through its nose.

She opens her eyes a fraction, then shuts them again.

It's that Dr Valentine. She doesn't like him. He was waiting for her when they got to Providence. And he's so *vain*. He brushes his silver hair forward to cover his bald spot, and he deepens his voice to make it more commanding, and he obviously believes that he has a penetrating stare.

He reminds her of a vampire. Dr Valentine Vampire, with his brushed-forward hair and his deep voice which he thinks is so commanding. But he doesn't frighten her. She can handle him with her eyes shut. In fact she's doing it right now, by making him think that she's fast asleep.

Everyone calls her a liar, and of course they're right. She's an expert at lying. She jolly well ought to be, she's had enough practice. So just watch her now.

'Mrs Lawe,' says Dr Valentine in his deep, firm voice. 'Mrs Lawe. Wake up.'

Slowly, hazily, she opens her eyes.

The doctor is leaning over her – commandingly, of course – and his face is so close that she can count the pores on his nose.

She gives him a drowsy little frown, as if she has indeed just woken up.

He pats her hand. 'There's a good girl. Now tell Dr Valentine how you feel.'

Slowly, dazedly, she blinks at him. Then she gives him a weak, scared, tremulous little smile. A sort of Clemency-smile. Yes, that's it. Let's pretend to be Clemency.

Out loud she whispers in a soft, trembly Clemency-voice, 'Th-thirsty, doctor . . . Very thirsty . . . Where am I?'

He gives a satisfied nod. 'To be sure, to be sure, of course you are thirsty. And no doubt hungry as well. You shall have a bowl of semolina directly, and a large glass of goat's milk.'

How perfectly horrid, she thinks. Out loud she murmurs, 'Thank you, doctor,' in a grateful Clemency-whisper.

'Excellent,' he says. 'Now you must be very good and lie here quietly, and do exactly as I say. And by and by, you shall begin to feel a great deal better.'

'Yes, doctor,' she whispers, and snuggles into the pillow and shuts her eyes. Your little Clemency-patient is so sleepy, doctor, and so confused. All this talking has tired out her poor weak brain.

He takes her pulse and feels beneath her jaw, and she restrains an urge to bite him on the wrist. Finally, with a satisfied 'Capital, capital,' he leaves the room, and a moment later she hears the key turn in the lock.

Yes, doctor, she thinks as she opens her eyes, I shall do exactly as you say. I shall drink my horrid goat's milk, and eat my horrid semolina. And then when I'm strong again, and it's night-time and you and Sinclair and the housekeeper are asleep, I shall clamber out of that window over there, the one with the louvres coming loose, and I shall sneak round behind the croton bushes and find my trunk and my clothes and my gun, and steal Sinclair's horse – or maybe the carriage-horse, or maybe yours, doctor, if I like the look of it – and that's the last you'll be seeing of me, Dr Valentine Vampire, with the commanding voice and the penetrating stare.

She stifles a spurt of laughter.

Is that the laudanum, making her silly? Oh well. It's really rather nice. But watch out, Sinclair. Your wife has become a drug fiend.

'Drug fiend,' she giggles helplessly into her pillow.

Eliphalet Tait is just about full up to the neck with wife trouble. All damn week that Phoebe's been lip-lashing and calling him spineless salt water nigger, just because they got nothing fancy to take for Free Come party over at Disappointment.

Well all *right*, he blazes into her, I go *get* you some fancy damn thing, woman!

Which is why he's been stumbling round all night long in this damn dark Providence Wood, chewing on bissy nut to keep himself awake, and trying to poach little something to sweeten her up.

Lord God, but it *dark* in here! All tangle-up with hogmeat and wiss and wild pine, he near to break his damn leg! Still, his luck's starting to sugar, for he's just caught himself three little bald-pates, all nice and fat.

And now he's at the edge of the wood, looking down on

buckra house in the moonshine. And he's just deciding to go and rest up in the stables till Cousin Sukey and old Aaron come awake and he can visit with them awhile, when he walks slap into spider-web, right slap across his face.

Now Eliphalet's not no fool. He knows this a warning sign: that little Master Anancy spider-man trying to tell him to stay back. So Eliphalet apologizes to spider-man for messing with his place, and thanks him for the warning. And he's just about to turn and go, when down below, out the buckra house, he sees a woman in white come creeping soft, soft, towards the stable door.

Eliphalet near to chokes on his bissy nut. Lord Master God! Is what all this now? *Buckra* woman creeping about at three o'clock in the night?

He gets down behind rockstone at edge of the trees, and peers over the top.

Even for buckra woman, she's walking strange: like she's all liquored up or dizzy or took sick. He wonders if maybe she's the wife of that pinch-mouth parson over at Fever Hill who maintains she's gone moonshine mad.

Hn, thinks Eliphalet. Mad, I don't know. But she wants bad to get away from her man.

He sees her go into the stable, then come out again riding horse – and she's not riding it sideways like up-class buckra women always do, but just like a man.

Peculiar strange, he tells himself. And he sits down in the deep darkness behind the rockstone to consider awhile.

He must a fell in sleep, for when he comes awake, Brother Sun's starting up into the big blue, and crac-cracs are buzzing roundabout, and jabbering crows are jabbering away in the thatch-palm above his head. And down at the buckra house there's a lot, lot a trouble.

Cousin Sukey's outside the cook-house wringing her hands, and old Aaron's running fast as he can for the stables, and that parson's pacing, pacing in the yard, looking angrified and yelling for his horse.

Eliphalet swallows hard, and stays careful still. Eliphalet, he tells himself, don't you get tangle-up in this. You stand up soft now, and take foot and run like black ant back to your own self yard. And you give Phoebe those bald-pates to make her sweet, and have nice little party over at Disappointment, and swallow your damn spit.

And you keep one careful fact in that head you got. Far as you concern, you never was here at all.

CHAPTER TWENTY-EIGHT

The dew had been heavy overnight, so his wife's trail was easy to follow.

For an hour he had tracked her, and despite the heat and the discomfort he had almost enjoyed the ride, for with every passing moment he felt more certain that he would find her. She was no match for him. Instead of going north towards Fever Hill she had headed east, in a transparent attempt to throw him off the scent. Did she take him for a fool? Or did she think that he lacked his brother's woodsmanship?

He reached a fork in the track, and reined in. Curious. She should have turned left, heading down through the hill-pastures of Turnaround, past Stony Gap, and through the cane-pieces of Glen Marnoch towards Fever Hill. Instead she had taken the right-hand track, heading south-east up a narrow path that wound into the waterless labyrinth of the Cockpits.

The Cockpits? Why? Was this some kind of broken-backed attempt to reach Eden across country? Or had she simply made the wrong choice and lost her way?

He dismounted, unhooked his water bottle from the saddle, and went to rest beneath the thorn tree that marked the parting of the tracks. The patchy shade brought some relief from the relentless heat. His head was throbbing, his mouth gritty with dust. The glare off the white rocks hurt his eyes.

He drank deeply, then moistened his handkerchief and

cooled his face and neck and wrists. He glanced up the right-hand track, and saw jagged white rocks and thorn-scrub, and the towering, eerily conical hills of the Cockpits. For the first time since he had started out, he felt a flicker of real unease.

He had always hated the Cockpits. Arid, demon-haunted, fit only for blacks. It enraged him when Mrs Herapath held forth about their 'untamed beauty – their savage and desolate allure'. What allure? They were the mouth of hell.

Still, he told himself, what of that? It's such rough country, she'll make slow progress. She can't be far ahead now.

He stoppered the water bottle and remounted and kicked his horse to a trot.

The morning wore on, and the track became steeper and narrower, forcing him to slow to a walk. Twisted thorn trees clung to the slopes. Beneath them the ground was a dreary confusion of tumbled boulders and spiky wild pine and the rampant, dusty creeper the blacks called hogmeat. The crickets pulsed to the throbbing in his temples. Midges thronged the air like tiny invisible demons.

And that constant feeling of being watched. Often he twisted round in the saddle, convinced that something was observing him from the rocks. But there was never anything there; or never anything that he could see.

He wished Dr Valentine were with him. But the doctor had returned to town the previous evening to check on his surgery, and Sinclair had been alone when the housekeeper had roused him with the news that his wife had gone. Some time before dawn she had stolen the carriage-horse and gone. But how? And *why*?

It hadn't taken him long to come up with the answer. Somehow, she had learned the truth about the pickney's death. Perhaps her sister had told her; perhaps she had found out by some other means. It didn't matter. The point was, she knew. And now she meant to tell the authorities, and bring him down.

He stood to lose everything. Position. Inheritance. Perhaps even his life. And all because of a Negro nobody and an hysterical woman.

'Calm, calm,' he whispered aloud. She can't have told anyone yet. All you have to do is find her. Take her back. And let Dr Valentine work his magic. *Depend upon it, Mr Lawe, she will be a different woman. Obedient, well regulated* – and compliant.

Ahead of him the track led down into a rocky hollow like a small natural amphitheatre, before snaking up the other side and round the crest of the hill. The hollow was puzzlingly familiar. Nothing more than a handful of thorn and calabash trees, and a tumble of enormous boulders. The rasp of the crickets was deafening in the noonday heat.

Ah, now he remembered. Years before, he had come here on a shooting trip with his brother and the old man. He disliked hunting, but on this occasion he had bagged more than his brother, so the memory was sweet.

He put his horse cautiously forward down the rocky slope.

And wasn't there, he wondered, something else about this place as well? Something vaguely unsettling? But what?

He was trying to remember when he rounded a spur, and came upon Madeleine.

She was sitting with her back to him beneath a calabash tree: head down, arms about her knees, as if exhausted, or taken ill. She hadn't heard his approach, but her horse, tethered a few yards behind her, raised its head from the thistles and pricked its ears.

Mouth dry, heart pounding, Sinclair slid from the saddle and tied his horse to a thorn bush, and moved silently forward.

He had passed her horse and was no more than twenty feet away from her when she turned and saw him. He froze. For a moment they stared at one another in silence.

'You,' she mouthed. Her lips formed a perfect O of alarm.

She was bizarrely dressed, no doubt having seized whatever had come to hand. A wide straw hat with white silk roses round the brim; a pair of cream calfskin ankle-boots; and a wildly unsuitable morning dress of flimsy white muslin painted with little bronze leaves. When she got to her feet, he saw how she swayed. She was still drugged. Thank God.

'Why did you run?' he said.

She backed away. 'After what you did? How can you ask?'

A cold weight sank within him. So now he was sure. She did know about the pickney.

He took out his handkerchief and wiped the back of his neck. 'You must know', he said, 'that you cannot run from me. You have nowhere to go.'

She threw a rapid glance over her shoulder, and took another step down the slope, stumbling on the uneven ground.

He held out his hand. 'Come. I'll take you home. We will forget all about this.'

Like a rebellious child she thrust out her lower lip and shook her head. Her eyes had the same animal watchfulness as her sister when he'd confronted her in the gallery. Yes, he thought, she is an animal, a frightened animal. She simply needs firmness, and all will be well.

Still holding out his hand, he took a step towards her. 'I can't let you tell anyone,' he said. 'Come, now. Be reasonable.'

She took another step back and lost her footing, and fell to her knees in a clump of hogmeat. The ground sagged beneath her as if she'd gone into a ditch. 'Sinclair . . .' she said. She sounded surprised.

'Come,' he said again.

The next few seconds seemed to stretch, and he took in the details with extraordinary clarity. He saw how the earth gently folded beneath her, and crumbled and began to fall away. He saw how she grabbed at the creepers around her with both hands. He heard the vegetable snap as they gave way, and the rattle of falling pebbles, and he saw the red dust rising to envelop her.

She looked up at him, her face blank with shock. 'Sinclair – I can't—' She clutched at the creepers and slid down, down, and disappeared into the choking cloud of dust.

The dust was blinding, all-enveloping. He whipped out his handkerchief and covered his mouth, and dropped to his knees and crawled towards the edge. He could hear nothing but the rattle of falling rubble and his own rasping coughs.

Through the red haze he made out a ragged hole some ten feet across, and as the dust slowly settled, he saw her at the bottom, lying in a mound of creepers and rubble. He leaned over as far as he dared. 'Madeleine? Are you all right?'

She coughed, and sat up, still coughing, and wiping her eyes. She touched her forehead and winced, and finally nodded. 'I – I think so. Yes.'

'The creepers must have broken your fall.'

She sneezed. 'What – is this place?'

'A sink-hole, I think. Yes, it must be. I remember now. They're everywhere around here. The creepers grow over the edge, so it's hard to see them. We were never allowed to come here as boys.'

Still probing her forehead with her fingertips, she got unsteadily to her feet. 'That', she said, 'I can understand.' She peered up at him. 'How am I going to get out?'

He had been wondering that himself. The walls were nearly sheer, and about eighteen feet deep. Far too deep for him to reach her by leaning over. He looked round for some creeper which might bear her weight but saw only hogmeat: as thin as knitting wool and brittle as honeysuckle.

Then an idea came to him. Sights and sounds fell away. He sat back on his heels and wiped his face with his handkerchief.

'Sinclair?' his wife called out.

No, he told himself. No. This is marsh-fire. A false hope sent by the Evil One to tempt the unwary.

'Sinclair?'

Unless, he thought. Unless it is not the Evil One who has put this into your mind. But God.

'I didn't push you,' Sinclair said as he peered down at her.

'Well I know that,' she snapped, rubbing the bump on her forehead. Her head was pounding, and the laudanum was making her nauseous, but strangely, the shock of the fall seemed to have cleared her wits. She felt sharper than she had done in days. And furious with herself. Of all things, to fall down a sink-hole. Now there was nothing to do but wait to be rescued – by the very man she had been trying to escape.

Sinclair was still peering down at her, solemn and un-blinking. He gave himself an odd little shake, as if to banish some unwelcome thought, then leaned down and extended his hand as far as he could. 'Here,' he said. She could hear the strain in his voice. 'See – if you can reach.'

She reached for him on tiptoe, but his hand was a good six feet above hers. She took hold of a creeper snaking up the wall, and tried to pull herself up. She had climbed a foot or so when the creeper gave way and she fell back painfully onto the rocks. She sat up, rubbing a bruised hip. 'It's no good,' she said. 'Do you have any rope?'

He shook his head. 'Only my belt. And that's not nearly long enough.'

'What about the stirrup leathers? And the reins? Couldn't you knot them together?'

Again he shook his head. 'They'd never hold. And we'd have nothing to tether the horses.'

Dizzy and sick, she put her elbows on her knees and forced herself to take deep breaths. 'Well then,' she said, sounding a lot more robust than she felt, 'I suppose you'd better go for help.'

Above her there was a lengthy pause. 'Yes,' echoed Sinclair. 'I shall go for help.'

She looked up at him. His face was dark against the glare. 'Come back soon,' she said.

He nodded. Then he was gone. Soon afterwards she heard the clatter of hooves disappearing down the track.

Hot, bruised and thirsty, she found a patch of ground without too many rocks, and sat down to wait.

It must be around noon, for the sun was directly overhead, and there was no shade to be had. Thank God she still had her hat. But why hadn't she had the sense to unearth her dust-coat from the trunk, and her riding habit, instead of this ridiculous morning dress? Already she could feel her shoulders burning through the insubstantial muslin.

After a while, a thin rind of shade appeared at the other side of the sink-hole. She crawled over to it. As she did so, something crunched softly beneath her hand. She remem-bered the passage on sink-holes in Sophie's gazetteer, and wished that she hadn't. Recalcitrant slaves tossed down here and left to die. She wondered if what had crunched beneath her hand was bones.

Don't be absurd, she told herself. That was sixty years ago, they'd be dust by now. Besides, there are hundreds of sink-holes in the Cockpits; how do you know it was this one?

She clasped her arms about her knees, and forced the thought of dying slaves from her mind.

She had more pressing concerns. Thirst was becoming a problem. Why hadn't she had the sense to make Sinclair throw down his water bottle? More proof – if proof were needed – that she was still affected by the drugs.

The afternoon wore on, and the rind of shade grew wider. Surely Sinclair would find someone soon? A labourer or a smallholder? Or perhaps he'd decided to ride all the way back to Providence to raise the alarm? But even so, he would be here soon. It couldn't be more than five or six miles to Providence.

She curled up against the wall and tried to doze. Her head was still throbbing from the knock she had taken when she fell. Her thoughts were tangled and confused.

When she opened her eyes, she was alarmed to see that the shade had eaten up most of the sink-hole floor. The breeze had dropped, and the creepers at the lip of the hole had stilled. In a few hours it would start to get dark.

That was when it hit her. Sinclair wasn't coming back.

Chapter Twenty-Nine

Cameron awoke before dawn, still drunk from the night before. Abigail sensed that he was not to be trifled with, and wisely stayed at the other end of the verandah.

At breakfast he snapped at Braverly, at the stables he snapped at Moses, and on the way to Maputah he snapped at Pilate. Three days had passed since he'd left Madeleine outside the church. Three days and three nights which had brought him no answers; only more questions.

The ride to Maputah took him past some of his best cane-pieces, but the sight did nothing to lighten his mood. He had thought that by rescuing Eden he was making peace with Ainsley's ghost. What a shameful piece of self-deception that turned out to have been.

For ten years he had scarcely given Ainsley's children a thought. When he'd remembered them at all, it had been with a sense of distant relief. He'd done the right thing by them, hadn't he? He'd given them half his patrimony; what more did they need?

It astonished him that he could have deceived himself for so long. And that dream. Why had he never grasped its meaning, when it was staring him in the face? Simply because he hadn't wanted to? Was that all it took to ignore the truth?

He studied the young cane trembling in the breeze. How could he have been so *blind*? She even looked like Rose. The same rich colouring, the same dark, almond-shaped eyes. And the same extraordinary blend of candour and secretiveness and naivety. Sinclair had told him once that she was not as innocent as she seemed. Well, perhaps that was true – but surely not in the way that Sinclair had meant. She didn't even know how to kiss.

The thought made him reach for his hip flask and take a long, burning pull of Scotch.

And to think that he had actually believed that she cared for him; that he reached something in her, as she did in him. God, he had been such a fool.

A flock of parakeets exploded from a guinep tree, and he watched them furiously beating their wings as they scudded across the sky.

The night before, as he had worked his way steadily through a bottle of rum, he had been so angry with her that a red haze had misted his vision. He had felt a physical need to do her harm. For lying to him; for leading him on; for not feeling as he did. And what *right* had she to ask him to help her sister? She had lied to him over and over again; she had no right to ask him anything. No right.

He was still carrying that anger inside him as he rode up the dusty red track in the harsh morning sun.

When he reached Maputah, he threw himself into work. He supervised the test run of the new still; he climbed to the boiling-house roof to check the repairs. The hours flew by. Gradually, the demons retreated. Some of the anger leached away.

After all, what crime had she committed? What had she done, except to make what was already a confounded mess just a little bit worse?

None of this was her fault. It was his fault: his and Jocelyn's. If they hadn't been so eager to sweep Ainsley's 'monumentally inconvenient bastards' under the carpet, none of this would have happened. Septimus would not have emptied the trust and left them with nothing. Sophie would not have fallen ill. And Madeleine would not have felt compelled to marry Sinclair.

But what could be done about that now? Nothing. Stay out of it. Try to forget.

The bell tolled for the noonday break, and he watched the

men settling down in the shade to tackle their lunchpails. He wondered what to do until the break was over and he could get back to work. He couldn't face returning to the house for a solitary meal that he didn't want, and it was too hot to go for a ride. An unwelcome image came to him of Sophie in Burntwood, and he pushed it away.

Just then, he noticed a stranger loitering under the poinciana tree at the entrance to the yard. The stranger was small and thin, in tattered dungarees and crumpled straw hat: plainly one of the poor white vagrants who wandered the countryside in search of a day's casual work.

Behind him, Cameron heard Oserius snort. 'White lubba,' the foreman muttered, wiping his mouth on the back of his hand and rising to his feet.

Cameron motioned him down. 'Finish your meal. I'll see him off.' He put his hands in his pockets and made his way across the yard. 'There's no work for you here,' he told the stranger. 'You'd better be on your way.'

'Din't come for a job, did I?' came the sharp retort.

Oh Lord, thought Cameron, this one's after a scrap. 'As I said,' he repeated in a firmer tone, 'there's nothing for you here. Now be off, there's a good fellow.'

'I got somethink to tell you,' said the stranger, belatedly snatching off his hat.

Cameron was surprised to see that he was much younger than he'd thought. Thirteen? Fourteen? It was difficult to tell, for poverty had hardened the thin face beyond its years. But the expression was oddly familiar: an edgy mix of belligerence and apprehension. Where had he seen that before?

Then it came to him. There had been boys like this in prison. Cynical, quick-witted and startlingly amoral, no missionary could reach them, no prison visitor make them see the light. What light? They'd been thieving since they could walk.

Cameron was intrigued. A Cockney street Arab on the Northside. What were the odds on that? And what are the odds, he reminded himself, that this wily little urchin isn't on the lookout for something to steal?

He put his hands on his hips and gave the boy a hard look. 'What's your name,' he said, 'and what are you doing on my land?'

The boy raised his chin and met his gaze. 'Don't matter who I am,' he snapped. He was making a good job of not looking frightened, but all the same, Cameron felt like a bully. Because he saw now that this boy was different from the Millbank lads. The worst of those had had something dead about the eyes, for they were long past feeling; but this boy's eyes looked bruised and exhausted, as if he'd felt too much.

'Very well,' said Cameron, 'we'll dispense with the introductions. Now what do you want?'

The boy licked his lips. 'You the parson's brother, yeh?'

'The parson . . . ? Yes. I suppose I am. What's that to you?'

'Miss Clemmy sent me.'

'Miss Clemmy? What the devil are you talking about?'

The boy bridled. 'She did. Miss Clemmy of Fever Hill. I seen her on Monday.' He flicked a sideways glance at the men in the yard, and lowered his voice. 'It's about Sophie. She's in the san, Burntwood san. That's what I come to tell you. You got to get her out.'

Cameron was too astonished to reply. What was Clemency thinking of, recruiting an urchin to run her messages?

And yet – on reflection, was that so bizarre? It wouldn't be the first time that she had befriended a waif. In the old days, he and Jocelyn used to tease her about her 'followers': mostly pickneys hoping for a ginger bonbon or a story or a chance to play with her cat. Few were sent away disappointed.

But that left the little matter of *Sophie*: an astonishingly familiar form of address for a street boy to use about one of his betters. How did he imagine that he could make so free?

Behind him, the men were watching them with undisguised curiosity. Cameron jerked his head at the boy to follow, and started up the road. 'I don't understand,' he said. 'Are you telling me that you know – that you claim some acquaintance with – Miss Sophie Lawe?'

Shading his eyes with one hand, the boy squinted up at

him. 'Well *I* can't get her out of there, can I?' he said, dodging the question. 'And the grandpa's in Kingston and won't be back for—'

'The grandfather?' Cameron cut in.

'The old man. The one they call Uncle J—'

'You said "the grandfather".'

Impatiently, the boy tossed his head. 'Yeh? So? Madlin's and Sophie's.'

The grandpa. The way the boy had said it. Casually dropping it in as if it were common knowledge. Cameron ran a hand through his hair. 'Did Mad— did Mrs Lawe send you?'

'Course not, how could she? Parson's gone and locked her up.'

'*What?*'

'Some place called Providence. Up in the hills. He says she's cracked, and he's put her on some kind of cure. Anyway she can't get out, so she can't—'

'Who told you this? Who are you? How the devil do you know Mrs Lawe?'

He'd spoken sharply, and the boy clenched his fists, bracing his scrawny frame for a fight. He seemed not to have noticed that Cameron was twice his size.

'Who are you,' Cameron said again, 'and how did you come to know Mrs Lawe?'

'Who cares who I am,' muttered the boy. 'And as for Madlin and Sophie – if that's any of your business – I got to know them back in London.'

In London? This urchin had 'got to know' Madeleine in London? But how? And what was he doing in Jamaica? Was there no end to what she hadn't told him?

'Point *is*,' the boy insisted, 'Madlin can't do nothink for Sophie. That's the point.' He seemed genuinely anxious, and he flushed under Cameron's scrutiny, as if such concern were a cause for shame. 'That's why I come,' he muttered. 'To tell you she's in the san. So now you can go and get her out. Yeh?'

Cameron did not reply. As he stood there in the sun, the lunacy of the situation came crashing in on him. Here he was, arguing with a child – a denizen of the slums – about the merits of rescuing another child, whom he hardly knew.

And surely that, he told himself, is – to borrow this creature's expression – 'the point'? You don't know Sophie and you don't know Madeleine. It was an illusion to think that you did.

'What do you expect me to do?' he said, feeling his temper rise. 'Ride up to Burntwood like some medieval champion, and break down the door?'

For the first time, the boy was lost for words.

'Perhaps you're not aware', Cameron went on, 'that Miss Sophie Lawe is my brother's responsibility. He is her legal guardian, not I.' As he said it, he felt himself colour with shame. Because he knew that it was just an excuse: an excuse to cover his anger at Madeleine.

Well, and what if it is? he thought. My God, hasn't she given you cause?

He turned back to the boy. 'Do you understand what it means to be a child's legal guardian?' he said. 'It means that he's the only one who can get her out.'

The boy was staring at him with his mouth open. Suddenly he looked very young. 'You *knew*,' he said. 'You already knew she's in the san. And you done nothink.'

'I don't need you', said Cameron between his teeth, 'to teach me my duty. Now be off with you. I've got work to do.'

The boy was shaking his head. 'I thought you was different. I thought, if Madlin likes him, he can't be the same as them others. Shit. I should of known.'

Cameron put down his head and gave the boy a look that made him flinch. 'I've let you have your say,' he said in a low voice, 'but don't imagine for a moment that I'll tolerate disrespect. Now do as you're told and get off my land.'

But the boy stood his ground, though he threw a quick glance over his shoulder to make sure of his escape. 'You're narked at Madlin,' he said. 'That's it, innit?'

'How dare you, you little—'

'You're narked at her, so you're taking it out on Sophie. What's the matter with you? You think Madlin done it for fun? All she ever done, she done for Sophie. Don't you know that yet?'

Bloody hell, thinks Ben. Now what d'you do?

He's still puffing and blowing after cutting the lucky up that hill. He didn't like the look of that brother's face one little bit. Them light-grey eyes, as clear as gin and sharp as glass. Them big hands clenched at his sides. Just itching to knock the stuffing out of him. If he hadn't legged it when he did, he'd be spitting out teeth right now, and wondering what bones *wasn't* broken.

What a sodding waste of time. What were you thinking of, Ben Kelly? Parson's *brother*? What's he care about Sophie? Him with his big posh house and his fancy horse and all them fields. You should of known better. You should of known they're all the same.

Still. That's not the point, is it? Point is, it's down to you now, and nobody else. So what you going to do about it?

Think. Think. Sophie's in the san. Who put her there? The parson. Of course. So if you take away the parson, then anybody can get her out. Madeleine. Grandpa. Even that Miss Clemmy could see to it. So what does that tell you, Ben Kelly? *Tells you to take away the parson, like you was going to in the first place!*

And it's all very well Madeleine saying it's not what Robbie would of wanted – but this isn't only about Robbie no more. It's about Sophie, too.

Shit but it's hot.

He goes to the side of the road and squats down under one of them flame-colour trees to think. Parrot on a branch looks down at him, like it's wondering if he's going to chuck a stone at it; it decides not to pross around and find out, and lifts itself off the branch and flies away.

Only trouble is, thinks Ben, watching the parrot cut the lucky up the road, only trouble *is*, Madeleine went and took the sodding gun. Bloody Madeleine.

Then all of a sudden he gets this idea. It's sort of killing two birds with one stone, so to speak.

Course, it'll mean going back the way he come. Sneaking past that brother again, and padding the hoof all the way to

Fever Hill. A good few hours on the road that is; be lucky to get there by dark. But that's all right. He's got the time.

He sits there under the tree, turning the plan over in his head and looking for holes. But whichever way he looks at it, it's not bad. Not bad at all.

CHAPTER THIRTY

She had tried everything she could think of, but nothing had worked.

She had tried making steps in the sink-hole walls by hammering wedges of rock into cracks. The limestone crumbled on impact, or splintered beneath her weight. She had tried ripping up her gown and plaiting a rope. Without scissors it was impossible to tear the muslin into even strips, and she managed only an unwieldy chain of knots. Nevertheless, she had tried throwing the 'rope' over a sapling which jutted halfway up the sink-hole wall. She had managed to haul herself a few feet off the ground before the sapling gave way.

Finally, she had tried shouting for help. She had given that up the soonest of all. It was frightening to hear her voice buffeted from wall to wall, with no reply.

She forced herself to sit down and think. How long since Sinclair had left? Five hours? Six? The breeze had dropped but the sky was still blue, the heat still intense.

Her face felt stiff, her eyes scratchy and sore. It was becoming difficult to think of anything but water. She'd had nothing since well before dawn, when she'd stolen a drink from the Providence cook-house. *Why* hadn't she thought to take anything with her?

But if she had, it would be out of reach now.

Just like Ben's gun.

That wretched gun. If she had it now, everything would

be different. She could fire off shots that would be heard for miles; she could shoot one of the john crows which wheeled overhead, and drink its blood.

If only she had that gun. She'd been rooting around in the trunk when she'd found it, neatly rolled in a pair of cambric combinations. She remembered bundling it up with her clothes before slipping out of the house and finding her way to the stables, but after that she'd forgotten all about it until she'd stopped to rest beneath the calabash tree, and found it in the saddlebag, and put it on the ground and stared at it. How alien it had looked, lying there in the dust. Why had she taken it? What had she imagined she could do with it?

No doubt Sinclair had found it when he'd gone to fetch her horse; and no doubt it would help him to justify what he had done. *She had a gun*, he would tell himself. *She meant to shoot me. I had no choice but to leave her.*

She kept seeing his face as he peered over the edge. Those bright, dispassionate eyes: like a child watching a minnow in a pail. *Look at the funny little creature I have caught. I wonder how long it will live?*

How long will it live?

Her head was throbbing, her lips cracked and sore. Once again she made a search for something to eat or drink. Shrivelled brown moss; mounds of dusty creepers spattered with bird-lime; the remains of the sapling: thorny, brittle and dry. She wondered if the creepers might be the 'hogmeat' that Sophie had told her about. If pigs could eat it, did that mean people could too? She broke off a leaf and chewed, but it was so bitter that she had to spit it out.

It occurred to her that she must cut a bizarre figure, in white canvas ankle-boots and sleeveless cambric combinations that only reached to the knee. Her gown had gone to make the rope, and her petticoat had got in the way when she'd tried to climb, so she'd taken it off. If only she'd had the sense to unearth her riding habit from the trunk. Then she could have used the skirt for a rope, and still had the trousers to protect her shins.

She sat back against the wall and shut her eyes. What did that matter now? What mattered was getting out of here, or finding some way of attracting help. A hunter or a passing smallholder, or a Negro on the way home from his provision ground. There must be someone about.

Then she remembered what the housekeeper had muttered when she'd brought in the tray. Some complaint about being forced to work over the Free Come holiday, the day after tomorrow.

She struggled to marshal her thoughts. The housekeeper had said that yesterday; which meant that tomorrow was the holiday. Which meant that there would be no Negroes passing by. There would be no-one about.

And no-one would come to search for her, because they all thought she was at Providence with Sinclair.

She pictured him telling the housekeeper that his wife had wandered off into the bush and was nowhere to be found. She pictured him riding down to Fever Hill to sound the alarm. She pictured Northside society tut-tutting over its afternoon tea. *Too dreadful, one can hardly bear to think of it. Apparently it was neurasthenia, and she simply wandered off. Poor Reverend Lawe! They say he's utterly distracted. Searched for days, poor lamb, but never found a trace. And what horrid bad luck that the rains were over, or she might have had a chance.*

She wondered how Cameron would feel when he heard the news.

And Jocelyn.

And Sophie. God, Sophie. Who would tell her? Would she even live long enough to find out?

When she opened her eyes, she saw that some of the blue had leached from the sky. How long till it got dark? One hour? Two? Would there be a moon? She couldn't remember.

She put out her hand and studied it. Her fingers were swollen, the skin so taut that it hurt to make a fist. If she didn't get out tonight, she would be too weak to do anything by morning.

Setting her teeth, she struggled to her feet. The blood soughed in her ears. Black spots darted before her eyes. She forced herself to begin again, to make another search for stones that might serve as wedges.

She found the rock she had been using as a hammer, and went to the part of the wall which was less sheer than the rest, where about four feet of her rudimentary ladder had survived. She found a crack about five feet up and started hammering in a wedge.

This time it went more smoothly than before. None of the wedges broke, the 'hammer' didn't crack, and after about half an hour she'd made a zig-zag of hand- and footholds snaking roughly halfway up the wall. Which still left about nine feet more from there on up, so she'd have to carry her hammer and the rest of the wedges with her and put them in as she went along; but she'd worry about that when she came to it. She made a sack of her petticoat, slung it over her shoulder, and filled it with all the stepping-stones she could find.

She was nearly five feet up before a wedge snapped, and she went down. She landed heavily on her side, and pain shot through her shoulder.

Winded, she lay where she had fallen. She smelt dust and bird-droppings and her own oniony sweat. She tasted grit, and something that wriggled before she could spit it out. Mosquitoes whined in her ears. It was getting dark.

Her throat was swollen, her lips sore. It hurt to swallow. It hurt to move. She wanted to cry, but the tears wouldn't come. She curled into a ball and dug her knuckles in her eyes. What do I do? she thought. What do I *do*?

No answer came. No heaven-sent voice whispering salvation in the wilderness. No half-forgotten survival hint now recalled in the nick of time. As far as she could remember, Robinson Crusoe had never fallen down a hole.

Eventually, she opened her eyes. In the twilight she was surprised to see a long gash down her left forearm. She groped beneath her for the rock that had done it.

Her swollen fingers closed on it painfully. But it wasn't a rock. It was a shackle. Rough with corrosion but still solid, and unmistakably a leg-iron: part of the section which encircles the ankle. She thought back to her first foray across the sink-hole floor. That soft, chalkily yielding crack of bone beneath her hand.

Heart pounding, she sat up. Her skin prickled with the sense of being watched. Someone had been here before her. Someone was down here still.

She strained to make out shapes in the gloom. And after a while they began to move, as shadows do when you look at them for long enough.

'I don't want to harm you,' she whispered. 'I just want to get out.'

The shadows stopped moving and became a listening stillness.

She felt warmth and wetness on her arm, and glanced down. She touched the cut with her fingertips. It had bled freely, but was already forming a scab.

The shadows watched, but didn't move.

She crawled over to her petticoat and tore a strip with her teeth to make a rough bandage.

The shadows kept to their side of the hole.

When she had finished binding the cut, her fingers were sticky and glistening. She sat cross-legged in the dust and turned her hands this way and that. In the deepening gloom, the blood looked almost black.

The shadows began to feel less of a threat and more like company.

At Cairngowrie House, she had pictured the taint as little grey flecks floating in scarlet. *It's in the blood.*

She thought about that now. She thought about waking up in her mother's cold, snowlit bed, and peeling back the blankets to reveal the great scarlet stain.

She thought about her mother on all fours on the rug. *Well, Maddy, we'll just have to do this on our own.*

She scowled at the blood on her hands.

Her mother had been wild, self-indulgent, undisciplined, and brave. She had hurt people and made enormous mistakes, and had reaped both the good and the bad of what she had done, and she had never blamed anyone but herself. When she'd got into trouble, she'd simply done her best to get herself out. *Well, Maddy, we'll just have to do this on our own.*

A noise above her made her start. A john crow had alighted at the edge, and was peering down at her, its eyes bright and dispassionate. She reached for a stone.

Behind her the shadows waited to see what she would do.

The stone clipped the edge of the sink-hole and tumbled harmlessly back to earth. With a squawk the john crow spread its wings and flew away.

'Come back tomorrow,' she shouted. 'I'm not dead yet.'

Chapter Thirty-One

Up in the rafters, a spider is spinning its web. It is working from the outside in, and will finish soon, unless a helper comes and brushes it away.

The spider has nearly finished when it disappears behind a shiny black face. 'Now chile,' says Nurse Fletch, 'be quick an take you medicine. I don' got all day.'

The medicine is oily and brown and tastes of ash, but the child swallows it in one gulp, for she is a good child, and doesn't want to go without supper again.

The inside Sophie watches the child take the medicine, and knows that it tastes of ash, but she doesn't say a word. The inside Sophie never speaks. If she did, the nurses would find her and take her away.

The inside Sophie watched when they took the child's clothes and strapped her to the bed, and gave her injections which made her jangly all over. The inside Sophie watched when they took Pablo Grey to the incinerator in the yard and burnt him, and the twisty black flakes flew up up up and crumbled to nothing, which is what really happens to you when you die. The inside Sophie watched when the child screamed and screamed until they gave her morphine which made her sick, and the nurses were vexed, and wouldn't change the sheets. The inside Sophie saw it all, but never said a word. The inside Sophie never speaks. If she did, the nurses would find her and take her away.

The child's bed is in the south gallery, with the rest of the female patients. She can't see out because of the louvres, but below them there are gaps between the balusters and she can see down into the yard, to the incinerator where they burnt Pablo Grey. And she can see up into the rafters where the spider is spinning its web, and she can see behind her to the wall where the gecko puffs up his scarlet ruff to attract the flies.

Once, the gecko fell plop onto the child's midriff, and beside her the old lady with the scabs on her arms burst into giggles. 'Oh!' she cried. 'A gecko in your lap! That means you shall have a baby by and by!' She went on giggling until the nurses came and gave her an injection.

The young lady in the other bed told the child not to mind old Mrs de Charmilly, who was sent here years ago when this was a clinic for nervous cases. The young lady was nice, with fluffy, colourless hair and glistening eyes, but she coughed a great deal. Once, her guardian sent her a little blue glass atomizing flask of cocaine to ease her throat, but she coughed so much that it didn't last long; and the day before yesterday she was taken upstairs for cautery, and hasn't come back.

The child has been here for ever and ever. Once upon a time there was a pretty sister who was brilliant at guessing games, and a nice lady in a floaty white dress, and a stiff old gentleman with thousands of books. But that was far away and long ago.

The child sleeps all the time now, except when she is woken by the nurses to take her medicine or her semolina, or by somebody coughing. After the medicine, everything becomes fuzzy. Fuzzy shadows and fuzzy strips of sunlight on the floor. Even the gecko is fuzzy. Noises are fuzzy too, although sometimes they become stretchy and loud.

Until now, there hasn't been much noise, except for coughing and sometimes the gurgly noise of a person trying to breathe. But now there is a great deal of noise. Old Mrs de Charmilly is screeching and biting her scabs, and the nurses are shouting and running about, and there are footsteps in the gallery: not the footsteps of the nurses in their cotton slippers, but someone in boots.

The child turns her head and sees a tall gentleman at the

other end of the gallery. The nurses are crowding round him and waving their arms, and the inside Sophie can tell that they are frightened, although she can't make out what they are saying.

The tall gentleman walks the length of the gallery very fast, with the nurses trailing after him, and now he is standing over the child, looking down. The inside Sophie knows him, but cannot remember his name. It has something to do with pilot-lights and a horse.

The tall gentleman doesn't speak, but the inside Sophie can tell that he is extremely angry, which is why the nurses are so scared. But the inside Sophie isn't scared at all.

The tall gentleman is undoing the straps on the child's arms and leg and around her splint, and wrapping her in a blanket and lifting her up, and carrying her along the gallery and down the steps and out into the sunlight, which makes the child blink.

Then the tall gentleman turns, and the child sees the nurses huddled on the steps. They aren't shouting now, but they won't come down from the steps, for they are too frightened.

Carefully, so as not to jar her splint, the tall gentleman passes the child to a helper. The helper smells sweaty and scared, and for a moment the inside Sophie thinks that the tall gentleman means to leave her behind. But then the helper lifts her high, high, and the tall gentleman takes her before him on his horse, and they are moving off down the carriage-way. She can't see much because of the blanket wrapped around her, but she can smell the horse and hear its hooves, and see the tips of its glossy black ears. *Pilate*, she thinks. The horse's name is Pilate.

After a while they reach the great iron gate, and it's shut, and the gatekeeper runs out and begins to shout and wave his arms about. Then the tall gentleman tells the gatekeeper a very bad thing, and after that there is no more shouting, and the gates open up, and they pass through.

Later, through a gap in the trees, the inside Sophie sees the sanatorium in the distance. She sees the pointy witch gables and the great windowless cutwind where they lock up the children and leave them to die. She watches the sanatorium for as long as she can, to make sure that it's really, truly gone.

The inside Sophie wants to tell the tall gentleman that she is glad that he came for her, but she can't, for the inside Sophie never speaks. If she did, the nurses would find her and take her away.

As Cameron drove the borrowed trap through the gates of Fever Hill, he glanced at the reddening sky and gave the reins an impatient flick. It would be dark soon, and he needed to see Sophie to safety before he could think of starting for Providence.

The sensible thing, of course, would be to postpone Providence until the morning. But he couldn't do that. He needed to know that Madeleine was all right. Which was irrational, he knew that. Why wouldn't she be all right? No reason. Except that since their fraught conversation outside the church on Sunday morning, she had allowed her sister to spend three more days in that appalling place, without making any further attempt to get her out. And that wasn't like Madeleine. Whoever she really was.

A mongoose shot across the carriageway, and Pilate swerved and tossed his head. Cameron gave him a slap with the reins and told him to quieten down. He turned to Sophie, beside him. 'He's just making a fuss', he explained, 'because he doesn't like pulling a trap. He thinks it's beneath his dignity.'

She turned her head and gave him her unblinking stare. The sedatives were wearing off and she'd lost that comatose look, but she hadn't said a word since they'd left the sanatorium. He was beginning to wonder when she would.

Soon after leaving Burntwood, he had realized the impossibility of taking her all the way to Fever Hill on horseback. No matter how slowly he rode, it would still be too rough on her knee. So instead he'd stopped at the first settlement they reached: a straggling little slum village called Simonstown. He knew the people there, and it wasn't too far from old Mowat's place, and Mowat – clever, over-sensitive, and vilely unlucky – had always been civil to him, and would probably lend him his trap.

He'd forgotten that it was Free Come eve until he rode into the village and found it heaving with preparations. Men were stacking green pimento wood by the barbecues for tomorrow's jerked hog, and bringing in baskets of breadkind and chochos from the grounds; pickneys were racing about under everyone's feet; and the women were hurrying to put the finishing touches to their new gowns, and making piles of hard-dough, and stoking the fires beneath great bubbling yabbas of fufu and gungo peas stew. The whole village smelt of cloves and thyme and wood smoke and anticipation.

They welcomed him like a holiday novelty that had arrived a day early, and crowded round to see the little cripple girl from Fever Hill. A man ran off to petition Mowat for the pony-trap, and another took Pilate to be fed and watered. Cameron bought a tumbler of rum punch for himself, and watched in relief as Sophie worked her way with painful concentration through a beaker of guava syrup and a bowl of stewed okra and yam. Then he paid a young woman a month's earnings to bathe her and dress her in her daughter's Sunday best: a flounced pink drill affair which must have looked delightful on a healthy little Negro girl, but transformed Sophie into an incongruous and extremely bony wax doll.

She submitted to everything with unnerving passivity, and only seemed to notice her surroundings at all when a very small pickney sidled up to inspect her, clutching his plaything to his belly. The toy was a little mule of plaited cane-trash, and Sophie stared at it with such intentness that the pickney took fright and ran away.

Cameron wondered what the straw mule meant to her. What had she been through in that place?

He could still smell the Lysol and the hopelessness. He could still see her sallow little face on the pillow, her eyes unfocused and frighteningly blank. She had been there for – what? Four days? Five? Surely that wasn't long enough for permanent harm?

And what if he was wrong about that? What if her lungs were already affected, and he could have prevented it if he'd acted at once, instead of delaying until a Cockney street Arab taught him a lesson in ethics?

He shot her an anxious glance. She was watching the cane-pieces whip past, her lips slightly parted, her eyes dull.

Ainsley's daughter. He still couldn't believe it. And yet all the evidence was before him. That fair hair. Those straight, intelligent dark brows. That hint of her grandfather in the determined set of her chin.

He remembered what Madeleine had said as they'd stood together outside the church. *She's his daughter, Cameron. Think about that. For eight years you've been up there in your self-imposed exile, having those nightmares and wondering why. You say you've forgiven him, but have you? Don't you think that if you'd really forgiven him, you wouldn't have visited his sins on his children by denying their very existence?*

I have forgiven you, Ainsley, he told the rippling cane-pieces. Look. Here's your daughter. I'm bringing her home.

It had been ten years since he'd driven up this carriageway. Ten years since he'd been anywhere near the house. Why so long? What had prevented him from simply riding up one day and making his peace with Jocelyn? He had wasted so much time.

I think you've become accustomed to living like this, she had told him. Separate. Isolated. *It's become a way of life.* She was right.

He passed a weeding-gang walking home across Bullet Tree Piece. They raised their hats to him, and turned their heads to watch his progress. Soon word would be all over the estate. *Mas' Camron try for come home.*

God, why was this carriageway so infernally long? Everywhere he looked, he saw the ghosts. Every tree, every cane-piece, was familiar as only a land learned in childhood can be. Off to the right was the guango tree which he'd climbed when he was nine, and lost his footing, and nearly throttled himself on a strangler fig. There to the left was Congo Walk, where they used to race their polo ponies and hold jousting tournaments. Beyond that was the Old Pond, where Jocelyn had taught them to swim. And up there on Clairmont Hill were the marl-pits, where a sixteen-year-old Ainsley had made himself into a luminous spectre for the Boxing Day masquerade – incensing his father, appalling May, and delighting Aristide Durrant's mischievous young daughter Rose.

They swept past the New Works, and suddenly the great house rose into view. Cameron caught his breath. The dilapidations were cruelly apparent: the broken louvres, the peeling paint; the great copperpots flanking the steps, which used to overflow with oleander, but now held nothing but thistles. But none of that mattered. This was still the only place he could remember calling home.

He wondered what sort of reception he would receive. Jocelyn was safely in Kingston, but what about May? And Clemency? He and Clemency had once been close; or as close as two people of vastly different natures could be. When Ainsley had run off, they had helped one another to cope. And when she'd lost her child he had watched her take refuge in a kind of deliberate madness, with her constant illnesses and her secret plans for the 'journey' that only he was allowed to know. He had pitied her, but he hadn't interfered, for behind the breathless little laugh and the propitiatory smiles there was a single-mindedness about Clemency which he couldn't help but admire.

The carriageway in front of the house was empty, except for Remus dozing at the foot of the steps. The mastiff recognized Cameron from his visits to the Burying-place, and heaved himself up to make way.

A harried-looking groom ran round from the servants' quarters, and opened his mouth to exclaim when he saw who it was, and thought better of it, and took charge of the trap. Cameron carried Sophie up the steps and into the gallery.

He was shaken by the wave of emotion which swept over him. The gallery hadn't changed at all. The same slatted amber light. The same battered old rattan chairs with their throws of the red and green Monroe tartan. The same never-to-be-forgotten scent of cigar smoke and orange-oil polish.

This gallery had been his first experience of Fever Hill, and the centre of his world when he was growing up. When he'd had nightmares, he would come out here and curl up with the dogs. When there was a storm, he would stand with Jocelyn on the steps and watch the rain sweeping the cane-pieces. And on his sixteenth birthday, the old man had poured him his first whisky and soda, and raised a toast. '*By fire and sword*,' he had declaimed, 'that's for the Lawes. *Death before dishonour*. That's for the Monroes.'

He put Sophie in the nearest armchair, and fetched a foot-stool to support her splint. As he did so, he realized that he'd put her in Jocelyn's chair. Here was the aged tapestry cushion, and the old throw of the McFarlane tartan, its heathery mauves and sage greens tempering the red. He remembered a stiff old gentleman settling a six-year-old boy on this same throw, and introducing him to a pair of mastiffs, and sending the helper for a bowl of red pea soup. If he shut his eyes, he could still taste that soup.

From the shadowy ballroom, the grandfather clock brought him back to the present. Half-past seven. It would be dark soon. Even by moonlight, it would be slow going up into the hills. He would be lucky to reach Providence by midnight.

As he was straightening up, a woman hurried round the corner of the gallery, feverishly searching for something.

She was elaborately dressed in a modish travelling-costume of crisp white brocade, and laden with all the accoutrements of a fashionable outing. In one hand she clutched a pair of white kid gloves, in the other a card-case, a scent bottle, and a handful of pearl-headed hatpins. Dangling from one wrist was a sumptuous hat brimming with white chiffon roses, while over the other arm hung a carriage-cloak of snowy silk damask, and – curiously, given the impending dusk – an ivory-handled parasol of white satin and lace.

Cameron saw with a pang that she had hardly aged since he'd last seen her. Still the same delicate, pretty features beneath the startling chignon of dyed grey hair. 'Hallo, Clemmy,' he said.

She gave a violent start, and her face froze guiltily, as if she'd been caught in some crime. Then guilt gave way to round-eyed astonishment as she recognized him. 'Cameron? Is that you?'

He went to her and reached for her hand, then – mindful of the accoutrements – awkwardly withdrew it. 'How are you, Clemmy?'

She opened her mouth, but no words came. The carriage-cloak slid off her arm to the floor, quickly followed by the gloves, the scent bottle, the card-case and the hatpins. Cameron stooped to retrieve the cloak, and put it over a chair. 'I got your message,' he said.

She looked blank.

'The boy? D'you remember?'

There was such bemusement in her china-blue eyes that he wondered if she'd heard.

He tried again. 'I went to Burntwood. I've brought S—'

'I can't find my purse!' she burst out. 'It was here a minute ago, I know it was, and now it's simply vanished!'

'Clemmy—'

'Oh, it's all such a *muddle!* I had everything perfect, perfect! But just as I was about to put on my hat I heard the carriage outside, so unexpected, I never thought he'd be back so *soon*. And now here I am discovered with all my special things, absolutely *discovered* . . . and May will be so *vexed*!' Her lips quivered, as if she might burst into tears.

Still the same Clemency, thought Cameron with exasperated affection. Plainly she was far more exercised over the loss of her purse than by his own unexpected arrival.

Knowing it was useless to rush her, he helped to retrieve the rest of her belongings from the floor and put them on a side table. She still hadn't noticed Sophie, who was gazing at her gravely from the depths of her incongruous pink flounces.

Cameron gestured to her and said, 'Look, Clemmy. See whom I've brought back.'

At last Clemency saw her. Her face crumpled, and her hand flew to her cheek. 'Oh, now I really don't know what to do! I prayed and prayed for this to happen – but May will be *so* vexed!'

Cameron suppressed a flicker of impatience. 'Forget about May. I need you to look after Sophie. Can you do that?'

'What? But you can't go yet! What about my purse?'

'You don't need your purse.'

'Yes I do. I—'

'Clemency, what would you do with a purse? You never go out.'

That brought her up short. 'I wasn't going out,' she said stubbornly. 'I was – practising.'

'Practising? For what?'

Frowning, she shook her head, as if she'd already said too much.

Then he remembered. The journey. The practice sessions. Oh, Clemmy, not now. 'Clemency,' he said firmly, 'it's time for you to give that up. You've got to stay here and look after Sophie. Surely you can see that?'

She shook her head, and two more hairpins clattered to the floor. A lock of grey hair came loose and tumbled over one shoulder.

'The fact is,' he said none too gently, 'there's no point to your journey. There never was. Your baby isn't in hell. Why should he be in hell? He didn't do anything wrong. He's in heaven. He's been there all along.'

She looked horrified. 'But that can't be right! May *told* me. She knows all about it. She—'

'May knows nothing about it. She isn't a priest. She's just a wicked old woman who likes to hurt people.'

She flinched. After decades in semi-darkness, reality was clearly too much for her. He wished he'd had the sense to tell her this years ago.

'Listen to me,' he said with mounting impatience. 'I don't have time to explain everything now, but I'll send Reverend Prewitt to you, and he'll tell you all about it, and you can ask him whatever you like, and then you'll know that I'm telling the truth. But just for now you've got to put it out of your mind, and think about Sophie. She needs you. She's had a bad time of it. Don't let her down.'

Her face worked. 'I don't know what to *do*. May will—'

'May will what?' said Great-Aunt May.

359

Oh hell, thought Cameron.

Great-Aunt May stood at the entrance to the ballroom, her hands serenely clasped at her waist. Despite the heat she wore a high-collared evening gown of iron-grey moiré, and long, narrow-fingered gloves of pewter kid. From the silver chain at her waist hung a collection of keys like those of a medieval châtelaine.

Her inflamed blue gaze flickered over Clemency, lingered briefly on Sophie, then locked with Cameron's. 'What', she said, 'is the meaning of this?'

'I should have thought that was obvious,' he said. 'I've brought Sophie home.'

May permitted herself the slight tightening of the lips that was her version of a smile. 'Against her guardian's wishes, no doubt.'

'Well, of course.'

May inclined her head as if he had paid her a compliment. 'Then she shall be returned in the morning.'

He opened his mouth to contradict her, but Clemency got there before him.

'Oh no!' she exclaimed. 'No no *no*! I absolutely will not allow that!' She rustled over to Sophie and plumped herself down in the adjacent chair. Then she realized whom she had just countermanded, and her jaw dropped.

'That will do, Clemency,' said Great-Aunt May, keeping her eyes on Cameron. 'Now go to your room, remove that preposterous attire, and dress yourself appropriately for dinner.'

Clemency drew a deep breath, and sat her ground. Her face was pink, and she was clearly astonished at her own audacity. After a moment she frowned and reached beneath her, and pulled out a small rectangle of white plush embroidered with pearls. 'Why, *here* it is! Look, Sophie, my evening purse! Isn't it beautiful? Do you see all the tiny pearls? And the dear little silver chain with the ring on it to fit over my finger, so that it won't get lost?'

Cameron glanced from her to Great-Aunt May, and realized with a sinking feeling that he couldn't leave Sophie with them. Which meant that he would have to take her all the way down to Olivia Herapath before he could even make a start for Providence. And with every passing minute, he was becoming more uneasy about Madeleine. The more he thought about Sinclair's 'rest cure', the less he liked it.

He was wondering if Sophie was well enough for another long drive, and whether he could persuade Doshey to give him a fresh horse from the old man's stables, when he was astonished to hear the familiar tapping of a cane approaching across the ballroom floor. My God, he thought, but he's in Kingston. Isn't he?

Then Jocelyn walked out onto the gallery, and drew himself up like a battered old eagle as he caught sight of Cameron and came to an abrupt halt beside Great-Aunt May.

The old man had always possessed impeccable self-control, and it did not fail him now. He contrived to look only mildly irritated at seeing Cameron in the gallery: as if he were merely an unwelcome caller who had arrived inconveniently close to the dinner hour. 'What the deuce', he said, 'is all this rumpus?'

May lifted her chin and waited for vindication. Clemency glanced fearfully from Cameron to the old man. Sophie ignored them all in favour of the evening purse which Clemency had placed in her lap.

Plainly, Jocelyn had only just arrived, for he hadn't had time to change out of his travelling clothes. He looked dusty and exhausted, and very much his age. But he took in May's glacial expression, Clemency's extraordinary outfit, and Sophie's sallow, unsmiling presence without a flicker. Finally, his gaze returned to Cameron. The sunbleached eyes gave nothing away.

For ten years they had avoided coming face to face. In town they always made sure to cross over to the other side of the street; at the few social events they both attended, they circled one another like hostile mastiffs unwilling to engage in an out and out fight.

For ten years Cameron had thought about this moment. He had worked out exactly what he would say, and how he would act. Now all that deserted him. 'I thought you were in Kingston' he muttered.

'Evidently not,' snapped the old man. 'I had a wire from Clemency. Now answer the question.'

Cameron gestured at Sophie, whose head was still bowed over the evening purse. 'Sinclair sent her to Burntwood. I—'

'I know that,' barked Jocelyn. 'It's a rum do, but there we are. You seem to have forgotten that he is her legal—'

'I don't care about that. What he did was wrong.'

'Wrong?' The silver brows drew together. 'And I suppose you're the man to decide that?'

Cameron bit back a retort. My God, he thought, some things never change. All it takes is two minutes, and we're at each other's throats.

In the ballroom, the grandfather clock struck the quarter-hour. An elderly helper in evening uniform appeared in the doorway and hovered at his master's elbow, with a salver bearing a crystal tumbler of whisky and soda. Jocelyn dismissed him with a jerk of his head, and turned back to Cameron. 'Be so good as to leave. We dine in a quarter of an hour. I'm dashed if I see any reason to put that off.'

'What about Sophie?' said Cameron.

The old man blinked fiercely. 'Not your concern. Sinclair's responsibility.'

Cameron drew a deep breath. 'Don't you think she's yours as well?'

Again the sharp eyes met his. It was impossible to tell what he was thinking. 'The child is Sinclair's responsibility,' he repeated, as if it were an article of faith.

A quarter to eight, thought Cameron, and if I don't cut the Gordian knot soon, we'll be here till next week. 'I don't have time to argue,' he said shortly. 'So I'm just going to tell you the truth, and then you can work out what to do.' He glanced at Sophie, then back to the old man. 'That's your grandchild. That's Ainsley's daughter.'

Jocelyn's eyes never wavered from his own.

From the corner of his vision, Cameron saw Clemency rise to her feet, then sit back doll-like in her chair. May had gone very still. Only Sophie remained oblivious, her fingers moving slowly over the pearl-encrusted plush.

'Jocelyn,' May said calmly, 'this is outrageous. Sinclair is the only one who—'

'Be *quiet,*' snapped Cameron. 'Haven't you done enough harm already?'

May's eyes widened with shock.

'You knew who she was,' Cameron told her. 'You've known for days. But you didn't see fit to tell Jocelyn – or, heaven help us, to get her out of that God-awful place.'

May opened her mouth to reply, then shut it again.

Cameron turned back to the old man. 'I need your assurance that Sophie stays here. No matter what Sinclair says.'

Jocelyn's shoulders seemed to have lost some of their parade-ground stiffness. He put out his hand and grasped the back of a chair.

Cameron saw how he clutched at it, and felt contrite. 'I'm sorry,' he muttered, 'I was too blunt. Madeleine was going to tell you, she'd have made a better job of it.'

Jocelyn dropped his gaze and scowled at the floor. 'You've said your piece. Now go.'

'Not until you promise that Sophie stays here.'

Jocelyn made no reply. Cameron wondered if he'd heard.

'Jocelyn,' said May, 'this has gone far enough. I will not tolerate—'

Enough!' barked Jocelyn.

Cameron didn't see the look which passed from the old man to May, but a moment later she dropped her gaze, and her gloved hands sought the chain about her waist, and Cameron saw how her fingers shook. If it had been any other woman, he would have pitied her.

Still grasping the back of the chair, the old man turned, and for the first time since Cameron had told him, he looked at Sophie. There was no softening of his expression. His face was concentrated and inward-looking. Perhaps he was beginning to feel the truth of what he had learned. Or perhaps, punctilious to the last, he was making up his mind to obey Sinclair's wishes, regardless of his own inclination, and send her back to Burntwood.

'What will you do?' said Cameron.

Jocelyn did not reply.

'Jocelyn—'

'I told you to leave.'

'Well I won't. Not until I know what you intend to do. Dammit, Jocelyn, if you mean to send her back to that place, I'll take her down to Falmouth right now, and have Olivia Herapath put her up.'

The old man ignored him. He couldn't seem to take his eyes off Sophie.

She raised her head from Clemency's evening purse and gave him her solemn stare. Her lips moved, but no sound came.

'What's that you say?' Jocelyn said sharply. 'Speak up. I can't hear a word.'

Her eyebrows drew together in a frown. She tried again. 'Uncle Jocelyn,' she said.

The old man blinked. His hand tightened on the back of the chair.

'They burnt Pablo Grey.'

There was a silence. Then Jocelyn cleared his throat. 'Did they,' he said. He let go of the chair, and squared his shoulders, and passed one liver-spotted hand over his waistcoat. 'Well. I dare say it was quick.'

Sophie's eyes never left his face. 'Can we build a monument?'

CHAPTER THIRTY-TWO

The john crow had been back three times, but after the moon had risen it hadn't come again. Patoo had taken over. His soft hoo-hoos echoed from hill to hill, and once, Madeleine thought she saw him: a darker darkness cutting across the stars.

In Jamaica the country people believe that if an owl flies into the house, a death will follow soon. Patoo frightens them; many don't even like to hear his voice.

He didn't frighten Madeleine. Nothing frightened her now. Not even the ghost that crouched in the corner, watching her hammer flat the last section of leg-iron.

She put down the stone and sat back on her heels to catch her breath. Mosquitoes whined in her ears. Moonlight cast strange shadows on the walls, and turned the blood on her fingers black. And at the edge of her vision, the ghost watched. A shape out of darkness, it only took form when she looked away, and dissolved into rubble when she turned to stare. But when she resumed her work it always drifted back.

There had been a time when it had frightened her. She had been frightened of everything, then. Of the darkness. Of the centipedes. Of the bones that crumbled chalkily beneath her hands. But now she felt no more fear. No more hunger. No more pain from the gash in her arm. Even thirst had become just another companion. Nothing was left except the stone in her hand and the fragments of iron she had found in the rubble, and her determination to get out.

A gecko scuttled down the moon-blue wall. She followed its progress for a moment, then raised her head and scanned her handiwork for flaws.

Before dark, she had added as much as she could to the crude progression of hand- and footholds from which she had fallen some hours before. She had managed about ten feet of it: four small ledges of stone, and three of iron – each jutting out no more than an inch, but wedged in securely enough to take her weight. Above that, the slope of the wall became gentler, which ought to make it easier – if she could get that far.

For that part she planned to rely on the last three pieces of stone which she would carry in her petticoat shoulder-pouch, and on the two best pieces of shackle. These she meant to use repeatedly, avoiding the risk of dropping them by tying them to her wrists with her bootlaces. There was no chance of her boots coming off during the climb. Her feet were too swollen for that.

But there wasn't much time. At present, the moon shone full upon this side of the sink-hole, but soon it would be in shadow. And she couldn't risk waiting till dawn, for by then she would be too weak to make the climb.

She tied the second bootlace to her wrist, and got to her feet, and from its corner the ghost watched in silent approval. She acknowledged it with a nod. Then she shouldered the pouch and began to climb.

He kept seeing his wife's face peering up at him.

There had been something animal in her expression. Yes, an animal in a trap, with no true awareness of its fate. But it was better so. Wasn't it?

Still in his riding-clothes, he lay on the bed and watched the slatted amber sunlight on the floor, and longed for sleep. He had never felt so exhausted. And yet he couldn't relax. His hands twitched. His thoughts teemed.

When would this torment end? He had never wanted her harmed. He had never wanted anyone harmed. He had never *done* any harm.

This is some sort of trial, he told himself. A terrible trial which God has designed for me. And it is because of who I am that I suffer so. If I were coarse and unthinking, I shouldn't be tormented. It is because I am finer, purer, and cleaner in spirit, that this is such torture.

He rolled onto his side and reached for the small amber phial, and poured enough chloral into an inch of water to put him out. He drank it in one slow swallow, and lay back and waited for the coming of the golden certainty.

The first wave was always the best. Soft warm radiance warming his flesh. Clarity and confidence suffusing his limbs. Power in his veins. He took deep, even breaths, and peace bathed him in its golden glow.

The truth is, he told himself, you haven't done anything wrong. All you did was try to help her. You risked your life in trying to reach her. But it was not to be. God *intended* you to fail.

He shut his eyes and drifted away, cradled on the gentle swell of a sunlit ocean.

The chimes of the clock wrenched him back to consciousness. He was in darkness. What time was it? Where was he? His head ached from the chloral. He felt oppressed by some nameless dread.

He rolled off the bed and stumbled to the window. Outside, the moon had risen, and all was peaceful and still. He must have slept for hours.

He remembered returning to Providence in the heat of the afternoon, and ordering tea. Then paying off the housekeeper and the stable boy and sending them away to spend the Free Come holiday with their families. And after that, nothing.

As he stood at the window, he heard the skitter of a horse's hooves down below. He couldn't make out much through the louvres, but as he froze, breathless and horrified, he heard the unmistakable sound of boots hitting the dust as a man dismounted. The clink of a bridle slung over a hitching-post.

He wiped the sweat from his face. No-one ever came this way. The track ended at Providence. Dr Valentine was safely in Falmouth, and the old man in Kingston; nor could it be a messenger from Fever Hill, for no black would ride like that in the dark.

He cast about for a weapon, and saw the candlestick beside the bed. As he took hold of it, he caught sight of himself in the looking-glass. His face was pale and resolute, his grip on the candlestick firm. The thing to remember, he told himself, is that no-one knows where she is.

Softly he made his way through the moonlit house towards the gallery.

A man had just climbed to the top of the steps. He was tall, with unruly fair hair, and although his back was turned, Sinclair knew him at once.

Heart pounding, he withdrew into the shadows behind the door. His dismissal of the servants now seemed the purest madness. He was alone in the dark with a man who coveted his wife and wished him nothing but ill.

Then he saw the horse tethered to the mounting-stone at the foot of the steps, and his apprehension turned to horror. The animal was sickeningly familiar: a big, clean-limbed grey hunter from Fever Hill. The old man's horse.

He spiralled down from a great height. His brother had been at Fever Hill – had been *received* at Fever Hill – and had so contrived to worm his way back into the old man's affections that he had come away with his very *horse*.

His skin prickled with loathing. His hand on the candle-stick became slick with sweat. In that moment he understood the urge to kill. He understood Cain.

His brother turned and saw him. 'You're up late,' he remarked.

Sinclair stepped out into the gallery. 'And you, brother,' he said.

His brother indicated the candlestick. 'You're not going to do much damage with that.'

Sinclair licked his lips. 'A curious notion. I was seeking a fresh candle.' He put the candlestick on a side table, and placed both hands on the back of a chair. Calm, calm, he told himself. This fool is no match for you.

But he couldn't get that image out of his mind. He pictured

his brother and the old man in the library, standing before the great oil painting of Strathnaw: smoking cigars and drinking whisky; planning the future; laughing at him. *Cameron, my boy, you were always the one I wanted for my heir. It was never Sinclair.*

Out loud he said, 'What brings you here at this hour?'

'I was worried about Madeleine,' said his brother, matching his conversational tone. 'I didn't like the sound of your rest cure.'

How blunt, thought Sinclair, how lacking in subtlety. 'I don't see why,' he replied. 'It was – is – entirely appropriate. And under the strict supervision of Dr Valentine of Cornwall Street.'

'Dr Valentine of Cornwall Street,' repeated his brother with solemn mockery. 'And is that where the good doctor is now? In Cornwall Street?'

'I expect him back in the morning.' It occurred to him that he was allowing his brother to cross-examine him, whereas an innocent man – or rather, a man with nothing to conceal – would have been outraged at such presumption. But his mind was only half engaged, still churning over the hideous notion of his brother at Fever Hill. The return of the prodigal son.

'Where is she?' said his brother.

Sinclair moistened his lips. 'By "she", I take it that you mean my wife.'

'Where is she?' said his brother again.

Sinclair's hands tightened on the back of the chair. 'My wife,' he said, 'is no longer here.'

He was gratified to see his brother's astonishment. Yes, he told him silently, you weren't expecting that, were you? You thought you could just ride up here and see her at any time of the day or night. How disagreeable to find that you cannot. 'She left,' he volunteered. 'She took a horse and left.'

'When? Where did she go?'

The exchange had put fresh heart into him. This was going to be easy. Why had he worried? 'I cannot be sure,' he said. 'But I imagine that she has returned to Fever Hill.'

His brother shook his head. 'I've just come from there.'

Sinclair allowed a silence to grow. Then he said, 'And what took you to Fever Hill?'

His brother threw him an impatient look. 'I brought Sophie back. And yes, I know you're her guardian, but I told the old man who she is, so from now on I don't think he'll be so ready to let you play the autocrat.'

Sinclair swayed. The child and the old man. Together. The child knew about the pickney. If she told the old man— He felt sick. Terror buzzed in his skull like an angry wasp.

No. Wait. If she had said anything, then his brother would be crowing about that too. Calm, calm.

He ran his fingers over his throat. 'I thought the old man was in Kingston.'

'Clemency sent him a wire,' snapped his brother. 'Now, when did Madeleine leave?'

His thoughts raced. There was still time. The child would be asleep all night; she couldn't tell anyone yet.

'What's the *matter* with you?' said his brother.

'What?'

'I've asked you three times, when did she leave?'

Sinclair thought for a moment. 'Some time around dawn.'

'*Dawn?* What the hell have you been doing?'

'Looking for her,' he said. He squared his shoulders. 'I have spent all day, brother, looking for her.' He indicated his dusty riding-clothes. 'As you can see, I've only just returned.'

Again that surge of power. This was easy. All he had to do was keep his nerve.

'Why didn't you send for help?' said his brother.

'I did. I sent the housekeeper and the stable boy. Which is why they are no longer here.'

His brother rubbed his hand over his face. 'D'you have any idea where she was heading?'

'North,' said Sinclair without hesitation. 'A field-hand saw her heading north. Which is why I assumed she was making for Fever Hill. But she must have taken a wrong turn, for when the field-hand saw her she was on one of the cane-roads around Caledon. No doubt that's why your paths didn't cross.'

His brother swallowed it whole. It was beautiful. 'Saddle

your horse,' he said, with that soldierly decisiveness which Sinclair had always detested. 'We're going to find her.'

'In the dark?'

'There's a moon.'

'My horse is lame.'

'Saddle another.'

Sinclair studied him for a moment. 'Very well,' he said. 'I shall fetch my hat.'

Why had he worried? This sugar-planter was no match for him. He would pass the test which God had designed for him, and he would prevail.

He *deserved* to prevail. He was an innocent man.

Still some hours till the sun comes up, and Evie has dropped asleep in the house, and Grace is sitting out on her step, sitting in the moonshine and looking at that fresh new grave at the back of the yard.

They planted him by the garden cherry tree, for he liked garden cherry; though not as much as he liked star apple. Only she got no star apple tree in her yard.

She got her pipe ready for a little smoke, and she got her bankra ready to do a little obeah, to ask again for a sign who kill her boy. She asked before, but no sign came. Maybe her heart still too confuse.

If only she could clean up this confusion in her heart. But she so tangle-up with mourning and worry-head and black monster hate, she about reaching her rope end. Can't find a way to balance off the feelings. Sagging tired and full of worry-head about Evie – that child not said two words since it take place – and black monster hate at whoever done this thing to her boy.

Strange, strange, the way things work out. The eve of First August just drawing to a close, and usually on that night, everybody singing and partying, to mark the day they mancipate the slaves. But not this night; not here roundabout. This First August eve, they been too busy keeping nine-night for Victory.

Last week, soon as word of the death went out, everybody came for the burying. Brother, sister, cousin, aunt. From all over Trelawny and from foreign they came. Moses from Eden, and Daniel Tulloch from Parnassus, cousin Martin that preach at Rio Bueno, and sister-in-law Lily, that teach Baptist school at Simonstown, and do a little myal on the side.

The nanas they helped Grace and Evie make the coffin-shirt, and dug the grave at the back of the yard. They dug deep, for pickney duppy stronger than a man's, and you got to make damn sure that he stay put in there.

They raised the coffin three times high before they laid him in the ground, and planted pigeon peas by the stone to hold him firm. Then they swept out the dead room, and left the lamp burning right through till the nine-night, so the duppy would know where to come.

But *when* to hold the nine-night? That the question. And it cost Grace some worry-head, figuring out what actual true day he died. In the end, Miss Clemmy said, Grace, you just ask your heart; your heart tell you the truth. And Miss Clemmy was right about that. Grace looked in her heart and counted to nine from there on up, and when it came out for the eve of Free Come, she knew it correct for true.

So for nine nights that pickney duppy been walking round-about, throwing rockstone, making trouble, putting hand on people. Then on the nine-night, this same night, he came home again, and everybody arrived back at the house, to keep him entertain.

Strange, strange. Grace done nine-nights out a count for other people, but she can't get use to the *strangeness* with her own self son. Course, that pickney duppy *not* her son, she know that. But still he is, and that the strangeness of it. Duppy not the *good* part of him: the good part gone way off in the Up (if there is a Up, and Grace not too sure, thinks maybe not, since not a damn thing ever came down from there except rain). It the bad part left down here which becomes the duppy. Everybody got a bad part. And when you die, it slips loose and becomes duppy, and goes round making trouble.

So on the nine-night, everybody arrived again. Brought lot, lot a food. Currie land-crab and pepperpot, cowfoot and beans and bammy cakes, hot pickle and run down. Brought rum and sorrel and ginger wine, and coffee sweet with cocoanut milk. And Grace and Evie, too, they were cooking since dawn. Hard-dough and roast breadfruit, jerked hog and rice and peas, johnny cake and chocho pie and cassava pone. And duppy own feast, too besides.

Dark falls, and everybody sitting round in the dead room, eating, singing, telling Anancy story. Waiting for duppy to come. Duppy feast spread out on banana leaf in the middle, nobody touch.

And roundabout midnight, old Cecilia said, I feel him oh I feel him: hot wind rushing through. And people started to shiver and shake, and Evie was near to crying, but couldn't; she just said in small muffle-voice, Where? Where?

And old Cecilia felt him – but Grace she *seen* him too. And he was one dirty little duppy, that true to the fact. No shoe, no Sunday best for him. Just the saggy old blue pants he liked so much, and the yellow shirt that never kept one button more than a day. And that look on him face when he just *knew* he done wrong, and waiting for her to catch him a wallop.

So then came the time for Grace to shoo him out to the graves; to tell him Go way and never come back. But she couldn't do it. She must a done it time out a count at other people nine-nights, but this time, with her own self son, she couldn't get out a word. And old Cecilia seen that and took it on, to give Grace time to get her spirit back.

Duppy, said Cecilia loud and polite, we know you come. We glad you come. Myself two times. See, Duppy, we give you feast. Boil fowl and white rice and good white overproof rum. We do everything for you.

Then Cecilia looked to Grace, to see if she better yet. And Grace nodded, for she was ready to take it on from here. But it *hard*. Hardest thing she ever did in life. She stood up straight, and put on her strictest voice – like she meant it this time, or he for trouble true, and she said, Duppy! Go on to you rest now, and not to do we no harm. We no want to see you again, duppy. So no come back. Mind me now, I say mind me. Done!

Then they got up and shooed him out the house, and Grace watched him fade, fade into the yard. And right that last moment she so wanted to call him back – for though he a duppy, he still part of her boy. But instead she stood her ground and swallowed her spit, and let him go.

After that they removed the duppy feast into the yard, and put cross-mark charcoal on the door and window – and then it done, and people commenced to leave. And Cecilia said, Well Grace, we done with Victory now. We shooed him to the grave and we planted him good. So now he at peace.

Well, Victory at peace now. True. But Grace, she the mother. She never know peace again.

Out of her bankra, she takes an old syrup bottle of dirt from the new grave, and some parrot bones, and some camphor that Miss Clemmy gave. Still some good few hours till the sun comes up, and she's getting ready to ask again for a sign who done this thing. Could be any sort a sign. Bird on the roof. Man in the road. Mark in the dirt. She'll know it when it comes.

She gets up and goes inside – soft, so as not to wake Evie and brings out a little bowl of scrip-scraps of lizard parts to help things along.

He used to fascinate with lizard, when a baby. Always trying to touch one, never could; they always too quick. But how he laugh! Sitting in the dirt, watching them chasing each other round and round the yard, fighting at their fierce little lizard-wars. How he laugh, laugh and clap him fat little hands.

He grew up so quick. One day baby, next day riding jack-mule, digging yams, picking rat coffee to sell. Last September, first day of school, Grace watched him walking off to Salt Wash with Evie, and it the proudest day in life.

And this night, Free Come eve, was always the favourite with him and Evie both. Staying up late, telling story of Nana Semanthe in slave time, and of great-grandfather Caesar that got killed in Black Family War, that buckra call Christmas Rebellion. Telling story of how Grace named Evie after the First Woman, and Victory after victory, simple straight, like in the Book. 'Victory that overcometh the world.'

Victory that overcometh the world.

Well, that all dead-bury now.

Grace lights up her pipe and starts setting out her things, to ask again for a sign who done this thing. She knows obeah and myal and church matter, too. She knows all kind a ways to ask.

So sign go come for true.

CHAPTER THIRTY-THREE

She lay back, gasping and staring at the moon. She was so relieved that she wanted to retch.

A trickle of pebbles rattled down into the sink-hole, warning her that she was still on the edge. She rolled onto her front and half-crawled, half-dragged herself away. The bootlaces snagged on the ground and cut into her wrists. She stopped to untie them, but her fingers were raw and shaking, and she soon gave up.

Once again she lay back, and felt the warm earth beneath her, and the warm night flowing over her. She watched a wilderness of stars spinning towards her.

Gradually, she became aware of something else beneath the ring-ring of the crickets. A faint, continuous roar, just on the edge of hearing. Was it a sound, or a vibration in the earth?

She strained to listen. There it was again. A river? She held her breath. The Martha Brae had its source in the Cockpits. Was that what she could hear? If it was, and if she had the strength to climb to the top of that slope – if she could find the river, she could follow it out of the hills.

She stood up slowly, and her head swam. She hadn't eaten or drunk for at least eighteen or twenty hours. She took a deep breath of the warm night air, and smelt sweat and dust and the coppery tang of the blood on her hands.

Twenty feet ahead of her, the calabash tree loomed in the

moonlight. She made out the boulder where she had rested, a lifetime ago. Around it thorn bushes, and the spiky rosette of a wild pine.

In Sophie's gazetteer it said that if country people get lost, they can sometimes get a little moisture from a wild pine.

She stumbled over to it, and fell to her knees in the dust. The spiny leaves dug into her palms, and the plant clung stubbornly to the earth – she had to rock it from side to side to loosen it – but at last it came free with a fleshy snap.

She broke off an outer leaf, and then another. A trickle of moisture ran into her palm. It was no more than an eggcupful, stale and gritty with midges, but when she gulped it down her thirst came roaring back. She snapped off another leaf and sucked the bitter sap. It would have to do until she reached the river.

The cane-fields can be eerie at night. The ghostly white slash of the marled track cutting through the dark. The tall, whispering cane. The certainty that if you get into trouble, there is no help to be had for miles around. In the cane-fields at night, it's easy to believe in duppies, and in the sorcery that can take a man's shadow and nail it to a tree.

Cameron led his horse down to the irrigation ditch, and thought about Madeleine out here on her own. Why had he allowed Sinclair to take her to Providence? Why had he wasted so much time?

For two hours they had been working their way north through the hill-pastures of Turnaround and Corner Pen – *No, sah, nobody see Miss Maddy heah about* – and down into the lonely cane-pieces of the Queen of Spains Valley. And always Sinclair rode beside him: silent, and very slightly aggrieved. As if this were some elaborate game which had gone on for just a little too long.

Cameron glanced over his shoulder and saw his brother standing at the top of the ditch, watching him.

He can't have done anything to her, Cameron told himself. He isn't capable of that. Of many things, perhaps. But not of that.

So why did he feel this tightening in the chest? This sense that events had jumped track and were veering out of control?

Above him, Sinclair tapped the reins against his thigh. 'This is pointless. I'm going back. I shall start again when it's light.'

Cameron led his horse back up the side of the ditch. 'You never expected to find her out here, did you?'

Sinclair put his head on one side. 'Of course not. How could one expect to find anything out here in the middle of the night?'

Cameron suppressed the urge to grab him by the collar and shake him. 'That's not what I meant,' he said. 'Tell me where she is.'

'If I knew that, why would I—'

'Tell me.'

Sinclair's pointed tongue came out and moistened his lips, but he made no reply.

I can't take much more of this, thought Cameron. He opened his palm and studied it, and clenched it into a fist.

He watched Sinclair draw the reins over his horse's head and put his foot in the stirrup and hoist himself into the saddle. 'For all I know,' said Sinclair, 'she's at Eden. Waiting for you.'

'For all you know, she's out here on her own in the dark.'

'We don't know that.'

'Well damnit, man, you said she was heading this way.'

'And perhaps she arrived safely at Fever Hill. Why don't you go and find out, brother? That's what you want, isn't it?'

Cameron ignored that. 'For a man whose wife is missing,' he said, 'you're showing remarkably little concern.'

'Why? Because I don't indulge in vulgar displays of emotion?'

'What's wrong with you? Don't you care?'

'Not nearly as much as you.'

Cameron lost his temper. One moment he was watching Sinclair gather the reins, and the next he was grabbing him by the belt and hauling him out of the saddle and throwing him to the ground with a *whump* that sent the horses squealing and the dust flying up.

A red haze misted his vision. He looked at Sinclair lying on his back, and as if it were really happening, he saw himself flipping him over and digging his knee into his back and grabbing him by the hair and pounding his face to a pulp. The blood roared in his ears. His palms itched to do it. It took a massive effort to put his hands behind his back, and step away.

Sinclair sat up gingerly, coughing the dust from his lungs. 'Have you completely lost your reason?' he said.

'Tell me where she is.'

Still coughing, Sinclair brushed the dust from his riding jacket. 'I don't *know* where she is,' he spat.

Cameron reached down and grabbed him by the collar and hauled him to his feet, and Sinclair's arm flashed out, and Cameron felt warmth and wetness opening up across his chest, and looked down and saw a dark diagonal stain blotting his shirt.

He dropped Sinclair and took a step back. Christ, he thought, he's got a knife.

He put a hand to his ribs, and it came away wet. A long, shallow slash that was already burning like the devil.

That's a good sign, isn't it? he told himself. It's the ones that don't hurt that mean trouble.

Sinclair had staggered back, and was staring at the knife in his hands.

'Put that thing down,' said Cameron.

'*You* attacked *me*,' muttered Sinclair. 'It wasn't my fault.'

'It never is,' snarled Cameron. 'Now put the bloody thing down.'

Sinclair shot him a look of pure hatred. 'You're glad I did it, aren't you?'

'What?'

'Now you can run squealing back to the old man, and tell him how wicked I am, how unfit to inherit—'

'Oh, for Christ's sake, no more about the inheritance—'

'What, you expect me to believe that you don't care?'

'Well I don't!' roared Cameron. 'Take it! Take the whole

bloody estate! I don't want it! I just want to find Madeleine!'

'Oh, you do want it,' cried Sinclair, 'You do! It's all you ever think about!'

Cameron moved forward and made a feint with his right hand, and Sinclair went for it, and with his left Cameron grasped his brother's wrist and gave it a vicious twist, and with a howl Sinclair dropped the knife, and Cameron caught it.

Now it was his turn to look down at the knife in his hands.

'You'd do it, wouldn't you?' cried Sinclair. He had fallen to his knees, cradling his wrist against his chest. 'Your own brother. And you'd kill me like a dog in the road.'

Cameron heard the night wind whispering through the dark cane. He saw the moonlight glinting on the still water of the ditch. He sensed the silent watchfulness of miles and miles of empty fields.

He remembered as if it were yesterday what it had felt like to kill. The soft elasticity of flesh giving way to iron; the terror and the disgust, and the incredible feeling of power.

'Your own brother,' whispered Sinclair. 'Like a dog in the road.'

Cameron looked from his brother's clammy face to the dull grey metal in his hand. Then he turned and flung the knife as far as he could into the cane. 'Get out of my sight,' he said.

The wild pine water had made her thirsty again, but it had also sharpened her mind. Sitting with her back against the calabash tree, she could think beyond footholds and hand-holds for the first time in hours.

The river is the first thing, yes. Follow the voice of the river. It will be light soon. And it doesn't sound too far. Perhaps a mile or so?

Find it. Sink into it. Drink until you can't drink any more. Roll around in that slippery red mud until you're sodden and cold, yes actually cold . . .

Then what?

Food and shelter and clothes and Sophie.

She struggled to recall the map of the Northside in

Jocelyn's library. From its source in the Cockpits, the Martha Brae made a great northwesterly loop towards Fever Hill, then veered east towards Eden for a mile or so, before once again turning north for Falmouth and the sea. She had a hazy picture of a bridge somewhere at the edge of the hills, and a fork in the track: one branch going north towards Fever Hill, the other east towards Eden.

At least – she thought there was a bridge. Or had she only imagined that?

It didn't matter. She knew what to do. She must find the river and follow it to Eden, and then make Cameron get Sophie back. It didn't matter that he had already refused. He would not refuse again. She wouldn't let him.

And what about Sinclair? What if he came looking for her?

She brushed that aside. She couldn't think about it now.

The crickets were ringing the low peal of the hour before dawn. The voice of Patoo echoed through the hills. In an hour or so it would be light.

Still with her back against the tree, she struggled to her feet. Something tilted beneath her heel, and she nearly lost her balance. She looked down to see what it was. It was small and silver-blue, and it had a cold metallic gleam.

The peace of the night blew away on the wind. She hadn't realized until now that she had been afraid of this thing. And afraid of herself, and of what she might do with it.

She stooped to retrieve it, and her fingers closed on the incongruous blue steel of Ben's gun.

Sinclair rode back to Providence shaking with humiliation and rage.

His mind teemed with fearful images. His wife's animal gaze. The crippled child telling the old man everything. The mockery in his brother's eyes as he threw away the knife. *I don't care about the estate.*

'You do care,' Sinclair whispered. 'You do.' He was so angry that he could scarcely breathe. Nothing was any good if his brother didn't care.

By four o'clock the hunting lodge at Providence loomed into sight. He ran up the steps to the gallery and poured himself a brandy and soda, and drank it pacing up and down. He had been tempted to go straight to Fever Hill – he'd even ridden that way at first, to throw his brother off the scent. But he knew that to go to Fever Hill now would be a mistake.

He wasn't safe yet. He would not be safe until he had gone back to the sink-hole and seen for himself that she was dead. Then he would be free to go to Fever Hill and deal with the child, and put an end to his brother's ambitions. Only then would he know peace.

The thought of going back into the Cockpits, alone and in darkness, was almost more than he could bear. But he told himself that this, too, was part of God's great test.

Cameron had been catastrophically wrong about Sinclair. He had been wrong about everything. And now, as he tracked his brother through the greyness before dawn, he fought the urge to overtake him and thrash the truth out of him.

It wouldn't work. For reasons he didn't understand, Sinclair would never tell him what he knew.

They were on a narrow track that wound ever deeper into the Cockpits. Why? Presumably because she had come this way – but why into the Cockpits, and why east? Towards Burntwood? Ah yes, that would be just like her. You won't help me get my sister back? Well fine. I'll do it myself. And if that means crossing the Cockpits on my own, then so be it.

He had been such a fool. What did it matter that she had lied to him? What did it *matter*?

He felt again that heaviness in his chest. The dread at what he might find.

The track became steeper, and he dismounted to lead his horse. The animal baulked at the slope, and as it tugged on the reins he felt the cut across his ribs opening up again. It was stiff and sore, and it made every breath hurt, but he was almost glad of it, for it kept him alert. He couldn't remember the last time he had slept; couldn't count the miles he'd ridden in the last twenty-four hours. And now this endless, unreal, stumbling journey into the Cockpits after a brother he'd never truly known until tonight.

He had been so blind. He had genuinely believed that Sinclair wasn't capable of harming her.

And what if she were the one who paid for that mistake?

The sky was beginning to lighten in the east when he crested the hill and found himself looking down into a dark hollow that seemed vaguely, troublingly familiar. Some distance below him he saw Sinclair's fair hair. He ducked behind a boulder, and watched Sinclair dismount and disappear round a bluff. It was too dark to see any more. He tied his horse to a thorn bush and started silently down the slope.

No sound of voices. No sound at all. Just the wind in the thorns and the distant hoot of an owl.

Sinclair emerged from behind the bluff – alone – and made for his horse, staggering a little. Cameron felt a cold wave washing over him. What had Sinclair seen down there? What had he done?

He watched Sinclair mount his horse and start briskly up the other side of the hollow. When he was gone, Cameron made his way down the slope and into the darkness at the bottom.

Day just about commence to light, and Grace must a dozed asleep, but then she comes awake with a start.

At first she thinks that everything fine: she sitting out on her step, neck little stiff, but everything fine. Then she sees the new grave by the garden cherry tree, and she knows it not fine, that it never be fine again.

Then she hears someone out in her yard. Who got the nerve to intrude on Victory nine-night? She starts up, hot and vex. Who there! she yells out. Go way! Get out a me yard!

A boy moves out from the shadows under the paw-paw trees. And Grace about to yell again, when she astonished to see that he buckra boy – only so poor and ripped about that he resemble dirty Congo nigger.

Hat in hand, he comes over to her, and she sees that he whistle-thin, with face tight-stretch and full of mourning, though he not like to show. And peculiar strange, him eye *green*, like puss-eye. Grace never put her sight on a boy like this, and she starts to consider if he some sort of sign.

Then she thinks again. This boy no sign. This just a damn intruding disrespectful buckra boy, and in her own self yard, on Victory nine-night.

Didn't I just tell you, she blazes out at him, get out a me yard!

But he just stands before her, straight and still. Not frighten. Not turn way him eye.

Sorry to trouble you, ma'am, he says, nice and polite. But Grace McFarlane the name you got?

Grace so surprise, she near forgets to stay vex. Cho! She says, with hand on hip. Where you from, boy, that you not know Grace?

I from foreign, ma'am, he says. He speaks polite, but Grace can see that he not accustom to speak polite. It costs him to try.

Where from foreign? she snaps out. From Kingston? You talk peculiar, boy!

He shakes him head. From island far way, ma'am. Ben Kelly the name I got.

He talks damn peculiar. And sounds more peculiar still when he tries talk potwah. Grace dislikes when buckra do that, for they only do it to crack a laugh – except for Cameron soldierman and Master Jocelyn, who both talk it since a boy. But this boy only does it for respect. And that all right.

She sits again on her step, and lights her pipe, and buckra boy stands and waits, full of respect. And that all right too.

She says, You walking late, puss-eye boy. This a bad place for buckra. Full a skull laughter and evilness and duppy.

Duppy? he says. That's like a ghost, yeh?

Hn! He not frighten easy; but he *un*easy, that plain to see. He takes deep breath and says, I got a deal to do with you, ma'am.

Grace so surprise, she near to choke on her damn pipe. A deal? What sort a deal she going to do with a meagre down-class mocho like this?

She about to blaze into him again, and he sees it, but still he decides to take a chance on life, and run on with what he got to say. You know the girl Sophie? he says. The sick girl up at the busha house? Well she thinks she's gone and lost her shadow.

Now Grace getting on for suspicious. What this buckra boy know about shadows?

Buckra boy lifts him head and says, I need for you to get it back.

Grace leans back and gives him a long, hard look. She says, You fooling me up, boy. Buckra begging after black medicine? Cho!

No, ma'am, he says, still respectful. I not fooling you up.

But Grace wants no more talk about little buckra girl. She wants no more talk at all. That fresh grave out in the yard, it staring, staring back at her. And all of a sudden her heart so full up with mourning and destroyful feeling, she about ready to burst.

Go *way*, she says. Get out a me yard.

But still he not to move. Just narrows him green eye, and says, Why won't you help, ma'am?

Damn, but he persistent! He just about wearing her down. Grace spits in the dust and says, All right, boy. I tell you why not, and then you go. Three reason why not.

She puts out three finger and starts counting off. First reason. Catch a shadow is trouble. Hear? Myal woman – that me – got to go at night to duppy tree where shadow nailed; got to give that tree eggs and rum, got to walk round and round singing to duppies that took shadow prisoner. Got to hold up bowl of water – do it right, just right – and maybe shadow jump in. Then got to run, shadow in water, all the way back. Wet cloth, put it on child head, and get shadow back inside. All that I got to do.

Second reason, says Grace, counting off on finger. Catch shadow, cost money. Cost six shilling. You got six shilling, boy? Don't appear to me you got six quattie. Not so?

Hn. He got no reply to that.

Third reason, she says. And best of all. Why I should help buckra child? Why I should help buckra child when my own self son dead?

By now Grace getting hot and vex, and wishing to hell this damn boy just get out a her yard.

But in her heart, she remembers that little buckra girl playing with her boy. Talking a stream, and telling him story. Making him laugh.

Too besides, that crazy child one time put hot quattie on her arm, just to discover whether buckra books tell the truth about if branding not to hurt.

So all this raises a crazy black confusion in her head till she don't know *what* to think. But still she hardens her heart. And she snaps out at him, So now you tell Grace a thing. You tell Grace why she *should* help little buckra girl.

And buckra boy looks at her long, long, and never turns way him eye. Because, he says, I got something you want.

That so surprises Grace, she drops her damn pipe, and for first time in days she cracks a laugh. She puts her hand on her hip and looks him up and down slow, slow, and she says, Boy, you got nothing I want. In a year or two, and maybe we see about that. But not this day. Oh, no.

But buckra boy just looks at her steady with him green puss-eye, and he says, Ma'am, you're wrong about that. You get Sophie's shadow back, he says, and I'll tell you who killed your boy.

CHAPTER THIRTY-FOUR

She was dizzy with hunger, and the chloral was making her sick. It was becoming harder to think in straight lines.

There was something important she had to do, but she couldn't remember what. Why was she out here, and why had she forgotten to put on her riding habit? What made her think she could tackle a jungle in her combinations?

As the sun rose, the heat became oppressive. Like an underwater swimmer she waded through the hot green shade. Bird calls echoed through the canopy. Mosquitoes whined in her ears. The crickets were deafening.

Strange how quickly the thirst had returned. Hours before, when she'd found the river, it had vanished in seconds. She had stumbled down the crumbling red banks and into the fast-flowing water, and in a few long, cool green swallows, the thirst had become a distant memory.

But then she'd forced herself back onto the track and started off again, and something had gone wrong. She'd been so absorbed in pushing through the undergrowth that she hadn't noticed that the track was veering away from the bank – until the moment when she'd turned, and the river wasn't there any more. She couldn't even hear it. She was alone in the high forest, with no idea where she was.

That had been hours ago, when it was just getting light. Since then she had been walking for ever. Pushing aside enormous waxen leaves crawling with ants; blundering through great glistening webs strung across the path.

The forest was a vast, indifferent presence, waiting to see if she would survive. A cinnamon-coloured streak shot across the path, and through the ferns she caught the feral red eye of a mongoose. She was in its world, not her own.

The revolver in its pouch bumped against her thigh. Why was it still there? She remembered standing on the river bank and deciding to throw it in. After that, nothing.

Her thoughts kept slipping back into the past. She brushed away tree-ferns like the one in the photograph of Eden on the piano. As she finger-combed her hair and plaited it clumsily into a braid, she was back at Cairngowrie House, lying on the apricot silk counterpane and watching her mother plaiting the same long, dark braid. Was she Madeleine or was she Rose?

At last she reached a clearing where dragonflies and hummingbirds swam in the dusty sunlight. Beyond the clearing the forest was thinning, and on a distant slope she saw a silk-cotton tree. Its great limbs were draped with strangler fig and Spanish moss, and orchids like little darts of flame.

Was that the Tree of Life? Had she reached Eden? Had she? *And deep in the forest stands the Tree of Life, and from its branches the creepers hang down to the ground, and at night after the rains they're speckled with fireflies, and you can smell the vanilla flowers and the sweet decay.*

Behind her a branch snapped. She spun round. But the clearing was empty.

Her mind flooded with clarity. She remembered why she was here and why she was frightened. Only Sinclair knew where she was. And if he found her, it was over.

Another twig snapped. She heard the clink of a bridle, and forgot to breathe.

She drew back into the shadows at the edge of the clearing. All was still. Only the dragonflies and the hummingbirds stirred. She waited. But nobody came.

It's all right, she told herself. There's no-one there. It's all right.

She stumbled out into the sunlight. Sharp, splintered light, and the rank smells of growth and decay. She made her way across the clearing to the deep shade on the other side, and stopped for breath beneath an ironwood tree. She tried to go on, but her legs wouldn't move. Black spots darted before her eyes.

Just a little rest, she told herself. A little rest, and then you can go on.

She curled up among the ferns beneath the tree and leaned back against the trunk and shut her eyes. She took deep breaths of the warm green air. She slept.

She dreamed she was back in the Forbidden Kingdom. She was curled up in the snow, watching Cameron riding away. He had almost disappeared from sight when she saw him turn his mount's head, and start back for her. She watched him dismount and come towards her through the long grass. 'I knew you would come,' she said.

'Thank goodness I've found you,' said Sinclair.

With a cry she woke up.

He stood on the path about eight feet away. He looked tense and frightened, and his eyes flickered over her, then darted away.

Sweat trickled down her sides. She sank her fingers into the leaf mould, and felt a tree root beneath her hand. Something real. Something to hold on to.

'Thank goodness I've found you,' he said again. Bizarrely, he sounded as if he expected to be thanked.

'You left me,' she said. 'You left me in that place.'

'I came as soon as I could.'

'Sinclair. I was down there all night.'

He blinked. 'I was delayed. When I reached Providence there was a message about your sister. She wanted to come home. I had to make arrangements to bring her back to Fever Hill.'

Did he truly expect her to believe that?

Behind him the clearing was weirdly peaceful. A dragonfly zoomed low over the ferns. Sinclair's horse put down its head and cropped the grass.

She wondered why he was keeping his distance. Perhaps it's the blood, she thought. Yes. That's it, the blood on your hands. He doesn't like the blood.

'Your sister is well,' he said, as if she had asked a question. 'Come. I shall take you to her.'

She pressed back against the tree.

'Come,' he said again.

'Why did you leave me in that place?'

'I didn't "leave" you.'

'Sinclair—'

Irritably he tossed his head. 'Why won't you believe me? Why won't you accept that what happened to that child was an accident?'

A cold wave washed over her. 'You said Sophie was safe. You said—'

'And so she is,' he snapped. 'You're always so eager to believe the worst! You never believe me. I'm your husband, you *should* believe me. It's your duty to accept what I say.'

She was hardly listening. *What happened to that child was an accident.* What did he mean? What had he done?

'I forgot about him,' he said tetchily. 'That's all. It was scarcely my fault. Why must you be so determined to tell the world?'

Her thoughts rearranged themselves in a swift, seismic falling into place. Victory in the hothouse. *I forgot about him. It was an accident.*

She remembered Sophie's silence after the little boy's death, and Sinclair's sudden decision to send her to Burntwood. She remembered what he had said at the sink-hole. *I can't let you tell anyone.*

It had a weird kind of logic, but it couldn't be true. What reason could he have for killing a child? He wasn't capable of such a thing. He wasn't violent. He was too fastidious for that.

And yet, she thought with a sudden sense of cold, he doesn't need to be violent for it to be true. All he needs is to have rolled a stone in front of a door and walked away. And he's good at walking away. You already know that.

She knew then that it was true. She had been wrong about him. Wrong, wrong, wrong.

'Enough of this nonsense,' he snapped. He put out his hand. 'Come with me at once.'

She drew her legs closer beneath her, and as she did so, the revolver in its pouch nudged her side.

Until then she had forgotten about it. But now in a heart-beat she took in its weight against her hip, and the fern brushing her calf, and the dappled sunlight on the path, and the oozing patches on Sinclair's throat where he had rubbed them raw. She took in the fact that she was alone with a man who had taken a life, and who perceived her as a threat; the fact that she had a weapon, and that she was going to have to use it. *Well, Maddy, we'll just have to do it on our own.*

I can't, she thought. I can't I can't I can't.

Yes you can, came the reply inside her head. You're a Durrant. This is what Durrants do. It's in your blood.

No-one will blame you for it. He left you to die, didn't he? He left a child to die, too.

And if you do it, everything falls into place. Sophie is safe, and you are free.

All this raced through her mind in the seconds while he waited on the path.

She slid her hand into the pouch, and her fingers closed on the smooth, warm steel. With a sense of disbelief she drew out the revolver and pointed it at him.

At any other time his astonishment would have been comical. His blue eyes widened, and his mouth fell open. He looked like an actor in a music-hall comedy.

With her back against the tree she struggled to her feet. She was shaking so much that she had to grasp the revolver in both hands to keep it steady. Am I holding it right? she thought. What do I do if I need to shoot? Just point and pull the trigger? Is that what I do? Is it?

'Turn round,' she said as levelly as she could, 'and go back the way you came. Walk. I'm taking the horse.'

He looked from her to the revolver, and back again. He seemed more vexed than alarmed. 'Have you taken leave of your senses? Give that to me at once.'

'Do as I say.'

'Don't be ridiculous. You're not going to—'

'I mean it, Sinclair.'

Please believe me, she told him silently. Please don't see

how terrified I am. Because this isn't a bluff. I really could use this thing.

And the worst of it – what frightened her most – was that she *wanted* to do it. All she had to do was squeeze the trigger – a single movement of one finger – and Sophie would be safe, and she would be free.

'Do you realize', he said, 'that you've just signed your own committal papers? Do you?'

'Go away,' she said.

'A deranged, half-naked woman pointing a weapon at her own husband? Do you know what they'll do to you? They'll lock you up for ever. You'll spend the rest of your life in a straitjacket.'

'Go *away*,' she whispered.

'A straitjacket,' he repeated, and started towards her.

She took aim and fired.

Cameron found her in a clearing, curled up beneath an iron-wood tree. In the green shade her face had an underwater pallor. He thought she was dead.

Then she opened her eyes and gave him a dark, unfocused stare, and the world tilted back into place.

He left his horse and fell to his knees beside her and gathered her into his arms. 'My God,' he said, 'my God.'

He felt her fingers digging into his back, her breath warm on his neck.

'You're shaking,' she said.

'No.'

'Yes. You are.'

He tightened his grip. He didn't want to let her go. He wanted to tell her what it had been like to see her lying there dead, but his throat had closed, and he couldn't get out the words.

She twisted out of his arms and touched his face with her fingers. Then she saw the scab on his ribs. 'What's this?'

'Nothing. I – got in a fight.'

She looked at him with solemn eyes, and he wondered if she was in shock. He had read that when people are in shock their pupils dilate. But her eyes were too dark to tell.

She wore only some kind of cambric undergarment, its elaborate pin-tucks and satin ribbons bizarrely at odds with the scratches on her arms and shins. Her feet were bare. She had taken off her boots and placed them neatly by her head.

'A fight?' she said. 'When? With whom?'

He took off his shooting jacket and put it round her shoulders. 'It doesn't matter. It's all right now. It's all right.' He knew that he was saying that to reassure himself.

For hours he had lived with the terror that she was dead. From that first moment when he'd stumbled down to the edge of the sink-hole and seen the pale, crumpled muslin at the bottom, and thought it was her. Then tracking Sinclair, knowing that his brother was tracking her. *Why* had he wasted so much time at the sink-hole? Why had he given Sinclair a head start?

Still sick with relief, he went to his horse and unhooked the water bottle. When he gave it to her, she took it in both hands and drank with the concentration of an animal. Her fingers were raw and crusted with blood, and round each wrist was a narrow cut that mystified him.

He tried to imagine what she had been through; how she had managed to get out of that hole on her own. My God, he thought, any man who calls them the weaker sex doesn't know women.

He took out his handkerchief and soaked it in water, and cleaned her hands as gently as he could. He seemed to find it far more painful than she.

He said, 'I heard a shot.'

She nodded.

'What happened?'

She sat back on her heels and clasped her arms about her waist, and he realized that far from being in shock, she was hanging onto her composure by a thread. 'I thought I could kill him,' she said. 'It turned out that I couldn't. I'm not – not who I thought I was. So I shot the tree instead.'

He followed her glance and saw a branch of wild almond hanging brokenly about fifteen feet up.

He scanned the empty clearing, and felt a prickle of unease. There was nothing to indicate that it had happened as she'd said. No sign that Sinclair had been in the clearing: no tracks, no horse manure, and most telling of all, no gun. That branch could have snapped in a strong wind or a heavy rain; that shot could have come from anywhere. Sound does strange things in the Cockpits. Besides, where would she have got a gun? It didn't make sense.

'What happened then?' he said.

She hunched her shoulders against the memory. 'He was terrified. He didn't realize that I'd missed on purpose. He ran back to his horse and rode away.'

'Where? Where did he go?'

'I don't know. Didn't you meet him on the path?'

He hesitated. 'Perhaps he took a different one. There are several in this part of the forest.'

She was watching him as he said it, and he saw the understanding dawn in her face. 'You don't believe me,' she said. 'I'm telling the truth. He was here.'

'I know. I—'

'Why don't you believe me?'

He put his hand on her shoulder but she shook it off. She reached for one of her boots and threw it at him. 'There,' she said. 'Now d'you believe me?'

Inside was a small Lee-Remington service revolver. In disbelief he took it out and emptied the chamber into his palm. There was one round missing.

'It's because I lied to you, isn't it?' she said, her teeth chattering. 'I lied to you, so you don't believe me.'

'No,' he said, 'no, that's not it at all.'

'I told you why I lied. I tried to explain—'

'Madeleine, look at me. No, *look* at me. What happened before doesn't matter. None of it matters. All that matters is that you're safe.'

She was looking at him as if she wanted to believe him, but couldn't.

'Sophie's safe too,' he told her. 'I took her out of Burntwood, she's with the old man. We'll go down to Eden, and get you some food and some clothes, and then we can go to Fever Hill and see her. Everything will be sorted out.'

'How?' she said harshly. 'He'll tell them one version, and

I'll tell them another. If you didn't believe me, why should they?'

'He won't be able to wriggle out of this. He—'

'Yes he will. He'll say I'm mad, he'll say I'm making it up.'

'Madeleine—'

'He can do what he likes, Cameron. He's the husband. He has all the power.'

'Not after what he did—'

'Yes! Even then! Don't you see? What he did won't have any consequences. It won't *matter*. That's how it works.'

'Everything has consequences,' he said.

Sinclair was enormously relieved when he reached the edge of the forest. But as he emerged blinking into the glare, he was startled to find that he didn't recognize the way ahead. The hills were steeper than he remembered, and criss-crossed with paths no wider than goat-tracks.

Still, he thought, no harm done. A glance at the sun gave him a rough idea of a northward course, and he put his horse forward along the most likely track.

Despite the heat of the afternoon, he was in excellent spirits. The moment she had brought out that revolver, he had known that he was saved. A half-naked madwoman brandishing a gun. Even if she survived, no-one would believe a word she said. And the beauty of it was that the sister would be tarred with the same brush. Insanity in the family; who would have credited it? Poor Reverend Lawe. What he must have suffered!

In the distance he saw a black man meandering into view, and his spirits rose still further. Here was a dusky messenger, sent by the Almighty to guide him home.

The man was only a country black, barefoot and in ripped dungarees and tattered jippa-jappa hat, and so dull-witted that he took some moments to grasp Sinclair's shouted enquiry. But he had the primitive's sure sense of direction, and readily indicated the track towards Fever Hill, before his own path took him out of sight behind a spur.

Humming under his breath, Sinclair put his mount forward.

Poor, handsome young Reverend Lawe. All Society would sympathize after what he'd endured with that woman. It would be easy to find another wife. And she would bear him a son, and his brother would be vanquished, and he would come into his inheritance at last.

As he rounded a bend, an animal shot across the track. His horse reared, and he lost his stirrups and fell.

For a moment he lay winded, listening to his horse galloping off down the track. Then he sat up, wincing and rubbing his head. There seemed to be no serious harm done. A bruised hip, a slight contusion at the back of the head, and a scrape across the left palm. His horse, however, was nowhere to be seen.

He got to his feet and retrieved his hat, and brushed himself off.

Glancing round, he saw with a start that a little pickney girl, a mulatto, was crouching on the slope above, watching him.

A stroke of luck, he thought. Here's just the creature to run and retrieve the horse.

He called to her to come down, but to his surprise she did not respond. He repeated the command more sharply. Still no response. Like some diminutive pagan idol she squatted on the slope, her garish yellow frock tented over her knees. He wondered if she were deaf.

He was not the man to tolerate disobedience, but for once he decided to let it pass. It was too hot to climb the slope and discipline her.

A short, uncomfortably warm walk down the track revealed that his horse was nowhere to be seen. He would have to go back and collar the pickney after all, and compel her to run for help. But when he retraced his steps, he was exasperated to find that she was no longer there. It was a confounded nuisance, but he would have to make his way on foot.

It was another hour before he could bring himself to admit that he was lost. Instead of leaving the Cockpits, he seemed to be heading deeper into them. The track had become narrow and treacherous: to his left the ground rose steeply, but to his right it fell away into a dizzying ravine. That simpleton must have pointed out the wrong path.

He stopped to rest by a thorn tree. The air shimmered with heat. The glare off the white rocks pained his head. The rasp of crickets assailed his ears – and behind it, a great, watching silence that he found peculiarly disagreeable.

Once again he struggled to his feet, and this time his heart leapt to see a man on the track, some distance ahead. He was saved: the man was white. True, he was as ragged and filthy as any backwoods black, but he was a white man none the less.

'You there!' Sinclair shouted. 'Come down here at once!'

To his consternation, the man made no move to obey. He stood on the track with his hands at his sides, silently watching.

Outraged, Sinclair started up the slope towards him. But as he drew nearer he saw that the 'man' was in fact just a boy: dark, scrawny and sharp-faced, and with an unsettling resemblance to the urchin from Fitzroy Square.

Which, he told himself angrily, is arrant nonsense. It's just that they all look alike.

But he couldn't help glancing about him for that other one, the hunchback with the flame-coloured hair. And for one unnerving moment he even thought he saw him, some twenty yards behind. But it was only the little mulatto girl who had watched him earlier.

This time she was accompanied by two tall blacks: hill Negroes, by the look of them. Relief washed over him. Now there were grown men to assist him instead of children.

He turned to find that the white boy had also been joined by blacks: a full-grown male, and three squat and ancient Negresses. The male was unremarkable, except that he resembled the simpleton who had pointed out the wrong path; but the Negresses were hideous. They wore the gaudy headkerchiefs and strident yellow and green print gowns so beloved of their kind, and their skin was so black that he couldn't make out their features. Faceless black totems, they sat on the path: their stubby arms clasped beneath their enormous breasts, and their horny feet stuck out, the soles showing obscenely pink.

A scatter of pebbles behind made him spin about, and he overbalanced and nearly fell.

Some thirty feet above him, another Negress stood looking down with her hands on her hips. She was younger than the others, and slender; but although her skin was mahogany, not sable, the glare was too bright to make out her face.

'You there!' he shouted. 'Come down and help me at once!'

She made no reply. She just stood there with her hands on her hips, a pose he found both unsettling and astonishingly insolent.

He wondered why she felt entitled to behave with such freedom towards a white man, and opened his mouth to administer a sharp rebuke.

But as he did so, she began to pick her way down the slope towards him, and as she drew nearer, he recognized her. And understood.

CHAPTER THIRTY-FIVE

March 1896 – eight months later

The service had ended and the congregation was filing out. Madeleine was preparing to make her usual swift retreat to the carriage, when Jocelyn put out his hand and touched her wrist. 'One moment, my dear.'

She turned and looked at him, and knew immediately what he would say. 'I can't,' she said. 'I can't.'

'Just talk to him,' he said gently.

They drew aside to make way for Clemency and Sophie, and watched them leave the church and disappear into the glare of the porch, their heads already turned to one another as they embarked on the sermon and the congregation, and whatever other thoughts they had been prevented from sharing by two hours' enforced silence.

Madeleine said, 'You promised you wouldn't engineer a meeting.'

'And I have not,' said Jocelyn. 'But since this is the only time when you go out, there's a good chance that he'll be here.' He paused. 'After all,' he added, and the corners of his mouth turned down in his version of a smile, as they often did when he mentioned Cameron, 'it's what I'd do.'

She opened her reticule, then snapped it shut again. 'What do you think I should do?'

He sighed. 'I don't know, my dear. I don't know what you want. What I do know is that this – reticence – of yours, this unwillingness even to see him, isn't making either of you happy. You're both in pain. And I'd very much rather that you weren't.' He frowned and tapped his cane on the flags, as if he'd just made a damaging admission. 'So yes, I think it would be a capital idea for you to have it out.'

What he hadn't said was that her 'reticence', as he called it, was hurting him too. He had no son and no legitimate heir; all he had were two illegitimate granddaughters and one adopted son whom he was gradually allowing himself to love again. It would mean the world to him if she married Cameron.

And she wanted to. More than anything. But the risk was too great. And the only way round it that she could come up with was too shocking to mention to anyone. She couldn't even tell Sophie. Or Clemency. Or Dr Pritchard.

She watched Jocelyn square his shoulders and give himself a little shake. 'We shall be by the carriage,' he said as he picked up his hat.

'Jocelyn—'

'By the carriage,' he said firmly. 'Don't worry. We shan't go without you.'

Cameron arrived at the church shortly after the service had ended. He had brought Abigail with him. A mastiff for moral support. If he hadn't been so on edge, he would have smiled.

The previous evening he had taken his Scotch and soda and made a tour of the renovations to the house. The missing shingles had been replaced, the new bathhouse was nearing completion, and the master bedroom finally had a bed in it – although from habit he still slept out on the verandah. But as he'd stood in the golden evening light surveying what had been achieved, he'd wondered if it would all be for nothing.

Duke Street was busy with churchgoers, and he had to search for a place to leave Pilate. Through the dust of departing carriages he spotted Cornelius and Rebecca Traherne on the other side of the road, talking to Jocelyn, Clemency and Sophie. Madeleine was nowhere to be seen. God damn it to hell. Not *again*.

Sophie caught sight of him and waved so vigorously that

she nearly fell over. She was wearing her new light walking-splint, of which she was immensely proud. 'Dr Pritchard has pronounced my lungs quite sound, and the tuberculosis practically *vanquished*,' she had told him on her last visit to Eden – which had been an historic one, for Clemency had brought her all on her own, and had absolutely driven the trap herself. 'I shall have a limp,' Sophie had told him, as if it were a badge of honour, 'but Grandpapa says it will take more than that to keep me from whatever I put my mind to. I have asked him to teach me to ride, and he has promised to see to it. But I expect I shall have to remind him several times, for he often forgets.'

Clemency had spotted him too, and shyly lifted a hand in greeting. He tipped his hat to her and forced a smile. She had remained loyal to the grey hair dye – 'such a soothing colour' – but was gaining daily in assurance, now that May had taken to spending all her time upstairs. With unnerving suddenness Jocelyn had transferred the management of the house to Clemency, and after a hesitant start she was beginning to overcome her fear. And her health had improved immeasurably, now that she had something to do.

Across the road, Sophie was patting her lap and calling to Abigail to come. Cameron gave the mastiff a nudge with his boot and she padded across, her tail lazily swinging, her head lowered for the expected caress.

'Grandpapa,' said Sophie, 'how do I get her to sit?'

'You don't,' said Jocelyn drily. He threw Cameron a glance, and the corners of his mouth went down.

Cameron nodded to him, but made no move to join them. He knew the old man would understand.

He turned and made his way up the church path, taking off his hat and gloves as he reached the porch. St Peter's was empty, except for Mr Mullholland the curate, and a trio of lady volunteers tidying the flowers. No Madeleine. Cameron swore under his breath. The curate shot him a look.

He went back into the glare of the churchyard. Since Sinclair's death he had seen her exactly seven times, and always in the company of others. For the most part she was edgy and monosyllabic, or worse: polite. And over the past five weeks, he hadn't seen her at all. He'd had to content himself with two brief notes, both pleading 'indisposition'. She was avoiding him. He couldn't work out why.

Since the funeral she hadn't left Fever Hill except to go to church. Nothing out of the ordinary there, he reminded himself. No respectable widow would make calls for at least a year after her husband's death. Except that with Madeleine, there was more to it than that.

It was as if she felt obliged to do penance: to Jocelyn for having lied to him; to Clemency for being the daughter of the man who had deserted her and the woman who had stolen him away; and perhaps also – and this was worst of all – to Sinclair's ghost.

In his darker moments, Cameron cursed his brother. He wished he could honestly grieve for Sinclair, but he was too conscious that, for his brother, death had been an escape. He would have been crushed by the public disclosure of his guilt. And as things had turned out, there had been no disclosure. Grace had said that she was content to let it lie.

Cameron had told her who had killed her son as soon as Madeleine had told him, the week after the funeral. 'In a sense,' he had said to Grace, 'one might regard Sinclair's death as – I don't know, perhaps an act of God?' Grace had studied his face for a long time, her mahogany features unreadable. 'Maybe so,' was all she had said.

He rounded the corner of the church, and saw Madeleine standing before the Lawe family plot, where a new stone commemorated Sinclair Euan Lawe, suddenly in a riding accident at the age of thirty-one.

With a spasm of anger Cameron saw that she was still wearing the dull black crape of deepest mourning. He'd been blunt about that, the last time they had met. 'Surely it's time to lighten the gloom just a little? Or do you propose to emulate the Queen, and remain in deep mourning for the rest of your life?'

'According to Clemency', she had retorted, 'one year of deep mourning is proper form.'

'Perhaps it was, twenty years ago,' he had said. 'Besides, since when were you guided by form?'

To that she had made no reply, and he had known that he'd gone too far.

In the end he had grasped the bull by the horns. 'I don't understand you, Madeleine. What is this about? You didn't love him.'

'No,' she had sombrely agreed. 'No-one did.'

To begin with, he had wondered if in some perverse way she felt responsible for what had happened to Sinclair. 'It was an *accident*, he had told her with deliberate bluntness. 'Why should you feel guilty because he lost his way and fell down a ravine?'

Then he realized that he was mistaken. It was not the manner of his brother's death which had brought about her withdrawal, but the fact of it. Sinclair's death had given her back her freedom. She had benefited from it. How could she not experience guilt?

Above his head a flock of grassquits squabbled noisily in a frangipani tree. As he passed, they rose in a cloud and flew away.

Madeleine had seen him, and was waiting composedly beneath her parasol of dull black silk.

He had to admit that she looked very well in mourning. Black suited her dramatic colouring, and gave her dignity and poise. It also reminded him disturbingly of Great-Aunt May.

As he approached her, the little family group that was laying a wreath at a nearby tomb turned discreetly away, and made strenuous efforts to display no curiosity whatsoever.

Madeleine flicked them a glance, then gave Cameron a meaningless smile and offered him her hand. He took off his hat and pressed her black-gloved fingertips and bowed, and they turned and started sedately for a more secluded part of the churchyard.

For a while they walked without speaking. To break the silence he said, 'Sophie looks well.'

'She is,' she replied. 'And she can't wait to show you her new treasure. Mrs Herapath gave it to her on Friday. It's a photograph of our mother.' Sophie and Clemency were becoming frequent callers on Olivia Herapath – who, while still cool towards Madeleine, was making rather a point of spoiling her sister.

Cameron said, 'I thought Olivia destroyed all her photographs of Rose years ago.'

'It turns out that she couldn't bear to part with this one, as it's the best portrait she ever took.'

'Except for the one of Hector, of course.'

She smiled. 'Of course.' She seemed perfectly at ease with him provided that they kept to neutral ground. It made him want to shake her. Here they were, making small-talk like a couple of acquaintances at a five o'clock tea, when all he wanted to say to her was, *Marry me. Promise that you'll be my wife. I can't go on like this, I need to hear you say it.*

'Cameron, I'm sorry,' she said with disarming suddenness.

He coloured. 'For what,' he muttered.

'I've treated you appallingly. The truth is, I haven't been able to talk to anyone. Not even you. I needed to think about things. To make sense of what happened.'

There must be more to it than that, he thought. But he decided not to press her yet. This was the most that she'd said to him in eight months.

'I know it's been hard for you,' she said.

'It doesn't matter.'

'Yes it does.'

They exchanged glances, and his heart leapt. Then she spoilt it by asking if he'd heard any news about Ben Kelly.

'Not as yet,' he said between his teeth. The boy had been seen shortly after the funeral, working his way towards Kingston on a coastal steamer, but since then all enquiries had drawn a blank.

'No doubt he'll turn up,' Cameron added. He knew that he sounded perfunctory, but he didn't care. Her concern for the scrawny little street Arab baffled him. She'd explained that they had been friends in London, in some incomprehensible way which made Cameron absurdly, humiliatingly jealous. And she had also admitted that for some unexplained reason the boy had followed her to Jamaica, and lent her his gun. His *gun*? Why the devil should a fourteen-year-old boy need a gun? But as to that, she either could not, or would not, say.

Once, he had demanded in exasperation if there was anything else that she hadn't told him.

'Probably,' she had replied. 'Is there anything about your own life that you haven't told me?'

Touché. That was one of the things he loved about her: that bluntness which could flash out without warning and take one's breath away.

They had reached the overgrown part of the churchyard behind St Peter's, and were drawing near to the Durrant graves: a handful of lichen-crusted tablets in an untended, disorderly cluster. Cameron watched her shut her parasol and loop its cord over her wrist as she stopped to read the legend on her grandfather's tomb. *Aristide Durrant, 1813–68. Of Your Charity, Pray for His Soul.*

'Madeleine,' he said, 'it's been eight months.'

Her eyes remained stubbornly fixed on the tomb.

'Eight months,' he repeated, 'and you've never allowed me to say it.'

'Cameron . . .'

'Well, this time you can't stop me.' He went to her and reached out and gently took her hand in his. She tried to pull away, but he kept his hold.

'People will see,' she muttered.

'No they won't. There's no-one about.' He was silent for a moment, looking down at her hand. Then he turned it palm upwards, and slowly unbuttoned the three little black jet buttons of her glove, and peeled it back. Then he bent and kissed the soft, pale skin on the inside of her wrist. He felt her tense; he heard the sharp intake of her breath. He caught the milky scent of her flesh.

Dizzily, he straightened up.

She was looking down at his ungloved hand grasping her black-sheathed fingers. Her dark brows were drawn together. Her mouth was set.

'You know that I love you,' he said, still holding her hand. 'You know that.'

She made no reply.

'And I thought – at least I hoped – that you—' He broke off. 'Marry me. I want you to marry me.'

Still no reply. Her head was bowed. She was biting her lip.

He drew her closer to him. 'I'm not asking you to name the day,' he said. 'If you want a long engagement, then you shall have it. I just – I just need you to tell me that some day, in the future, you will be my wife.'

At last she raised her head and looked at him. To his dismay he saw that her face was pale and agitated, her eyes bright with tears. She put her free hand on his chest and gently pushed. 'Not here,' she said.

'Madeleine—'

'Not *here*.' With a kind of violence she twisted from his grasp and turned, and took a few unsteady steps, and put her hand to her temple and smoothed back her hair.

And as he watched her, a terrible feeling of risk swept over him. He realized that if he could not bring her to accept him now, today, he would have lost her for ever. His life without her would stretch before him as a meaningless blank. He would never stop wanting her. He would never want any other woman. He would end up like Jocelyn: hopelessly longing for a love whom he had lost decades before.

He felt as if he were standing at the top of a high cliff, looking down over the edge. 'If you've stopped loving me,' he said, struggling to keep his voice steady, 'it would be kinder to tell me now. One word will be enough. I'll do whatever you say. You can tell me to go the devil and I'll do it. I'll never trouble you again. But God damnit, Madeleine, just tell me.'

'I haven't stopped loving you,' she said over her shoulder. 'You know I haven't.'

'Then *what*?'

She shook her head. 'We can't talk about this now. Jocelyn's waiting—'

'And he'll go on waiting. He doesn't mind.'

'This isn't the right place. People might—'

'They don't matter. Nothing matters but this. You can't put it off any longer. I won't let you.'

She turned away.

Again he had that appalling sensation of risk. He fought the urge to take her by the shoulders and shake her until she told him what was holding her back.

At last, to his incredulous relief, she simply nodded. 'You're right,' she said. 'We can't put it off any longer. Come. Let's walk.'

They turned and took the path that ran the length of the churchyard, heading for the silk-cotton tree at the end.

When she still made no move to begin, he decided to help her. He said, 'I've been trying to work out what's troubling you.'

He felt her turn and look at him, but he kept his eyes on the path. The silk-cotton was still in bloom, and he watched her black skirts stirring the creamy white flowers that littered the gravel. 'It seems to me', he went on slowly, 'that if you do still care for me, then whatever's troubling you must have something to do with – I'm not sure exactly what, but perhaps you feel some – disinclination – for marrying again.'

He threw her a glance, and saw that he had guessed correctly. He thought, well, one can hardly blame her for that; not after Sinclair. He cleared his throat. 'You said something once', he went on, 'that's stayed with me. You were talking about Sinclair, and you said, "He's the husband. He has all the power." Is that what's troubling you? Do you fear that as your husband I might have too much power?'

'No,' she said quickly, 'it isn't that. I do – trust you.'

He caught the hesitation in her voice. 'But I'm not far off, am I?'

She turned her head and studied the tombstones in the grass. He saw her fingers tighten on her black kid reticule, and open the clasp, and snap it shut. 'When two people marry,' she said at last, 'neither of them has any real idea whether it will work. And if it goes wrong, there's no way out. It's irrevocable.'

'True,' he said slowly. 'But I don't see what—'

'That's what happened when I married Sinclair. We made each other miserable, but we were trapped.' She caught her

407

lower lip in her teeth. 'I couldn't bear it if that happened with you. I just couldn't—'

'But why should it?' he broke in. 'Why should we make each other miserable? I'm not Sinclair.'

She glanced up at him and gave him her quick wide smile. 'Of course you're not.' Then the smile faded. 'It's not you I'm worried about.'

'What do you mean?'

But she shook her head, and turned away.

He had never felt so mystified. She seemed to be blaming herself for something: something that she couldn't even bring herself to name. And how was he to counter that?

'Madeleine,' he began, 'I don't pretend to have understood Sinclair. But I do know that whatever went wrong between you, it wasn't your fault. There was something in him that wasn't – that would never be right. And it began a long time ago. Long before he met you. I don't think we'll ever know what it was, but—'

'I'm not sure about that,' she put in, startling him.

'What do you mean?'

She dug at the gravel with her heel. 'After he was killed, I thought I knew what had gone wrong.' She glanced about her to make sure that no-one could overhear. 'I thought', she went on in a whisper, 'it was because of Victory. Because he – Sinclair – believed that I might turn him over to the authorities. But then I realized that it wasn't only that. It couldn't have been.' She paused. 'He had a horror of me from the very first night we were married. No, don't interrupt. I know it's true. There was something about me that truly horrified him.'

That was so absurd that he nearly laughed. 'Well, I can assure you that there's nothing about you which "truly horrifies" me.'

'But you don't know that, do you?' she said quickly. 'You don't know that for sure.'

'Yes I do. I—'

'And you *won't* know for sure until we're married. And then it'll be too late.'

Now he was well and truly adrift. He had thought that he

was following her at last, but she had lost him again and headed off into unfathomable water.

She was still opening and closing that wretched reticule. He wanted to snatch it from her and throw it into the bushes. Then he saw her taut face, and felt contrite. Whatever the problem, it was making her just as unhappy as it was him. He longed to help her, but he didn't know how.

'With Sinclair', she went on, twisting the reticule in her fingers, 'it went wrong from the very first night. I didn't perceive that to begin with. Or – perhaps I did, and I just didn't want to admit it. But I've thought about it a great deal since, and I know that I'm right. It went wrong because—' She broke off.

'Yes? Because of what?'

She flushed. 'Because of – that.'

Oh, dear God. This was going to be even harder than he'd thought.

They walked on a few paces in silence, neither of them looking at the other.

He cleared his throat. 'So your – concern', he said, 'is that the same sort of thing might happen to us.'

She turned to him, and he saw that she was fighting back tears. 'Well, it might, mightn't it? I mean, how do you *know*, absolutely *know*, that it won't?'

He opened his mouth, then closed it again. 'Well,' he began awkwardly, 'as regards – um, that side of things – one can usually sort of – I mean, if there's real regard, if there's love . . .' Now it was his turn to colour.

'But there's no guarantee,' she insisted.

'Well – I suppose not, but—'

'I won't take that risk. No, not with you.'

'But Madeleine—'

'What, and have you look at me the way he did? As if I were some sort of monster? No. I can't. How can I do that?' Her tone was decided.

His heart sank. Once again he stood at the edge of the cliff. 'Then what do you suggest we do?' he said. 'You can't possibly want to end things between us simply because of some theoretical risk that it might go wrong.'

She didn't reply.

'Tell me that's not what you want,' he said. 'Look at me and tell me that.'

She raised her head and met his eyes. 'No,' she said. 'That's not what I want.'

He drew a shaky breath. 'Then what the devil are you talking about?'

They had reached the end of the path, where the silk-cotton tree towered overhead. She came to a halt, and turned her parasol in her fingers, and stood there stabbing at the gravel with its point. He sensed that she was nerving herself to say something, but that she couldn't bring herself to do it.

'Madeleine,' he said. 'Whatever it is, you've got to tell me—'

'I'll only marry you', she broke in with peculiar intensity, 'if we find out beforehand whether it's going to be all right.'

He blinked. Then understanding dawned. Jesus Christ.

'Wait a minute,' he said when he'd got his breath back. 'Are you telling me that you'll marry me if we – if we sort this side of things out first?'

Again she stabbed at the gravel. 'And *only*', she added, 'if it turns out that it's all right.'

He raised his head and looked up into the branches of the silk-cotton tree: at the vivid emerald leaves and the creamy white flowers against the brilliant, tender blue of the sky. How beautiful, he thought. The most beautiful sight he'd ever seen.

He turned back to her, and reached out and took her hand in his. Then he met her eyes, and gave her a slight smile. 'I think,' he said, 'I can agree to that.'

THE END

The Shadow Catcher is the first book of the *Daughters of Eden* trilogy, and the second novel in the series will be published by Corgi Books in 2003.

Acknowledgements and Author's Note

First and foremost, I owe a special debt of thanks to my cousins Alec and Jacqui Henderson of Orange Valley Estate, Trelawny, Jamaica, for their unfailing help, hospitality and good humour when I was researching this book.

I'm also most grateful to my aunt, Martha Henderson, for the loan of many invaluable old books on Jamaican history and folklore – and to my uncle, Ian Henderson (who sadly died before the manuscript was finished) for his insights into life as it used to be lived in Jamaica.

I'd also like to thank the following for their very kind help: Mary Langford and Enid Shields, both distinguished members of the Jamaica Historical Society, who gave so generously of their time in taking me round Kingston and its environs; David and Nicky Farquharson, who showed me over their beautiful estate at Hampden (after a never-to-be-forgotten rainstorm); Diane and Mark McConnell, who were so friendly and welcoming at their gloriously situated great house at New Hall; and also Christina Mantle, Patricia Gould, and David Wiggan. In addition, I must also mention Abigail the mastiff, who took time off from her duties to follow me about at Orange Valley, and graciously allowed me to include her in the story.

Finally, I should deal with a few points concerning the narrative itself. The principal Jamaican families and properties featured in the book are entirely fictional, and I have taken some liberties with the local geography around Falmouth in order to accommodate the estates of Eden, Fever Hill, Burntwood and Parnassus. As regards the *patois* of the Jamaican people, I haven't attempted to reproduce this precisely, but have instead tried to make it more accessible to the general reader, while retaining, I hope, at least some of its colour and richness.

Michelle Paver

Michelle Paver was born in Malawi but has lived for most of her life in Wimbledon. After gaining a first in biochemistry at Oxford she became a lawyer, and was for five years a partner of a large City law firm. She has now given up the law to write full time. Her previous novels, *Without Charity* and *A Place in the Hills*, are also published by Corgi. *A Place in the Hills* was shortlisted for the 2002 Parker Pen Romantic Novel of the Year award.

To find out more about Michelle Paver and her novels visit her website at www.michellepaver.com.

Also by Michelle Paver

WITHOUT CHARITY
A PLACE IN THE HILLS

and published by Corgi Books